Mrs Hudson and the Blue Daisy Affair

Martin Davies grew up in north-west England. All his writing is done in cafes, on buses or on trains, and all his first drafts are written in longhand. He has travelled widely, including in the Middle East, India and Sicily. In addition to the Holmes & Hudson Mysteries, he is the author of four other novels, including *The Conjurer's Bird*, which sold over 150,000 copies and was selected for the Richard & Judy Book Club and *Havana Sleeping*, which has been shortlisted for the 2015 CWA Historical Dagger award. He works as a consultant in the broadcasting industry.

Also by Martin Davies

A Holmes & Hudson Mystery

MRS
HUDSON
AND THE
BLUE DAISY
AFFAIR

MARTIN DAVIES

🔟 CANELO

First published in the United Kingdom in 2021 by

Canelo
Unit 9, 5th Floor
Cargo Works, 1-2 Hatfields
London, SE1 9PG
United Kingdom

Print ISBN 978 1 80032 528 9
Ebook ISBN 978 1 80032 527 2

Look for more great books at www.canelo.co

Printed and bound in Great Britain by Clays Ltd, Elcograf S.p.A.

Today I had an unexpected visitor.

When the bell rang, I was at work in my study, at my little desk overlooking the park. It's some years now since I retired, but students still send me papers, and there still seems a lot to do, so the interruption wasn't altogether welcome.

As I opened the door, I saw an old man standing there. He could have been anyone. But when he said my name, I recognised his voice. He said he had come to apologise. And we both laughed.

So we walked in Hyde Park and watched the little boats on the Serpentine, and talked about the crowded years that had passed since we'd last met. We said goodbye at the Victoria gate. He was only passing through. It would surely be our last farewell.

Tonight I am supposed to be going out. There will be friends and laughter and people who love me. But I find myself looking out over the park, where the lamps are peeping through the twilight, and thinking instead of other times and other people, and of tiny blue flowers that look — just a little bit — like daisies.

Part I

Scandal in Salisbury Street

Chapter One

George Dashing returned to London at the beginning of the most glorious autumn, when the streets were full of sunshine and the afternoons were heavy with a soft, lazy heat.

I remember when I heard the news. It was a morning of intense, golden loveliness, and the trays of the flower girls were bright with early asters. Mrs Hudson, on discovering a strange purple stain in the bathtub, had rolled up her sleeves and sent me on the morning's errands, and I had been overjoyed to go. After the longest, most stifling summer in memory, the city seemed revived by a new-found crispness in the air, and house after house was being reawakened from its August slumber; as I made my way down Baker Street that morning, all around me shutters were being pulled back, windows thrown open, and dusters shaken like little waves of greeting from open bedroom windows. Even the cab-drivers seemed more cheerful, and when I scurried across George Street rather too hastily, causing the driver of an on-coming hansom to pull back on his reins, I was rewarded, not with the customary scowl, but with a gruff '*Go carefully, Miss,*' and a nod of the head.

And it wasn't only in my own street that the long lull of August was coming to an end. All across the city, it seemed, a returning population had brought with it a rich cargo of bad behaviour and criminal intent, from minor misdemeanours to grand larceny, and this, in turn, had seen a notable rise in the number of intriguing new cases being brought to the attention of Mr Sherlock Holmes. After a woefully quiet summer, this change was as welcome as it was sudden, and only that morning I had been obliged to turn away two callers without appointments, either of whom, had they come a month earlier, would have been whisked immediately and without ceremony into the presence of the great detective.

But now there were simply more demands on Mr Holmes' time than even the greatest detective could satisfy, and so he was enjoying the luxury of choosing which puzzles to ponder, which mysteries he wished to address. And he had a rich array from which to choose – this was the autumn, you may recall, when he unveiled the sensational truth about the true heir of the Beauchamp estate, then astonished everyone, only a few days later, with his explanation of that perplexing business of the Romford hieroglyphs.

For me, it was a welcome change. Gone were the pacing footsteps and the long silent mornings, and the agitated squeal of Mr Holmes' violin at twilight, replaced by the knocking of countless callers and a new sense of busy-ness, one that revived us all. Of course, the greater the number of comings and goings at Baker Street, and the greater the number of dusty feet upon our stairs, the more work there was for me; that morning I had jobs to do, and errands to run, and really no time to take in the beauty of the morning. But it was a beauty that was hard to ignore, and everything, from the ring of horses' hooves on the cobbles to the twittering of the sparrows on the rooftops, seemed fresh and lively and exuberant. A baby waved from a pram, a gentleman raised his top hat to me with a flourish; on the corner of Portman Square, separated from me by the bustling carriages and the rattling victorias, a lady handing out leaflets marked 'Votes For Women' gave me a little smile as I passed.

It was after that, as I paused to straighten my bonnet, that I heard the newsboy's cry.

'*News! Get your news! Mr Dashing recalled from Montenegro! Vows to fight for downtrodden masses!*'

Looking along the pavement to where the lad was standing, I saw two finely dressed ladies of middle years pause in their conversation and reach for their purses. Both took copies of *The Clarion*.

'It's true, madam,' I heard him say to one, 'the gentleman's back all right. Saw him myself, this very morning, in Regent's Park.'

Then, with what might almost have been a wink, he touched his cap and resumed his crying.

'*Mr Dashing returns! By-election next for Society favourite!*'

And of course, for many people, it *was* exciting news. It was impossible to live in London in those years and not know of the handsome George Dashing – young, rich, charming and brilliant, with eloquence and wit to match. In fact – as so many people loved to point out – every bit as dashing by nature as he was by name. And very often that name seemed hard to escape; people interested in politics talked of him as the rising darling of the liberal cause; in sporting circles, he was famous as an amateur cricketer of considerable skill; in fashionable society, I was assured, he was considered one of the three most eligible bachelors south of Carlisle. So his abrupt departure a year before, on a diplomatic mission to the Balkans, had been the cause of widespread lamentation, and – if rumour were to be believed – a number of broken hearts.

But for me, that day, George Dashing was no more than a name, albeit a rather good one, and my list of errands was lengthy: first to Palfrey's with an order for fish, then to Lamingtons' for cold meats, then to Throok's, Ostermann's and Bromley's, and finally, if there were time – and I was determined there *would* be time – a little stroll in Hyde Park before I was expected back in Baker Street. There, I still had stairs to sweep, and floors to mop, and door-handles to polish. But the brightness of the day couldn't be denied. The floors would have to wait.

Unfortunately, the service at Ostermann's, which was usually so prompt, proved rather slow that day, so it was a little after eleven o'clock by the time I reached the park, and, after the freshness of early morning, the slow autumn heat was already beginning to build. I paused to tie a ribbon in my hair, one I had brought with me specially, then made my way briskly through the drifting pedestrians, until I reached the bandstand.

No band was playing yet, but on a bench nearby, smartly dressed in collar and tie, his nose in a newspaper, sat a familiar figure.

Many years before, in less happy times, I had been rescued from the dirt and mire of the London streets by a boy barely older – and not much cleaner – than myself, but it was hard to recognise any part of that boy in the figure on the bench. Scraggs was no longer the grocer's boy, no longer even a gawky teenager, but a pleasant-featured and rather good-looking young man. Years of trading from behind a barrow had equipped him with strong arms, quick wits and a straight back, as well as the wherewithal to purchase for himself a very respectable suit of clothes – although it was not one he wore often, and when he did it always took me by surprise.

Seeing him in it, that day in the park, it almost seemed there was nothing left of that urchin I'd first met, until he looked up from his newspaper and noticed me watching him, and smiled, and the smile hadn't changed at all, and the sun was shining, and he was still Scraggs.

'Morning, Flot,' he called out cheerfully, scrambling to his feet and wrestling the newspaper under his arm. 'Glad you could make it. Thought it would be a nice morning for a stroll, and since I had some business up this way... The old dragon's let you out for a bit today, has she?'

I gave him a swift poke in the ribs.

'None of your cheek, Scraggs. I told Mrs Hudson that I might come here for some air after Bromley's, and she said that was a very good idea. Now, are we going to walk, or aren't we? And are you going to tell me why you're all dressed up?'

He offered me his arm.

'Oh, nothing important. Just a bit of business.'

He was up to something, I knew him well enough to know that. And well enough to know that there was no point pressing him any further, for a little while at least. So we strolled under the trees towards the Serpentine, chatting idly about the shortage of best cleaning paste at Bromley's, and the limited supply of good feather dusters at Throok's. When we passed another news-stand, the subject turned to Mr Dashing, and his sudden return to London.

'There's something peculiar going on there,' Scraggs told me, a little frown on his face. 'That Dashing fellow has a house on Weston Square, and when I came through there this morning there was no sign of the usual constable

9

who does that beat. Instead, there were four coppers I didn't recognise, each patrolling one side of the square, whistling to themselves as though it was the most ordinary thing in the world. And, on top of that, there was a man selling sweets from a barrow, a chap I'd never seen before, and I reckon I know every barrow between here and Lambeth. Seems to me there's something up.'

But I had no sense of foreboding. One young gentleman, however much loved by the ladies, surely couldn't stir up that much trouble, and if Mr Dashing's return added to the general melting-pot of London excitement, then I was quite happy to have him back.

'But what about old Sherlock?' Scraggs went on, as we paused to watch the ducks. 'I hear he's busy trying to work out who gets the Beauchamp inheritance?'

'It's true,' I assured him, 'and as all three of the triplets look exactly alike, it's causing all sorts of headaches. And he's supposed to be looking into that odd business with the Egyptian writing too, so we've got a different chimney-sweep tramping up the stairs every twenty minutes. Mrs Hudson says that until things quieten down a bit, we'll never get the carpets properly cleaned.'

Scraggs grinned.

'Well, perhaps things *will* quieten down a bit. With Mr Holmes so busy at the moment, his clients might start going somewhere else.'

He handed me his newspaper, folded open on a page of small advertisements.

It was easy to see which one Scraggs intended me to read. It was printed at the foot of the centre column, in confident larger type:

Laurence Martin, Consulting Detective. Modern methods, guaranteed results, testimonials

But I only laughed. It was becoming quite the thing for ambitious young men with time on their hands, or for unscrupulous adventurers seeking an easy fortune, to attempt to emulate Mr Holmes' methods – but none of them had ever achieved any particular success. That bright autumn day, watching the ducks on the Serpentine, I gave almost no thought at all to Laurence Martin. It struck me as highly unlikely that I – or anyone else – would ever hear the name again.

I returned to Baker Street that afternoon with a light heart. My errands were complete, there had been time for a stroll around the Serpentine, and the streets seemed to be smiling at me. I don't recall exactly where my thoughts had led me by the time I approached our front door, but I was undoubtedly a little lost in my imaginings, because it was not until I reached the top of the area steps that I became aware of the young woman watching me.

She was standing at the end of our railings furthest from the front door, in a position where she could look down into the area, and from the angle of her body she might have been doing exactly that, until distracted by my arrival. She was, perhaps, twenty years of age or a little older, in a plain bonnet. The manner of her dress suggested a servant on her day off, and at first I thought she was lost and about to ask for directions, so hesitant and anxious was her manner. But seeing that I'd noticed her, she seemed to make a decision, and advanced a pace or two in my direction.

'Excuse me, Miss,' she began, and I noticed her voice was not strongly accented, perhaps the voice of someone born and raised in one of those outlying areas now viewed as part of London but which, a generation before, had still been villages and fields. 'Excuse me, Miss, are you employed here?'

I told her that I was, but as I spoke her eyes were moving from me to the area below, as if trying to make a decision.

'In the service of Mr Sherlock Holmes? Then perhaps...' She gave a little cry of anguish. 'If only I knew... If only I had someone to advise me! Is he a *kind* man, do you know?'

I told her that I thought he was, although a busy one, and often impatient, and rarely very tactful, and frequently off-hand in his manner, and generally fonder of facts than of feelings.

'Then I must not... I *should* not...' I thought she was about to turn away, but almost immediately changed her mind. 'But I'm so afraid! And perhaps *you* could advise me whether or not Mr Holmes... But no! How could you possibly know? I must go. I must.'

Again she began to turn away from the railings, but this time she paused to dab at her eye with a handkerchief and I was able to reach out and lay my hand on her elbow.

'Please,' I told her, 'you're upset. I think you should come inside, just until you are calmer. Mrs Hudson is in – she's the housekeeper here – and she is famous for her sound advice.'

'Then, perhaps...' She allowed me to lead her to the top of the area steps, where she paused and pushed her little handkerchief into the wrist of her glove. Where the glove rode up, I glimpsed a narrow red scar. 'You see,' she went on, 'I used to be in the service of... No, I must not say his name! But I must explain. I was in the service of a gentleman and his family, and that gentleman has a son...'

I led her down the steps as she talked, but halfway down she suddenly stopped.

'No, I must not! If I speak of it, he – they – will be so angry! And perhaps I am not in danger at all!'

I turned to soothe her, but, before I could say a word, she had taken flight, back up the steps and into the street. On the pavement, she paused and looked back at me.

'Please! Say nothing of this! I am probably mistaken. Only, please, if anything... If anything *happens*, then do please tell your employer I was here!'

And with that, she was gone, leaving no name and no address. Leaving nothing, in fact, apart from one thing. Later that day, when I went out to shake the dusters, I noticed a little pale scrap of fabric beneath the area steps, a scrap of fabric that turned out to be a slightly soiled ladies' handkerchief. It was a common enough object, of thin cotton, hand-hemmed with lilac thread, but I remembered immediately whose hand I had seen it in.

It bore, however, no initials or insignia, and no clue that might lead me to its owner.

–

It seems strange, looking back, that such an incident did not particularly unsettle me. In any other household, a housemaid accosted in such a way would surely have made a great deal of fuss, raising a commotion that would almost certainly have reached the ears of her employers. But so accustomed was I, in those days, to the strange habits of the callers at our house, so used to encountering hesitancy or nervousness, understatement or exaggeration, that I quickly put the whole episode out of my mind. The young woman might very well return, and if she did, I would renew my efforts to persuade her to share her story; if she did not – and there was something in the manner of her departure that made me think she probably wouldn't – well, there was little that I or anyone else could do about it.

I found the house very quiet. Mr Holmes, it turned out, was on his way to Romford in the company of a rat-catcher named Slake, while Dr Watson had been dispatched to the British Museum with half a dozen burly policemen to stand guard over the Rosetta Stone. Neither would return before sunset. So when I continued down the area steps and into the welcoming sanctuary of Mrs Hudson's kitchen, an unusual calm prevailed. And in the very centre of that calm, at our heavy kitchen table, stood Mrs Hudson herself, a solid beacon of strength and serenity, stirring currants into the dough of a pound cake.

Seated beside her, on a very low stool, was a lady I didn't recognise, an elderly lady, bespectacled, with a very serious expression, and incredibly tiny. She rose as I entered, blinking slightly, in the manner of someone who has been talking a great deal and had just been interrupted.

'So, as I say, Mrs Hudson, I would be grateful if you would give the matter some thought, and if you do wish to sign the petition, you will find it in the Temperance Hall in Dover Street. Now, I should wish you a good day.'

'Mrs Welland, this is Flotsam.' Mrs Hudson was clearly not going to allow her visitor to skimp on the formalities. 'Flotsam is something of an expert on chemicals, aren't you, Flotsam? She and I will no doubt read your leaflet together, as soon as we are at leisure.'

Having not previously looked up from her mixing bowl, she now pushed it to one side and allowed herself a smile in my direction, brushing her hands together as she did so.

'Flotsam, this is Mrs Welland, who has been telling me of the great dangers posed to children in this city by the confectionery being sold to them. She has a petition she wishes us to sign.'

I was aware that the lady in question was looking at me with a degree of suspicion. Her manner, and her slightly peremptory air, gave the impression of someone rather haughty, and it occurred to me that she was perhaps someone who had once been in service herself, but in a very superior position; someone who was therefore not accustomed to being introduced, in a formal manner, to housemaids.

'Well, of course, every signature helps,' she acknowledged, with a little nod in my direction. 'And when Mrs Hudson has explained to you the nature of some of the confectionery being sold on these streets...' Her voice began to change, as though she were beginning to address a public meeting. 'Confectionery adulterated with all sorts of toxic colourings, Flotsam, to achieve the gaudy colours so popular with the young! Red from cinnabar powder, for instance, or green from Verdigris, to give only two examples. Toxic chemicals that damage the inner organs and poison the body! When these things have been explained to you, then I am sure you too will wish to lend your name to our cause!'

She finished with her voice uplifted, as one who concludes a rousing speech, then looked embarrassed again, mumbled a hasty farewell, and was gone.

'A good woman, Flottie,' Mrs Hudson remarked as the door closed behind her, 'although not one I would necessarily choose as a companion for a lengthy train journey. And her visit was not a brief one – I confess I began to despair of your return. Now, there's a clean apron behind the door, and a jar of Cheadle's polish in the cupboard. Though perhaps a bite to eat first – I daresay you were too busy rushing to the park to think about food – and then those doorknobs.'

I blushed slightly, because I wasn't sure whether or not Mrs Hudson knew I'd gone to the park to meet Scraggs. I hadn't actually mentioned it, but sometimes not mentioning something can make a thing more obvious, and Mrs Hudson often just *knew* things. So I hurried to the door and took a little longer than necessary to tie my apron. Only when I was sure I was no longer blushing did I turn back to the room, and then, perhaps by way of diversion, I picked up the little pile of leaflets left by our visitor on the kitchen table. They were headed '*To Petition Parliament to Increase the Number of Food Inspectors by Four Hundred Persons, this being the Number Required to Properly Enforce the Sale of Food And Drugs Act of 1875, and Thereby to Improve the Safety of the Population and to Better Protect them from Pernicious Chemical Adulterations of Many Sorts*'.

'It is not a rallying cry that trips easily off the tongue, is it, Flotsam?' Mrs Hudson shook her head a little sadly. 'I suspect that anyone hoping to fire up the passions of the British public needs a rather more memorable slogan. But meanwhile, let us give thanks for the excellent and unadulterated Sage Derby that awaits you in the pantry. It is a gift from Lord Memblesbury, who, although somewhat eccentric in his devotion to his herd of Friesians, is a man who can undoubtedly be trusted when it comes to cheese.'

Satisfied that preparation of the pound cake was complete, she reached for a cloth and began to wipe down the table.

'Now, those doorknobs won't clean themselves, Flottie, my girl, and Mr Holmes and Dr Watson are in such a state of high excitement over this Romford business that I don't imagine any of us will be in bed before midnight. We must have everything ready for a late supper, and the tea tray ready too, although with the gentlemen not expected back till so late, I don't suppose we'll be troubled by any callers.'

Which just goes to show that Mrs Hudson, although a good judge of cheese, wasn't necessarily always right about everything.

Chapter Two

It was, however, true that our two gentlemen were both home late that evening, and both of them in exuberant mood. Mr Holmes was the first to arrive, a little after nine o'clock, blowing lightly on his fingertips as I took his cloak.

'It has turned chilly, Flotsam,' he informed me, 'and there is fog on the river. In fact, the perfect evening for burglary. Which is,' he added with the faintest of smiles, 'precisely how I have spent the afternoon.'

I took his hat and cane, and raised my eyebrows slightly, but knew better than to interrupt.

'The rat catcher was correct, you see.' The great man's air of satisfaction was unmistakeable. 'And therefore the meaning of the last hieroglyph was obvious. Fortunately, on that particular street in Romford, only one house had a green door, and equally fortunately, it also had an unlatched upstairs window and a sturdy drainpipe to the rear, so I was able to enter without difficulty. It was the work of a moment to verify that the Canopic jar was empty, and I was comfortably seated in a hansom cab heading back to the station before anyone was the wiser. I feel certain that Dr Watson will have had an exciting time of things at the British Museum.'

He checked his watch.

'But we still have thirty-seven minutes until he returns. He cannot possibly make it home a minute sooner, and were he to take five minutes longer, I would begin to fear that our plan has failed. No, no violin tonight, Flotsam. Two bottles of brown ale, one of Mrs Hudson's stand pies, and the day's post, I think, so that you can read it to me as I eat.'

This suggestion, which would have bewildered most housemaids and shocked a great many of them, was not as surprising as it may sound. Lately Mr Holmes had taken to treating me, when Dr Watson was absent for an hour or so, as a convenient substitute, as if my position in his household was simply to support his detective endeavours in whatever manner he required, and oblivious of the fact that, even when a problem was particularly baffling, the dirty dishes still needed to be washed.

That particular evening, as I perched in Dr Watson's armchair with the day's correspondence on my lap, there was not yet a fire in the study, but the lamps were lit, wrapping the room in a warm glow, and the shutters were closed against the night, so that for the first time since the previous spring a familiar feeling of evening comfort prevailed there. But the letters received that day offered little to interest the great detective and a great deal to annoy him. While I scanned them for anything urgent, obscure or intriguing, Mr Holmes demolished a cold pork pie and grunted his disappointment.

'*Another* missing briefcase, Flotsam? It beggars belief that such an enormous number of people leave items in railway carriages, and that so many of them seem unaware of the excellent lost property systems operated by our railway companies. A note to... Mr Prendergast, is it? A simple note to Mr Prendergast, suggesting he visits the offices of the Great Western, will suffice, Flotsam, should you have a moment later on. What else?'

'Eight more letters about the Rutland murder, sir, all suggesting that the butler must have been responsible.'

Mr Holmes gave a little gasp of exasperation and dabbed some mustard from his chin.

'The *butler*? Have they not read the newspaper reports? The butler is left-handed, allergic to cats, and cannot sing. He is no more guilty of slaying the vicar than you are.'

He thrust his empty plate onto the floor and rose to his feet.

'And is there anything further, Flotsam?'

'Only two bills, sir, and a letter from a Mr Jones asking for your help in finding his missing dog.'

'Very well.' Mr Holmes brushed the crumbs from his waistcoat and took out his watch. 'You may leave the bills in the hip bath, Flotsam, and if your schedule allows it, I would be grateful if you could send a note to Mr Jones suggesting that he places a notice in the personal columns of the daily newspapers, offering a small reward for his animal's return. Now, it is precisely thirty-eight minutes since I returned home, and, if I am not mistaken, those footsteps you hear approaching the front door belong to our good friend Dr Watson, which means that one of us should begin to prepare a large glass of brandy and shrub.'

Not only was Mr Holmes correct about the brandy and shrub, it was also true, as he had predicted, that Dr Watson's evening had been an eventful one.

'Nabbed the fellow in the Assyrian section!' he announced proudly, as I took his coat. 'Never had any idea we were expecting him, Flotsam. Whistling, he was! We only had to step out from behind that big stone lion to catch him red-handed. Easy as eating a pie! Speaking of which…'

He looked at me hopefully.

'I'll bring something up, sir,' I assured him. 'And Mr Holmes has already poured you a drink.'

Dr Watson pursed his lips slightly at the news.

'He has, has he? Very good of him. He'll be pleased to hear we've got the red-headed chap out of the way, won't he? That just leaves Lady Galbraith and the fishmonger, and Holmes says before the end of November one of them will have to show their hand.' He paused. 'Mixed me a drink, did he? Very thoughtful of him. Though, between you and me, Flotsam…' He allowed himself a slightly guilty grimace. 'Between you and me, he tends to mix them a little on the weak side.'

The rigours of the evening had clearly sharpened the doctor's appetite, and he made short work of the pie, following it with a plate of sliced ham, some blood sausage from Wilson's, a bowl of cucumbers and half a bottle of burgundy. It was while I was clearing away the remnants of this repast that the two gentlemen's contented musings on the day's events were interrupted by a knock at the front door.

'Good lord, Holmes!' Dr Watson exclaimed, leaning back in his armchair and rubbing his stomach contentedly. 'Callers? At this hour? You'd better go and find out what they want, Flotsam. And it had better be important, eh, Holmes?'

The great detective, who had just a moment earlier taken up his violin, gave a quick nod.

'Bring up their card by all means, Flotsam, but I fear we shall not be receiving visitors. We have a very full day ahead of us, and shall need our rest.'

But when I opened the front door, I was surprised to discover, not one, but two callers waiting on the front step, and two extremely smart coaches pulled up in the street beyond, one on each side of the road, so that passing traffic had to slow to squeeze between them. It wasn't clear which of the two men standing in front of me had been the one who knocked, but, from their dress, both were clearly coachmen, and one was particularly striking in a smart green livery. And from their expressions it was clear that they had not arrived together by design, because each was scowling at the other, and when I opened the door to them, each thrust a calling card towards me with ill-disguised competitiveness.

'For Mr 'Olmes, Miss,' the man in green told me, thrusting a card into my left hand. 'I'm to wait.'

'For Mr *Sherlock* 'Olmes,' the other declared, pressing the card into my right. 'On most important business from the 'Ome Office. And my instructions is to wait till Doomsday if needs be. Besides...' He gave the other a look of utter distain. '...I was 'ere first.'

The other – the larger of the two – straightened.

'Who was first and who was second, I wouldn't like to say, Miss, but it was me that knocked, and that's what counts.'

So I returned to the study with both cards presented very properly on a small silver tray, and explained that there were in fact two callers rather than one, that each caller was waiting in their own coach, and that it was a matter of dispute which one had the prior claim.

The first card Mr Holmes plucked from the tray was the one presented by the smaller of the two coachmen.

'Sir Joseph Croxton,' he announced, raising an eyebrow. 'What do you make of that, eh, Watson?'

'Croxton? The civil servant?' Dr Watson puffed out his cheeks. 'Well, they say he practically runs the Home Office, don't they, Holmes? And a very good friend of the Queen, if the rumours are to believed.'

'So I've heard, Watson. One of those men with more power at his fingertips than any peer or politician, but who can walk through a crowd unrecognised. I wonder what brings Sir Joseph out at this hour?'

Dr Watson, who was now rested and well-fed, ventured over to the drinks tray.

'Well, we'll have to see him, Holmes, won't we? Can't say 'no' to a man like Sir Joseph Croxton.' He helped himself to a comfortable measure of old Scotch. 'So who is the other caller, Flotsam?'

But I was unable to tell him, for the simple reason that the other calling card was unlike any I had ever been given before. It was simply a vacant rectangle, green on both sides, without a single word of any sort printed upon it.

–

For all my years in Mr Holmes' service, I could never be quite sure which things would annoy and which fascinate him. I'd already decided that the blank green card would be one of the former, and half expected him to tear it in two on the spot. Even as I watched him examine it, it would have been easy to conclude that it held no interest for him. Only when he finally looked up did I realise the opposite was true, for his eyes were bright and a very faint smile played at the corners of his lips.

'Here, my friend,' he said, passing the object to Dr Watson, 'what do you make of this?'

His companion turned it over once or twice, peering at it intently, before passing it back.

23

'Must be some kind of joke, Holmes,' he concluded. 'But not a very funny one. You say the fellow who sent this up is waiting in his carriage, Flotsam?'

'Yes, sir, on the other side of the road, just across from our front door. It was his coachman who delivered the card.'

'Well, I've got a good mind to go and throw the thing back in his face. What does he mean, sending up a bit of nonsense like that?'

'He, Watson?' Sherlock Holmes held the card close to his face for a moment. 'You are sure our caller is a man?'

His friend gave a careless shrug.

'Well, I suppose it could be a woman, Holmes. Can't see what difference it makes. Shall I go down and send them on their way?'

But Mr Holmes held up his hand.

'Steady, Watson. Not so fast, if you please. What if I told you that the owner of this card is a lady of advancing years and considerable fortune, and that she has stopped here tonight on her way home, having spent her evening attending a public meeting in support of Women's Suffrage? During the course of that meeting she has learned a piece of news that worries and disturbs her. Oh, and she walks with a stick in her left hand, of course.'

If Dr Watson was surprised by any of those assertions, he certainly didn't show it. He simply looked a little relieved.

'Ah, so you know her, do you, Holmes? Even so, it's a bit of a rum time to call.'

Sherlock Holmes allowed himself a small smile.

'I assure you, my friend, that I know no more about the lady than is revealed by this calling card.'

And, to my alarm, he turned to me.

'What do you make of it, Flotsam?' And with those words, he handed the card to me for examination.

'Well, sir…' I began. I had been long enough in service in Baker Street to have heard the great detective make many similar revelations, and this was not the first time he had challenged me in this way. Even so, it was difficult not to feel a little nervous when asked. 'The coachman was wearing a green livery, and although it was dark, I think his uniform might have been the same green as the colour on this card. So, just by itself, the colour of the card is perhaps a clue to its owner?'

Mr Holmes nodded briskly.

'Go on. Anything else?'

I studied the little card more closely, determined not to miss any detail.

'Well, sir, it's of very fine quality. Its weight and edging both show that. So it's reasonable to think that the person who had such cards made must be quite wealthy.' I sniffed. 'And it has a very faint scent, sir, like a woman's perfume.'

On hearing this, Mr Holmes smiled happily, then took the card from me and passed it back to his friend.

'You see, Watson, this calling card is not quite as blank as you thought. As Flotsam so rightly points out, it is an object of the highest quality, suggesting a person of considerable fortune. And that perfume tells us a great deal.'

He held it close to his nose for a moment.

'This is no ordinary fragrance, Watson. I have mentioned before that the ability to recognise a trace of perfume can sometimes prove vital in a case, and for that reason I make it my business to familiarise myself with all the newly fashionable fragrances. This one, however, is no recent concoction. It is, I believe, none other than the famous *Fleurs de Bulgarie*, a fragrance as distinctive as it is expensive. Have you heard of it?'

'I can't say that I have, Holmes.' From his expression, I gathered that Dr Watson's knowledge of ladies' perfumes was no more extensive than his knowledge of French cookery or ancient Greek verbs.

'If you had, Watson, you would know it is not the perfume of a young woman. *Fleurs de Bulgarie* was all the rage back in the days when Aberdeen was Prime Minister, and I would warrant that nowadays very little of it is sold to ladies under sixty years of age.'

'I may be no expert, Holmes,' Dr Watson agreed, 'but I do agree that a lady's perfume says a lot about her. I once shared a railway carriage with a very charming young woman who smelled of cinnamon and vanilla. Very fetching, she was, but it was a long journey, and for much of it I was gripped by an almost uncontrollable urge to get off the train and order an ice cream.' He gave his head a little shake. 'So, then, Holmes, our caller is a wealthy, older lady. But what of the rest? How can you possibly know how she has spent her evening?'

'Think about it, Watson!' The great detective waved one hand towards the windows that overlooked Baker Street. 'Flotsam has told us the lady is waiting in her carriage on the opposite side of the street. Now, if that lady had been sitting at home when suddenly seized with the desire to consult us, is it likely that she would have ordered her carriage and then roused herself at this hour, and come in person to Baker Street, without an appointment, on the off chance that she might be seen? It is one thing for Sir Joseph Croxton to behave in that way – he is on duty, as it were, and he knows he *will* be seen – but a less eminent person would have surely penned us a note begging for an audience, and had a servant run out to deliver it. Her presence here in person suggests that she was already out and about, somewhere north of here, when she made the decision to call upon us on her way home.'

'North of here, Holmes?' Dr Watson looked up sharply. 'Can't tell from a card which direction she's travelling in.'

'But we can tell by the position of her carriage, Watson. Flotsam says it is pulled over on the far side of the street, and as we have heard no carriage turning, we can assume that she approached from the north, on the left-hand side of the street. So she was heading south, towards the centre of town, which is exactly where you would expect to find the townhouse of a woman as wealthy as this one.'

Dr Watson pursed his lips and seemed about to speak, but Mr Holmes hurried on.

'Now, where, north of here, might an aristocratic old lady have passed her evening until this hour? She may, of course, have been dining at one of the big houses around Regent's Park, or in one of the respectable streets south of Marylebone Road. Yet, had she been entertained in any such household, this hour of the evening would seem, not too late, but rather too early for her to be returning home.'

Dr Watson rubbed his nose.

'People do seem to dine later and later, nowadays, Holmes, I'll give you that. But if she's an elderly lady, it would be perfectly natural for her to excuse herself early.'

'Of course she *might* have done that, Watson.' The great detective sounded slightly impatient. 'And she *might* have been returning from a jaunt around Primrose Hill in a bid to exercise her horses. But these things are surely less likely than the alternatives, especially when you consider that the Scriveners' Hall on Melcombe Street invariably closes its doors at half past ten o'clock, and that you yourself, Watson, have more than once commented upon the increased number of carriages heading past our door shortly afterwards. As we have both observed, this phenomenon is particularly marked on Tuesdays, when the hall hosts the proceedings of the Explorers' Club, and on Fridays during the season, when Lord Salter-gate's Thoroughbred Society gathers there. But this is a Thursday, and on Thursday evenings, if memory serves, the Scriveners' Hall is given over to a meeting of the London Society for Women's Suffrage.'

He paused, as if to allow us time to absorb this inform-ation.

'And then, of course, there is the colour of the card. Were Mrs Hudson present she would no doubt recognise it at once because she knows these things, but I believe it is the colour commonly known as Swarkstone green. I came across it many years ago, when investigating that fellow Mattley, the society portraitist who took to burglary. A tiny smear of paint on a windowsill gave him away in the end, because an expert was able to testify that the colour was a particular shade of green, one that Mattley had been using half an hour before in his portrait of Sir Oliver Stephens. Its name derives, I seem to recall, from the colour of the famous dining room at Swarkstone Abbey.'

'Swarkstone Abbey...' Dr Watson pondered this. 'That's the Hastings' place, isn't it? So this particular shade of green might suggest a connection with the Hastings family?'

'More than that, my friend. When a visiting card of this colour is sent up by a rich and elderly woman whose coachman, as Flotsam has observed, wears a uniform in the same shade, then it would appear to be more likely than not that our visitor is none other than Lady Hastings herself, who, as you are no doubt aware, also happens to be extremely prominent in suffragist circles.'

'Lady Hastings…' Dr Watson considered this for a moment, then clicked his fingers. 'Of course! Sir Humphrey Hastings' widow. And she does walk with a stick, doesn't she? Well known for it! Well, only one way of finding out, Holmes!'

The great detective smiled broadly and reached for his pipe.

'My thoughts exactly.' He turned to me. 'Flotsam, please show her up. And kindly inform Sir James Croxton that we shall be happy to receive him in…' He appeared to be calculating something in his head. 'We shall be happy to receive him in around seventeen minutes' time.'

Chapter Three

It says a great deal for my faith in Mr Holmes' deductive powers that I was not at all surprised when the elderly lady handed down from the grand carriage on the opposite side of the street was indeed Lady Hastings of Swarkstone Abbey and Belgrave Square – a fact confirmed when the lady herself handed me a second card as I assisted her up the steps to our front door. Despite her stick – a rather beautiful ebony wand topped with a perfect agate sphere – she moved awkwardly, with a very marked limp, and it was not until she was safely inside that she dismissed her coachman.

'I shall manage the stairs perfectly well, Folkestone,' she told him. 'There is a good strong rail, and if I need you, I shall send for you. What is your name, child?' she went on, looking me up and down.

'Flotsam, ma'am.'

'And how old are you, Flotsam?'

'Seventeen, ma'am,' I told her, although I should really have said 'about seventeen', because no one knows exactly when I was born.

'I think between us we can rise to the challenge, can't we, Flotsam? Folkestone is broad, and the stairs are not. We will do better without him.'

I had expected, from her title and her carriage, a very grand lady, but Lady Hastings seemed quite the opposite.

Frail, certainly, and short of stature – she stood no taller than my shoulder – but her eyes were bright and full of good humour, and when she wobbled slightly towards the top of the staircase, she seemed to have no objection when I instinctively placed my hand on her shoulder to steady her.

'That's right, girl,' she said briskly, 'give me a bit of a push. I am clumsy as a sack of potatoes, and have no objection to being heaved about like one. At my age, dignity is an over-prized virtue. Now where is that famous detective?'

In my years at Baker Street, it was my privilege to show many distinguished visitors into Mr Holmes' study, and it was surprising how often, when faced with the great man himself, their self-confidence appeared to diminish. That, however, was certainly not the case with Lady Hastings. After exchanging the usual compliments with Mr Holmes and Dr Watson, she asked me to help settle her into the armchair reserved for visitors, and as I did so she spoke only to me, chattering about the difficulties of arranging old bones into modern furniture, and directing me exactly where to place her stick. When finally comfortable, she handed me her reticule and gestured towards a small foot-stool in the corner of the room.

'Now, Flotsam, I would like you to bring that here and sit beside me, and be ready to administer to me the small red pills you will find in my bag. I will signal if I need one. They are for when I feel faint. There are some blue ones too, but those are for a quite different problem.'

Finally, she turned her attention back to her hosts.

'Pardon me, gentlemen, but it is convenient for me to have someone on hand to administer to me, and, as I have no maid of my own present, I trust you will have no objection to this excellent girl of yours attending me. If Flotsam cannot be trusted to be discreet then you should not employ her, and, besides, nothing I have to say tonight is particularly confidential. You see, I have long held the view that if we treat young women in service as though they do not exist, then they will begin to believe that of themselves. Yet I am sure, were you to take the trouble to investigate, that you would discover in your female staff many unexpected skills and talents.'

It is greatly to Mr Holmes' credit that he offered no protest in his own defence, simply nodding gravely.

'Then if you wish it, my lady, Flotsam shall remain.' He offered a little nod in my direction. 'Now, we are already aware that you have come to us directly from a meeting about the suffrage, and that you have learned something there that makes you wish for our assistance.'

The old lady looked delighted.

'Excellent, Mr Holmes! Your talents have not been exaggerated.' She chuckled to herself. 'I knew the blank card would appeal to you. It is an old trick, taught to me back in the Forties by a rather scandalous Italian countess. She maintained that brilliant people were always too busy to give audience to strangers, and that the less you told them about yourself, the better the chance that they might see you.'

She allowed herself another chuckle.

'I admit that she used the device for purposes that today would be considered highly immoral, but things were different back then, and she was Italian.'

Sherlock Holmes cleared his throat quietly.

'Perhaps, my lady, if you tell us what's troubling you, we can see how we can be of assistance.'

'Get on with it, you mean?' She nodded briskly. 'Yes, of course, Mr Holmes. You have someone else waiting. Now, you will have gathered I am passionate about the issue of votes for women?'

Mr Holmes had taken up his favourite position by the fireplace, leaning against the mantel and toying with a pipe he didn't attempt to light.

'Of course. I had the privilege of hearing you speak to a packed house in Manchester in April of last year.'

I confess this rather surprised me, and it certainly surprised Dr Watson, who had been about to drain the last drops of Scotch from his glass, but paused with it halfway to his mouth.

Lady Hastings had clearly not been expecting it either.

'Really, Mr Holmes, you astonish me. I have heard so much about you, but I had never heard that you took an active interest in the political issues of the day.'

'In our line of work, everything is of interest, isn't it, Watson?' The great man rapped his pipe against the stone mantelpiece. 'Although I confess that I was present on that occasion in a professional capacity, pursuing a fugitive disguised as a member of the Primrose League. But I found your talk perfectly sensible, my lady, and your arguments both cogent and logical.'

'Aha! Such compliments!' Lady Hastings looked delighted. 'Tread carefully, Mr Holmes. When my comrades and I detect a convert to the cause, we pursue him most doggedly! However, if you had attended our meeting at the Scriveners' Hall this evening, you would have heard no speeches at all, for the gathering was convulsed by news of the utmost importance. You have heard, gentlemen, of Mr George Dashing?'

I confess I raised an eyebrow, although later I realised the coincidence was not so great – Mr Dashing's return was the subject of a great many conversations that evening.

'The son of the Marquis of Heswall?' Mr Holmes pondered the name. 'A radical politician, is he not?'

'And something of a society favourite,' Dr Watson added, rising from his seat and moving over to the drinks tray. 'Packed off to the Balkans, wasn't he? They say the Prime Minister wanted him out of the way. A good-looking fellow too, by all accounts, and admired by the ladies. I suppose it's a case of Dashing by name, dashing by nature, eh?'

He noticed the slightly pained expressions on the faces of both Mr Holmes and Lady Hastings.

'Ah. Heard that before, I daresay. Anyway, my lady, what has the fellow been up to now?'

'You have clearly not read today's newspapers, gentlemen.' The old woman looked surprised. 'You see, George Dashing is back. The Foreign Office have recalled him from Montenegro.'

That piece of news, which hadn't seemed particularly significant to me when I heard it that morning, clearly gave the two gentlemen cause to ponder.

'Back, is he?' Dr Watson mulled this over. 'Well, that ought to shake things up a bit in Westminster. You think they'd have wanted to keep him out of the way for a bit longer than that, wouldn't you, Holmes?'

'Indeed you would, my friend. But I rather think Mr Dashing has been too clever for them. He could hardly have turned down the posting – that would have seemed churlish and not very patriotic – but from what I've read, ever since he set foot in the Balkans, he has been making it impossible for the Foreign Office to keep him there.'

'You are quite right, Mr Holmes,' Lady Hastings told him. 'Mr Dashing has given a series of speeches, and has written a number of letters to the Balkan newspapers, all of them criticising the Tsar of Russia. In particular, he has persistently accused the Tsar of oppressing his peasantry, and has speculated openly about what would happen if the agricultural workers there rose against their masters. In Russia, of course, Mr Dashing's attacks – which fall little short of inciting revolution – were considered extreme provocations.'

'Good lord!' Dr Watson, having poured himself a substantial measure of brandy, remained at the drinks tray. 'Can't have that sort of thing, can we? Inciting revolution! Provoking the Russians! Why, the fellow could start a war!'

Lady Hastings gave him an approving look.

'That is, I believe, exactly what the Foreign Office are afraid of. In short, Mr Dashing gave them no choice but to recall him. It is the end of his diplomatic career, of course, but he never really cared for that. His interest has always been in politics, and, in many ways, he returns with his reputation enhanced. He has denounced tyranny abroad, and now he is back to do the same at home.'

'And yet,' Mr Holmes mused, 'I fail to see why his return should cause such particular excitement in the ranks of the London Society for Women's Suffrage. I have never heard him spoken of as a particular supporter of your cause.'

Our visitor nodded again, then turned to me and indicated that she required a handkerchief from her reticule. This she used to dab daintily at her brow and temples before continuing.

'You are right, Mr Holmes. Mr Dashing has never shown any specific interest in the cause of Women's Suffrage. He is not against us, of course, and our hope is that he might be persuaded, in time, to make a public stand on our behalf. But nevertheless his return is of the most enormous importance for us, not because of what he himself will do, but because of what his return will *prevent*. You are familiar with the Paternoster Society, gentlemen?'

Outside, a carriage rumbled by and a horse whinnied, but I barely heard them.

'Of course we are, aren't we, Holmes?' Dr Watson looked pleased. 'Even I've heard of it. Lots of clever sorts who come up with political ideas, isn't that right?'

Lady Hastings nodded.

'It is indeed. A society of political philosophers, renowned for its select membership and its considerable influence. The annual Paternoster Lecture is reported in newspapers and journals around the world, and has an enormous effect in shaping political opinion. And you may recall that shortly before he departed for the Balkans, George Dashing was elected the Society's president.'

Our visitor returned her handkerchief to me with a smile.

'I hope all this talk is not too tedious for you, Flotsam? I know these are weighty matters.'

With that, she patted my hand and turned back to her hosts.

'Old Samuel Saunders-Smith had been president for forty years or so, and when he finally turned up his toes, the contest to replace him was a bitter and divisive one. The obvious candidate was, of course, Sir Henry Catanache...'

I noticed a little shudder pass through her.

'…A most odious man,' she went on, 'a person resistant to all change, a man who sees in every liberal cause, not a beacon of hope but a canker of revolution. He is an avowed enemy of the cause of Women's Suffrage, and of every alteration that might make this country more equitable and more just. For such a man to become President of the Paternoster Society would have been a disaster for us. But, thankfully, many of his fellow Society members felt that a candidate with more enlightened views should be found, and to everyone's surprise they turned to young George Dashing. The vote was very close, I believe, but Mr Dashing prevailed. Sir Henry, to his fury, was elected instead to the post of vice-president.'

Mr Holmes was still standing by the mantelpiece, but I sensed he was growing a little impatient, as though all this talk of political movements and manoeuvres was of very little interest to him.

'So, Lady Hastings, from your point of view, an excellent result,' he observed.

'So it seemed, Mr Holmes. But Mr Dashing's foreign posting changed everything. It is written into the constitution of the Paternoster Society that the annual Paternoster Lecture will always be delivered by the Society's president, or, if he is for any reason unavailable, by the vice-president. For the last year, therefore, with Mr Dashing away, it has been assumed by everyone, including by the man himself, that Sir Henry Catanache would give this year's lecture, which is traditionally delivered on the first Friday in November. And we had it on good authority that Sir Henry intended to deliver a vicious attack upon the very principles of the Women's Suffrage movement.'

The old lady sighed, and in that moment, her pale face picked out by the lamps, I noticed how tired she looked, and realised just how much her cause really meant to her. She was not, as I had believed at first, a rich woman with a hobby, playing at politics and public meetings as a form of entertainment, but someone working to the very edge of her strength for something she believed.

'Sir Henry would have shown us no mercy,' she went on. 'And for all his faults, he is an eloquent speaker. It is undoubtedly true that, were he to use the Paternoster Lecture to deliver a savage rebuttal of our movement, then the damage would be dreadful to contemplate. All those doubters, all those wavering MPs who are so nearly convinced, all those fair-minded men who are beginning to see the logic of our cause… All of them might turn their backs on us in an instant when shown the lurid picture of doom Sir Henry Catanache intends to paint!'

Moved by her anguish, Dr Watson put his glass down and reached out to pat the arm of Lady Hastings' chair.

'Come now, my lady,' he soothed, 'there is surely no need to upset yourself. As you've just explained, Sir Henry will no longer be giving the lecture.'

Our visitor looked up at this, and there was a determined look in her eye.

'That is why I am here, Doctor. At tonight's gathering, jubilation was unconfined. The news of Mr Dashing's return, and the realisation that Sir Henry Catanache will no longer be able to use the Paternoster Lecture to attack us, these things were being cheered to the rafters, by myself as much as by anyone.'

She paused and gave a little shake of her head.

'It was not until I came to leave that it struck me. You see, there are many people in this city of ours who find themselves deeply threatened by our cause, many disgruntled and angry individuals who might, if provoked, go to almost any lengths to stop us. A small, unsavoury handful of these individuals invariably find the time to demonstrate their anger outside our meetings. We have become accustomed to their presence, and have learned to ignore the unpleasant epithets they aim at us as we take our departure. But this evening, Mr Holmes… Oh, I know you will think me a foolish old lady, but this evening, when I came to leave, there was nobody there. Not a single soul. Not a single voice raised in protest.'

She gave another little shake of her head.

'It was as the carriage came away that I fell to wondering what had become of them all. What had made them abandon their weekly protest? What had suddenly changed? And then I thought of Mr Dashing.'

'Ah!' Dr Watson's face had brightened. 'I see your point. I had an uncle once who was bothered by flies in the breakfast room. Used to solve the problem by putting a bucket of manure in the hall. No offence to Mr Dashing, of course,' he added hastily, 'but I take it that you think the attentions of these undesirables is now being directed elsewhere?'

Lady Hastings nodded graciously.

'Indeed, Doctor. Because, you see, there are many ruthless and unscrupulous people who would give a great deal for Sir Henry Catanache to deliver the Paternoster Lecture this year, to use it as a weapon to attack our movement. And tonight, gentlemen, I realised how easy it would be for them to make that happen. If, in the next six weeks, any misfortune or accident were to befall Mr Dashing – if for any reason he were unable to give the Paternoster Lecture himself – then Sir Henry would have the floor once more, and all our celebrations would have been misplaced.'

Until that moment, I don't think it had been clear to me – or to the two gentlemen – precisely why Lady Hastings had called at Baker Street that night. But now I began to understand, and I realised with a sinking feeling that there was little Mr Holmes could do to help. The same thought had clearly occurred to the detective himself, because he placed his pipe gently on the mantelpiece, and turned to her with a curiously gentle expression on his face.

'So you have called here tonight to enlist my services in keeping Mr Dashing safe until this lecture of his is delivered?'

'I confess, Mr Holmes, that was precisely what I had in mind.' Lady Hastings leaned forward in her chair. 'As my carriage turned into Baker Street this evening, it occurred to me that if there was one person in London who would be able to confound our enemies, you were that man. Were Mr Dashing to entrust himself to your care for the next six weeks, I feel certain that he would be able to take the lectern for the Paternoster Lecture without mishap and unscathed.'

Mr Holmes nodded, but I could see he was a little embarrassed.

'But you have not yet put this to Mr Dashing? Because, unless he agrees to be helped, there is little anyone can do for him. You see, Lady Hastings, my methods have enabled me to solve various perplexing and complicated problems in the course of my career, but they have their limits. For instance, they cannot prevent someone from setting upon Mr Dashing with a weighted stick next time he steps outside his front door, nor from waylaying him in a dark alley on the way home from his club, nor from shoving him under a speeding carriage next time he attempts to cross Piccadilly.'

'Holmes is quite right, my lady,' Dr Watson confirmed. 'You see, there are only two of us, and we can hardly be expected to guard the fellow every waking hour from now to November. It sounds as though Mr Dashing would be better served by a team of stout manservants with hefty cudgels, or some vigorous constables assigned to special duties.'

But Lady Hastings did not seem utterly downcast.

'Of course, sir, I anticipated some such response. I know that you are a detective, Mr Holmes, not a Praetorian Guard. But, you see, I have a terrible feeling that Mr Dashing is in danger. I cannot explain it, but I feel certain that some dark force will attempt to prevent him from speaking.' Lady Hastings leaned further forward still, as if to look her host more clearly in the eye. 'And I know that if any such dark force is at work in this city, sir, if any secret conspiracy is being plotted, then I would trust you, more than anyone else in London, to ferret it out.'

It was an impressive compliment, and for all Mr Holmes' apparent unease, I could see that he was not unmoved by it.

'My lady,' he told her, with a slow bow of his head, 'I can offer no guarantees as to Mr Dashing's safety. If he has concerns, I would advise him to go to the police, because the vigilance of the local constabulary can count for a great deal in this city. But occasionally we do hear rumours, here in Baker Street, of criminal acts being plotted, and we shall be more than usually attentive to them in the coming weeks. I give you my word.'

'That is exactly what I wished to hear!' Lady Hastings patted my hand fondly. 'Now, remember, my girl, even the smallest part of an enormous engine is vital to its successful operation. So whether you are blacking a hearth or brushing a stair, never forget that, in your own small way, you are also helping a great man to work his brilliance.'

I liked Lady Hastings, and came to greatly admire her campaigning work, but when I reported this last remark to Mrs Hudson, it was greeted with a narrowing of the eyes and a twitch of the eyebrows that was every bit as eloquent as any campaign speech ever given.

Chapter Four

Sir James Croxton, when finally admitted to Mr Holmes' presence, did not seem put out by being made to wait. I had imagined someone as important as Sir James would be a commanding presence, capable of striking fear with a gesture or freezing a soul with his glance. But seen in person, the great man – famous even to me as one of Her Majesty's most trusted advisors – was a rather unassuming individual with a round face and greying whiskers, who, but for his very perfect suit of clothes, might just as easily have been a butcher or a grocer as an eminent statesman. This impression was strengthened by the fact that he still carried a copy of *The Times* under his arm, as though he had just got down from a passing omnibus. His manner was brisk but friendly and he acknowledged his hosts with a firm nod of the head.

'It is good of you to see me, Mr Holmes. Dr Watson.' He cast a look around the room. 'Especially at such a late hour. I know you are busy men.'

His eye alighted on the little tray of glasses and decanters, and appeared to linger there.

'Flotsam,' Mr Holmes ordered, 'please help Sir James to a drink. What will it be, sir? Whisky and soda water? Very good. And I should begin by apologising, sir, for keeping you waiting so long this evening.'

But Sir James waved the apology away with a little flick of his wrist.

'Not at all, Mr Holmes. I noticed the Hastings carriage across the road from mine, and assumed that for Lady Hastings to be calling at such an hour, the matter must be an important one.'

The great detective acknowledged this with a discreet nod of the head, and pointed his guest to one of the vacant armchairs.

'Lady Hastings is an admirable woman,' Sir James went on, 'but I'm afraid, however pressing the matter she has brought to you tonight, the business I wish to discuss must take precedence. It is a matter of the greatest national importance, and it is the personal wish of a certain extremely illustrious individual that you give the matter your full attention.'

With that he raised his eyes towards the ceiling, suggesting that the individual he alluded to, if not the Deity in person, was someone who in terms of eminence at least came very close.

'Then you must tell us more, sir.' Mr Holmes took up his familiar position by the mantelpiece and with a wave of his pipe invited his guest to continue. But Sir James, having received his whisky and soda, paused and cast another pointed glance in the direction of the drinks tray, where I still lingered, awaiting instructions.

'That will be all for now, Flotsam,' my employer told me in a very kindly way. 'But I believe there is some silver that requires your attention. Please leave the study door a little open behind you, if you will. I find the room grows stuffy.'

It was a peculiarity of the arrangements in Baker Street that directly opposite the gentlemen's study stood a very small box room where Mrs Hudson stored the silver-ware. It had long ago been discovered that anyone at work in that small room could, when both doors were ajar, hear with perfect clarity what passed in the study – a fact that greatly amused Mr Holmes, who had never shared the common reluctance to speak freely in front of servants, and who, for the sake of his own convenience, was perfectly happy to honour me and Mrs Hudson with a great deal of confidence.

And so it was, with a knowing nod and an air of gentle amusement, that I was dispatched to the silver cupboard that evening, and if Sir James Croxton thought it peculiar that I should be set to polish silver at that time of night, he didn't show it. In fact, I think he quickly put me completely out of his mind, for before I had even left the room he had begun to explain the reason for his visit.

'Mr Holmes,' he declared, his voice suddenly more decisive and more purposeful, 'I have come here tonight directly from Downing Street. It is the dearest wish of Her Majesty, and of her ministers, that for the next two months, or until the Paternoster Lecture is safely delivered, you will personally undertake to ensure the safety – from attack of any sort, by his enemies, or by the enemies of this country – of a certain Mr George Dashing.'

This was, I confess, something of a surprise. That two people as different as Sir James Croxton and Lady Hastings should, on the same night, ask for assistance in exactly the same matter, was unlikely enough. But, as I worked away furiously in the silver cupboard on an old and very tarnished candelabra, it quickly became apparent that each had very different reasons for the same request. For Lady Hastings, Mr Dashing's continued good health was vital to the cause of Women's Suffrage; for Sir James, Mr Dashing's continued good health was a question of national honour, and vital to the precarious peace that prevailed in Europe.

'You see, Mr Holmes, the man is a menace.'

The two slightly open doors allowed me a surprisingly wide angle of vision into the study, wide enough for me to see that Sir James had, in one sip, taken a good measure out of his whisky and soda.

'A charming gentleman of enormous talents, excellent company, a good head in a crisis, but a menace of the very worst sort. You will be aware that his father, the Marquis of Heswall, is a gentleman of somewhat conservative opinions?'

'Rather more than *somewhat*,' Dr Watson exclaimed. 'Didn't he once horsewhip a house guest for appearing at dinner in the wrong-coloured socks?'

'So they say.' The words were cautious, but the expression on Sir James' face suggested that he gave the story at least some credence. 'The father and son are cut from very different cloth, so perhaps it is not surprising that Mr George Dashing has deliberately espoused more liberal views.'

Our visitor sighed.

'I have no objection to a modicum of liberalism, Mr Holmes. Some of my dearest friends are Liberals. But George Dashing has taken it upon himself to become the darling of the downtrodden and the defender of the masses, to play the part of rabble-rouser at every opportunity. You might think such behaviour would make him an outcast from polite society, yet he's so impeccably bred, and so utterly charming in company, that he remains feted in the very best circles, even as he is cheered at the factory gates. And now he has gone and tweaked the nose of the

Tsar, and if we're not very careful, there's going to be the Devil to pay.'

'You refer, of course, to Mr Dashing's pronouncements in the Balkans, championing the cause of the Russian peasantry.' Mr Holmes' voice was calm and measured, but I could tell that his brain was already in action, working out the precise reason for Sir James' visit.

'Indeed.' The great statesman cleared his throat, a little uncomfortably, it seemed to me. 'And it is hard to over-state the incendiary nature of his remarks. The Russians, Mr Holmes, are not like us. They do not tolerate dissent, and nor do they allow insults to go unpunished. Did you read, last spring, of that Spanish writer who wrote a novel comparing the Tsar to Caligula? He was found dead, hanging by his bootstraps from his own weather vane. And before that, the Hungarian revolutionary who called for land redistribution in the Ukraine? Yes, that's right, Dr Watson, you remember the case. Went missing one night after giving a lecture in Pest, and was found a month later in his cellar, choked to death with his own pamphlets.'

'Good lord, Sir James!' The horror in Dr Watson's voice was unmistakeable. 'Are we to understand you feel Mr Dashing is in similar danger? Here? In London?'

'That is precisely what we fear, Doctor,' his visitor replied. 'And we have every reason to believe that some such outrage is already being plotted.'

I saw the shadow of a smile pass over his features.

'Of course, there are some people in this country – some people in eminent positions, even – who would argue that Mr Dashing has brought this upon himself. People who feel that the removal of Mr Dashing from the public discourse would make their lives very much easier. But, damn it, Mr Holmes, we're not having that! No, sir, we're not Spain, we're not Austria-Hungary! No Russian assassin shall be allowed to ply his trade upon these shores and get away with it!'

So genuine was his outrage, so clear his conviction, that I found myself also feeling rather stirred. That morning, George Dashing had been little more to me than a slightly amusing name – now he seemed to stand for something so important that no effort should or could be spared to ensure his safety.

After another full-throated sip of his drink, Sir James continued, his voice a little lower, but in no way less passionate.

'If we were to allow agents of the Tsar to come over here and murder a prominent member of the British establishment, Mr Holmes, well, I hardly need tell you what that would do our prestige, to our standing among nations! How could our allies have confidence in our guarantees, if it were known that we could not even guarantee the safety of our own citizens in our own capital city? We would be little better than a laughing stock, and worse still, our enemies would be encouraged to believe that any outrage might be perpetrated against us. Which is why Mr Dashing *must* be able to give this year's Paternoster Lecture. It is widely known that he intends to use it to repeat his anti-Russian views, and we have reliable intelligence that agents of that power are preparing to prevent him from ever reaching the podium.'

Mr Holmes, still in his familiar position by the mantelpiece, appeared to nod in understanding, but even from my distant position I could see that his brow was furrowed.

'Forgive me, Sir James. I understand perfectly why you would wish to foil any plot against Mr Dashing's person, and why an assassination of the sort you describe, here on British soil, would be a terrible blow to our standing and reputation. But I don't fully understand why that should bring you here. As Dr Watson remarked earlier this evening, there are only two of us. In a crowded street, the assassin's blade comes without warning. We cannot guarantee to shield Mr Dashing from every danger he may face. But you, sir, you have all the resources of this great nation at your disposal. You can surround Mr Dashing with police officers. You can escort him around town with a regiment of infantry if you choose. I fail to see how Dr Watson and I can greatly improve upon that.'

In reply, Sir James reached for the copy of *The Times* that was still wedged rather awkwardly under his arm.

'I already know, Mr Holmes, that you take an interest in the personal columns of this newspaper. Is that not so?'

Mr Holmes confirmed this with a nod, and it was certainly true. He had often told me that the only really important news in the whole paper was to be found in those parts known as the agony columns, which contain innumerable private and anonymous messages, a great many of them in code, all of them intended to defy the understanding of the general public while conveying a very particular message to a particular person or loved one. And of course, Mr Holmes was not alone in this. It was often said that the personal column was the most widely read section in the whole of *The Times*.

Sir James gave his rather crumpled copy of the paper a little shake, then passed it to Mr Holmes, explaining that he had marked with pencil the entry that was of interest.

'*Maya to Aldan*,' Mr Holmes read... '*He has returned. You know we cannot be happy while he remains. Now you must act to save us.*'

He looked decidedly unimpressed.

'That would seem a fairly unremarkable communication of its kind,' he observed drily, passing the newspaper to his companion, 'with nothing obvious to distinguish it from a great many messages that appear in such columns. What do you make of it, Watson?'

Dr Watson appeared to deliberate carefully.

'Well, Holmes, I suppose "he" could be George Dashing, but he could equally be just about anyone else. I suppose, Sir James, there's a reason why this one has caught your eye?'

Our visitor nodded gravely, and reached inside his jacket to retrieve a folded slip of paper.

'There is indeed, Doctor. Firstly, you should know that *Maya* and *Aldan* are the names of rivers in the eastern provinces of Russia. Secondly, printed here is a pair of similar messages for you to consider.'

Dr Watson took the folded paper from him, and read aloud.

'*Lena to Tobol. I act tonight. There will be no more insults. Tomorrow, those who seek him will know which way the wind blows.*'

From my vantage point in the silver cupboard, I could see the grave expression on Sir James' face as he listened.

'That message appeared, in Spanish, of course, in the Madrid dailies on the day Marcelo Pedraza was horribly murdered and hung from his own weather vane. Many similar messages preceded it, of course, and all of them, with hindsight, could be seen to relate to the assassination.'

'And Lena and Tobol?' Mr Holmes asked sharply.

'Are both eastern Russian rivers, Mr Holmes. As are the River Uda and the River Selenge. Read on, Doctor.'

Dr Watson narrowed his eyes slightly as he continued.

'*Uda to Selenge. Tonight he speaks for the last time. He shall be made to eat his words.*'

'Translated from the Hungarian, I take it?' Mr Holmes asked, looking thoughtfully at his guest.

'Indeed, Mr Holmes. It was the culmination of an exchange of messages placed in the *Budapesti Hírlap* newspaper. Nagy Sandor, the anti-Russian activist, was choked to death with his own political writings.'

Still in his armchair, Dr Watson was looking troubled.

'But surely, sir, if the personal columns were really being used in this way – if foreign agents were actually using them to communicate – wouldn't they try a bit harder to hide the content? Those columns are full of messages that no one can make head nor tail of. Surely any sensible spy would take the trouble to do something similar?'

As he spoke, he picked up the crumpled copy of *The Times* and ran his eye down the front page.

'Look, here's one. I'll read it to you. "*Mark – GQCLRQGJCRRC PQQGLACKWPCRSPL.*" I mean, what on earth is anyone to make of that? Whoever Mark is, he could be planning to plant gunpowder under Buckingham Palace and nobody would be any the wiser!'

'On the contrary, my friend...' Mr Holmes took the paper off him rather gently and studied it. 'Codes of this sort attract a great deal of attention. I can guarantee you that a hundred amateur cryptographers are already at work ferreting out the meaning of this very code. For such enthusiasts, the agony column of *The Times* is the richest imaginable resource, providing countless hours of challenge and amusement at very little cost. Am I not right, Sir James?'

The great man nodded his assent.

'We know from reliable intelligence, Mr Holmes, that the agents of a certain foreign power have been instructed to avoid elaborate ciphers in these public forums. It has not escaped their attention that the German Admiralty was transmitting messages masked by a very complex code in the pages of the *Paris Gazette* last year, only for the details of its North Sea manoeuvres to be revealed by an elderly pork butcher near Nîmes who had taken to cryptograms as a means of enlivening his retirement. Ever since then, our experts tell me, it is now generally assumed that the more innocuous a message, the less attention will be paid to it, and the more likely that it will go unnoticed.'

Mr Holmes clearly felt this sensible, for he rapped his pipe smartly on the mantelpiece.

'But now your people have noticed a new pair of Russian rivers, running their course here in London. It is well spotted, Sir James, although of course we cannot be certain that they flow from the same source as those others. Nevertheless, I would like the opportunity to peruse them at my leisure.'

'I have had the entire correspondence copied here,' Sir James explained, passing Mr Holmes a second sheet of paper pulled from his pocket. 'All we ask of you, sir, is that you study these messages – and any that follow in the days and weeks to come – with the most minute scrutiny, looking for anything that might help us to understand our enemies' plans, and to protect Mr Dashing, whether from assassins abroad or from enemies at home.'

He rose from his chair, and Mr Holmes straightened, his face grave.

'It might be sensible for me to meet Mr Dashing in person,' he told his visitor, 'to see what precautions can be taken. Perhaps such a meeting could be arranged?'

Sir James Croxton bowed.

'I shall ask Mr Dashing to call tomorrow,' he promised.

But Mr Dashing did not call the next day, nor the day after. In fact, as I was to learn for myself, although he was an extremely obliging gentleman in a great many ways, he did not much like to be told what to do.

'I'm not sure that the whole thing isn't a load of nonsense!' Dr Watson snorted irately. 'Coded messages, foreign spies, all on the front page of *The Times*? Why, if it was anyone other than Sir James Croxton suggesting it, I'd be telling him that he'd been reading too many novels of the stupidest sort!'

It was some minutes short of midnight, and Mr Holmes had already retired, leaving his companion to seek refuge in Mrs Hudson's kitchen, where he was able to enjoy a glass of the Warburton's port, the one which, in the housekeeper's words, was far too good ever to send upstairs. While Dr Watson sat back in one kitchen chair, his slippered feet resting comfortably on another, Mrs Hudson and I put the last touches to the day's tidying. Both of us were accustomed to the gentlemen's late hours, and with the fire still blazing, the kitchen looked warm and welcoming, and immaculately well-ordered.

On the table in front of the doctor, now marked by a neat tawny ring made by the bottom of his glass, was Sir James Croxton's piece of paper, the one on which was printed all the messages from Maya to Aldan and back again. Seeing that nothing now remained to be done but a little tidying up around the draining board, where Mrs Hudson was already engaged, I ventured to wipe my hands and pull up a chair so that I could take another look at that strange series of communications.

They were, at the same time, both oddly innocent and rather disturbing, depending on which meaning you chose to find in them.

> Maya to Aldan – Awake! He who threatens us is to return. Be vigilant. I shall write again.

> Aldan to Maya – I have seen. I am in readiness. Instruct me.

> Maya to Aldan – You are my great hope. Be vigilant.

> Aldan to Maya – I wait.

> Maya to Aldan – He has returned. You know we cannot be happy while he remains. Now you must act to save us.

Dr Watson cradled his port tenderly, and waited until I pushed the paper aside.

'You've got to admit, Flotsam, that we're being asked to believe in a pretty strange kettle of fish. Wouldn't you say so, Mrs H?'

'There *is* something a little bizarre about it all, sir,' Mrs Hudson agreed as she rubbed at the draining board with a china gauze, 'but it can't be denied that the agony columns are used for many strange purposes. By paying a few shillings at the offices of one of the advertising agencies, anyone can now share their thoughts with the world, safely and anonymously, regardless of how peculiar those thoughts may be. Such an arrangement inevitably allows all sorts of bad behaviour to flourish.'

'But foreign spies? Here in London?' To calm himself, Dr Watson took another sip of the Warburton's. 'I'm prepared to believe that all sorts of atrocities have been perpetrated in foreign parts, Mrs H, but George Dashing is a British citizen and a pillar of fashionable society. You're not telling me that he's about to be horribly butchered on a British street?'

Mrs Hudson was now rubbing at the tiles behind the draining board and appeared absorbed in her task, but I thought I noticed the smallest of furrows appear upon her brow.

'If you are asking me whether I think there may be a plot against Mr Dashing's safety, sir, then I'm afraid I really couldn't say. But I have heard one or two stories about the gentleman – an acquaintance of mine was once second parlour maid to the Marquis of Heswall – and none of them suggest that caution is one of the young man's greatest qualities. A very charming gentleman by all accounts, but rather a reckless one, I'm afraid, sir, who rather tends to invite controversy.'

A final tile remained, and she seemed to have found upon it a most intractable stain, for she was scrubbing at it with great determination.

'As a consequence,' she concluded as she rubbed, 'I would imagine that if you and Mr Holmes have really been entrusted with delivering Mr Dashing safely to the Paternoster Lecture in six weeks' time, you may find you have rather a challenge on your hands.'

But that night, comfortable in the warm glow of Mrs Hudson's kitchen, it seemed hard to believe that a gentleman as eminent as Mr Dashing could really be in any danger. And, as Dr Watson had said, the idea of Russian spies and foreign assassins exchanging messages in the columns of *The Times* seemed little short of absurd.

Besides, it had been a long and busy day, and lulled by the warmth and the late hour, my eyes were growing heavy.

I had a vague idea that something else had happened that day, something I'd been planning to mention to Mrs Hudson. But what with hieroglyphs and suffragists and Sir James Croxton, and Scraggs in a suit, and ducks in the park, and that funny woman worried about sweets, it was hard to remember what. It probably wasn't very important. I'd tell her in the morning, I thought, as I crept into bed, my head already beginning to nod.

But I didn't tell Mrs Hudson in the morning. In fact, with so much going on, the woman on the area steps completely slipped my mind.

Which is why, when I was eventually reminded of her, it all seemed much too late.

Chapter Five

It would be wrong to say that the next few days passed quietly for, on the Sunday following the visits of Lady Hastings and Sir James Croxton, Mr Holmes called upon the Lord Chancellor and revealed to him the true identity of the Beauchamp heir. During the commotion that followed, it was difficult to go outside even to run an errand because of the crowds that had gathered to cheer Mr Holmes, and Mrs Hudson decided instead that we should exhaust our existing supplies of beeswax and turpentine with a thorough clean of the gentlemen's study. While we worked, in order to avoid both the crowds and the turpentine, Dr Watson took himself off for two days' walking in the South Downs, and Mr Holmes, somewhat grudgingly, removed himself to the kitchen with his violin and a book about head wounds; within a few days, the crowds, finding nothing to see and nobody to cheer, had drifted away without a trace.

During that time, I don't think I thought very much about Mr Dashing. Sir James Croxton's tale of foreign spies seemed less believable with every day that passed, and the visit of Lady Hastings, with her deliberately melodramatic calling card and her vague sense of foreboding, began to feel a little unreal, like the sort of artificial confection found in the pages of foolishly far-fetched romances. After all, the truth was really very simple: Sir Henry Catanache had planned to deliver a political speech, and now that speech was to be given by George Dashing instead. In the bright sunlight of an autumn afternoon, it all seemed rather ordinary and not very important and perhaps even a little dull.

In the lull that followed, we were all given a little chance to catch our breaths. Mr Holmes and Dr Watson re-occupied a remarkably clean and tidy study, and although Mr Holmes complained that the jars containing organs had been removed from the mantelpiece, and Dr Watson grumbled that the freshly laundered antimacassars were itchy, both seemed largely pleased that they could now find places to set down their newspapers without knocking over stacks of tatty notebooks or vials of strange liquids. Mr Holmes, although he rarely allowed himself to show it, seemed extremely gratified by the public reaction to his latest triumph, and took to sending me out for the early and late editions of the newspapers, which is perhaps why the story in *The Clarion*, which appeared not long after Lady Hastings' visit, struck such a jarring note.

I remember the morning well. The two gentlemen had already breakfasted by the time I took up the papers, and I found them kneeling on the hearth rug, studying a large and complicated diagram.

'The London sewer system,' Mr Holmes explained, without looking up. 'Dr Watson and I are attempting some calculations. You may leave the papers by my chair, Flotsam. Or better still, you may look through them yourself, and read to us any items of interest you find. *The Times* first, I think.'

And so I settled down in Dr Watson's chair and looked through *The Times*, reading out the headings of some stories and skipping others. I had done this before, and had a shrewd idea which articles the gentlemen would find interesting. While I did so, Mr Holmes and Dr Watson pondered the diagram.

'There has been an incident in the Black Sea, sir. A Russian fishing vessel has collided with a British dreadnought. And there's been more fighting in Macedonia. The French ambassador in Serbia has issued a strongly worded statement. And in Lincolnshire there has been another theft of empty sherry casks from Grimsby docks. Shall I read that one, sir?'

'If you would, Flotsam. It sounds as though the Sleaford gang has re-awoken from its slumbers. But first, Watson, what about this route here?'

He moved his finger along various lines of the diagram, while Dr Watson frowned.

'I suppose that might work, Holmes, but I don't see how the fishmonger could have got home from Fleet Street. And Lady Galbraith would have started out much further north.'

And so we went on. An item about a missing Danish opera singer and another about the Pembrokeshire strangler were of particular interest to Mr Holmes, but he paid little attention to the business pages, and when I read out that Mr Raffles had taken nine wickets against the Free Foresters in his last game of the season, he simply tutted and rolled his eyes.

'And what about our Russian friends?' he asked. 'Anything new today?'

'Yes, sir, but only a short one, from Aldan to Maya: *I still await instructions. Then I will act.*'

'Neither shall win any prizes for their prose, shall they, Watson?' Mr Holmes looked decidedly unimpressed. 'And no word yet from Mr Dashing, Flotsam?'

'No, sir. But there's something about him here. "*Mob in Weston Square. Police officers yesterday dispersed a small group of individuals causing a disturbance outside the home of diplomat and by-election hopeful Mr George Dashing. Placards marked* Go Back To Montenegro *were seized. It is believed the individuals making the protest are opposed to votes for women.*"'

Dr Watson looked a little startled.

'Sounds like the group of undesirables Lady Hastings warned us about, doesn't it, Holmes?'

'It does, Watson.' The great detective nodded. 'Although they don't yet sound like a threat to the gentleman's life. Let us hope that they will now go back to their preferred occupation of shouting at ladies outside meeting halls. Anything else, Flotsam?'

'Only a line stating that Mr Dashing definitely plans to stand in the Winchester by-election next month, sir. And I heard from the coal boy that he dined at the Mecklenberg last night. But there's been no sign of him calling here.'

After *The Times*, I went through *The Telegraph* and *The Standard* in the same way, and finally I turned to *The Clarion*, where a particular story caught my eye.

'Consulting Detective Displays Brilliance!' I announced happily.

Mr Holmes raised an eyebrow.

'Still more about the Beauchamp affair? I would have thought everything to be said about the matter has already been said. But if *The Clarion* wants to sing our praises further, we can't complain, can we, Watson?'

'Not at all, Holmes.' But Dr Watson had noticed a sudden and dramatic change in my expression. 'I say, Flotsam, is something wrong?'

I licked my lips because my mouth seemed to have gone very dry. I had a horrible feeling that somehow I was to blame.

'It isn't about the Beauchamp inheritance, sir. In fact, it isn't about you at all. It's about someone else. I'm sorry to say... That letter I wrote to Mr Jones...'

Sensing my distress, Dr Watson rose from the hearth rug and took the paper from me, then carried it to the window to read it.

Consulting Detective Displays Brilliance
New Star Eclipses Old
Cornwall Mews to Become New Baker Street?

The editor of this journal has been staggered this week by an astonishing display of deductive brilliance by a consulting detective hitherto unknown to him, and unknown to the general public.

Until the emergence of a certain Great Man of Baker Street, the profession of consulting detective was unknown in Great Britain and, indeed, in the wider world. For some years now, this country has gloried in the knowledge that the world's greatest detective was a product of these shores. But no Titan strides the globe unchallenged forever, and it would now appear that a rival to the Baker Street Brain has been found a little further south, in the unlikely environs of Kensington.

This momentous discovery was occasioned by an unhappy domestic event. The editor of this journal has long enjoyed the companionship of a faithful canine that answers to the name of Scrap, a Trawler Spaniel, a dog of advancing years but most affectionate disposition. This greatly loved animal, a faithful friend to his owner and the willing playmate of his children and grandchildren, enjoys, every day, without exception, a morning constitutional in the leafy surroundings of St James's Park. In this walk Scrap is accompanied by his cherished master who, invariably, rewards himself for his exertions by pausing near the York Gate to purchase tobacco of a certain highly prized type. While this transaction takes place, it is Scrap's custom to remain outside the shop premises, tethered and obedient, while he gratefully rests his ageing and increasingly infirm limbs.

Imagine, then, the great wailing and gnashing of teeth when, one day a fortnight since, Scrap's loving master emerged into the sunlight having secured his daily dose of the divine weed, only to find his faithful friend DISAPPEARED. In vain did he search, in vain did he call! Of his canine companion there was no sign. Not for a moment did he maintain the notion that his 'little Scrap of fur' had made off of his own volition, for the tether had been most firmly secured, by the knot commonly known as 'the log binder'. In short, he was forced to conclude that his companion in his matutinal excursions has been STOLEN.

Naturally, every appropriate step was taken, and within hours a letter had been dispatched to the Great Mind of Baker Street, begging for the assistance of its renowned deductive powers in reuniting master and hound. But alas, all that was received by way of reply was a letter, signed by a minion — a most kind, solicitous and delicately worded letter, it is to be admitted — to the effect that the Genius of Baker Street was too busy to attend to the matter, and suggesting instead that a newspaper advertisement, and the offer of a reward, might be the desperate dog owner's only hope.

This advice was rapidly taken, and readers may have seen just such a notice in the pages of this very journal. Scrap's name was stated, and also his description, for he is that rare type of Trawler Spaniel possessed of a red coat, with a white waistcoat, rather than the black coat more commonly associated with the breed.

Fortunately for our distinguished editor, one reader who viewed the notice was a Consulting Detective newly established in Cornwall Mews, one LAURENCE MARTIN, who, taking pity upon the suffering of Scrap's grieving master, applied his own genius to the problem. And what spectacular deductive powers Mr Martin is now seen to possess! With the permission of this GREAT NEW-FOUND DETECTIVE TALENT, we reproduce the letter than gave such great hope to those who were in despair!

'Dear Sir', Mr Martin wrote, 'I cannot pretend to know the identity of the thief, but from the details in your advertisement I feel certain I can reunite you with your lost dog. I suggest, this coming Saturday, from mid-morning onwards, you position yourself at the Victoria Gate of Hyde Park. Remain vigilant, and look out for any young man of sombre aspect dressed in mourning. One such, I am persuaded, will be in the possession of your dog, Scrap.'

To this heartening communication the remarkable gentleman added a kind-hearted rejoinder.

'The individual you encounter, although certainly a thief in fact, will not, I feel sure, be a criminal by custom, and I strongly suspect will yield up your dog without objection. I would ask you to treat the culprit with compassion rather than contempt.'

Dear reader, you can imagine with what joy these instructions were acted upon, and the amazement that abounded when events unfolded precisely as this new Great Thinker had predicted. A small association of 'Scrap-seekers', led by the creature's master, assembled at the given time at the given spot. Only a few minutes after they had taken up their positions, they witnessed a young man in mourning-clothes approaching, his expression downcast, with the beloved canine trailing on a leash at his heels. The fellow was confronted, and yielded up his ill-gotten prize, not with defiance, but with tears of sorrow and regret. The tale he told his captors was so tragic, his remorse so heartfelt and his countenance so pitiful, that, to a man, those who had seized him agreed to release him, not with cuffs and curses, but with genuine good wishes for his future welfare. The joy of dog and master on being so happily united can be readily imagined.

But what of Kensington's new-found Genius? How had he been able to facilitate with such uncanny ease the lost dog's return? Surely to do so, he must have had some prior knowledge of thief or dog or both?

These questions occupied Scrap's master, so he wrote to the new detective, begging for an explanation of how he had achieved such a remarkable outcome. The reply, which Mr Martin in his modesty requests we do not publish here, was detailed, clear and astonishing in its simplicity. All, when laid out calmly in writing, appeared so simple and straightforward; yet without a GREAT MIND to order those things, all had been opaque!

Mr Martin, it must be noted, has not sought financial reward for his efforts on Scrap's behalf, acting, he states, entirely out of goodwill. Nor has he sought fame, tending, if anything, to shun publicity rather than to seek it.

And so, while many seeking enlightenment will no doubt continue to turn their steps towards the famous Oracle of Baker Street, the editor of this journal, and all those who have been privy to these events, have no

hesitation in advising that there now resides
in London a rival GENIUS whose deductive
powers are every bit as great – if not greater –
than those of their better established compet-
itor.

Mr Holmes listened to all this quietly, and when the reading was finished, I was the first to speak.

'Oh, Mr Holmes, sir! This is all my fault. It was me who wrote Mr Jones that letter!'

'Nonsense, Flotsam!' The great man calmly folded the diagram that lay on the hearth rug, then rose to his feet. 'You wrote precisely as I instructed, and wrote very prettily, if that account is to be believed. I confess it did not occur to me that the Mr Jones who had lost his dog might be Arthur Frederick Jones, editor of *The Clarion*, but even if it had, my response would have been exactly the same.'

'But what of this Martin fellow?' Dr Watson asked, look somewhat aghast. 'They're making out that he's every bit as clever as you are, Holmes! Why, I'd like to read that letter, to see how he explains himself! And after all, at the end of the day, he's only found a lost dog!'

But Mr Holmes had taken the newspaper from him, and was browsing it thoughtfully.

'Trawler spaniel... Unusual red coat... Clearly infirm... Grieving widower... Hyde Park... Yes, I can see how he reached his conclusions.'

Then he gave a little shrug and returned the paper to his friend.

'But no need for you to be downcast, Watson. I have never claimed a monopoly on logic, and, besides, this is simple stuff – for all *The Clarion's* excitement, there's no great genius on display here, only some clear thinking and common sense. With an advertisement such as this to boost his standing, I daresay Mr Martin can expect an increase in callers in the coming days, and I wish him well. But he needs to be aware that his new-found fame will pass quickly enough unless greater triumphs than this one are laid at his door. Mr Martin will need more than just a tale of missing pets if he wishes to live long in the public's attention.'

And with that crisp assertion, he handed his folded diagram to me then turned to his companion.

'Come, Watson. You and I are going to examine the sewer that runs below Fleet Street. And so, Flotsam, if the editor of *The Clarion*, or of any other daily newspaper, should happen to come calling today, you will know exactly where to direct him.'

Chapter Six

Mr Holmes was surely right to think that a newly established consulting detective, without either a previous
reputation or an eminent sponsor, might struggle to
remain for very long in the public eye. But to my great
surprise, Laurence Martin's name did not fade away that
autumn, but seemed to grow in fame with every week
that passed.

Three days after the tale of the rescued Trawler Spaniel
appeared in *The Clarion*, I made my way from the kitchen
in Baker Street to the grand town house of the Earl of
Brabham in Bloomsbury Square, where, once a week,
I was given a lesson in science by the earl's nephew,
Mr Rupert Spencer. This most unlikely arrangement had
been in place ever since those days, long ago, when Mrs
Hudson had rescued me from the streets and replaced my
rags with the tidy trappings of a scullery maid. For Mrs
Hudson believed in education, especially for girls. 'Young
men, even very ignorant ones, enjoy all sorts of freedom,
Flotsam,' she used to tell me, 'but without some learning,
a young girl finds herself trapped below stairs forever.'

And so a campaign was begun to expose me to all sorts
of knowledge, from reading and writing to history and
geography, and Mrs Hudson's extensive range of acquaintances were pressed into service for a number of subjects:
French from various ladies' maids as they passed through

town; botany from the curate of St Luke's; even some Latin from the Irish knife-grinder, who Mrs Hudson paid in pastries. He would sit and eat them by our kitchen fire, talking of Virgil and Ovid, and telling tales of the fall of Troy, all in a soft Cork burr.

Once Mrs Hudson felt I had a sufficient grounding in reading, writing, arithmetic and polishing, and that I had learned enough of manners and deportment to pass, if not for a lady, at least for someone who was not quite an urchin, her thoughts turned to the physical sciences.

Mr Spencer, a good-looking young gentleman of some standing in scientific circles, had known Mrs Hudson since he was a boy, when she was in service at the big house in Brabham-on-Sea. Back then, her discretion in the matter of various broken windows had clearly made a favourable impression upon him, not to mention, as the gentleman once confided in me, a certain occasion when a number of waterfowl from the local duck pond were released into the drawing room minutes before the Brabham Summer Ball. His avoidance of punishment that day was a miracle that left the young Mr Spencer feeling he owed a debt of gratitude, and many years later, when he learned he was to give weekly lessons to Mrs Hudson's young *protégée*, he may perhaps have had misgivings, but he didn't demur.

Which was why, that morning in Bloomsbury Square, dressed in my very best clothes, I called at the front door, not the rear, and was shown into the library by Reynolds, the butler, who whispered me a few words of warning.

'You will find Miss Peters waiting for you, Miss,' he told me, 'and she is in a state of considerable excitement.' He cleared his throat, and lowered his voice yet further. 'She has been in such a state, if I may say, ever since the news reached us of Mr Dashing's return to London. But I believe it is something quite different that is on her mind this morning. No doubt she will tell you all.'

Miss Hetty Peters, ward to Mr Spencer's uncle, the Earl of Brabham, also resided in the house on Bloomsbury Square, and was obliged, for reasons of propriety, to accompany me during my lessons. I found her pacing to and fro across the rather beautiful Isfahan rug that filled the centre of the room.

'Flottie! At last! Thank goodness!' She advanced upon me and greeted me with a warm embrace. 'You are just the person I wanted to see! I've been worrying about it all morning. I keep trying to think about bonnets, but then I start imagining everything changing and nothing being right anymore. Tell me...' Her voice softened, as though she were addressing someone in mourning. 'How *are* things in Baker Street?'

I told her that things were very busy, and that Mrs Hudson and I had started work on the tiles in the pantry.

'But what about Mr Holmes, Flottie? Is he very worried?'

I considered this.

'He was a bit impatient with Dr Watson this morning,' I admitted, 'but I don't think he's particularly worried about anything. Are you thinking of the Romford thing? He seems very sure that he will have an answer to it in no time at all.'

Miss Peters gave a little gasp of impatience.

'But what about his *rival*, Flottie? He must surely be worried about him?'

'You mean...?'

I was still, even then, not entirely sure what she meant, and Miss Peters rolled her eyes, then took me by the hand.

'Mr Martin, of course! It's making me terribly anxious.'

As she talked, she led me over to the leather sofa by the fossil cabinet.

'You see, Flottie, last night I was at a little gathering at the Framlinghams. You wouldn't really call it a *party*, and it certainly wasn't a *soirée*, but there was some music, and a little bit of dancing, and Drusilla Framlingham made a terrible fool of herself by wearing a peach dress with pearls and chasing after Matthew Hemmings, even though everyone knows he's practically engaged to her cousin, who wore a very perfect dress in a lovely sort of midnight blue and looked so utterly charming that no one could imagine why she would even think of marrying a chunky old boot like Matthew Hemmings, even if his father *does* own every sheep in Suffolk. Or is it every cow in Cambridgeshire? I never can remember. A large number of animals, anyway, and somewhere rather flat.'

'And Mr Holmes' name was mentioned, Hetty?' I guided her gently back to the subject.

'But, no! That's just the point, Flottie. His name wasn't mentioned at all, not even once. It was as though he didn't exist. All anyone wanted to talk about was the amazing Mr Martin!'

I confess I was surprised. However heart-warming the story of the rescued pet, it seemed unlikely to me that, among Hetty's friends, it could come close to rivalling Drusilla Framlingham's pearls as a topic of conversation.

'So they are still talking about the missing spaniel?' I asked.

'The what? Oh, the dog thing.' Hetty waved her hand airily. 'Well, yes, everyone knew all about that. People love a story about a faithful hound. But the thing is, Flottie...' Her other hand, which was still holding mine, gripped my fingers more tightly. 'The thing is…' She took a very deep breath. 'The thing is, *Mr Martin has found Patricia Knibling's diamonds!*'

The effect upon me of this dramatic declaration was diminished by the fact that I had never heard of Patricia Knibling and knew nothing of her diamonds. But clearly, to Miss Peters, it was an event of the most enormous significance.

'Oh, really, Flottie, surely you *must* have heard about it? I mean, it was all top secret, of course, because the Kniblings didn't want it to get out, but Frank Fosdyke knew, and so did Laetitia Parker-Tomlinson, so it was very quickly the sort of secret that *everyone* knows, but which is still a secret because everyone is too discreet to talk about it, except to other people who understand that it's *that* sort of secret.'

She paused for breath, then carried on with a rush.

'Anyway, it all happened about three weeks ago, at Trenthams, which is the Kniblings' house in Sussex. The Kniblings were putting on one of their lavish entertainments to celebrate the birthday of their youngest, Violet, who is fifteen and the pretty one, and Patricia Knibling wore those famous diamonds of hers, which are marvellous stones but just a little bit spoiled by being in such ugly settings. And of course everyone knows that Patricia Knibling is terribly absent-minded, and that her family try terribly hard to hide the fact, ever since that night at Chatsworth when she slept half the night in old General Matteson's bed without either of them noticing, just because his bedroom door was cream-coloured and so was hers.'

Miss Peters allowed her face to brighten for a moment at the memory, then collected herself and continued.

'Anyway, there they all were, having a jolly good time at Trenthams, because, to be fair, the Kniblings never stint on the entertainments, and there's always champagne on the terrace, oceans of it. Then, half-way through the evening, Patricia Knibling decides to take off her necklace because she says it's heavy and always makes her skin sore, and, of course, that's just the sort of thing she *would* do, because she's quite as vague about etiquette as she is about everything else, and because, as she told anybody who would listen, it was only going to be for a moment.'

Miss Peters looked at me and shook her head sorrowfully.

'Only, of course, Flottie, it wasn't for a moment, was it? Because then she forgot to put it back on, and for quite a long time, according to everyone who was there – and practically everyone *was* there – she carried it around in her hand like a string of glass beads, and then quite suddenly she realised the diamonds weren't in her hand anymore, and she had no idea *where* they were, and nor did anyone else, and, well, to sum it all up, Flottie, they had completely disappeared!'

'Stolen?' I asked, astonished. A scandal of that sort would be almost unprecedented, yet it seemed impossible that an object of such enormous value could simply be mislaid.

Miss Peters sighed.

'Well, that's just it, Flottie. Nobody knows. But the sort of people invited to Trenthams aren't the sort who usually steal diamonds, and most of the servants have worked for the family for about a thousand years, so it seems more likely that Patricia Knibling simply put them down somewhere peculiar. That's certainly what her parents thought, because they absolutely refused to go to the police. Instead, the family all moved back up to London while the servants searched the house from attics to cellars, but by the start of this week they were on their seventh search, and no one had found even the tiniest trace of a diamond, and the Kniblings were going to be ruined by the scandal, because if the necklace *was* stolen then one of their guests was a thief, and, if it *wasn't* stolen, then their daughter would be held-up as a laughing stock for the rest of her life. And it was then that one of their callers brought with him a copy of *The Clarion* with the dog story in it, and suggested that they might do worse than dropping a line to Laurence Martin, asking for help.'

I had, of course, known where Miss Peters' tale was leading, but even so I felt a sinking feeling in my stomach. It had been my letter that had steered the editor of *The Clarion* towards Mr Martin, and now, as a result, it was that detective's name on everyone's lips.

'At first, Mr Knibling wasn't sure,' Miss Peters went on, 'because he didn't want a stranger to know that his daughter left priceless diamonds lying around. But Mrs Knibling liked the fact that Laurence Martin had solved the dog thing from a distance, without poking about in the closets, as she put it, so a note was sent that same evening, and a reply came back by return asking that Patricia Knibling should write a full account of everything she remembered from the moment she took off the neck-lace.'

Miss Peters paused to tuck a stray tendril of hair behind her ear.

'Well, obviously, Flottie, that could have taken forever, because all her recollections were very vague but she had rather a lot of them. So her sisters sat down with her and helped her piece things together, and according to Frank

Fosdyke it was the most rambling thing he'd ever read, but they finished it late that night and it was sent off straight away.

'Of course, Flottie, I don't think they really thought Mr Martin would help, because how could he? He's never met the Kniblings or been anywhere near Trenthams, and the house had already been turned upside down several times by the servants. But I think they all felt better for doing something. And then the next morning a small boy arrived with a telegram. Laetitia Parker-Tomlinson told me what it said, and I knew I'd want to tell you and Rupert about it, so I memorised it. Wasn't that sensible?'

I agreed that it was, and begged her to go on.

'Very well then. I suppose there were lots of "stops" and things, and words left out, like there are in telegrams, but Laetitia P-T didn't bother with them, so neither shall I.' She lowered her voice into an impression of booming male tones. '"*Can assume servants competent and guests honest? If so wire Trenthams immediately. Instruct gardener to search dense foliage directly beneath terrace approximately twelve feet from West Steps.*"'

I felt the fingers on my hand tighten even more.

'So now you can see why I'm so worried, Flottie! Poor Mr Holmes! What will he do when he is no longer the detective everyone turns to? He won't like it all, will he? I hate to think of him scraping along, looking for missing husbands and stray cats and things, and if things get really bad for him he may have to move from Baker Street, and then what will happen to you, Flottie? Oh, I know you will be all right really, because Mrs Hudson could choose om a hundred positions at the click of her fingers, and course she'd take you with her wherever she went. k how much you'd miss Mr Holmes and all his escapades! We all would! Really, Flottie, I cannot bear to think of this Laurence Martin taking his place!'

I placed my other hand on hers and squeezed back, rather touched by her anxiety.

'Truly, Hetty, I'm sure everything will be all right. Mr Holmes won't worry about a little competition. So am I to understand, then, that the Kniblings followed Mr Martin's advice and that they really did find the necklace where he told them?'

'I'm afraid so.' Miss Peters gave a little sniff and raised her chin as if to calm herself. 'Completely out of sight, under a big clump of hydrangeas, exactly where he said. Trenthams is famous for its hydrangeas, apparently, and now they're even more famous than they used to be, although, if you ask me, Flottie, the Knibling Hydrangeas sound horribly carnivorous, don't they? But last night, they were all anyone wanted to talk about – them and Laurence Martin, of course. Rather more about him, in fact, because detectives are a lot more interesting than shrubs, even with diamonds under them, especially after a glass or two of sparkling hock. And the story will be in all the evening papers today, because there's no danger of any scandal now the diamonds have been found, and the Kniblings know it's quite safe to tell the newspapers everything, because all anyone will want to talk about will be Mr Martin's astonishing abilities, and not the fact that their daughter is the most scatter-brained child in the whole of the Home Counties. Oh, there's Rupert! Rupert, I'm just telling Flottie about Mr Martin and the diamonds.'

The gentleman who advanced into the room wa[s] an undoubtedly good-looking man of around thirty-fiv[e] years of age, with brown hair and brown eyes, and a pleasant smile as he held out his hand.

'Good morning, Flotsam. Hetty here has been worrying all morning about Mr Holmes' rival, and it certainly seems that gentleman has pulled off rather an impressive trick on behalf of the Kniblings. I will be fascinated to hear how it was done.' He grinned broadly. 'Personally, however, I'm very grateful to Mr Martin. This is the first morning for a week when I have not had to listen to a breathless commentary on the latest doings of a certain George Dashing.'

'Rupert!' Miss Peters bounced up and down in her seat. 'Really, Flotsam, you mustn't listen to a word. Rupert is simply being a beast. I don't deny that Mr Dashing is rather better looking than most young men, and has rather superior manners, and is a *much* better dancer than any of them, but I don't believe I talk about him at all really, or at least not very often, and even if I do, it's perfectly normal to wonder where a fashionable gentleman of that sort likes to dine, and whether I'm likely to meet him, and what I should wear. And Rupert, if you *dare* to say that thing of yours about him being dashing by nature, I swear I shall hit you with this book about the Stone Age, I really shall.'

Mr Spencer looked at the large leather volume that lay on an incidental table just in front of us and seemed reluctant to take the risk.

'My apologies, Hetty. I was mistaken. However, in my defence, your lack of interest in Mr Dashing is extremely well disguised, and, among young ladies of your acquaintance, quite possibly unique.' He looked across at me and smiled. 'Incidentally, Flotsam, Mr Dashing is said to enjoy the company of young ladies who are widely read, and although you will find this hard to believe, only yesterday

I came across Hetty with a novel in her hand. A coincidence, of course, but a decidedly curious one.'

'Really, Rupert!' Miss Peters reached for the tome in front of her, and, I think, would probably have thrown it at Mr Spencer had it not proved far too heavy to lift. 'The novel has absolutely nothing to do with George Dashing. Well, almost nothing to do with him. It was given to me by Angelica Tipton, who is always reading startling romances about dowdy governesses who rescue handsome young noblemen when their horses bolt, then marry them.'

She looked at Mr Spencer, who was holding in his hand a book about chemical elements, and sighed to herself.

'So, anyway, when I mentioned I was in the mood to read a book, just because I *did* happen to be in the mood to read a book, Angelica told me of something everyone was talking about. So I borrowed it, and started it, and I was expecting shapely calves splattered with mud and a lot of dark, glowering looks, but it turns out her book is by some foreign Count Something, and although it says it's about war and peace, really it just seems to be a lot people with funny names talking to each other, and it's terribly long, which makes it awfully heavy to carry about. Perhaps you could read it, Flotsam,' she added hopefully, 'and then tell me what happens?'

Sensing I was at a loss for a reply, Mr Spencer turned to me.

'I hear a rumour, Flotsam, that Mr Holmes is also taking an interest in the fortunes of Mr Dashing?'

I attempted to look discreet, because even in Bloomsbury Square it was hardly my place to chatter freely, but before I could mumble any sort of response, Miss Peters had tossed her head and uttered a little exclamation.

'Rupert, that isn't at all fair!' She turned to me, all blue-eyed outrage. 'He knows all about it already, Flottie. That stuffy old Croxton man has a private secretary who went to school with Rupert and the two of them are thick as thieves because they both hunt beetles in their spare time, and people who hunt beetles always seem to like other people who hunt beetles, presumably because they have no one else, although what the beetles have ever done to deserve it, I really don't know.'

Mr Spencer acknowledged this with a polite nod of the head.

'It's certainly true, Flotsam, that everyone in Whitehall seems to be talking about a plot against George Dashing. And at the Aristaeus Club, it's impossible to get a copy of *The Times* because everyone is desperate to read about Maya and Aldan.'

'Oh, really, Rupert!' Miss Peters bounced up from her seat and snatched the newspaper from his hand. 'With so many really *interesting* messages to choose from, why would anyone bother with those two? It's all so *drab*. I don't believe they're Russian spies at all. They are probably just two unhappy and unfortunate people with unpleasant families, living in Balham or Wimbledon or somewhere unutterably soulless, and you should all just leave them alone. If you want excitement, what about *Emma to Jack*? Or *Miss F.W.*, with her little messages about pressing flowers which I'm told aren't about pressing flowers *at all*, and which, when you realise that, are so incredibly racy it's impossible to read them at all without blushing. There was one about a blossoming gladiolus...'

Mr Spencer coughed in a very pointed manner.

'Perhaps not now, Hetty.' He looked at his watch. 'And if we are to have a lesson at all today, we had better begin.

At your suggestion, Flotsam, I thought we could look at chemical pigments. I have some rather toxic substances laid out downstairs, so perhaps if you two ladies would like to lead the way...?'

And for the next hour or more, watching colours change and gases form, my mind full of chemicals and poisons, I didn't think even for a moment about the fate of Mr George Dashing.

Chapter Seven

Thinking back upon the many cases brought to Mr Holmes in Baker Street, it isn't difficult to recall a great many clients who were, for all sorts of different reasons, in great personal danger. But it is hard to think of any who appeared less concerned about it than the elusive Mr Dashing.

A week after Sir James Croxton had begged Mr Holmes to help ensure the young man's safety, we had still seen no sign of him at Baker Street. Notes had been dispatched, both to Sir James and to Mr Dashing himself, urging that a meeting should be arranged, but despite Sir James' earnest assurances that the young man had promised to call, no such visit was made. From the young gentleman himself, there was only silence. We knew, from the great many mentions of his name in the newspapers, exactly where he was dining, the names of his dance partners, and even what he was wearing, but he showed no sign of including Baker Street in his daily itinerary.

Those days were nevertheless busy ones, and Mr Holmes and Dr Watson made great strides in the case of the Romford hieroglyphs. But finally, after five days of hearing nothing, Mr Holmes decided that he and Dr Watson should call upon George Dashing in person. They returned hot – for the golden weather continued, and it was another very warm afternoon – but also rather cross.

'Fellow refused to see us,' Dr Watson muttered irritably, handing me his hat. 'Servant had been told to tell us that Mr Dashing was uncommonly busy just now but would call upon as at some point this month! Might be dead by then, mightn't he, Holmes?'

'Sir James Croxton certainly seems to think so.' He looked across at me. 'Remind me of this morning's message, Flotsam...'

'Yes, sir. *You must make sure he goes away forever. Only then can the sun smile upon us*,' I quoted.

Mr Holmes seemed to ponder this as he passed me his cane.

'Well, we can't do much about it if Mr Dashing refuses to talk to us, can we, Watson? We'll continue to keep an eye on the messages in *The Times*, just in case anything else catches our eye, but otherwise I fear Mr Dashing's fate is in his own hands.'

'Doesn't feel right to be doing nothing, though, Holmes.' Dr Watson's brow was furrowed. 'What do you say we go and have a word with Sir Henry Catanache? You know, Mr Dashing's arch-enemy? Remember what Lady Hastings told us about those thugs outside her meetings? If they're planning anything against Mr Dashing, Sir Henry might have heard some sort of rumour.'

The great detective smiled at this.

'If a man like Sir Henry were aware of such a plot, he would surely have raised the alarm, my friend. Unless, of course, he were one of the plotters, in which case he is hardly likely to confess as much to us.' But then, perhaps seeing his friend look a little downcast, he clapped him heartily on the shoulder. 'But you are absolutely right that he should be interviewed, Watson. You shall call on him this evening. I have that pile of volumes about the

Rameses Anachronism which need to be returned to the Pharaonic Society. You can deliver them this evening, then stop by at the Catanache residence after that.'

Dr Watson looked slightly perturbed.

'But what about you, Holmes? Won't you be coming?'

'If you remember, my friend, I solemnly promised Lord Carnarvon's secretary that I would call later today. You are worried, perhaps, about managing all those volumes alone?'

Mr Holmes' gaze turned to me.

'Flotsam, Dr Watson will need your assistance this evening with some extremely bulky books. Would you be so good as to ask Mrs Hudson if she can spare you for an hour or two after dinner?'

–

Mrs Hudson said that she could, and I was pleased. It would not be the first time I had helped Dr Watson run an errand, and I always enjoyed his company, finding him both restful and amusing at the same time. But before I could go, there were various tasks to be completed and the kitchen floor to do, while Mrs Hudson set off to visit various elderly acquaintances who were, apparently, in great need of blackberry vinegar for their rheumatism. When she was gone, I finished the floor, then continued my ongoing work in the pantry, scrubbing at the grout with Mrs Hudson's home-made paste and a narrow brush.

With the house so quiet, it was soothing work. I had propped open the area door to allow the rich warmth of the afternoon to drift in, and from beyond the quiet of the house, the noise of the streets trickled in, muted and soft. Any footfall on the area steps must have been a very soft one, for no sound of that sort reached me in the pantry.

It was therefore rather a shock, on returning to the kitchen, to find a very finely dressed young gentleman in the narrow little area, just outside the kitchen, perched casually on the fourth-from-bottom step, smoking a long and elegant cigarette.

So outraged was I by this singular intrusion, that I didn't really notice much about him in that first instant. Instead I stepped sharply to the door, still in my stained apron, still with a smear of dirt across one cheek, and demanded to know what he meant by it, lurking by our door in such a way.

On hearing my voice, he straightened hastily, pulling off his hat with one hand while throwing down his cigarette with the other, smartly extinguishing it with the tip of one shiny leather boot.

'I do beg your pardon,' he replied, meeting my eye and smiling an open and frank smile, 'but I was waiting for someone to come. I felt certain that someone would, with the door being open like that.'

He was, I realised, an extremely handsome young gentleman: very dark hair; an open, honest face; dark brown eyes; full lips and the broadest of smiles; and all of it wrapped up in an air of gentle and infectious good-humour. Before he'd even finished speaking, I could feel myself smiling back.

'My name is Dashing — George Dashing,' he went on, 'and I was wondering if Mr Sherlock Holmes was at home?'

Unlikely though it may sound, I do believe I noticed the gentleman's voice quite as much as his face on that very first meeting — a soft, rich baritone that seemed somehow warm and familiar, like an old song, as though you had always known it. Much later, looking back on events, a certain lady once told me that whenever she was in conversation with George Dashing, she felt like a dog having its stomach tickled, which is perhaps a little shocking, especially given how many young ladies would have gladly had their actual stomachs tickled by him. But it is certainly true that he had a nice voice.

'Mr Holmes is… Well, sir, I'm not sure…'

My confusion was evident, and the gentleman smiled again.

'Yes, I know, I should have knocked at the front door. And by not doing so, I have placed you in an awkward situation. But, you see, I've promised someone that I will call here, and a gentleman always tries to keep a promise. Yet, at the same time, I don't really want to meet Mr Holmes very much, because if I meet him, I shall feel honour bound to do what he tells me, and I have a strong suspicion that it won't be very much fun.'

His eyes met mine as he talked, in a way so natural and so friendly that I found myself swallowing rather more than usual.

'My plan in coming down here,' he went on, 'was to seek out someone who could tip me the wink. Because if Sherlock Holmes is out, I shall call at the front door in the proper manner and leave my card. But if he's at home, rather than risk a lecture, I shall simply tiptoe away and come back another time when I've got a better chance of missing him.'

He concluded with a self-deprecating smile, as though aware of his own absurdity, and I rather think I giggled. Certainly, it never occurred to me not to enter into his conspiracy.

'Mr Holmes *is* in, sir,' I told him, lowering my voice, 'but I believe he plans to be out later in the evening, if you wished to call then?'

The gentleman replied with a little bow.

'I am greatly in your debt. And your name is…?'

'Flotsam, sir,' I told him with a little curtsy, and I rather think I blushed as I said it.

'I am greatly in your debt, Flotsam, and I shall do as you advise. But first, I'm expected at my club, and I must go there by a circuitous route. Because, do you know, Flotsam…' And here he too lowered his voice, greatly adding to that sense of a shared and secret understanding. 'Do you know, Flotsam, and you may think me very odd for saying it, but I rather think I was followed here today. And not by anyone in the least bit sinister or romantic, but by a stout little man in a bowler hat with a very indifferent moustache.'

And with a further little nod, the exquisite Mr Dashing was gone.

It was only afterwards, as I returned to the pantry, that various thoughts occurred to me. For instance, it struck me that, for once, all Miss Peters' bubbling excitement about a good-looking gentleman newly arrived in town might actually be justified. Also, as I reached for Mrs Hudson's grout paste, I confess that I wondered for the very briefest of moments if perhaps Mr Dashing's great warmth and friendliness that afternoon might possibly – just possibly – have been in some part due to me; a suspicion I instantly put out of my head.

Only then did I remember that a number of quite prominent people believed George Dashing was genuinely and greatly in danger. And with that thought came the realisation that, by so foolishly assisting him in avoiding my employer, I had perhaps made my own, very real contribution to the peril in which he stood.

–

It had been arranged that Dr Watson and I should set out for the library of the Pharaonic Society at eight o'clock that evening. Before that hour, I had every opportunity to tell Mrs Hudson of my strange encounter by the area steps, and to confess in full the details of my indiscretion. Certainly I would have done so promptly in my younger days, for I had grown up never having, and never wanting, any secrets from her. But when I remembered how I had blushed on telling Mr Dashing my name, and how I had quite willingly volunteered the information he sought, I was filled with a mixture of shame and embarrassment that it was all too painful to think about. But at the same time, and in a peculiar way, it was a very tiny bit exciting too.

So instead I asked Mrs Hudson about the Catanache family, and she was able to tell me a surprising amount.

'For I used to know their housekeeper quite well,' she explained, 'although it's been a year or two since I saw her last, and she has retired since. The Catanaches are a very old English family, Flotsam, for all their exotic name. It's said the first Catanache came back from the Holy Land with Richard III, and Sir Henry Catanache is a staunch defender of the family name and traditions. How well do you know your garden flowers, Flotsam?'

For a young girl raised in the city, I was surprisingly knowledgeable about flowers, but I didn't know as much as Mrs Hudson, who had, in her time, seen some of the great English gardens at close quarters, and had provided tea and fruit cake to their gardeners.

'The catanache is a little blue flower,' she went on. 'In this country they call it 'Cupid's Dart', and put it at the front of borders, but in warmer climes, I'm told, it grows on waste ground like a weed. Hence the motto of the Catanache family – "*Love and our arrows from the wilderness strike*".'

She pursed her lips slightly.

'Which may sound romantic enough in these modern times, Flottie, but no doubt sounded rather more sinister during the Crusades. Anyway, the Catanache family uses the flower as their emblem and you'll see it everywhere in their house on Cuthbert Square – on their crest above their front door, even moulded into the railings outside. People call it the Blue Daisy of the Catanaches, though, of course, it isn't really a daisy at all.'

'And what about, Sir Henry, ma'am?' I asked. 'Lady Hastings made him sound terribly fearsome and not very nice.'

Mrs Hudson, who was polishing teaspoons, considered this for a moment.

'I suspect Sir Henry is like a great many men of his sort, Flottie – rather too grand for his own good, and not at all accustomed to having his opinions challenged. Which means that anyone who *does* challenge his opinions must clearly be an idiot or a revolutionary. He probably considers George Dashing to be both.'

I opened my mouth then, and was about to confess that Mr Dashing hadn't struck me as either of those things, but the clock chimed eight, and I heard Dr Watson on the stairs, and it was time for me to go.

–

The large volumes Mr Holmes had mentioned proved to be very large indeed – far too large to be bundled together with string because simply lifting any one of them by itself was a challenge, and lifting two or more together would have been quite impossible. However, a hansom cab was hailed, and a helpful cab-driver even lent his assistance by offering cheerful advice about angles and stacking.

Eventually, with the help of Mrs Hudson and the boot boy from across the road who happened to be passing, the five great volumes, all carefully wrapped in oil cloth, were stored on the floor of the hansom, where Dr Watson and I were able to rest our feet on them.

'Almost certainly the best use they've been put to for some time,' the doctor commented bitterly, as we got underway. 'For between you and me, Flotsam, they're far from being gripping prose, and I'd wager my lucky necktie that no one has looked at them for a good fifty years, and probably longer. We found dead moths in them of a kind that Holmes says has been unknown in London since before the Industrial Revolution.'

He was, however, careful not to repeat this observation when we arrived at our destination, where a small army of young men in livery was awaiting our arrival with expressions of great deference and seriousness. Between them they carried away the great tomes in next to no time, handling each with such exaggerated reverence that I felt a little guilty not to have done the same. When the last of them was gone, and when appropriate farewells had been said, Dr Watson gave a great sigh of relief.

'That's that, and I'm pleased to see the back of them. And now to the Catanache residence in Cuthbert Square, Flotsam. Probably won't be long. I'll just ask Sir Henry a few questions, you know the sort of thing. And, er...' My travelling companion was suddenly embarrassed. 'Given Sir Henry's views about, er, well, women, Flotsam, it might be better if you stay in the cab. Would love to have you with me myself – sure you'd know exactly what to ask – only, the thing is, I can't see him consenting to see anyone who isn't his idea of a proper person, you know, and as an Army man, I just about qualify. But, well, you're a girl and a, um, well, you know. He's a terribly dry old crust in every way, or so I'm told.'

It was very gracious of Dr Watson to feel such an apology was necessary, for it had never occurred to me that my role that evening should extend beyond helping him with the books and keeping him company between his visits. Sir Henry Catanache, who had made it his personal crusade to deny all women the vote, was hardly likely to allow a visiting housemaid into his house except through the rear entrance, and even then only if she had business with the cook.

But murder changes things. Even just the accusation of murder.

And things changed forever in the Catanache household that very evening, at almost exactly the moment the cab containing Dr Watson and I drew up outside their front door.

Chapter Eight

As soon as our hansom pulled into Cuthbert Square, we could tell something unusual was taking place.

Cuthbert Square is one of those lovely, hidden squares of London that always seem quiet and leafy and strangely forgotten. No carriages pass through it on the way to somewhere else; no pedestrians use it as a short cut. Street hawkers and barrow boys give it a miss, for there is no business to be done there. The garden in its centre is green but not showy, a calming rectangle of grass and shrubs, and in summer its five or six ancient London plane trees dapple the square with a soothing, dancing shade. Its solid Georgian houses are home to families that are both rich and respectable, but are rarely in the forefront of fashion. The excitements of the Season leave Cuthbert Square unruffled, and the great balls and gatherings happen somewhere else.

But that night, on one side of the square, there was a great deal of commotion. I saw one of the great front doors wide open, and light flooding out of it into the street, where a crowd of onlookers had gathered, and where a dark, rather ominous four-wheeler was already parked. It was to that same front door that our hansom cab delivered us, and, as we slowed to a stop, I dimly remember noticing the ornate railings, with their elaborate ironwork twisted into countless posies of tiny flowers.

'Good lord, Flotsam!' Dr Watson exclaimed, viewing the scene in front of us in bewilderment. 'Something's up.'

The assembled crowd had now stopped peering into the hallway of the Catanache residence and had turned its attention to us, staring with unabashed curiosity. I noticed that they were being kept in place, just off the pavement, by two police constables, who were also studying us carefully, and with some suspicion.

'Well, I can't leave you on your own out here,' my companion concluded, taking in the scene. 'Better come with me, Flotsam, and we'll find out just what's going on.'

It says a great deal for Dr Watson's quiet dignity that the crowd parted to let us through, and when one of the constables stepped towards us, my companion favoured him with a smart nod of greeting.

'Dr Watson of Baker Street, here on confidential family business,' he stated briskly, and whether the officer recognised the name or was simply impressed by the confidence of the speaker, he touched his hat and allowed both of us to pass without a word.

The scene that confronted us that night, as we climbed the steps to the open door, was like a moment from a melodrama, with each character carefully arranged around the stage, each of them positioned so as to afford us the perfect view.

At the very centre of the scene, standing on the lower steps of a grand staircase, stood a young man of about twenty-eight, fair-haired and bespectacled, in evening dress. His mouth was open as though about to speak, perhaps to one of the two burly police constables who stood beside him, who each held one of his arms in a firm, two-handed grip. Below him, and to his left, a very finely dressed lady lay partly slumped on the marble floor, her head and shoulders raised by an older gentleman, also in evening dress, who cheeks were puffed out and purple with anger. An elderly butler also knelt beside the fallen woman and was waving a bottle of smelling salts beneath her nose.

Strangely, though, despite the dramatic poses of those characters, the person my eye was most drawn to was a small, slightly dishevelled man of middle years wearing a crumpled suit, with sandy hair and a sandy moustache and rather unremarkable features. He was standing to the right of the scene, and holding up his hand, as if for silence.

'Forgive me, sir,' I heard him say, his voice very calm and strangely confident. 'But you must allow me to proceed.'

At this, the lady on the ground gave a little shriek and the gentleman beside her cursed audibly, but undeterred, the man in the crumpled suit turned to the gentleman on the stairs and spoke loudly and clearly.

'Oscar Catanache, I am arresting you for the murder of Thomasina Trubshaw, one time parlour maid at this address. I would ask you to come with us quietly, sir, so as to minimise any unpleasantness.'

Then, when the younger man said nothing, but merely looked from one face to another as if in panic, the inspector addressed his constables.

'Take him away, lads. I'll finish up here, then head back to Salisbury Street to put things to bed.'

It was only then, when the constables began to lead the young man down the steps and towards the door, that the other actors in the tableau appeared to come to life.

The older man, whose face had grown even more purple, exploded in rage.

'Oscar! Don't take another step! This is an outrage! An outrage!' He rose to his feet, leaving the butler to assist his wife into a sitting position. 'This jumped-up little man talks of evidence! Evidence! I've never heard such drivel! Tell him, Oscar! Tell him that it's nonsense. Tell him that you've never even heard of this woman!'

Oscar Catanache, still escorted by the constables, had now come to within a few feet of the front door, only a few paces from where Dr Watson and I were standing, just on the other side of the threshold. At his father's command, both he and the constables came to a halt, and I saw for myself the sad smile on his face as he turned back to face his father.

'I'm afraid I can't do that, sir,' he said simply. 'I can, with all my might, assert my innocence. And I am sure that the truth will come out. But I cannot deny knowing the young woman in question. Rather more than that. You see...' And here his sad smile turned sweet. 'You see, father, at one point she and I were very nearly engaged to be married.'

And with that, he allowed the constables to lead him from the hallway to the waiting carriage, brushing past Dr Watson as they went.

The effect of this remarkable confession on the young man's father was dramatic. When I turned back to the brightly light hall, I saw the colour in his cheeks had faded to white, and his shoulders had slumped, like someone who had just received a very hard blow to the stomach.

'Engaged? Engaged?' he mumbled, but by now Lady Catanache was on her feet and addressing herself to the police officer. Her voice was a good deal less irate.

'You must forgive us, Inspector…?'

'Merivale, ma'am,' the little man reminded her.

'You must forgive us, Inspector Merivale. You can imagine this has come as a terrible shock to us. We had no idea that my son had any… any *connection* with this woman. But of course he is innocent of this terrible charge.'

While her husband grew paler, the colour was now returning to Lady Catanache's cheeks.

'It is all clearly a dreadful mistake,' she went on. 'Oscar would never hurt a fly. And now you have met us, now that you know who we are, I'm sure you will be able to reconsider matters.'

But Inspector Merivale was standing firm.

'I'm afraid not, my lady,' he began. 'You see, the evidence…'

'Pah! Evidence!' Sir Henry Catanache had quite suddenly regained his colour, as if infuriated by the word. 'The man is clearly an imbecile, Mabel. I've known for years that there's not a man at Scotland Yard capable of tying his own shoelaces. The whole of London knows it! Evidence, by Gad! The only evidence here is that we can't trust our own police force. Just look at the newspapers if you don't believe me – every day they're full of talk of gentlemen detectives doing the police's work for them!'

At this, the police inspector, who until then had remained admirably calm, seemed to uncrumple himself, straightening up until he suddenly stood an inch or two taller than before.

'The evidence I speak of, sir, will be put before a magistrate, and it will be he who decides on its merits. But to be honest, sir, when you have read the letters, seen the evidence, spoken to the witnesses… Well, sir, let's just say you don't need to be a Sherlock Holmes to put the pieces together.'

It was at this moment that Dr Watson announced our presence in the doorway with a discreet but pointed cough.

'Lady Catanache, gentlemen, forgive me for intruding. My name is Dr John Watson, and I am a friend and colleague of the man just mentioned. I mean, of Mr Sherlock Holmes. I happened by chance to be calling this evening on quite another matter, but if you need any assistance in this unfortunate affair, Sir Henry, then I am sure Mr Holmes and I would be delighted to help in any way we can.'

I'd often observed how Dr Watson, when in the company of Mr Holmes, enjoyed playing a very deliberate second fiddle to his friend, and it was sometimes easy to forget how very dignified and impressive he could be when the occasion demanded it. Certainly, on this occasion, his entrance was rather magnificent. Lady Catanache gave a little gasp and held her hand to her chest as if holding in a great spasm of relief. Inspector Merivale gaped in surprise. And Sir Henry Catanache, after a pause in which his face betrayed utter astonishment, advanced across the room to shake the doctor's hand.

'My word! What astonishing timing! You have come to us in the very hour of our need, Doctor!'

As he spoke, he drew Dr Watson into the hallway, and I, uncertain what to do, stepped in after them, before the butler closed the door behind us. Sir Henry, however, was far too overwrought to notice.

'You may have heard, sir, that this man... this inspector... has just taken away my son on a murder charge. Murder, of all things! Seems the boy might have been mixed up with the wrong sort of woman, and I imagine some dirty-minded conclusions have been drawn, so please, I beg you, let us send for Mr Holmes at once. I'm sure the two of you will have no trouble at all in clearing up this little misunderstanding.'

In this assertion he was supported by his wife, who had joined her husband and was now clinging in a rather desperate manner to Dr Watson's arm, echoing her husband's plea for help. And Inspector Merivale, far from appearing to resent my companion's intervention, also appeared pleased to see him. Having recovered from his initial surprise, he approached Dr Watson and held out his hand.

'An honour to meet you, sir,' he said warmly. 'I've had the privilege of working with Mr Holmes in the past once or twice, in that business of the St Pancras picture-framer, for instance. And if it helps reassure Sir Henry, then I'm only too happy to lay the matter before you two gentlemen. After all, evidence is evidence, and I know Mr Holmes to be as fond of it as I am.'

Sir Henry, although still in high colour, appeared somewhat mollified by the reasonableness of this, and so, in this bizarre and rather haphazard way, Mr Holmes and Dr Watson acquired a new case. Indeed, there was talk of sending a boy for Mr Holmes that very hour, for Sir Henry was adamant that investigations on his son's behalf should begin at once. It was only when Lady Catanache grew faint again that wiser counsels prevailed, and it was agreed that Mr Holmes should call the following morning, when things were calmer.

'For it is a very grave case, sir,' the inspector reiterated. 'Very grave indeed, and I would be more than happy if the young gentleman were able to explain everything away. But in the meantime, questions must be asked, sir, and evidence must be gathered. Evidence of innocence, evidence of guilt, which ever it may be, but it must be gathered.'

'And I promise you again, sir,' Dr Watson reassured Sir Henry as we made to depart, 'that you may sleep easily tonight. If your son is indeed innocent, as I've no doubt he is, then I'm sure it won't be hard to prove it. Why, I daresay we'll have him home by tomorrow night!'

It was then, perhaps, while I was still standing unnoticed in the hallway of Sir Henry Catanache's elegant home, that I first felt a whisper of anxiety about what came to be known as the Blue Daisy Affair. Dr Watson was a man who liked to see the good in people, and as a trait it was admirable. But whether Sir Henry's son would be home quite as soon as he suggested seemed to me highly uncertain. Because, I realised, there was one thing we didn't yet know, one hugely important thing.

We didn't yet know whether Oscar Catanache was innocent or not.

—

By the time Dr Watson and I left the Catanache residence, calm had returned to Cuthbert Square. The ominous police carriage was gone, and so too were the crowds, having eventually wearied of staring at a closed front door. The distant rumble of carriages and the clip of horses' hooves on busier thoroughfares seemed very far away, and between us and them lay a soft, leafy silence. We were alone – but for the energetic figure of Inspector Merivale, who was standing on his tiptoes and running his fingertips along his moustache.

'A grave business, sir,' he repeated thoughtfully. 'And although I may have sounded confident in front of the old gentleman – men of his sort need to be handled that way, I find – there is one aspect of this unpleasant affair that worries me.'

He moved his fingertips from his moustache to his chin, and began to stroke his jawline outwards, towards his ears.

'Oh, that's not to say I don't have evidence,' he went on. 'It's exactly as I said, sir. I have a good deal of evidence of a certain sort. But even so... Look, sir, I have to return to the scene of the crime now, and I was wondering if perhaps you would like to come with me and see for yourself. We can walk if you wish, or hail a hansom, and on the way I can tell you all the details.'

And then, to my astonishment, he turned to me and raised his hat.

'It's Miss Flotsam, isn't it, Miss? I thought I recognised you. A good policeman never forgets a face. I've seen you before, you see. That night in Charing Cross Station when we nabbed the foreign spy. A good piece of work, that. Not that you'll have noticed me, 'cos as you'll remember, there were a lot of us there that night. It was quite an occasion! Mrs Hudson certainly knows how to throw a wake, doesn't she, Miss? I trust she's well?'

I told her that she was, but, to be honest, I was so taken aback by being recognised that I think I rather mumbled.

'Well, if the doctor here is agreeable to my plan, you'd better come with us, Miss. I don't imagine Mrs Hudson would thank us for sending you home alone at this hour, and although it's a gruesome scene, I know from that night in Charing Cross that you're not one for a fit of the vapours. And don't worry, sir,' he added, as Dr Watson seemed about to intervene, 'because I know what you're going to say, but it's not as bad as I've made it sound. That's the problem I have, you see, sir. The problem I mentioned before. The problem I have, sir, is that I don't have a corpse.'

Chapter Nine

Looking back on that long night, it is hard be sure just how late it was when we set off for Salisbury Street, the three of us squeezed into a rather rickety hansom. To find it, we had walked south from Cuthbert Square in search of busier places, and it must have been nearly eleven o'clock before we were on our way. But despite the advanced hour, I'm ashamed to say I didn't feel even the slightest bit weary. To a young girl eager for excitement, the London night seemed full of adventure, and I gave little thought to the true meaning or the true nature of any horrors that might lie ahead.

'But I don't understand, Inspector,' Dr Watson was saying as we turned eastwards into Oxford Street. 'You've arrested a young man for murder – and an extremely well-connected young man at that – and yet you say you have no body? Without a victim, how can you even be sure there has been a crime?'

'Well, sir, it's like this.' As he talked, Inspector Merivale's eyes never left the road ahead, constantly scanning the streets in front of him and the premises on either side, as though he had trained himself to be always alert and always observing. 'At about five minutes past three o'clock this afternoon, one of my constables on The Strand was approached by a lady.'

The inspector paused, still looking ahead, but apparently a little embarrassed.

'Well, that is to say, sir, by a woman, for I wouldn't go so far as to call her a lady. And not what you would call a respectable woman, by any means. In fact, she was a person already known to the officer in question, for on more than one occasion he's had dealings with her, for drunkenness, mainly, and once or twice for being in fights. Now this woman is the proprietor of a run-down house on Salisbury Street. Left to her by her husband, I'm told, who was quite a different sort of man and successful in the root vegetable trade. But the place has been neglected since then, and she lets it out as rooms. It's the sort of place where no one stays for long – mostly it's passing salesmen, but not of the affluent sort, or seamstresses up from the country, looking for work.'

The centre of town was still busy, and, as Inspector Merivale talked, we were making slow progress, often at a walking pace, while the driver waited for carts to unload or while slow victorias trundled along at their leisure. The three of us were rather squeezed together on the hansom's seat, and, with Dr Watson in the middle, I had to lean forward to watch the inspector as he continued his tale.

'So this woman, a Mrs Grace by name, approached my officer and told him quite a tale. She said that there'd been murder done at her house in Salisbury Street, and that he had to come to break down the door so that she could get in and clean up and get the room ready to let again. Ready to let to someone *un-murdered*, was how she put it. Well, my constable, whose name is Benson, asked her who had been murdered and when, and she said it was a Miss Trubshaw, and that she'd been killed three nights before, and that her body had been taken away by the murderer. 'I seen him taking it,' she told him a number of times, 'and I know who he is, and everything'. And when young Benson asked her why it had taken her so long to report such a thing, she said she thought having the police around would be bad for business, and that her friend Mr Wickes had said the same thing. But by this morning she'd had a chance to reflect on things, and thought perhaps she should report it, as it had finally occurred to her that a dead woman doesn't pay rent.'

Inspector Merivale allowed his eyes to relax their vigilance for a moment, and looked across at me with something of a smile.

'You might meet her for yourself when we get there, Miss. She has a lot to say.'

Then his eyes returned to the road in front of him, as though once again on watch.

'Of course,' he went on, 'young Benson is a sensible chap and assumed this Grace woman was just addled with drink. But to avoid a scene, he agreed to go with her back to her home, to reassure her that nothing was really amiss. When he reached the house in question, he found the door of Miss Trubshaw's room locked, and there was no reply when he called out. And, of course,' Inspector Merivale observed with a shrug, 'there's nothing strange about that. The young woman would very likely be out in the middle of the day. But when Benson listened at the door, there was something about what he heard that unsettled him. A strange sort of silence, he said, which sounds like nonsense to me, although generally he's a sound enough fellow. But then, as well as that, there was the buzzing of flies.'

I had no way of knowing, that night, whether or not Inspector Merivale was a competent detective, but it did strike me that he was quite good at telling a story.

'Yes, a buzzing of flies. Awful loud, it was, according to Benson, and he didn't like it at all. So he decided to kick open the door.'

He paused for a moment, as our hansom slowed to avoid a pothole, then, as our progress resumed, he took up the tale again.

'He was right about the flies, I'm afraid. We've had the windows wide open ever since, and there's still hundreds of them buzzing around in there. And what had attracted them? It was blood, sir. A great deal of blood. There were blood stains on the floor, and blood all over the bed sheets. Soaked in it, they were. Dried, of course, by then, but there was no doubting what it was. You could smell it. Like someone had slaughtered a small pig in there.'

'But Inspector,' Dr Watson interjected, 'you know perfectly well that without a body, the bloodstains themselves don't prove a murder. I don't know anything about this Miss Trubshaw, but for all we know she might *actually* have slaughtered a pig in there! Back in my Army days, I once had to share quarters with a man who made his own black puddings.'

Inspector Merivale nodded wisely. He had clearly anticipated some such objection.

'That's very true, sir, and as a policeman I've known people get up to some strange things in their lodgings. But there's more.'

We had left Oxford Street now, and were already some way down Regent Street, approaching Piccadilly Circus. Despite the late hour, the streets were busier than ever. It gave Inspector Merivale a lot to look at.

'First of all, there's the letters. We found certain letters in the lady's room. Letters she'd received from a gentleman friend, and one letter she'd written but hadn't quite finished. The gentleman friend, of course, is Oscar Catanache, and we have his name in his own handwriting to prove it. It's pretty clear from these letters that while this Trubshaw woman was working as a parlour maid at the Catanache house, the two young people formed some sort of connection.'

At this point, the inspector let his glance flicker in my direction and, although it was hard to tell in the shadowy gaslight, I think he blushed a little.

'A connection of the romantic kind,' he explained. 'Very passionate, it would appear, at least at first, although it seems the passion was greater on her side than on his because the last letters grow a little ugly. He tells her it's all over and that she must never bother him again. She evidently persists. He grows colder. She becomes over-wrought. He tells her to calm down. She doesn't. Finally he tells her he will do whatever it takes to silence her pestering and remove her from his life.'

Inspector Merivale reached inside his jacket and produced a small notebook, which he opened and angled to one side, so that the light of the streetlamps would fall on it more fully.

'Her last letter – the unsent one – is a sorry little thing,' he told us, looking at the open page. 'I took the precaution of jotting down one or two passages. The original had, well, *splatters* on it. "I have read your threats, my darling Oscar," she wrote, "but can only repeat that nothing you can do or say will ever make me renounce our love. I will never let you go. I will be yours forever, whether you want me or not. I will never let you forget the perfect love we've shared. When you come to me tonight, I know you will be angry…" And that's all,' the inspector concluded. 'We can't say why she never finished it, but we know that Oscar Catanache *did* call on her in Salisbury Street on Tuesday evening, because there are witnesses.'

'The drunken Mrs Grace?' Dr Watson asked drily.

'Yes, sir. And her friend, Mr Wickes. They were together in Mrs Grace's room when Mr Catanache arrived, shortly after eleven o'clock yesterday evening. I fear Mrs Grace's establishment is not entirely respectable, sir. That is to say, the lady does nothing to prevent her lodgers from entertaining visitors of the opposite sex in their rooms, at any time of the day or night. Individual rooms have keys, but the main door is mostly unlocked and people can come and go as they please. It would seem that Oscar Catanache had come and gone on a number of occasions in the last few weeks.'

'How could they be so sure that the man they saw visiting Miss Trubshaw was Mr Catanache?' Dr Watson asked sharply.

'Because he had previously introduced himself to them, sir, and because Miss Trubshaw had spoken of him quite freely. That night, though, according to Grace and Wickes, there was something furtive about his manner. Mrs Grace said that he seemed to be trying to avoid notice when he arrived. And despite the warmth of the weather at the moment, he was wearing a scarf wrapped high around his face, completely covering his nose and mouth.'

'Aha!' Dr Watson sounded triumphant. 'So they couldn't be *sure* it was him. Could have been any fellow of the same build with his face disguised!'

Inspector Merivale nodded again, but once again I felt sure he had foreseen his companion's argument.

'Both claim to have recognised his waistcoat, sir. A rather colourful affair with very bright, distinctive buttons.'

'But really, Inspector...' Dr Watson sounded a little impatient. 'A waistcoat? You've said yourself that Mrs Grace is a drunkard, and I can't believe this Mr Wickes is much better. Is it wise to place so much credence on their testimony?'

'Perhaps not, sir. But the house across the street from Mrs Grace's is the residence of one Mr Boldacre, a retired book-keeper who once worked for one of the ministries in Whitehall. He claims to know Oscar Catanache by sight, on account of his once calling at Cuthbert Square over some administrative matter. Mr Boldacre is teetotal, sir, and something of an invalid, with insomnia one of his complaints. He therefore spends many hours, day and night, peering out of his window.'

The inspector paused to pull a face, then went on.

'Snooping, if you ask me, sir, but I can't complain. There's many a murderer has been brought to justice by the local busy-body. Anyway, this Mr Boldacre also saw Mr Catanache arriving in Salisbury Street that night, sir, at five minutes past eleven. He also remarked on the waistcoat the gentleman was wearing, and what's more, he saw Mr Catanache approach the building *without* the scarf over his face. Watched him pause a door or two away to put it on and adjust it. Well, sir, I imagine there was no power on earth that would have dragged him away from his window after that.'

'So he saw Oscar Catanache leave?'

'He did, sir, but not until very much later. Not till about one o'clock in the morning, when the street was very quiet. That time would appear to be right, sir, because that's the time Mrs Grace says too. It would appear she and Mr Wickes were still, er, *active*, at that hour, and when they heard someone bumping down the stairs, they peered out of the bedroom window to see who it was.'

'And they are sure it was Mr Catanache?'

'All three witnesses are sure of it, sir. And they agree on the other details too.'

'Other details, Inspector?' I noticed, perhaps for the first time during that journey, a note of anxiety in Dr Watson's tone.

'Mr Catanache had arrived carrying a stout cane, sir, the sort with a heavy silver ball for a handle. But he wasn't carrying it when he left, sir. At least not so as anyone could see it. But he was carrying something quite different instead. Something about five or six feet long, and wrapped in a dark blanket. So heavy that he had to carry it over one shoulder, sir, and heavy enough for him to struggle a little under its weight.'

All three of us were quiet for a moment, and I felt a little shudder run through me. Suddenly, and for the first time that night, our journey no longer seemed to me an adventure. The matter was deadly serious, after all. And apparently rather horrible.

'I take it, Inspector,' Dr Watson said after a moment longer, 'that you believe the corpse of the unfortunate young lady was wrapped in that blanket?'

'I do, sir.' Inspector Merivale looked grave, then brightened. 'Of course, any number of things could be carried in such a way. Perhaps Miss Trubshaw had asked him to carry off a Persian carpet, or some bags of coal, or a sack of spuds, and had wrapped them in a blanket for convenience. Unlikely, of course, but I've nothing against an open mind. But there is one more detail I haven't yet

108

mentioned, sir, something Mrs Grace noticed. Of course, it's tempting not to take too much notice of what Mrs Grace says, given her character, it's just that everything else she's told me about that night has been confirmed by Mr Boldacre, so I can't altogether dismiss this one last thing. It was something she saw, sir, as Mr Catanache carried his bundle out into the night. She says she noticed that behind the gentleman's back the blanket had slipped open a little, and, where it had slipped, she caught a glimpse of something protruding. And she is fairly adamant, sir, that what she saw protruding was a woman's stockinged foot.'

Another pause. Longer and quieter than the last.

'And all three witnesses are certain it was Oscar Catanache they saw carrying this thing?' Dr Watson asked eventually.

'They are, sir. Of course, Mr Catanache denies it. In the short interview I had with him this evening, he denied being anywhere near Salisbury Street that night. But when a man has been clearly identified by three separate witnesses... Well, sir, as I always say, evidence is evidence.'

Squeezed together as we were in the narrow hansom, I could feel Dr Watson stirring uncomfortably.

'And yet, Inspector, you and I well know that cases of mistaken identity *do* occur. The hour was a late one, the street was dark. Mr Boldacre is unwell. Mrs Grace and Mr Wickes were almost certainly drunk. At night, in the shadows, slim, well-dressed young gentlemen with their faces hidden can all look much alike.'

'That's very true, sir,' Inspector Merivale conceded, 'and people can mishear things too.'

'Mishear things?'

The anxiety in Dr Watson's voice was now a good deal more marked.

'Yes, sir. A name shouted out in the night, heard through an adjoining wall... Well, it's just possible that a mistake *could* be made, couldn't it, sir? Especially if the person hearing it was half-asleep at the time. The only thing is, sir, that the person I'm thinking about claims to have been wide awake, and to have particularly good hearing. She's a singer in the Music Halls, sir, by name of Elsie Tanner, and her rooms in Salisbury Street share a wall with Miss Trubshaw's.'

'And I take it, Inspector, that she claims to have heard something that night?'

'She does indeed, sir. She says the time was around midnight. She knows that because she had come in at twenty-to, and gone straight to bed. She hadn't begun to doze off before she was startled by Miss Trubshaw's voice from the next door room, very loud and very frightened, she says. Raised in a cry, it was, to use her phrase. Of course, we can't be sure this Elsie Tanner has got it right, sir, but she is very certain about what she heard. And what she says she heard, sir, was this...'

Again, the police inspector reached for his notebook.

'One moment, sir, I have it here. Yes, here it is. The words she says she heard were these: "*No, Oscar, no! Please! Please don't! Please! No!*" Then, after that, sir, a little gasp or scream. Then nothing else at all. Apparently it didn't occur to Miss Tanner to get up, or to intervene in any way. After all, as she points out, you hear all sorts in lodgings, and it isn't usually murder. Hearing nothing more, she concluded that the argument was over, and she allowed herself to fall asleep. And that was the last anyone has heard of Miss Thomasina Trubshaw.'

The house in Salisbury Street where the hansom cab dropped us proved every bit as drab and soulless as Inspector Merivale had led us to believe. A scuffed front door, guarded by a police constable, led to a dirty hallway, bare of any furniture whatsoever. The once-fine doors that led away from it were chipped and worn, and disfigured by ugly locks, which had clearly been added at a later date. A staircase that would once have been solid and respectable had succumbed to neglect and misuse, with no runner or stair-rods, foot-worn treads and missing spindles in its rail. The only light was from a pair of police lanterns, one at the foot of the stairs, the other at the top, which threw a pale and rather ghastly light.

Nothing about the hallway, though, was as ghastly as the scene that awaited us in Miss Trubshaw's room, where even in the dead of night, flies still buzzed, lazily and heavily, around another pair of lanterns. No steps had been taken to remove the blood-stained linen from the bed, nor to mop the rust brown stains from the floor-boards. A small table that had once stood beside the bed now lay on its side, with various objects scattered beside it – a broken glass; a candlestick and candle, the two no longer joined; a lady's handkerchief; and a pot-pourri of dried rose petals, now strewn on the bare floor.

There was little other furniture, only a cheap writing table and chair, which clearly also served as a dressing table, another wooden chair drawn close to the window, a cheap washstand and chamber pot, and a battered wardrobe of dark wood, its doors closed. On the iron bedstead, above a thin mattress, was a single blood-stained pillow and, just as horribly stained, a pair of thin sheets.

The three of us stood near the threshold, silent for a few moments, taking in the scene, before Inspector Merivale stretched up on to his tiptoes then stepped into the room, waving his arm in a flourish of welcome.

'Please,' he said. 'Come in. Look around. I will be as delighted as you if you can prove the young man innocent, and it may be that there's something here I've missed. Some new evidence, contrary to all the rest. My men have noted how things were found, so you may search as you please. Here, take the lanterns.'

I think Dr Watson and I were equally at a loss. Dr Watson had reassured the parents of Oscar Catanache that their son's arrest was a mistake which could quickly be rectified. Inspector Merivale had taken him at his word, and was offering him every opportunity to review the evidence for himself. But now the two of us stood facing each other in that horrible room, each holding a lantern, and neither of us had any idea of where to start. Mr Holmes, I thought, would have produced a magnifying glass, would have studied window latches and skirting boards, and would no doubt have produced within minutes a dazzling explanation of his client's innocence. But we were simply bewildered.

'Ahem. I'll start in here, perhaps,' my companion muttered and, stepping to the wardrobe, cautiously opened its doors. But he was greeted by nothing more informative than a short rail with three women's dresses hanging from it, and a column of narrow shelves on which were stored, neatly folded, various items of ladies' accoutrements and undergarments. I saw Dr Watson step back hastily, his embarrassment evident in his demeanour. 'Or perhaps over here,' he went on, moving apparently at random to the washstand and holding his lantern above it.

And it was then that the little glint of metal caught my eye. It must have been something to do with the way the light fell when the lantern was held high in that particular corner, and had I not been standing in exactly the right place I would never have seen it. In clear morning light, it would probably have been obvious – but these rooms had been searched late in an autumn afternoon, when shadows were long and a tiny object lodged between floorboards, slightly under the bed, would already have been lost in deep shadow. I think you could have looked quite hard during the afternoon and not have noticed it.

'Over here, sir,' I said quietly. 'There's something between these boards.'

'Aha!' Dr Watson moved swiftly from the washstand and knelt by my side. 'Look at this, Inspector! Flotsam here has found something that your men appear to have overlooked. Here, let me see if I can fish it out with my pocket knife… I wouldn't be surprised if this is the bit of evidence we need to prove our young man's innocence.'

But then he held the item up, into the light of his lantern, and his face fell. Because the little disc of metal he held in his hand was very beautiful and extremely distinctive, and absolutely not the sort of thing we'd hoped to find. It was an exquisite waistcoat button, adorned unmistakeably and very perfectly with the Blue Daisy of the Catanaches.

All three of us in that room were still for a moment. The button resting in Dr Watson's palm looked back at us, innocent and lovely. It was only a button. And although it was the least ugly thing in the whole room, it didn't *prove* anything.

Then Inspector Merivale stepped forward towards Dr Watson and I stepped back towards the head of the bed, and the spell was broken.

'I'll take that, if I may, sir,' the inspector said gently. 'I daresay it belongs to Mr Catanache. Could have dropped it here on any visit, of course. Although it's strange that the young lady never noticed it. When the morning sun comes in through that window, you'd think it would be easy to spot. But perhaps she wasn't the observant sort. And perhaps she never swept the floors. Although I notice there's not much dust in the corners, so I suppose someone must have swept in here not long before the night in question.'

He examined the button for a moment longer, then pushed it into his waistcoat pocket.

'If I were desperate to make a case against young Oscar Catanache, sir, I'd say that button must have been dropped after the light had faded, or else it would have been noticed at the time. And I'd say that the following morning, with all the light from that window, Miss Trubshaw must surely have noticed the button lying there, had she been here to notice it. And if she *had* noticed it, well, it's hard to imagine her just leaving it there, isn't it, sir? And, of course, that might suggest to some people that Oscar Catanache was in this room on the very last night it was occupied, as the neighbours claim. But, of course, sir, I've nothing personal against the young man. I'm quite prepared to believe there's another reasonable explanation, if someone were to offer me one.'

But Dr Watson said nothing, and the inspector looked across at me.

'Why! Whatever's the matter, Miss?' he asked, suddenly startled. 'You look like you've seen a ghost.'

I was still standing near the top of the bed, by the overturned table, but by now I had picked something up and was holding it in my hand.

'No, sir. No, not a ghost. At least, not really. It's just that… This…'

And I held the object out to him.

It was a lady's handkerchief, the one that had been lying on the floor by the broken glass and the spilled rose petals. The first time I'd looked at it, I'd taken very little notice of it, but this time, stepping away from the button, something had made me look down, and I noticed it again. It was a very ordinary object, of thin cotton. But now I saw it had been hand-hemmed in lilac thread.

I had once seen one exactly like it – dropped by a nameless woman by the area steps in Baker Street, on that day I'd walked in the park. A woman who'd told me she feared for her life.

'I think, sir,' I told the inspector hesitantly, 'I think the dead lady… Miss Trubshaw… Well, sir, I rather think I may have met her.'

Chapter Ten

It was two o'clock in the morning when Dr Watson and I returned to Baker Street, and the night had turned cold. By then, the streets were quiet. In Orchard Street, a black cat dashed across the road in front of us with a loud mewing, and in Portman Place the rattle of our cab caused a flurry of rats to scatter from a pile of rotten vegetables, presumably dumped there at the end of the day by a disgruntled barrow boy. I remember shivering then, and shivering a great deal throughout that journey. Perhaps because the night was cold.

But in Baker Street a lamp still burned above our familiar front door, and in Mrs Hudson's kitchen a fire blazed, lit specially to welcome me.

'For you've had a long day, Flotsam, and whatever has occurred, a warm drink and a warm bed will do you good.'

And so, once Dr Watson had been helped to a tumbler of whisky and had disappeared to bed, I sat at the old kitchen table, revelling in the soft, golden glow that warmed me and soothed me in equal measure, and told Mrs Hudson everything that had passed, from the handkerchief dropped by the distressed young lady some few days before, to the moment of recognising a second handkerchief, surely stitched by the same hand, in that dreadful room in Salisbury Street.

'She came here because she was frightened, ma'am, and I let her run away. If only I had made her stay! Perhaps then this terrible thing would never have happened.'

Mrs Hudson, who had been adding hot water to a glass of rosehip syrup, carefully placed the kettle on the trivet by the stove then took a seat beside me.

'Come now, Flottie. Whatever has happened, whatever has been done, you of all people are not to blame for it. You will meet plenty of people in the course of your life who want to make you feel responsible for things that are not your fault, so don't you get into the habit of making it easy for them.' She gave my hand a little squeeze. 'You did what you could – you always do – and no one can do more. Now, let me just check that I have things straight. Young Mr Catanache is under arrest, you say?'

I explained that he was, and that Dr Watson had promised to get him released, before we had any idea of all the evidence against him.

'Well, don't you worry about that, Flotsam, because I think there's a very good chance the young man really will be released in the next day or two. This inspector – Inspector Merivale, did you say? He appears to have been a little hasty in making his arrest, and I would think a great many inquiries need to be made before he can go to a magistrate. I'm not saying that nothing bad has happened, Flottie. I'm not even saying that no-one has been murdered. But for the moment no one can be sure that Miss Trubshaw isn't at large and in good health. From what you've told me, no one even knows for certain that she is missing. I imagine that Scotland Yard will need to try quite hard to find her before they can persuade a judge that she is dead.'

'But, ma'am, I can't help thinking…' And here I broke down a little, because I could hardly bear to admit it even to myself. 'I can't help thinking that she must be dead, and that Mr Catanache must have carried away her body. Because according to the inspector, a great many people saw Miss Trubshaw arrive home the previous afternoon, but not a single person can be found who ever saw her leave.'

I felt a comforting hand come to rest upon my shoulder.

'Hush, young lady. You've witnessed a great deal too many horrors this evening, and have imagined a great many more. But tomorrow Mr Holmes will call upon the Catanaches, and will no doubt also visit Salisbury Street, and if it makes you feel any better I will drop a line to Mrs Fenton, who used to be the housekeeper in Cuthbert Square. She may have something helpful to tell us. She often used to mention the Catanaches in our little chats, and she's never said anything to suggest that Oscar Catanache was the sort of young man who might go off the rails. And as for all the rest, well, a great many mysterious and baffling things occur in this city of ours, Flottie, and a great many of them are never explained. But not all of them are murder, remember, so it's perfectly reasonable for us to hope that perhaps there may be some other explanation.'

And with those words of comfort clutched close to my heart, I allowed Mrs Hudson to usher me to my little cupboard bed, a glass of rosehip syrup still warm and steaming in my hand.

—

The next morning, much to my surprise, I overslept. Instead of a night haunted by dark visions, I seemed to have slumbered deeply and peacefully, and Mrs Hudson had done nothing to rouse me, so it was not until nearly eight o'clock in the morning that my eyes opened and memory of the previous day returned.

It was a shockingly late hour to be getting up, and I washed and dressed in something of a panic. But a smell of frying bacon proved reassuring, and when I rushed into her presence still blinking and yawning, Mrs Hudson appeared as calm and serene as ever.

'Good morning, Flotsam,' she greeted me, from one end of the kitchen table, where she was sitting surrounded by notepaper and envelopes, writing letters. 'There is breakfast waiting for you in the oven, and Mr Holmes waiting for you upstairs, so you haven't a minute to lose.'

'Mr Holmes, ma'am? Waiting for me?'

Mrs Hudson's eyebrow twitched slightly.

'That's right, young lady, you heard me correctly. A lot has happened since you went to bed. There have been messages from Sir Henry Catanache and Inspector Merivale for Mr Holmes, Dr Watson has gone out already, and those arrived for you.'

She nodded towards the mantelpiece, where a little bunch of very perfect marigolds were arranged in a jug, as fresh and bright as the morning outside. I saw an envelope next to them, with my name written on it in a bold and decisive hand. Mystified, I took it down and opened it, and found inside a very short note.

To my co-conspirator. I called last night when the gentleman was out. I have you to thank. Please accept these with my compliments – GD.

As I read, I was aware of Mrs Hudson's presence, and I could feel myself blushing a deep and burning red. Hastily, I crumpled up the note and stuffed it into the pocket of my apron.

But when I turned round, I found Mrs Hudson had turned her attention back to her letters, and I hurried to retrieve my breakfast from the oven. As I placed it on the table, Mrs Hudson signed off the note she was writing with a flourish, then pushed it slightly to one side.

'To Mrs Fenton,' she explained. 'She's bound to know at least something about any former parlour maid of the Catanaches. She has retired now, as I think I said, and is living in the country, and this is a little note asking her if we could call.'

It was hard to imagine that a retired housekeeper, however well she knew Miss Trubshaw, would be able to tell us very much about the terrible events in Salisbury Street, but even so I found Mrs Hudson's words hugely comforting. They told me that my worries of the night before, which had seemed to rest so heavily on my shoulders, were in fact to be shared. It was very hard not to feel confident about things when you knew Mrs Hudson was on your side.

Perhaps that is why I had such a good appetite for breakfast. The bacon disappeared in only a few mouthfuls and was followed, at Mrs Hudson's insistence, by an apple and a small bowlful of stewed pear.

'Now, off with the apron, into your best things, and upstairs with you, young lady,' she told me sternly. 'Mr Holmes will be impatient to be off.'

'Best things, ma'am? Am I going out?'

Mrs Hudson nodded.

'Indeed you are, Flotsam. Inspector Merivale's note invited Mr Holmes to join him at Scotland Yard this morning, for an interview with Oscar Catanache. But Mr Holmes had already promised to attend the Catanache residence this morning, and seemed eager to get there at the earliest opportunity – 'while the trail is still fresh', was the phrase he used. Sir Henry's note begged him to call at any hour, and said that his staff had been told to offer him every assistance, although Sir Henry himself will not be at home until much later in the morning. So Dr Watson was dispatched to Scotland Yard, and Mr Holmes is eager to have someone with him who can talk to the junior servants without frightening them. There is something about Mr Holmes' method of questioning that tends to reduce scullery maids to tears.'

'So is that to be me, ma'am?'

I knew Dr Watson to have an excellent manner for such things, and it was hard to believe I could properly take his place.

'Was I wrong to suggest it, Flotsam?' Mrs Hudson studied me carefully. 'No, of course I wasn't. You will do very well. And in the meantime, I intend to visit old Tom Mallows. I have some marmalade for him.'

'Tom Mallows?' I asked eagerly. The name was familiar. 'Will *he* be able to tell us something about the Catanaches? Or about Miss Trubshaw?'

'Certainly not, Flotsam. Tom Mallows is an old friend, who used to make the finest sausages north of the river, and I owe him a visit. Mind you,' she continued, and one of her eyebrows twitched very slightly, 'he still lives above his old shop, just off The Strand. So I daresay, since I'm going in that direction anyway, I might have a little wander around the area, just to see if anything strikes me.'

I had expected to find Mr Holmes full of that restless energy which often gripped him when a new case was beginning. After all, Sir Henry Catanache was much in the public eye, and for his son to be accused of murder was sensational news. But Mr Holmes' energies were still largely directed towards the Romford case, and, by comparison, he appeared to consider the events in Salisbury Street rather mundane.

'Dr Watson woke me up at the crack of dawn to give me a full account,' he told me rather grumpily, as I perched on a chair in his study, waiting while he cleaned his pipe with a little wire brush. 'Watson seems to think that the Catanache boy is the victim of some terrible misunderstanding, but when I asked him what evidence supported that view, he could only mutter something about the boy having a very honest face.' He grimaced. 'Well, they said the same thing about the Watford Poisoner, and he fed arsenic to his great aunt because he disliked her Christmas puddings.'

His pipe apparently clean, Mr Holmes blew into the bowl, and then began to polish it against his waistcoat.

'So I made it very clear, Flotsam, that I was willing to look into the case, but that I could make no guarantee that our investigation would be helpful to Oscar Catanache. It might, of course, be quite the reverse.'

'Like last night, sir,' I pointed out, 'when I found the button that Inspector Merivale had missed. *That* wasn't very helpful to Mr Catanache.'

Perhaps Mr Holmes detected a note of regret in my voice, because he was quick to reassure me.

'I'm sure Merivale would have found it for himself eventually, Flotsam. He is a good detective on the whole, and – unusually for a Scotland Yard man – he is open to the appliance of new scientific methods to the investigation of his cases. But I'm afraid if he hopes for extensive assistance on *this* case, he will be disappointed. We are just getting to the bottom of those hieroglyphs, and I will need to spend a great many hours over the next few days in Billingsgate, observing the fishmonger. And then, of course, I promised Sir Joseph Croxton that I would keep an eye on George Dashing too, although how we're supposed to do that when I've no time to follow the personal columns and the fellow deliberately avoids me, I don't know. Rather annoyingly, Flotsam, he called last night when we were all out.'

For a moment, I think, I studied the pattern in the rug very carefully, and hoped I wasn't expected to reply.

'No, I'm afraid Merivale can't rely on very much of my time,' Mr Holmes concluded. 'But I shall ask Dr Watson to assist him whenever he can.'

I swallowed and took a little breath, and looked up.

'About Mr Dashing, sir... Is he really in danger? I mean, I noticed there was another message in the agony column this morning.'

'Was there really?' The great man spoke so airily that it seemed to me he must already be losing interest in the Dashing case.

'Yes, sir. *Maya to Aldan – He threatens us with his falsehoods. He must go.*'

The society pages were also full of the fact that George Dashing had danced a great deal the previous evening with Lady Annabella Clary, but I didn't mention that.

'*He threatens us with his falsehoods...*' Mr Holmes considered this for a few moments. 'You know, Flotsam, I find it hard to share Sir Joseph's interest in those two.

If they are indeed Russian assassins, they are taking their time over things.'

'Then you don't think there really is a plot against Mr Dashing, sir?' I asked hopefully.

'Oh, I think it is highly likely that the Tsar's people would like to take their revenge. They are a ruthless bunch. And it seems certain from those other examples Sir Joseph showed us that they have, previously, used newspaper advertisements to communicate with their agents.' Mr Holmes patted his pockets, as if to check that the contents were all in order before setting out. 'But if Maya and Aldan are our pair, then the authorities already have an eye on them, and I can only really help Sir Joseph by studying all the other personal advertisements in detail, to check that nothing is being missed. But I simply don't have time for that at the moment. So, for now, we shall just have to hope that any plot against George Dashing is still in its early stages. When I've got to the heart of this Romford business, I shall give the matter my full attention.'

I confess that I didn't find this answer altogether reassuring. In fact, I think I spent a great deal of the cab ride to Cuthbert Square, when I should no doubt have been considering the plight of Oscar Catanache, worrying instead about the sender of my marigolds.

Mr Holmes didn't seem to notice.

–

Despite the excitements of the previous evening, Cuthbert Square stood in the warm morning sunlight as calm and quiet as ever. The day already had the beginnings of the heavy autumn heat that makes an Indian summer, and the leaves of the London plane trees were motionless, without a breath of wind to stir them. The square smelled of warm earth and late honeysuckle and just a little bit of dry horse dung, and it was as hushed as always – as we stood by the Catanache's front door, I could hear quite clearly the quiet humming of the man watering window boxes on the far side of the square.

The door was opened to us that morning by the house-keeper, a Mrs Howden, who looked gaunt and anxious, and who welcomed Mr Holmes as though he was a saviour sent from heaven, telling him over and over how shocked she was by what had happened, how outraged she was by the police, how she would be willing to pledge with the blood of her first-born that Mr Oscar was an innocent angel, and how delighted the whole household was that Mr Holmes was going to sort things out. At this point she turned to me and paused, apparently not sure what to make of Mr Holmes' choice of companion.

'This is Flotsam,' Mr Holmes told her briskly. 'That is, *Miss* Flotsam. She will be accompanying me.' And without further comment, he strode past Mrs Howden into the hallway.

It is strange how the passage of a few hours can change a place. The previous evening, that hallway had seemed to me the grand stage of a theatrical drama, lit by gaslight and peopled with characters who seemed every bit as grand and theatrical as the scene itself. Now, with the dappled morning light behind us, it was just the average hallway of a house of that sort, in muted shades of green and grey, and furnished with a quiet, unobtrusive opulence.

Mr Holmes stood in the middle of it, and took command.

'I understand Sir Henry is not at home at the moment? Very well then, we should like to begin with some questions. I shall interview the butler and the young man's valet, while Miss Flotsam here will speak to the housemaids. But first, a few questions for you, Mrs Howden. I understand Thomasina Trubshaw was employed here as a parlour maid until quite recently. Is that correct?'

'Yes, sir, until two months ago.' The housekeeper appeared to grow less wordy now she was on more familiar ground. 'She gave her notice at the same time as Mrs Fenton, who was the housekeeper here before myself.'

Mr Holmes eyed her keenly.

'So you are relatively new here?'

'That's right, sir. Mrs Fenton had been housekeeper here for a great many years, but a little while ago she came into some money, an inheritance from a relative, and decided that she wished to retire. She was good enough to put a word in for me here, sir, and I started at the beginning of July.'

'So you didn't ever meet Thomasina Trubshaw yourself?'

'No, sir.' Mrs Howden sounded slightly regretful, as though disappointed to have been deprived of such a sensational acquaintanceship by so narrow a margin. 'Trubshaw had been appointed by Mrs Fenton, you see, sir, about a year before, and the two of them left together.'

'And is that unusual? For the two of them to leave together?'

Mr Holmes knew a good deal about murder weapons but rather less about the comings and goings of staff in a big house.

'Not really, sir. It does sometimes happen like that. The other parlour maid left too – she'd been with Mrs Fenton for years, I'm told. So, what with the scullery maid leaving to get married last month, and the footman taking it into his head to join the army, there's been a fair bit of turmoil below stairs since the start of the summer. But I like to think nothing's been noticed by her Ladyship, sir. She takes very little interest in household matters.'

Mr Holmes considered this.

'So who then, of the existing staff, would have known Miss Trubshaw most intimately?'

'Well, sir, it's funny you should ask that question, because that's just what we were asking ourselves, only an hour or two before you came.'

Mrs Howden looked delighted by her own prescience.

'And the thing is, sir,' she went on, 'that there's not many of us here who knew her at all, really. There's Cook – that is, Mrs Wilkinson – who has been here for years, sir, so it's her as knew Trubshaw best. The boot boy says he knew her, but he's making it up, because Cook never lets him come further than the scullery door. Hendricks – that's the butler, sir – he was laid up down at the country seat with gout for most of last year, so we had an agency man doing for us up here. So apart from Cook, well, it's only her Ladyship's maid and Mr Oscar's valet who've even met her, and Grimsby – that's the valet, sir – is seventy if he's a day and doesn't take much notice of the rest of us. And as for Bertrand, the lady's maid – or *Mademoiselle* Bertrand, as she likes to be known – she's so far above the rest of us that she probably doesn't even know our names, so I don't suppose she and Trubshaw ever exchanged a word.'

'Very well. Then we shall start with the cook.' Mr Holmes looked around him, taking in the neat trappings of the hall, the understated testimony of an extremely affluent existence. 'I understand, Mrs Howden, that

Mr Oscar was out for the whole evening on the night in question, and not back till the early hours?'

For the first time, the housekeeper looked hesitant.

'That's right, sir,' she told him guardedly, 'but there's nothing unusual in that. Mr Oscar is often out late. He lets himself in with his own latchkey, so I don't suppose there's anyone here who could tell you for sure what time he came home.'

'And, tell me, Mrs Howden, how many of the servants do you think were aware of Oscar Catanache's dalliance with the last parlour maid? Was it much discussed below stairs?'

Mrs Howden looked shocked and a little outraged, and pressed her lips together very firmly before replying.

'Well, really, sir! As if we would! What a thing to say, sir! Mr Oscar is a gentleman, and I can't believe he has ever been anything but honourable in any of his dealings. Oh, I've known young men that weren't like him, I certainly have, sir.' Her voice rose as she warmed to her theme. 'The sorts of so-called young gentlemen as would dally with a servant girl without any thought of what was to become of her after they'd gone on their way. But Mr Oscar isn't like that at all, sir. A most thoughtful, gentleman, sir!'

'Of course, they said that about the Bedfordshire Puppy-Drowner,' Mr Holmes pointed out a few moments later, after Mrs Howden had left us to fetch the cook. 'The most thoughtful gentleman imaginable, and widely known for his kindness to animals. Even the vicar said so. Yet when his activities were at their height, it's said that there was scarcely a live puppy to be found in any village in the county.'

Mrs Wilkinson, the cook, proved to be a substantial figure of very few words. Yes, she had known Trubshaw.

128

Yes, she had been pleasant enough. No, she had not been a very good parlour maid, and she was surprised she'd kept her position as long as she had. No, she was not surprised that she had turned a young man's head, because she was pretty enough, with a narrow enough waist, and a bit more educated than most. As a cook of forty years' standing, she had seen it happen before. She would see it happen again. Over forty years old and homely – that was, according to Mrs Wilkinson, the only safe way for a parlour maid to be.

As for Mr Catanache, she knew next to nothing of him. The other servants spoke well of him, he liked chops, he'd never sent back even a mouthful of food, and if it were true that he *was* a murderer then none of us were safe in our beds.

The boot boy had even less to add. He was unsure whether Miss Trubshaw was tall or short, dark or fair, handsome or plain, although he thought perhaps she might have been all those things. Mr Holmes sent him on his way with a rather generous twopenny bit and a warning about making things up.

Mademoiselle Bertrand, Lady Catanache's maid, was a tall, slender creature who, when she finally deigned to see Mr Holmes, made it quite clear that she considered detectives of any sort to be sordid little men of a kind she would much prefer to avoid. Did she know Miss Trubshaw? Of course she did not. Why would she take the trouble to know a parlour maid? She did not look for friends in servants' halls. Could she describe her? Not really. Of average height, she thought, and no doubt English-shaped, but she couldn't recall. Probably dark. Was she pretty? Evidently so, in some way, for she had ensnared the affections of a wealthy young gentleman.

But young gentlemen aside, who really noticed a parlour maid's looks? Mademoiselle Bertrand herself would be unable to pick her out of a crowd.

All these interviews took place in the hall, but Mr Holmes asked to meet the valet, Mr Grimsby, in Mr Oscar's very grand rooms on the first floor. These faced out over the Square, and were light and airy, but were decorated with a lot of rather heavy gilding and some very ugly portraits that rather spoiled the feel of the place. As soon as we were left alone there, the air of detachment that Mr Holmes had hitherto maintained slipped from his shoulders, and he was instantly in action, moving swiftly this way and that, from the writing desk to the bed, then to the various windows, and on to the mantelpiece and the fireplace. There, crouching on one knee, he beckoned for me to join him.

'Tell me, Flotsam, in your experience, in a house such as this, how often would the fireplace be cleaned out?'

'Every morning, sir, by the chamber maid.' My years spent in the company of Mrs Hudson had given me a firm grasp of the housekeeping routines of every kind of establishment, from public houses to palaces. 'In wintertime she would clear out all the ashes, get everything clean and polish the brass, then lay a new fire for the evening.'

'But there is no fire laid here, Flotsam.' Mr Holmes indicated the empty grate.

'No, sir. In spring, when no more fires are needed, the grate is cleaned and polished and left unlaid until the following winter.'

'So let us imagine it is the last fire of spring, Flotsam, and a small fragment of ash falls from the grate at the back, landing in such a way that the grate itself hides it from immediate notice. What are the chances, Flotsam, that the fragment would remain unnoticed for the whole summer?'

I considered this for a moment.

'In a properly run household, the chances are very small, sir. A maid clearing out ash from the fire as part of her daily duties may perhaps miss a little bit from one day to another, but when the fire is put to bed for summer, it would be cleaned and checked very thoroughly.'

This answer appeared to please Mr Holmes greatly.

'So look here, Flotsam.' And he lay flat on his stomach to reach behind, then a little underneath, the grate. When he drew back his hand, he held in his fingertips something no bigger than his thumbnail, pale at the centre but charred and flaky around the edges. 'Not paper, Flotsam,' he told me, his interest clearly piqued. 'Fabric.' He handed it to me. 'A scrap of linen, at a guess.'

I thought he was right, although what it may once have been was impossible to tell.

'Now, you were at Salisbury Street last night, Flotsam. I'm told there was a great deal of blood. Inspector Merivale asks us to imagine all that blood was the result of a violent attack upon Thomasina Trubshaw. Were that the case, is it your opinion that the perpetrator of the attack would also have been stained in some way?'

I agreed that he would, and Mr Holmes thought for a moment.

'There is something interesting about that blood, Flotsam. But let us, for a moment, follow where it leads us. On a dark suit or frock coat, bloodstains may not show, especially by candlelight or gaslight. A man might possibly walk the streets like that unobserved. And at home, the next day, the stain might not stand out without closer examination. But his cuffs, Flotsam… His cuffs…'

At that point, and in that undignified position, with both of us kneeling by the grate, we were interrupted by the arrival of Grimsby, the valet of Oscar Catanache. He was, as Mrs Howden had said, an elderly man, mostly bald, with grey side whiskers and an anxious, slightly puzzled expression, and slightly parted lips that made him look a little like a trout.

'Oh, sir!' he began, on seeing Mr Holmes. 'How glad we are to see you! It is a terrible thing, the thing they've done to Mr Oscar. I simply cannot understand it. But now you are here, sir, I know things will be put right. Oh, thank you for coming, sir!' And he advanced to grasp the hand of his visitor, who had now risen to his feet and was looking distinctly embarrassed.

'Yes, yes, my man.' Mr Holmes freed his hand and cleared his throat. 'We are here to ensure justice is done, you can be sure of that. And, with that aim in mind, perhaps we may be permitted to ask you a few questions? Tell me, is your master particularly sensitive to the cold?'

'The cold, sir?' Mr Grimsby was clearly flummoxed. 'Why, no, sir. Far from it. Many is the time he's left the house in terrible weather refusing even a top-coat, saying that there was nothing so invigorating as a nip in the air.'

'So he would not have been in the habit of calling for a fire to be lit over the summer months? Not even in the last day or so, when the nights have been growing colder?'

The valet blinked in bewilderment.

'Why, no, sir! It has been the hottest summer anyone can remember. And Mr Oscar abhors a hot bedroom. He would no more call for a fire in September as he would call for an overcoat in the bath.'

'Very good.' Mr Holmes cast me a glance of satisfaction. 'Now, a word about the young man's clothes. You look after them, I take it?'

The old man nodded, still clearly confused and a little concerned by Mr Holmes' questions.

'What was Mr Catanache wearing four evenings ago? A dark suit, was it not?'

'Alas, yes, sir. Of rather a stylish cut.'

'Alas?' The great detective looked at him sharply. 'You are suggesting that something untoward has befallen it?'

'Indeed, sir. Mr Oscar regularly frequents the boxing halls of the East End, you see, sir, and as you can imagine, evenings there can be extremely rowdy affairs, and not for the faint hearted. Sir Henry greatly disapproves of it as a pastime, and threatens to cut his son's allowance if it continues, so Mr Oscar doesn't advertise his visits. His allowance is an extremely generous one, sir, so generous that Mr Oscar rarely spends the half of it, but the threat to reduce it is one that Sir Henry employs whenever he is in a high temper.'

'And Mr Catanache's dark suit?' Sherlock Holmes steered him back to the subject.

'Well, sir, as is often the case, Mr Oscar was in very late that night, so it wasn't until the morning that I was able to clear up his clothes. When I did, he told me not to bother getting the frock coat cleaned because he had been seated in the front row of the Empire Hall, right beside the ring, and after a particularly bloody bout, the trainer of the losing fighter had managed to splash his dirty bucket over those seated at the front. I explained to Mr Oscar that the laundry would almost certainly be able to clean the garment in a satisfactory manner, but he told me that he didn't want anyone at the laundry saying anything

133

that might get back to his father, and that he didn't much fancy wearing it again after that anyway. He said, instead, that I was to give it to the rag-man when he called on his daily round.'

'And did you?' Mr Holmes asked eagerly, and I understood the importance of the question. But the old valet simply looked a little affronted.

'Of course, sir. That was Mr Oscar's wish. I bundled it up myself, along with some other rags, and an old pair of flannels which Mr Oscar had torn playing tennis.'

'I see.' Mr Holmes turned to me. 'Given the efficiency of the rag trade in this city, Flotsam, I fear there is little chance of retrieving it, but if you remind me, I will suggest to Inspector Merivale that he gets his men on the case. Now, tell me, Grimsby,' he went on, turning back to the valet, 'did you notice anything in particular about the frock coat as you bundled it up?'

'I did not, sir.' Grimsby said it firmly, as if perhaps he was beginning to understand the direction of Mr Holmes' questions. 'But, as you can imagine, sir, given what I had been told, my inclination was to keep it at arms' length. I simply placed it in the sack with the other clothes, sir, and I used tongs to do it.'

'And what about Mr Catanache's cuffs and collar? What did you do with those?' Mr Holmes had moved to the window, and as he asked the question, he appeared to be studying the window-catch very intently.

'They would have been collected by the maid first thing, sir, in order to catch the linen collection. Those items, and shirtfronts, and under-garments in general, go to the laundry in Delph Street every morning, sir, and are returned later the same day. Outer garments and, I believe, all items of ladies' wear...' Grimsby looked a little embarrassed by the reference. '…are collected by Frobisher's twice a week, sir. Frobisher's are excellent with the finer fabrics and the more delicate tasks.'

'And tell me, Grimsby,' Mr Holmes continued to examine the window, 'how many pairs of cuffs does Mr Catanache own?'

I wondered if this question might prove beyond the old man, but the valet merely looked surprised by it.

'Why, thirty-five pairs, of course, sir. Seven pairs each of formal, formal dinner, casual, outdoor and cotton.'

'Excellent, Grimsby. And for a night at the Empire Hall, I take it he would have been wearing a pair of his formal cuffs? If that is so, let us move on to Mr Catanache's waistcoat. Was that bundled up for the rag man along with the frock coat?'

'Oh, no, sir.' Mr Grimsby seemed pleased that it had been spared that ignominy. 'Mr Oscar gave no special instructions for the waistcoat, sir, so I put it aside to be sent to the laundry.'

'And where is it now?'

Mr Grimsby took the fob-watch from his pocket.

'Frobisher's do not collect for another hour, sir, so I assume it is still downstairs.'

'Then I should like you to fetch it for us, Grimsby. And while you are about it, please could you bring up all seven pairs of Mr Catanache's formal cuffs, and also his cane, the one topped with a heavy silver ball? He does own such a cane, does he not? Excellent, then I would like to see it. And could you also accompany Miss Flotsam downstairs? I would like you to introduce her to the housemaid who cleans this room. Flotsam will have one or two questions for her.'

It was probably a good thing that Mr Holmes hadn't attempted to interview the housemaid himself, for she proved to be a willowy and waif-like figure of unusually nervous disposition, who appeared to find *me* a terrifying and awe-inspiring figure. One word from Mr Holmes might have deprived her of speech altogether.

The two of us were of similar ages, but despite my assurances that my station in life was really no different to hers, she resolutely refused to call me Flotsam, and accompanied everything she said to me with a little bob, as if I were the lady of the house.

Her name was Esther, and it was she who had filled the position vacated by Thomasina Trubshaw. Although by name a parlour maid, she was more properly a maid-of-all-work, sharing cleaning and parlour duties with a second maid. According to Esther, she and the other maid, Matilda, had started in Cuthbert Square within a couple of days of each other, but the arrival of police in the house the night before had brought an end to their collaboration. Matilda, Esther told me, had given notice and left the house the following morning, on the grounds that she hadn't come to London to be murdered by no one or nobody, not even if he *was* a gentleman.

Esther seemed secretly rather pleased by this develop-ment, her fear of me replaced briefly by a fragile smile as she explained that the two of them shared a room at the top of the house, and that Matilda snored like a foghorn on the Thames. Neither of them had ever known Trubshaw, nor had they had any dealings with Oscar Catanache, short of serving him at dinner and cleaning his room in the mornings.

'He was a very fine gentleman, you see, Miss,' she explained timidly, already using the past tense, as though Mr Catanache's appointment with the hangman was a foregone conclusion, 'so he'd never have spared a thought for the likes of us.'

I didn't like to point out that he had evidently spared more than a thought for Thomasina Trubshaw. Instead, I moved on to the subject of fires, at which a look of wonder spread across Esther's face.

'But however could you have known, Miss?' she gasped, the look of awe intensifying. Because earlier that week, she told me, she had been surprised to find a little pile of ashes in Mr Catanache's grate. Not the remains of a proper fire, she was at pains to point out, just a very little pile, and my knowing about such a little thing like that made her feel right proper giddy.

As for Mr Catanache's cuffs, she had no recollection of anything unusual on the morning in question. She didn't particularly remember adding them to the laundry bag, but nor did she remember *not* adding them.

'For to be honest, Miss, there's so much to do of a morning, and I've done those cuffs and collars every day, day in day out, I don't even notice that I'm doing them.'

And I could certainly sympathise with that. As I explained to Mr Holmes, while we waited for Grimsby to bring up the waistcoat and cuffs, anyone accustomed to daily drudgery knows exactly what it's like to have done a dozen things of a morning, and yet to have no recollection of doing any of them.

'Indeed, Flotsam. While a maid would almost certainly notice the presence of bloodstains on a cuff, the absence of the cuffs altogether – well, that's a very different thing, and might easily go unnoticed by a busy person whose thoughts are elsewhere. I'd be prepared to wager a guinea against a shilling that Grimsby can't produce all seven pairs of cuffs.'

And it was immediately evident, from the valet's obvious distress on his return, that Mr Holmes' prediction was correct.

'I just don't understand it, sir,' the old man kept repeating. 'There are only six pairs in the closet. And Mr Oscar cannot be wearing a pair, because he was in formal dinner cuffs when that horrible policeman took him away. But any pair sent for laundering would most certainly be back by now, for I have never known the people in Delph Street make any sort of mistake. So there *should* be seven pairs in the closet, there really should. I can't think where the missing pair could be.'

I think that was the moment, looking at the dismay on the old man's face, when I realised how very dark things really were for Oscar Catanache. Inspector Merivale might yet release him until a body was found, but the inspector's men were searching the river as we spoke, and the Thames, though rarely in any hurry, is surprisingly generous at giving up its dead in the end. And even if they found nothing this month, this year, this decade, the shadow of guilt would surely hang over the young man for as long as the scene in Salisbury Street was remembered, his own personal and inescapable cloud of ignominy.

That was before Mr Holmes asked to see the young man's silver-headed cane, the one he had been seen carrying into the house in Salisbury Street – only to be told by an almost tearful Grimsby that Mr Oscar had apparently mislaid the cane somewhere, at his club, perhaps, or on the floor of a hansom, the old man suggested hopefully.

And it was also before we inspected Oscar Catanache's waistcoat – the bright, distinctive waistcoat of sky blue and gold which, in Salisbury Street, had so easily caught the attention of Mrs Grace and Mr Wickes and Mr Boldacre.

Because, of course, as I think I'd expected all along, the waistcoat brought to us that morning was missing a button. An exquisite, metal button, judging by those that remained, and one adorned very beautifully with a bright blue daisy.

Chapter Eleven

Mr Holmes did not linger for very long in Cuthbert Square after his examination of the waistcoat, and we had left the house before Sir Henry Catanache returned.

This seemed to me to be a very good thing, because the discoveries we had made there were hardly of the sort to set a father's mind at rest, and my own doubts in the young man were growing by the hour. After all, as Inspector Merivale would have said, evidence was evidence, and my only encounter with Oscar Catanache had been a fleeting one, so I'd had no opportunity to form an opinion of the young man. My exchanges with the young lady in Baker Street on the other hand had been vivid and – with hindsight – difficult to forget. It was hard not to recall the fear in her face and the panic in her voice as she had fled up the area steps. *That gentleman had a son... If I speak of it, he – they – will be so angry...*

And then the little handkerchief, hand-stitched with lilac thread. It had been a sorry little object at the time, lying under the area steps, but infinitely more pathetic now that I had seen its companion. Sometimes I found myself imagining her at work, carefully stitching them, putting such care into her labours; and then I would remember that terrible scene in Salisbury Street... Just thinking of it, I would find a lump rising in my throat.

So, all in all, it was a great relief to find myself leaving Cuthbert Square and heading, on foot, back to Baker Street. I returned there alone, for Mr Holmes had arranged to meet Inspector Merivale in the rooms on Salisbury Street, where, he told me, he and the inspector would discuss a microscopic examination of the premises. Inspector Merivale, it seemed, was a believer in the power of science, and a believer in Mr Holmes too – a comforting thought that morning, because when I reached Baker Street I found Mrs Hudson sitting at the kitchen table taking tea with her old friend Mr Rumbelow, a copy of *The Times* spread open before them.

Mr Rumbelow was a portly gentleman of late middle years, and a solicitor of some standing in his profession. He was also the person who had first brought to Mrs Hudson's attention the vacancy in Baker Street that she had filled ever since. When the two had first become acquainted – over a missing angler and a stuffed pike, if Scraggs was to be believed – Mrs Hudson had been the housekeeper at a very grand establishment; and Mr Rumbelow seemed to feel personally responsible for the fact that, through his intervention, she now found herself at the mercy of Mr Holmes' peculiar ways. It was a guilt that often manifested itself in the form of small liquid gifts, and that morning I noticed on the draining board a rather fine-looking bottle of Madeira, which had not been there when I left.

'It is too bad, Mrs Hudson, too bad,' Mr Rumbelow was complaining as I entered the cool kitchen from the bright sunshine of the area. 'This, er, person, this Mr Martin, has done only a fraction of the things Mr Holmes has done, yet he is suddenly being hailed as the greatest detective in London! It seems most wrong, most wrong. "*Jewel Theft Thwarted*" indeed!'

Mrs Hudson rose and welcomed me, as calm and as unruffled as ever, then pointed me to a chair and poured me tea.

'It seems, Flottie,' she explained, 'that Mr Laurence Martin has achieved another notable triumph. After studying the agony columns of *The Times*, he has alerted the police to a plot to steal jewels in Hatton Garden.' She indicated the article they had been reading. 'A series of notices from one Old Ebenezer to his nephew attracted his attention, apparently, culminating in this one.'

I studied it carefully.

> **Old Ebenezer to his Nephew — The time is ripe to make your fortune, young man. The treasure is adjacent. I have provided you with the tools. Now you must use them. 37HGrhclrwllcX.**

'According to *The Times*, Flotsam, Mr Martin had been following these notices for some time, and, feeling certain that matters were coming to a head, wrote to Scotland Yard to warn them. He understood the last part to mean "37 Hatton Garden, right hand cellar wall, where marked with an X".'

I watched one of her eyebrows twitch, then right itself.

'And when the police attended that address, Flottie, sure enough, they found that the cellar had been rented to a bespectacled, bearded gentleman — now vanished — who wished to use it to store his wine collection but had actually filled it with a collection of pickaxes and whatnot. Had those tools been used to dig through the cellar wall at the point where the X was marked, the digger would have found himself in the vaults of one of London's more prestigious diamond dealers.'

Mr Rumbelow, who had been shaking his head as he listened to Mrs Hudson's explanation, now cleared his throat.

'Ahem. Ahem. I hope you will forgive me, Mrs Hudson, if I express some doubts about Mr Martin's genius.' He sounded a little put out by this other detective's success. 'That is not to say that he has not provided a useful service in this case. A very useful service, very useful indeed. But surely, Mrs Hudson, some element of luck must have played a part? Could such a message in the agony columns not have meant a great many things? That is to say, is there not surely some evidence of, er, guesswork, in play here?'

But Mrs Hudson was reading the article again, her brow furrowed, and I noticed one of her eyebrows twitch again as she read.

'I find myself increasingly interested in Laurence Martin,' she stated at last. 'And it is certainly true that his star is burning very brightly at the moment.' Then she looked up and addressed Mr Rumbelow. 'As for this particular case, sir, then, no, I don't believe there was any guesswork involved. It seems to me that anyone who had noticed Old Ebenezer's messages, and who had taken the time to follow them, could, with sufficient intuition, have discovered their meaning.'

'But isn't that something your gentleman usually does, Mrs H?' Mr Rumbelow was looking a little dismayed. 'I thought Mr Holmes was a great one for spotting mysteries in those columns?'

Mrs Hudson refilled all three teacups, then rose to put the kettle on the stove.

'These last few weeks, sir, Mr Holmes has barely had time to even look at a newspaper. And it's hard to imagine that changing for a while, at least while the Romford affair is still demanding so much of his time, never mind this business in Salisbury Street.'

'Ah, yes!' Mr Rumbelow seemed to brighten. 'I've heard a bit about that. My old friend Peebles – of Huntley, Peebles & Cadwallader, a highly respectable firm, as you probably know – my old friend Peebles is the Catanache family lawyer and he assures me that young Mr Oscar will be home in no time, at least for a while. It is hardly my place to say it, indeed it isn't, but it would appear Scotland Yard have got ahead of themselves in making the arrest, and the Home Secretary is, well – and I mean to imply nothing untoward, you understand – he is a very good friend of Sir Henry Catanache.'

The solicitor paused to mop his brow, although the kitchen was lovely and cool, and he didn't appear to be perspiring. I rather think he did it out of habit.

'As a matter of fact, Mrs H,' he continued, 'I have heard a good many rumours that the whole thing is a plot against Sir Henry. You know, an attempt to get at him through his son. A good many people – that is to say, I'm *told* that a good many people, and certainly a good many people at the Empedocles Club – feel that Sir Henry's enemies want to silence him. There is, you see, a general feeling – although not, of course, one I would endorse myself – that George Dashing isn't entirely reliable, and that sooner or later he will go off on one of his romantic escapades, leaving Sir Henry to give the Paternoster Lecture.'

'I see.' Mrs Hudson considered this thoughtfully. 'There does seem to be a huge amount of interest in this lecture, and in who gives it, doesn't there, sir?'

Mr Rumbelow nodded sagely, and returned his handkerchief to his top pocket.

'Quite so, Mrs Hudson. Quite so. It is hard to exaggerate the significance of the Paternoster Lecture. There is a general feeling that Sir Henry, were he allowed to give the lecture this year, would swing the Members at Westminster firmly against an extension of the suffrage, meaning that votes for, er, women...' He looked a little awkward, as though unsure about using the word in mixed company. '...That votes for women would be put back years, if not forever. He is, you see, a rather prickly individual, but an excellent speaker, and his opinions carry huge weight in Parliament.'

He gave a little sigh, one that suggested to me that perhaps Mr Rumbelow held rather more liberal views.

'And, of course, Mrs Hudson,' he went on, his face displaying genuine anxiety, 'there are fears that Mr Dashing, were *he* to give the lecture, might use the platform to stir up hostility towards Russia at a time when the Tsar is badly needed as an ally. I'm told that passions are running very high in public meetings – very high indeed – with quite as many people against Sir Henry making the speech as there are against Mr Dashing making it. But were *neither* of them available to give the lecture, Mrs H, then the constitution of the Paternoster Society dictates that the Secretary, Mr Hildegard, would take the podium. And old Jeremiah Hildegard only ever talks about his great passion, which is the evolution of Roman Law, so instead of high drama, we'd have the dullest Paternoster Lecture for years.'

The newspaper was still spread out in front of me, and as Mr Rumbelow spoke, my eye fell upon a particularly relevant headline.

Incendiary Speech by Former Envoy.

It certainly seemed that George Dashing, regardless of his own safety, was intent on stirring things up. But before I could read any further, Mr Rumbelow had risen to leave.

'As I said earlier, Mrs Hudson, I am free this afternoon, so do please feel free to send young Scraggs along to see me. It is always a pleasure to be of assistance, ma'am. Quite so, quite so.'

'Scraggs?' I asked, the moment Mr Rumbelow's portly figure had disappeared up the area steps. 'What on earth does Scraggs want with Mr Rumbelow, ma'am?'

But Mrs Hudson had taken up a polishing cloth, and had set to work on the sherry glasses, apparently unmoved by my undisguised curiosity.

'That, Flotsam,' she told me firmly, 'is surely something you should ask him yourself.'

Before I could object, she nodded pointedly towards the tea tray.

'There's those things to wash up, young lady, and do it sharpish, because we're on our way out. It is set to be another beautiful afternoon, and you and I are taking a train to the country.'

-

Mrs Fenton, for many years the faithful housekeeper of the Catanache family, had retired from service to the village of Market Steepleford, the sort of village that exists only in the imagination, on biscuit tins, and in certain rare folds of the English countryside, with black-and-white Tudor houses jostling together around an ancient church, a public house of honey-coloured stone, a pond, ducks, roses still in bloom, and a little stream running away across the lane and into the meadows.

All this could be reached by train in a little over fifty minutes from Waterloo Station, so there was hardly enough time for me to sink into my seat, give Mrs Hudson's arm a squeeze, study my fellow passengers surreptitiously, choose and consume a bright green humbug from a bag offered to me by the young man opposite, say goodbye to the thinning suburbs of the city, then note the gold softness of the wheat in the fields and the rough yellows of the stubble, before the lurching pressure of the brakes began to slow us one final time, and we had arrived at Market Steepleford. I loved a train journey.

I had already been told that Mrs Fenton's retirement from service had been prompted not by age or weariness, but by a rather substantial legacy from an unexpected great aunt, and her house in Market Steepleford bore this out; for it was not at all the cramped cottage one might imagine as the modest reward for a lifetime of service, but a very perfect little Georgian house standing confidently beside the rectory, with a view of the church to one side and of tumbling meadows to the other. Here she lived with a certain Miss Evans, who for many happy years had served alongside her as a parlour maid, and who now accompanied the housekeeper to Market Steepleford.

'We do employ a girl to do some of the work, and another to do some of the cooking,' Mrs Fenton explained to us as she ushered us into her neat little drawing room, 'but we do a lot of it ourselves. Old habits die hard, you see, and we like our privacy. Besides, making the bed feels very different when it is your own bed you are making, doesn't it, Livvy?'

Anne Fenton proved to be a tall and rather thin woman in her fifties, with a sharp and angular face, who on first glance struck me as rather intimidating, as all good house-keepers should. But when she smiled her features melted into surprising softness, and her eyes were suddenly warm. Olive Evans, her companion, was, by contrast, a round and generously proportioned woman of perhaps some ten years younger, with a gentle face that always came to rest in a smile. The two clearly shared a bond of great warmth and affection, and more than once, when one found the conversation troubling, the other would take her hand.

The two settled us in the drawing room, on a sofa that faced the church, and Miss Evans brought in tea and a stand of small iced cakes and biscuits, while Mrs Fenton addressed the business that had brought us here.

'I can't say how glad I am to see you, my dear Mrs Hudson, for we have had the police inspector here, and I don't know what to think. We are terribly worried for Thomasina, aren't we, Livvy?'

'Terribly,' Miss Evans concurred, carefully placing down the tea tray. 'Anne had already thought of writing to you, Mrs Hudson, hadn't you, Anne?'

'I had. Because of course I still remember how you found that man who bred racing pigeons, Mrs Hudson, when everyone thought he must have been eaten by rats. And we so hope you can do it again, because we're both very fond of Thomasina, aren't we, Livvy, and of course we don't believe for a moment that young Mr Oscar has harmed a hair of her head. But all the same, from what the inspector has told us, things look terribly bad for her, and we're terribly worried about her all the same.'

'It would help us both greatly,' Mrs Hudson explained, a piece of strawberry shortbread in her hand, 'if you could tell us everything you know about Thomasina Trubshaw, and, indeed, about Oscar Catanache too.'

And it turned out that, between the two of them, they knew a very great deal.

'For I dandled her on my knee when she was a tiny baby,' Mrs Fenton explained, 'and I suppose I have felt a little bit responsible for her ever since.'

The story was, in some ways, a rather touching one of friendships honoured and duty done. Mrs Fenton, as a very young woman, had served as a housemaid alongside a certain Maisie Bute, a pretty but rather romantic girl given to terrible lapses when it came to laying out dinner settings. As Anne Fenton had never laid an incorrect dinner setting in her life, the two became rather surprising friends, a friendship drastically altered by the appearance on the scene of a seller of knives and steel goods by the name of Thomas Trubshaw.

'He was little more than an apprentice salesman when he first stumbled across Maisie,' Mrs Fenton told us, 'somewhere near the water in Hyde Park. But he was always going places was Tom Trubshaw, or thought he was at any rate. The tales he told her of his inventions, and of how they would live together like a lord and lady, well, if you believed the half of them, you would expect him to be a duke by now. And, well, Maisie...'

'...Maisie married him,' Miss Evans concluded. 'Didn't she, Anne?'

'She did.' Miss Fenton allowed herself a little sigh that was both sad and fond at the same time. 'Terribly in love, she was. She gave in her notice and moved to Croydon with Tom, and in what seemed like no time little Thomasina was born. A big, fat, chubby child she was, and I confess that my heart warmed to her.'

However, Mrs Fenton's acquaintance with the young Thomasina Trubshaw was brought to a close by the abrupt departure of the Trubshaw family for Italy, where, Maisie told her, a famous industrialist was interested in Tom Trubshaw's ideas about non-tarnishing silver cutlery. Mrs Fenton had waved them all off at Victoria Station, and that was the last she ever saw of her friend.

'She did write,' Mrs Fenton conceded, 'but not very often. Her first letter came some six months later, and very excited it was. She and Tom had been given a lovely little house in Turin, with an Italian servant girl and three bedrooms. She said she was becoming quite the lady, and I was glad for her, even though, in my heart of hearts, I was always worried that it couldn't last.'

But for a long time, it *did* seem to last. Mrs Fenton heard nothing for another year, and when the next letter came it was as cheerful as the first.

'Then nothing for ages, for so long I'd almost forgotten about little Maisie Bute and her child. My own letters went unanswered, of course, but I didn't take it person-ally, for Maisie was never one for writing, and never greatly organised. It must have been five or six years later when I heard from her next, and that letter was sent from Marseilles. From it, I had the impression that Tom Trub-shaw's career in Italy had not been particularly smooth. There was the suggestion that the family had moved on, from Italy to France and back again, more than once, and that their fortunes had fluctuated, but all was now well, Maisie insisted, and little Thomasina was growing up like the daughter of a gentleman, with a pretty singing voice and already a love of reading.'

Mrs Fenton paused in her narrative for a moment, to take a sip of tea and to nibble at a Shrewsbury biscuit, and Miss Evans took up the tale.

'It was April when we heard from her again, wasn't it, Anne?' she told us. 'April of last year, that is. A very sad letter it was. She wrote to tell us she was unwell. Not unhappy, mind, for she had her husband and daughter at her side, and she was resigned to her fate. But she was terribly worried about her Thomasina, and what might become of her in the future.'

Mrs Fenton nodded, and dabbed the corner of her mouth with her handkerchief.

'The truth is, Mrs Hudson, that Maisie was a loving and lovely soul, but never a practical one, and she had allowed Thomasina to grow up happy and beloved, but without a practical plan for her future. She had been raised as a gentleman's daughter, with no thought of preparing for a career of any sort, and yet she never had the slightest prospect of any inheritance to support her were she to be left alone. At the end Maisie came to see her mistake, and her last letter was a touching one, begging me to do what I could for Thomasina if the day ever came when she was left alone in the world.'

'Needless to say, Anne replied by return,' Miss Evans explained hastily, 'promising that little Thomasina could always turn to her. And I like to think that letter was a comfort, for only a few days after she received it, Maisie... Maisie...'

'Maisie passed away, Mrs Hudson.' Mrs Fenton took a deep breath. 'Although we didn't learn of her passing until early in the summer, when a letter arrived from Calais, from Thomasina herself.'

Both women sighed then, and it was easy to imagine the consternation the letter had caused. At the age of nineteen, Thomasina Trubshaw had been left alone. Her mother's death had been followed only a few weeks later by her father's, whose health had been precarious for many years. Between them they left her nothing but wonderful memories, no more clothes than would fit in a small suitcase, and a train ticket to London. A lifetime lived constantly moving between different foreign cities had left her without close friends, or even reliable acquaintances, to whom she could turn. And so she was returning to England, a country she barely knew, in the hope of finding a safe harbour.

But her prospects were bleak. She had no references and no skills in musical instruments or in drawing to recommend her as a governess, and an upbringing spent trailing from foreign town to foreign town in the wake of her impecunious father was not one which recommended her to respectable families. In the household of a genteel English family, 'foreign parts' is rarely considered a respectable address. Her letter informed Mrs Fenton that she would be arriving at Victoria Station the following morning.

The retired housekeeper shook her head at the memory, then looked up at us and shrugged.

'Well, what was I to do, Mrs Hudson? I had a little put away as savings, but not enough to support a young woman in London for any length of time. And finding respectable work for her was not going to be an easy task. Yet without it she would have been homeless, and at the mercy of the streets.'

She gave a little shudder at the thought, and so did I. I was no stranger to being alone and penniless on the streets of London, and Mrs Fenton did not have to elaborate. The plight of Thomasina Trubshaw had been extreme, and the thought of what might have awaited her was more than enough to make me shudder.

'So I chatted to Livvy here,' Mrs Fenton continued, 'and we agreed that between us we could manage it, and then I told Lady Catanache that I'd found a promising new parlour maid. By rights we didn't need a second maid, we needed someone to help Cook in the kitchen, but Thomasina had never set foot in a kitchen in her life, and Cook wasn't the sort of woman to agree to an untrained skivvy getting under her feet. So Lady Catanache agreed that an extra parlour maid would be extremely helpful if we were sure that between us Livvy and I could give Cook the help she needed, and it was all arranged. And then I went to meet the morning boat train.'

Mrs Fenton paused, and I watched her smile as she relived that moment of meeting. It had clearly been a happy one.

'The thing about Thomasina,' she said softly, 'is that she is genuinely a very special person. I had worried about how she would take to my plan, I'd worried she might have all sorts of airs and graces, and I'd worried that even if she came around to my proposal, it might be impossible to pass her off as a parlour maid, even one of limited experience. But I could tell right away, at that first meeting, that I had nothing to worry about. Her warmth and her cheerful spirits stood out, even at that difficult time, and when she heard that a position had been created for her, and that a little bedroom at the top of the house was to be hers, her relief was beautiful to behold. She gave me such a hug, right there on the platform, that I didn't know what to do with myself.

'And full credit to the girl,' Miss Evans went on, taking over the narrative, 'she threw herself into things like an actor learning a part, didn't she, Anne? So willing to learn, she was, and not afraid of hard work, though her hands were so soft that I don't think they ever did harden up, did they, Annie? But she never complained about any of it, not even when she burned her wrist on the grate so badly that it left a scar. Within two months, we'd made quite a passable housemaid out of her, hadn't we, Anne?'

Mrs Fenton nodded, rather proudly, I thought.

'She was certainly a quick learner, Livvy. And she fitted in very easily. I'd been afraid she'd be too *exotic*, you see. But she had no foreign airs or accent or anything, nothing that would tell you she'd lived abroad for so long – apart from her not liking the cold, of course, and sleeping with a blanket on even through the summer because she said it was never properly warm in England. But I don't think the family ever noticed there was anything unusual about their new maid, did they, Liv? Which shows how well you trained her.'

At this moment, Mrs Hudson, who had been listening to the story with her brow slightly furrowed, cleared her throat.

'But one member of the family *did* find her different from previous housemaids,' she pointed out.

Mrs Fenton acknowledged this with a solemn nod of her head, but Miss Evans, who was sitting next to me, shuffled uncomfortably in her seat and her pretty round face flushed a little.

'Well, yes, that's true, of course,' she agreed. 'It was ever so unfortunate, wasn't it, Anne?'

Her friend thought for a second or two before replying.

'Unfortunate, yes. But, of course, Mrs Hudson, with hindsight, not altogether surprising. I blame myself for not anticipating it. Mr Oscar was a handsome and kindly young man, with little time for the silly young ladies he was introduced to by his mother. Thomasina was pretty and lively minded and vivacious and, of course, she quite literally didn't know her place.' She paused, as if to give us time to understand her meaning. 'The thing is, Mrs Hudson, you can teach someone like Thomasina to *act* like a housemaid, but there was no changing the person underneath. For her it was all an adventure, an exciting part to play. She took the part very seriously because she knew her livelihood depended on it – but inside she was still that lively, independent young woman growing up in exotic places.'

'And you became aware that the two young people had formed a connection?' Mrs Hudson asked.

'Oh, yes! Well, not at first, not until she was top over tail in love with him, and he with her. By then she couldn't help sharing it, and to her credit she knew that it was not good news, for Sir Henry Catanache of all people would never allow his son to marry a housemaid, and Mr Oscar was far too honourable to continue the connection if there was no prospect of marriage. She was in a right state when she came to us, wasn't she, Livvy?'

'A right state, yes, Anne. She said she had to go away forever and cut all ties with him, for it was intolerably cruel for them both to remain under the same roof. The poor thing! We felt terribly to blame, for it was us who had put her in that position, and now her heart was broken. But of course it can never end well if a housemaid becomes entangled like that.'

'Please, Miss,' I interrupted timidly, for it was a question I was desperate to ask, 'did Mr Oscar not consider going against his father's wishes and marrying Miss Trubshaw anyway?'

Both ladies turned to me with the same look on their faces – not an unkind look, but rather one of gentle pity, as though my innocence touched them.

'Young lady,' Mrs Fenton told me gravely, 'Mr Oscar is far too sensible a gentleman to consider any such thing. What prospect could there possibly be for such a couple were they to go ahead? Cut off from his family, shunned by polite society, their children condemned to the same fate... Oh, I know in the romantic novels they would find their happiness in a cabin in the wilderness, but in real life the wilderness, for those unaccustomed to it, is rarely conducive to a happy marriage.'

'And do not think,' Miss Evans added hastily, 'that Mr Oscar's decision was motivated by money, for although he enjoys an enormous allowance from his father, it is widely known that he has lived simply and invested wisely, and through his maternal grandmother is a wealthy man in his own right. But he is also a believer in family affections and family duties, and although he and his father rarely see eye to eye on any topic, Sir Henry is still his father nevertheless, and Mr Oscar would feel it a great wrong to pursue his own happiness at the cost of his family's.'

Mrs Fenton nodded her agreement.

'It is as you say, Livvy. Mr Oscar feels his duties to the family keenly, and would feel deeply unhappy were he ever to marry without the approval of his parents.' She sighed for the umpteenth time. 'And so there you have it, Mrs Hudson, the whole unhappy story.'

But I could tell from the tiny crease in Mrs Hudson's brow that she didn't feel the story was yet complete. She waited while Miss Evans offered me the cake stand, and only after I had chosen a tiny Star of Jerusalem did she continue her questioning.

'So I understand, Mrs Fenton, that when Miss Trubshaw took you into her confidence, she and Mr Catanache had already agreed they could never be together. Did it ever seem to you, then or later, that she regretted that decision?'

Remembering the acrimonious letters found in Miss Trubshaw's rooms, I expected Mrs Fenton to reply in the positive, but instead she simply shook her head.

'Not at all, Mrs Hudson. Thomasina was young and high-spirited, but she was not naïve. She understood as well as I did that without Sir Henry's consent the two of them could never be happily married.'

'I see.' Mrs Hudson appeared to ponder this for a moment. 'And did she in fact cut her ties with the young man straightaway? Did she leave without giving notice?'

Again, Mrs Fenton shook her head.

'At first she was determined to, wasn't she, Livvy? But this all happened just at the time I came into my inheritance, and I myself was already planning to give notice. Livvy too, for there was no question of us being separated, was there Liv? And between us we persuaded Thomasina that it would be more discreet to give proper notice and to leave when we did. I did suggest that she might join us here in Market Steepleford, but by then her mood had changed and she was seeing the positive side of things. She told me that she had saved a little in her year of employment, and that she would make her own plans. Of course, had I known that she intended to move into those grubby rooms in Salisbury Street, I would have insisted in finding something better for her.'

One of Mrs Hudson's eyebrows appeared to twitch a little.

'So you would say she was in reasonable spirits during her last days in Cuthbert Square? Some people might have expected her to be tearful, or bitter, or both.'

'Oh, she was tearful when she first told us, wasn't she, Livvy? But never in a self-indulgent way,' she added quickly. 'She was just a young person feeling the pain of a very deep wound. And then, within no more than a week, her mood changed and she began to talk of the future, and how she might go try her luck out in the Colonies somewhere. I don't think, from that point on, we ever heard her talk of Mr Oscar again.'

Mrs Hudson's eyebrow gave another, almost imperceptible, twitch, then she turned to me and asked me to describe the young woman I had met by the area steps in Baker Street. Both Mrs Fenton and Miss Evans listened carefully, but seemed uncertain how to respond.

'Well, that *could* have been her,' Mrs Fenton concluded. 'Indeed it does sound very like her, particularly the clothes you describe.'

'The young lady Flotsam encountered was very afraid,' Mrs Hudson told her sombrely. 'Afraid of violence from a young man or his family. Afraid for her life.'

'Then it was *not* Thomasina,' Mrs Fenton said decidedly. 'It is absurd to think that she ever harboured any such thoughts.'

'The handkerchief, please, Flotsam.'

Mrs Hudson said the words with such great seriousness that the room seemed suddenly very silent. I reached into my reticule and handed to Mrs Fenton the scrap of fabric I had found by the area steps.

But that silence was nothing to the silence that followed, as the retired housekeeper held the object between her fingers and looked down at it as if seeing a ghostly apparition. I noticed that her cheeks were suddenly very white, and there was a strange choking sound in her voice when she looked up and spoke.

'I recognise this beyond any shadow of doubt,' she told us quietly. 'This is most certainly the handkerchief of our Thomasina.'

Chapter Twelve

The train back to Victoria was sparsely occupied, but it was not until two stops after Market Steepleford that Mrs Hudson and I had the carriage to ourselves. By then the golden afternoon had turned into a deep and thickening dusk, and the windows of our carriage hid all traces of the rushing countryside, giving us back only a pallid reflection of our own faces.

'Mrs Fenton seems a very kind woman,' I began tentatively, the moment we were alone, 'and I can't help but feel that she in some way deserved her inheritance, because she was so very kind to Miss Trubshaw. It seems a shame that Mr Fenton is no longer alive to enjoy her retirement with her.'

'*Mr* Fenton, Flotsam?' Mrs Hudson looked rather amused. 'Have you forgotten that a housekeeper is always referred to as 'Mrs', whether she is married or not? And Mrs Fenton has never been one to contemplate matrimony. She and Miss Evans are very happy as they are. But she has indeed been a good friend to Thomasina Trubshaw, and I fear she is now very anxious about her. Even more anxious now, in fact, than she was before our arrival. We must do what we can to alleviate her concerns.'

'But, ma'am…' I paused, looking for the right words to express my own fears. 'Ma'am, perhaps her concerns are justified. If you had seen that room in Salisbury Street…'

I tailed off, trying not to think of it. 'And I can't help thinking that Mrs Fenton and Miss Evans didn't know Miss Trubshaw half as well as they thought, because she *was* frightened, ma'am. And those letters from Mr Catanache, the ones Inspector Merivale found in her room, prove she *was* upset and that she *didn't* want to let him go.'

'And yet, Flotsam…' I realised Mrs Hudson was smiling at me through the reflection in the glass. 'And yet, I have always considered Mrs Fenton to be a perceptive and sensible woman.'

However, set against a room awash with blood, I found those words of little comfort. I think Mrs Hudson could sense as much.

'Now, Flotsam, don't be downcast. There is still a great deal about this whole business that we don't understand. And if Mr Rumbelow is right, Mr Oscar Catanache will be released tomorrow, and then we might finally get to hear his version of events. In my experience, people are a good deal more inclined to talk fully and frankly in Mr Holmes' study than in a police cell with a huge bobby looming over them. And if the young man is as innocent as he says, then it is greatly in his interest that the truth is discovered quickly, before the newspapers become aware of it.'

But that, alas, was not to be the case, for as we stepped down from our carriage at Victoria Station, the news-boys were already at work, noisily advertising the evening editions.

'News!' one of them cried, waving a copy of *The Clarion* in our direction. 'Read the latest news! Bloodbath in Salisbury Street! Housemaid slaughtered! Politician's son in custody!'

And from that moment on, there was probably not a person in London who hadn't heard at least some of the details of the Blue Daisy Affair.

-

If anything, the contents of the newspaper proved even worse for Oscar Catanache than the newsboys' cries suggested, as we discovered when we had lit the lamps and closed the shutters and spread *The Clarion* open on the kitchen table. Neither Sherlock Holmes nor Dr Watson was at home, so we were able to take our time, which was just as well, as there seemed to be a great deal in the evening press to worry us.

A full two columns of *The Clarion*'s evening edition were given over to the mystery surrounding Thomasina Trubshaw, and I was struck at once by how much detail the article contained. The scene in Salisbury Street was vividly described, the connection between Miss Trubshaw and Mr Catanache was hinted at in no uncertain terms, Inspector Merivale's name was included, as was the time and location of Oscar Catanache's arrest, and so too – to my great alarm – was the discovery at the scene of a button bearing the Blue Daisy design. I suppose few people knew as much about the night in question as I did, but the writer of the article seemed to know very nearly as much, and seemed to have no doubt about Oscar Catanache's guilt. The conclusion of the piece was particularly damning.

'This newspaper understands that Scotland Yard have not yet laid any charges against any individual, acting on the perverse belief that they cannot yet be certain a crime has been committed. This newspaper, always a voice of caution, can nevertheless conclude without fear of contradiction that the wretched maid has undoubtedly been struck by the Dart of Cupid. And on this occasion we very much fear that its impact has proved fatal.'

'Why, ma'am!' I exclaimed, outraged. 'The Dart of Cupid is the other name for the Catanache flower! They are as good as saying that Oscar Catanache is guilty!'

'They are, Flotsam.' Mrs Hudson studied me curiously. 'But have you not, at various times, found yourself tempted to say the same?'

'Well, yes, perhaps,' I confessed, a little abashed. 'After all, as Inspector Merivale would say, evidence *is* evidence, ma'am. But I would never have shouted it out like this, not until everything has been properly investigated. And I'm sure you would never say it aloud either, ma'am, even though you must sometimes be thinking it.'

'No, Flottie,' Mrs Hudson told me quietly, her voice very firm. 'That is not at all what I am thinking. Now, tell me, my girl, have you noticed this item in the Stop Press?' And she indicated the place in the newspaper with her finger.

> **Stop Press: Politician George Dashing survives carriage accident. Report reaches us Mr Dashing shaken but uninjured after brougham overturns at speed. Faulty harness blamed.**

I read it aloud, aware as I did so of a faint blush rising in my cheeks.

'Mr Dashing is safe, ma'am! That's very good news. But what do you make if it, ma'am?'

Mrs Hudson rose from her chair and moved towards the kettle.

'I don't know what to make of it, Flotsam,' she told me, 'but that sounds like Mr Holmes at the front door now, and both of us still in our going-out clothes. There's no time to change now, Flottie, so you had better just throw on an apron, then open a bottle of brown ale, and I will cut some sandwiches. Judging by this evening's newspaper, Mr Holmes is shortly going to find himself a good deal busier than he was before.'

The great detective arrived home that night looking a little tired and a little worn.

'It has been a long day, Flotsam,' he told me. 'After our visit to Cuthbert Square I accompanied Inspector Merivale to Salisbury Street. Then I was required at the Admiralty, to explain the implications of the Beauchamp inheritance for our shipping interests in the Adriatic, and then I'd arranged to meet Dr Watson at the British Museum, only to find that he has been summoned to Aldershot on some regimental business that will detain him overnight. So I had to take on his sentry duties in the Ninevah Gallery myself, and it proved a long and dispiriting vigil. Now, a bottle of brown ale, you say? Excellent! Please bring it up with the evening papers, and a bowl of hot water for my feet.'

It seemed clear to me then that Mr Holmes was not yet aware of the contents of those papers, nor of the great wave of activity that was about to engulf him, but I thought he might at least be allowed to enjoy his brown ale in peace. However, before the kettle had even boiled for his hot water, the first caller of the evening had knocked on our door, bringing a sharply worded note from Sir James Croxton.

Mr Holmes opened it by the unlit fire, his bottle of ale perched on the mantelpiece, while I waited to see if there was a reply.

'Dear me! Sir James clearly wrote this with a well-loved pen, sitting at a desk crowded with other papers, and in such haste that he didn't wait to find his reading glasses before he began. See how cramped the movement of the pen is, Flotsam, and how worn the nib? And the misplaced crossings of the 't' here, and again here?'

'But what does he actually *say*, sir?' I asked, unable to make out the message as he moved the paper to and fro.

'Let's see... Deeply concerned... Disappointed at our inaction... Grave disquiet in the Cabinet... Frankly alarmed... Mr Dashing's life in increasing peril... Coming to see me tomorrow... One would have to say, Flotsam, that Sir James sounds extremely displeased.'

I told him as gently as possible about the line of late news in *The Clarion*, but Mr Holmes seemed surprisingly unimpressed by it.

'If *that* incident is causing Sir James such consternation, then I can only say that he must learn to hold his nerve. The people who assassinated Marcelo Pedraza in Madrid and Nagy Sandor in Budapest are not the sort to disguise murder as a carriage accident. No, they want the world to know what they have done. They want to shock, Flotsam, and they want to be feared. And no one is going to fear them very much if George Dashing breaks his neck crashing his own brougham.'

'Yes, sir,' I agreed, for I could see the sense in this. 'And I think you must be right that they had no hand in Mr Dashing's accident, because the messages from Maya to Aldan haven't suggested any such thing.'

'Ah, yes! Our friends in *The Times*...' Once again, Mr Holmes sounded distinctly unimpressed. 'Now, I suppose I really must get round to seeing this Dashing fellow, mustn't I, Flotsam?'

After a moment's thought, he drew a fountain pen from his pocket and scribbled some words on Sir James' note, then folded the paper in half and handed it to me.

'Perhaps this will do the trick,' he told me with a faint smile. 'Would you be so good as to deliver it to Mr Dashing first thing tomorrow, Flotsam? You will find his address in the Gazette.'

I had barely begun to reply before we were interrupted by another knock at the door, and another note to be conveyed to my employer, this time from Inspector Merivale at Scotland Yard.

'My word, Flotsam,' Mr Holmes commented as he ran his eye over it, 'the inspector seems even more agitated than Sir James. He is deeply disturbed... Extremely concerned about information being made public... Intrusion of the press... Assumption of confidentiality... Wishes to discuss the matter with me tomorrow. I can only assume, Flotsam, that the evening newspapers will again cast some light on our friend's perturbation?'

So I explained about the article in *The Clarion* and the way it hinted at Oscar Catanache's guilt, while supplying its readers with a great many details about the scene at Salisbury Street.

'Well, if Inspector Merivale is suggesting that *The Clarion* received its information from any of us here in Baker Street, I shall be delighted to disabuse him of the notion, and in no uncertain terms,' Mr Holmes replied stoutly, before taking a long swig of beer from the bottle.

'No reply to this one, Flotsam. And what on earth is it now?'

This last question was prompted by a disturbance in the street below. Judging by the noise, a carriage that had been travelling at some speed was being pulled to an abrupt halt directly outside our front door. From where we stood, we could hear the shout of the coachman and the protest of the horses, followed by the bad-tempered thump of a carriage door, and a voice – a rather angry one – giving some indistinct orders. Arriving at the window together, we were in time to see Sir Henry Catanache stamping up the steps to our front door.

As a vigorous knocking began, Mr Holmes sighed.

'Why is Watson never here for the angry ones?' he asked sadly. 'His is such a calming presence, while I invariably make them angrier still. But your presence will undoubtedly help to keep the man civil, Flotsam, so apron off before you show him up, please, and on no account leave us alone together, however forcefully Sir Henry demands it.'

I confess that I felt extremely apprehensive as I made my way downstairs, because I was not at all sure that Sir Henry Catanache, of all people, would be calmed by the presence of a woman in the room as he gave vent to his feelings. But perhaps I was wrong, for when the door was opened to him by a young woman who wore neither uniform nor apron, he appeared a little taken aback.

'Good evening, Sir Henry,' I greeted him, and I can honestly say that speaking those words sent a little thrill through me, because Mrs Hudson had trained me well, and the correct way for a maid to address a visiting gentleman was second nature to me. To ignore it so blatantly felt strangely bracing. But, that evening, seeing his angry and scornful expression as he stood in front of me, and remembering his views about the proper place of women, I felt myself filling with a strange and sudden pride, a pride that made me draw myself a little higher and meet his eye, and to greatly enjoy the sensation of not calling him simply 'sir'. If Mr Sherlock Holmes was willing to forget, on some occasions at least, that I was not a housemaid, then I was willing to do the same – and most especially if it discomforted a man like Sir Henry Catanache.

'Good evening,' I said again. 'Mr Holmes saw you arrive and asks that you should join us upstairs.'

He had little time to reply, and his confusion lasted at least until he had followed me into Mr Holmes' study, where the great detective advanced to greet him.

'We have not yet met, Sir Henry, but I am Sherlock Holmes and I shall endeavour to be of service. This is Miss Flotsam. Dr Watson is not here tonight, so I have asked her to join us.'

Sir Henry looked at me, and it was not a pleasant or friendly look.

'Harrumph!' he snorted. 'Your secretary, I suppose? I can't say I approve. You are no doubt aware of my views on suitable occupations for the fairer sex. A gentleman's secretary should be a young man of good family seeking to make his way in the word, and no nonsense about shorthand-writing will ever change that! But so long as she is discreet and sits quietly, and doesn't interrupt us, I have no objection. But tell me, sir...' And here he brandished a copy of *The Clarion*. 'Tell me, sir, just who can I trust to be discreet in this day and age?'

His voice was rising, and although Mr Holmes attempted to reply, Sir Henry carried on, the words flooding out of him.

'My family is ruined, sir! My son is found guilty in the press, and in every tavern in London! Why, there is a mob outside my house at this very moment, crying murder, and threatening to smash my windows! Our reputation is in shreds! And how? How has this come about? Scotland Yard assures me that no one there has spoken out of turn. I trust my family, I trust my servants, but I have to say, sir...'

And here he broke off, leaving the sentence unfinished, his newspaper still raised like a stick.

'...That you do not trust me?' Mr Holmes concluded drily. 'Come, sir, your distress is understandable. Please take a seat...'

'I will *not* take a seat!' Sir Henry exploded. 'I have to say, sir, that you have a peculiar way of going about your business, with your young females and your snide questions, and your contempt for a gentleman's word! On the night my son was arrested, Dr Watson assured me that you would be swift to prove my son's innocence, and such is your reputation that we had no hesitation in believing him. But what has happened since?'

The colour was deepening in Sir Henry's cheeks and, as he continued, his hand holding the newspaper began to shake.

'Inspector Merivale informs me that it was one of *your* agents who discovered the button, previously overlooked, that places my Oscar at the scene of the crime. There is an absurd allegation that the murdered woman had previously come to this very address, claiming that my son was a danger to her. The police are now talking about missing cuffs and ashes in the grate, both of which add to the case against my son, and both of which, sir, had gone unnoticed until *you* pointed them out! My word, sir, if this is how you go about saving an innocent man, I should hate to see you prosecuting a guilty one!'

Mr Holmes appeared unmoved by this tirade, but I noticed he had turned a little paler and I could sense his anger. But when he spoke, his voice did not betray it.

'I can tell, sir, that Scotland Yard has not yet shared with you the full extent of my infamy. Did Inspector Merivale not mention to you that he and I have conducted a microscopic examination of the rooms in Salisbury Street? The inspector is very open to new ideas, and I was able to demonstrate how somebody's fingertips can leave distinctive marks which are not always visible to the naked eye. We were able to discover finger marks belonging to two separate individuals, sir, and I strongly suspect those marks will prove to be those of your son and of Thomasina Trubshaw. But try as we might, we could find no others. Nothing to suggest that a third person had ever been present in those rooms. The evidence, you see, grows stronger against your son by the minute.'

To my surprise, instead of enraging Sir Henry further, the detective's words appeared to deflate him utterly. He let out a long breath, lowered his copy of *The Clarion*, and without another word dropped heavily into the armchair he had previously scorned.

'My God, Mr Holmes, it is a nightmare come to life,' he declared, not loudly or angrily, but with desperation in his voice. He sounded exhausted. 'Oscar and I disagree about every subject under the sun. Our arguments are famous. It was imbecilic of him to become entangled with a woman of that sort. But I love him with all my heart,

Mr Holmes. He is my own dear boy, and I know beyond a shadow of doubt that he is innocent of this crime. If only this were over, if only he were free of it, I have promised myself I will never argue with him again. I would give everything I own to have him back, free, and untainted by this terrible business.'

Mr Holmes signalled me to the stool by the window, then took the armchair next to his visitor. When he spoke, his voice was surprisingly soft.

'Do not despair quite yet, Sir Henry. It is true that the evidence against your son mounts by the hour, and if my investigations prove to me that he is guilty of a crime, then I shall have no hesitation in saying so. But believe me when I say I see cause for hope. We shall continue to give the matter our fullest attention.'

But instead of finding this speech comforting, Sir Henry simply looked pained.

'I'm afraid, Mr Holmes, that I have already taken certain steps…'

He shuffled awkwardly in his armchair, clearly embarrassed.

'My wife, you see… Well, Mr Holmes, before all this business happened my wife and son had both enjoyed reading about the rise of this new man, Laurence Martin. They talked about him a great deal. So when I saw the newspapers tonight, and when I heard how all your investigations had tended to deepen the plight of my son, well, Mr Holmes, before I came here tonight I yielded to my wife's urgings and wrote to Mr Martin, begging to engage his services in place of yours. He is to call at Cuthbert Square at noon tomorrow so that I may tell him everything I know.'

'I see.'

Mr Holmes rose from his armchair and returned to the mantelpiece, where he stood, his face away from us, fiddling with his pipe. I had seen my employer faced with many strange situations in my time, but never with this one.

'I understand you wish me to take no further action on your behalf in the matter of your son and Miss Trubshaw, Sir Henry. Very well. But it is only fair to give Mr Martin the benefit of all the facts we have learned to date. I have no intention of calling upon the gentleman myself. It might be seen as an attempt to interfere. And Dr Watson will be out of town tomorrow. But Flotsam here – Miss Flotsam – knows quite as much as I do about this matter. I suggest that she joins you in Cuthbert Square at noon tomorrow, to make sure that Mr Martin has all the information we can give him. That is, Miss Flotsam, if you are available to help out Sir Henry in this matter?'

Sir Henry opened his mouth and looked across at me in confusion, and I met his gaze for a few moments.

'Yes, Mr Holmes, I believe I can make myself available.'

In any other circumstances, I am certain Sir Henry would have protested most violently and volubly at the idea that any member of the opposite sex could or should come to his aid in such a way, especially not a very young one who was a complete stranger to him in every way. But in his embarrassment at having just dispensed with Mr Holmes' services in favour of a rival detective, he seemed only too happy to acquiesce to any suggestion that might relieve the awkwardness of the situation.

He didn't look at me when I showed him out, but he didn't sneer either. I felt some progress had been made.

–

After closing the door upon Sir Henry, but before I could return upstairs, I heard Mrs Hudson calling to me from the kitchen. On joining her there, I found one of the double-sized trays laid out on the table, and already laden with food: a bottle of claret, tongue sandwiches, a hefty slab of Stilton cheese, a French salad, some slices of ham, a bowl of pears and one very perfect peach. Beside the tray, on a small silver salver, lay a sealed green envelope. Not just any shade of green, I realised. Most definitely Swarkstone green.

'It arrived while you were in with Sir Henry,' Mrs Hudson explained. 'I heard the carriage pull up and was able to intercept it before they knocked. I rather think, Flottie, it will contain some ripe thoughts from Lady Hastings about Mr Holmes' negligence in allowing George Dashing to drive his own brougham. But I can't see any need to take it up straightaway. Any further scoldings can surely wait till morning. Now, I believe some hot water was required?'

I carried up the bowl of steaming water for Mr Holmes' feet while, behind me, Mrs Hudson manoeuvred the enormous tray up the staircase. We found our employer standing by the window in unusually pensive mood.

'I confess it is a novel experience, Mrs Hudson,' he told her as she set down the tray. 'I have had various prospective clients leave this room declaring that they would rather go to the Devil; but I have never before had one tell me he would rather go to a different detective.'

'An unwise decision, I am sure, sir.' Mrs Hudson said it very firmly, as though it were a considered opinion rather than a commonplace comfort. 'After all, Sir Henry knows very little about the elusive Mr Martin. As far as I can gather, sir, Mr Martin has yet to appear in person in any of the cases I have read about. His solutions are invariable sent in written form.'

'Well, he will appear tomorrow, Mrs Hudson, at twelve noon in Cuthbert Square, and Flotsam will be there to meet him, won't you, Flotsam?'

'Yes, sir.' I bobbed politely. 'But, sir, are you really going to give up on finding out what happened in Salisbury Square that night?'

The thought appalled me. It seemed to me that somehow I owed it to Thomasina Trubshaw to discover the truth. But to my relief, Mr Holmes was smiling.

'I don't think I ever promised that, did I, Flotsam? I simply confirmed that I would not be acting in the matter *on Sir Henry's behalf*. But I have a growing suspicion that his son is innocent of any crime, and the more the evidence against him mounts, the more that suspicion grows. And I certainly don't intend to let an innocent man go to the gallows.' He turned back to my companion. 'I should also add, Mrs Hudson, that Flotsam here was magnificent tonight. Sir Henry is the sort of man who likes to cow young women, particularly ones of inferior rank, and Flotsam refused to be cowed. She made me very proud.'

And so unprecedented was this compliment, so unexpected and so out of the blue, that I felt my cheeks suddenly burning the brightest red I'd ever known, and the room suddenly seemed breathlessly hot, and I had no idea where to look, torn between the edge of the hearth rug and one corner of the skirting board. So totally unbalanced was I, almost to the point of stupefaction, that I was only vaguely aware of the exchange that followed, as Mrs Hudson poured the claret and prepared to withdraw.

'May I ask, sir,' she asked, her voice low, 'what first persuaded you that Mr Catanache is not perhaps as guilty as the evidence against him suggests?'

By now Mr Holmes was looking incredibly weary, but he managed a wan smile.

'Of course, Mrs Hudson. If you must know, it was the blood.'

He looked across at her, awaiting her response.

'Indeed, sir.' Mrs Hudson adjusted the napkin around the claret, then straightened and brushed her fingertips together, ready to depart. 'Especially since Mrs Fenton maintains that Thomasina Trubshaw used to complain of the cold at night.'

In my confusion I may have been mistaken, but it seemed to me that for a moment the two of them looked at one another, and then both nodded.

Part II

The Rival

Chapter Thirteen

I woke the following morning feeling strangely excited, but for a moment was unable to remember why.

Then I recalled that I had been tasked to deliver Mr Holmes' note, very first thing, to Mr George Dashing, and instantly I felt myself blush. I seemed to be doing a good deal of blushing at that particular time, and yet I can honestly say I am not generally prone to it.

Of course, it was also the day I was due to come face to face with the mysterious Laurence Martin in Cuthbert Square, but – although exciting in itself – it was not that appointment which had me leaping from my bed with unusual vigour, nor that one which saw me washed and dressed in half the usual time.

Mrs Hudson seemed unsurprised by my brighter than usual start, merely gesturing me towards some slices of bread and butter, and a bowl of fruit that was waiting for me on the kitchen table.

'No chores this morning, Flotsam,' she told me briskly, 'because you have that errand to run for Mr Holmes, and on your way there you are to call at Bloomsbury Square, where Miss Peters will find you something to wear for you visit to the Catanache house. Which isn't to say that there is anything wrong with your own clothes, young lady, but I think things will go more smoothly there if you appear less like a housemaid in her Sunday best, and more like the sort of young lady Sir Henry is accustomed to seeing in his drawing room.'

Faced with the prospect of so many joyful and exciting things in such a short space of time, I couldn't help but feel a little bit of guilt too, and I mumbled something about beating the carpets, but Mrs Hudson was having none of it.

'The carpets will wait for you, Flottie,' she promised, 'and don't worry about the front step either, because Mrs Macfarlane is popping over at ten o'clock to give me a hand with things. Her people are still out of town, and I think she's eager for a good natter. There's no word yet about when Dr Watson will be getting back, and Mr Holmes has already gone out, so we should have a quiet morning.'

'Has Mr Holmes gone to see Sir James Croxton?' I asked, remembering his enraged message of the night before.

'On the contrary, Flottie, Mr Holmes seems very eager to avoid Sir James and Lady Hastings and Inspector Merivale for a long as possible, so he has taken himself off to Romford. So as I say, you've no need to worry yourself about the morning chores. There *is* one other thing, though.' Mrs Hudson, who had been wiping the top of the stove, appeared suddenly very intent upon a mark she had found there. 'Young Scraggs was round here at the crack of dawn asking if you'd have time to meet him in Piccadilly, by the statue, at eleven. There's something he wants to tell you.'

I looked at the clock and did a quick calculation. So long as I was not too long with Miss Peters, there should be more than enough time to get over to Mr Dashing's town house in Weston Place, and still be in Piccadilly in time to meet Scraggs. Ever since seeing him in his best suit, that morning in the park, I'd known he was up to something. Perhaps now I was to find out what.

That morning was another very fine one, and London felt like a city in high spirits as I made my way across town towards Bloomsbury. In Bedford Square an ice cream seller had already taken position in a brightly ribboned boater, and by the British Library an old lady feeding the pigeons smiled to herself as they nibbled from her hand.

I had expected Miss Peters to greet me that morning in high excitement, for she liked nothing better than dressing up, and dressing others gave her almost as much pleasure as dressing herself. But instead, when Reynolds ushered me into the hallway of the house in Bloomsbury Square, I was struck by the unusual silence.

'Miss Peters *is* expecting you, Miss,' he reassured me. 'We received Mrs Hudson's note at breakfast and Miss Peters could barely finish her kipper, such was her excitement. However, since then she has suffered a relapse.'

'A relapse?' I asked, startled. 'Is she ill?'

'No, Miss. Miss Peters is *never* silent when she's ill. The truth is much more unusual. Miss Peters is engrossed in a novel.'

He shook his head sadly.

'There were signs as early as Sunday night when she was strangely silent in the library for an hour. But for the last two days, she has been affected very badly. She barely speaks, disappears into quiet corners at all hours and doesn't hear anyone who addresses her. If anyone does succeed in attracting her attention, Miss, she looks at them as though she were somewhere else entirely. And yesterday she wore the same dress all day.'

'Good lord! It's not the book she was telling me about, is it? The very long one?'

Reynolds nodded gravely.

'Yes, Miss. By a Count Tolstoy, I believe. A tale of passion, heartbreak and spiritual enlightenment set against a background of the Napoleonic Wars, or so my researches would suggest.' He shook his head sadly. 'You see, Miss, Russian literature is all very well for those accustomed to it, but for Miss Peters, coming to it, as it were, without defences, well, it is all proving far too much.'

And with that, he opened the library door very quietly, waited until I was inside, then tiptoed anxiously away.

I found Miss Peters curled up in one of the leather armchairs by the window, the book in one hand, a tightly balled handkerchief in the other. She showed no sign of knowing I was there, so I gave a little cough, at which she immediately held up her hand to silence me. I noticed she was breathing very quickly, and finally gave a little gasp and slammed the book shut.

'There's going to be a battle at Borodino, Flotsam!'

With these words, she rose swiftly from her seat, and began to pace across the Persian rug.

'And it will end badly, I just know it! Prince Andrei will do something brave and stupid, I'm sure of it, and Pierre is there too, and he's bound to get caught up in it, and Natasha will lose them both!'

And to my great surprise she skipped across the room and embraced me very tightly.

'I really don't know how I will bear it, Flottie, but Rupert says when it is all too much I should take a break and practise breathing, which *sounds* ridiculous, because breathing isn't something that anyone really needs to practise, but which is actually really quite good advice, because when I breathe very deeply and slowly, I *do* feel better, and of course if they can go through it all, so can I, because I don't even need to fight Napoleon or tend the sick or marry my uncle's cousin, or anything like that. And, oh my goodness, is that the time! We have to find you some clothes, don't we, Flotsam, because Mrs Hudson says you're meeting Sir Henry Catanache, though why anyone wants to look nice for *him*, I've really no idea!'

And with that she took me by the arm and led me upstairs, giving me as we went a detailed description of the Battle of Austerlitz.

I'd worried that it might be difficult to curb Miss Peters' enthusiasm on the subject of clothes, afraid that she would want to take up the greater part of the morning dressing me in over-elaborate costumes. But a little part of her was still in Moscow, awaiting Napoleon's advance, and we settled with surprising speed on something both sensible and relatively sober – something which, I suspect, had been worn by Miss Peters very rarely, if at all.

'It makes you look like a librarian, Flotsam,' she decided, 'but a very fetching and rather well-dressed one. Or like one of those women who works at *The Lady*. I can't imagine how I come to own it.'

But for all their subtlety, the fabrics were sumptuously soft, and in them I felt transformed into someone poised and stylish. When Miss Peters crowned her efforts with a hat that was simultaneously simple *and* fashionable, I might have been anyone.

Miss Peters seemed pleased with her efforts too, but when I confided that my next errand was a visit to Mr Dashing in Weston Place – news that would once surely have made her explode with excitement – she simply sniffed.

'I really can't admire a man of that sort, Flottie,' she declared loftily. 'Rupert says he wants to start a war with Russia, which is a terrible thing to want to do, and simply shows that he cannot appreciate the Russian *soul*. And anyway, Uncle says we tried that in the Crimea and it all ended badly, and led to a lot of gangrene and poems and nurses, so I really don't think anyone will agree to do it again, whatever Mr Dashing says.'

And with that, she said a distracted farewell and returned to her book.

Thanks to Miss Peters' new-found love of foreign literature, I reached George Dashing's townhouse in Weston Square much earlier than I'd expected. His front door was opened to me by an elderly footman with sandy hair and a very large forehead, who took my name somewhat suspiciously, and told me he would find out if Mr Dashing was at home – a pretence rather ruined by the appearance at that very moment of the gentleman himself, trotting down the stairs in blazer and boater, looking as cheerful and carefree as the morning.

'Who's that, Smithers? Someone from Sherlock Holmes? You'd better show them in.' And he paused at the foot of the stairs to hold open the drawing room door. 'Come this way, Miss…'

He paused, waiting for me to supply my name, and then his expression changed into one of happy astonishment.

'Why, I know you! Flotsam, my Baker Street ally. I confess, I barely recognised you. Is it rude of me to comment on the transformation?'

Once again, I felt myself flushing, and then – embarrassed by my own embarrassment – flushing a second time. So I stammered something about conducting some business for Mr Holmes, and passed him the note, the one from Sir James Croxton on which Mr Holmes had scribbled a short message.

Mr Dashing read it quickly, and smiled.

'Why, your Sherlock Holmes is perhaps not the killjoy I had expected!' he declared. 'Have you read this?' And he handed me the note.

I recognised Sir James Croxton's agitated scrawl at once. Above it, Mr Holmes had added a very simple one-line message:

'*If we want these people to leave us alone, we had better be seen to be working together. SH.*'

Mr Dashing retrieved the note and grinned.

'Put like that, I shall be delighted to meet him. You had better tell Mr Holmes that he can call here any afternoon between three and five o'clock. I will make sure I am at home. And now, Flotsam, I am taking out a boat on the Serpentine. It is a beautiful morning, and I love to row! I was supposed to be accompanied by a certain young lady, but her father – an earl, no less – dislikes my politics and has walled her up in the keep of the family castle, or some such thing. So I shall row alone!'

He stretched his arms out in front of him, as though already reaching for his oars, then paused in mid-stretch as a thought occurred to him.

'Unless, of course, you would care to join me? I'm sure Mr Holmes would not begrudge you an hour on the water, and Smithers will have prepared an excellent hamper.'

I explained that I simply couldn't, that I had other things I must do, and other places that I needed to be. But Mr Dashing was insistent.

'Come, it is still early, there is surely time for a short outing before your other engagements. And besides, I have a terrible presentiment that something bad might happen to me if I row alone. The assassins that line the shores of the Serpentine will undoubtedly seize their opportunity. How will Sherlock Holmes explain to the world that my dreadful murder could have been avoided if only his special assistant hadn't refused to accompany me?'

Although it was easy to shrug off Mr Dashing's nonsense, he *was* right that it was still early in the day. It would certainly be possible to spend an hour on the water and still meet Scraggs, with time after that to walk on to Cuthbert Square. And the morning *was* very beautiful, and I had always longed to go out on one of those boats, and there was something about Mr Dashing's urging that was both frivolous and earnest all at once, making it very easy to say 'no' if I wished to, but also very, very easy to say 'yes'.

So I said 'yes', and we rowed on the Serpentine.

That doesn't sound like a very amazing thing, of course, and there were other boats out that day too, on water that was sprinkled with sunshine, where the air was fresh and the city felt very near and a hundred miles away, all at the same time. And in many ways, it was really rather an *ordinary* thing: a young man helping a young girl into a boat, a little giggle as it lurched beneath them, then a push away from the bank, and an easy pull on the oars, and out into open water. I'd seen it happen before, many times.

But this time, the young man was not just any young man. He was the most talked-about young gentleman in the whole of London. And the young woman was me. I can't pretend I didn't notice the many glances in our direction as we walked together down to the water that morning, and I'm sorry to say that I didn't altogether dislike them.

There is something undeniably intimate about a rowing boat in mid-water. Oarsman and passenger sit face to face, knees only a few inches apart, and although few places are as public as the middle of the Serpentine, in a strange way few places feel more private.

Had I been the heroine in a romantic novel, I would undoubtedly have found myself shy and tongue-tied on such an occasion, but it wasn't like that at all. Mr Dashing was easy to talk to. He asked me a lot of questions – about myself, and my life at Baker Street, and about what it was like to share a roof with the world's most famous detective – but just as often our conversation simply flowed from the things around us, the things we saw out on the water, or the little snippets of sound that reached us from the shore. He seemed delighted to discover how much I had read, but in a relieved way, not a condescending one, explaining that if he ever mentioned Cathy Earnshaw or Maggie Tulliver to the young ladies of his acquaintance, they would nearly always look around the room, wondering if that pair had been invited.

He was particularly intrigued when he discovered that my most pressing appointment that day was at the house of Sir Henry Catanache, his great rival.

'You *do* get about, don't you, Flotsam?' he declared with a smile, pulling hard on both oars. 'Flitting between both sides of the great political divide in the course of a single morning. But it is a sorry business,' he went on more sombrely, 'this affair in Salisbury Street. I have no reason to love Sir Henry Catanache – he once described me as a youthful goitre threatening to permanently disfigure a familiar and well-loved face – but I would not wish this upon him. From what I read in *The Clarion*, things look bleak for his son. I suppose his only hope is for helpful witnesses. I was actually on The Strand myself that night, and so were a great many other people. Let us hope somebody noticed something that will exonerate him.'

He rowed on in silence for a moment, but perhaps he realised that the mention of Salisbury Street had dampened my spirits, for when he spoke again it was in a more jovial tone.

'There is one good thing that has come of it, though, Flotsam,' he told me. 'With this thing hanging over him, Sir Henry is hardly likely to be giving the Paternoster Lecture, even if I were locked in a cellar for a month by agents of the Tsar. You know, I've a good mind to step aside and let Jeremiah Hildegard give his talk on Roman Law instead. There are many people in Westminster and beyond who would consider that the best possible outcome.'

Although he said it with a smile, his words reminded me of the danger he was in.

'But surely, sir, you must be a little worried by what Sir James Croxton says? About foreign spies plotting to attack you?'

'I beg you, Flotsam, please call me George. Two fellow boaters can surely dispense with the formalities?'

I watched him for a moment, while his head was turned aside to follow the sweep of his oar.

'I shall call you Mr Dashing,' I compromised. 'For this morning, at least.'

'Very well, *Miss* Flotsam.' He laughed, still watching his oars. 'For this morning, at least.'

'But really, sir... Mr Dashing, do you not think you should be a little cautious about the dangers?'

'Perhaps I should.' He faced me again, and gave a great heave on both oars which sent us surging forward towards the middle of the lake. 'Although the greater part of me thinks Sir James is an ass. But shall I confess my shameful secret, Miss Flotsam?'

He raised the blades from the water and let us glide for a moment in perfect silence.

'The truth is that you don't become the third most eligible bachelor south of Carlisle by keeping a low profile, and a name like mine comes with certain expectations. The more people call me Dashing, the more dashing I feel I have to be.'

I laughed at that, and let my fingers trail in the water as the boat gradually slowed, but although Mr Dashing smiled there was a certain earnestness in his voice as he continued.

'Ah! You laugh! But you should be feeling sorry for me, Miss Flotsam. When I dance all night with society beauties who have never read *Jane Eyre*, it is not because that is my calling, nor even my inclination, it is simply a sense of duty to the family name. You smile because you cannot see the heartache! But I am a martyr to my Dashing forbears! Never resting because always Dashing! And you, my fair Desdemona, should be pitying me for all the dangers I have passed as a consequence.'

I blushed a little at that (again), and laughed, but was not to be outdone.

'Well, I'm afraid I should be pitying you forever, Mr Dashing, because it would be a terrible shame for you to deny your father and refuse your name.'

He laughed aloud, warmly and freely.

'Ah, but one day I shall do almost exactly that, Miss Flotsam! I shall be new-baptised! When my grandfather, God bless him, finally shuffles off this mortal coil, my father will become Lord Thingwall, and I will be the Marquis of Heswall. Then my Dashing days will be over, and I shall dash no more! I shall retire very sedately to a lodge in the woods, or to a villa in the Tuscan hills, and breed sheep, and read books, and grow dahlias.'

In the very middle of the lake, where the water was at its widest, my companion stowed his oars and, from the little wicker carrying-case that Smithers had provided, produced raspberries, peaches, Garibaldi biscuits and a flask of homemade lemonade, which we drank from champagne saucers. Around us the park grew hotter and busier. Young ladies in animated conversation strolled arm in arm, while elderly gentleman taking their morning constitutionals mopped at their brows with brightly coloured handkerchiefs. Small boys chased butterflies, nursemaids tutted, and little girls fluttered this way and that in white summer dresses. But they were a long way away, and I felt strangely detached from them all, drifting in a little private world.

'It's lovely here,' I told him, and Mr Dashing took his time to reply, looking around at all that he could see.

'Yes,' he said, not at all flirtatiously, but with surprising seriousness. 'Yes, it is lovely.'

Then neither of us said anything for a little, both of us looking out in different directions as we sipped from our glasses.

'You are a strange creature, Flotsam,' Mr Dashing said at last. 'A veritable chameleon. When I sent you those marigolds, it was no more than a gallant gesture to a pretty housemaid. But it turns out you can hold your own in a conversation as well as any lady of my acquaintance, and far better than the earl's daughter who was supposed to be sitting where you are. And, also unlike her, you don't mind laughing – properly laughing. And you know your Shakespeare.'

'Only the famous bits,' I confessed.

'Those are the only bits anyone knows. Now, come on, glasses away, and let's see if we can catch up with that duck!'

Of course, we stayed out far longer than we'd ever intended. I suppose that was inevitable. To be fair to Mr Dashing, I think he lost track of the time in the same way I did, because he looked most genuinely horrified when he glanced at his pocket watch and found the time to be a quarter to eleven, and he certainly put his back into the return journey, pulling so hard on the oars that he couldn't really speak.

But even so, it was only two or three minutes short of eleven by the time we reached the shore, and I knew with a sinking certainty that I was far too late to honour both my appointments. As we hurried to the park gate, which suddenly seemed a very long way away, Mr Dashing insisted that he could hail me a cab, that if the traffic was good I could be in Piccadilly perhaps only twenty minutes late. But I knew it was impossible. Even if I did catch Scraggs before he gave up on me, I'd be very hard pressed to make it from there to Cuthbert Square on time. Whereas, if I went directly there, I would be in Cuthbert

Square in good time, unrushed and calm instead of hot and out of breath.

Sir Henry Catanache simply could not be let down. Scraggs would understand.

On reaching the park gate, Mr Dashing stopped a cab with the first click of his fingers, then handed me in.

'Cuthbert Square, please,' I told the driver.

Chapter Fourteen

The carriage ride to Cuthbert Square gave me a good amount of time to calm myself, and the serenity of the old square helped too. Arriving with a quarter of an hour to spare, I was able to take a little turn through the garden at its centre, listening to the quiet hum of the city in the background, and to a blackbird singing overhead, and there, in the shade of the old plane trees, I shut my eyes for a moment, took a deep breath, and composed myself.

I felt genuinely sorry for missing Scraggs, and annoyed with myself for forgetting the time, and there was no denying that the little knot of guilt inside me had felt uncomfortably solid as I drove away from the park gate. But in the hansom cab it had begun to shrink a little, and there, in the soft, green coolness of the square, it began to dissolve altogether. After all, I could see Scraggs later on, or the following day, or whenever he chose to pop in to Mrs Hudson's kitchen, and he would understand that my appointment with the Catanaches was one that couldn't be missed. Meanwhile, Mr Dashing had agreed to meet with Mr Holmes, and I was where I should be, so all was well, and my little boating trip had done no harm to anyone.

And the sunlight on the water really *had* been very beautiful.

In that warm weather, many of the windows facing into the square were open, their sashes pulled right up, so at noon I could hear the clocks in the different houses begin to chime together in a slightly ragged chorus. Prompted by them, I advanced up the steps of Sir Henry's house and rang the bell.

The footman was expecting me and, after a short wait in the silent hallway, I followed him through the large doors on the left, which opened into an airy and sunlit drawing room, where Sir Henry Catanache was waiting with his wife.

It was the first time I had seen Lady Catanache since the dramatic moment her son had been taken into custody, and it was very clear that she had no recollection of my presence in her hallway that night. Nor had she properly understood the surprising nature of Sherlock Holmes' representative, for as I entered the drawing room I heard a hushed whisper, hastily cut off.

'A *girl*, Henry? Can that be right?'

I heard Sir Henry mutter something in reply as he rose to greet me, but the only words I could make out were *Holmes* and *perverse*.

'Miss Flotsam,' he began, 'how good of you to come.' For all his views about women, on this occasion at least I couldn't fault his manners. 'This is my wife, Lady Catanache. Mr Martin has not yet arrived, but he has confirmed by messenger that he will be with us shortly. I imagine you will be able to answer any questions he has of you in very short time, and then we won't need to detain you any longer. I'm sure Mr Martin will be eager to get to work.'

Lady Catanache leaned towards me, as if to examine me more closely.

'You are very young, I perceive.' She sounded worried. 'Tell me, young lady, can it really be right that a girl of your tender years is exposed to all the criminal horrors that you must surely encounter in your work? Are you not afraid that such employment will coarsen you, and perhaps make it harder for you to find a husband?'

Many people asking that question would have met with outraged indignation, but I sensed that Lady Catanache meant it kindly, and was asking out of genuine concern. I had just begun to explain to her that many young women were exposed to much greater horrors than I was, through poverty and powerlessness, when a knock was heard at the front door and, after a pause of quite a few moments, the footman reappeared.

'The, er, the person you were expecting is here, sir,' he explained, looking, I thought, oddly flustered.

'Mr Martin?' Sir Henry gestured impatiently. 'Well, show him in, man! Show him in!'

I think his wife and I both shared his impatience, and the next few moments passed in a strained and expectant silence, as the three of us waited with barely disguised anticipation for the entrance of Mr Holmes' rival. I was, I realised, strangely nervous at the prospect.

After all, by then, we had all of us read the name of Laurence Martin on numerous occasions, and we had heard it discussed too, because speculation about this new detective was not confined to readers of *The Clarion*. In offices and omnibuses and public houses all over London people were reading about the Knibling Diamonds or the Hatton Garden Plot and wondering what this new man was like and what he would do next.

Yet, although we had heard so much about Laurence Martin, he remained a figure of mystery. No one knew what manner of person he was, whether he was tall or short, bearded or bald, broad or narrow-shouldered. I hoped he might be old and scholarly, and already close to retirement, a fond foil to Mr Holmes, rather than a fierce rival. And I feared he might be the very opposite – young and strapping, and already appalling in his arrogance.

But the person who entered Sir Henry's living room a few seconds later was clearly neither of those things. Poised, straight, graceful, chin held high, the new arrival was certainly no elderly scholar, but equally obviously was not the smugly confident man-about-town I had dreaded. I had imagined Laurence Martin many ways, but none of them had come even remotely close to the truth.

The person who was ushered into Sir Henry Catanache's drawing room that day was young, slim, elegantly dressed – and a woman.

A rather striking woman at that, with pale skin, dark hair arranged in the latest fashion, brown eyes, and an expression of amusement in her smile. She was wearing what I recognised at once to be the latest Paris fashions, with gloves of cream lace so exquisite they would have made Miss Peters weep with envy. She was, I estimated, no more than twenty years of age.

Sir Henry was the first to speak, and even his good manners couldn't hide his bewilderment.

'Er, madam,' he began, rising hastily to his feet. 'You must forgive us, but we are awaiting an important visitor. If you would be so good as to explain to the footman your business here, I'm sure we will be delighted to welcome you at another time.'

The young lady raised her eyebrows and gave him the most charming of smiles.

'Ah, my apologies. But, you see, I received a letter from Sir Henry Catanache asking me to call here at this hour.'

The words were spoken in a strong French accent that seemed to me the perfect accompaniment to her Parisian clothes.

Sir Henry was, for a moment, totally nonplussed.

'Well, I am Sir Henry Catanache,' he conceded, 'but there has clearly been some mistake, madam. We are expecting a gentleman by the name of Laurence Martin.'

The young lady's face seemed to clear and brighten, as though everything was suddenly clear to her.

'Ah! You mean the eminent detective! The one whose name is in all the newspapers, who has just prevented a great jewellery robbery in Hatton Garden! The one who revealed the location of the Knibling diamonds without even visiting the Knibling family home!' She smiled very sweetly. 'Yes, that is me.'

'*You*, madam?' Sir Henry spluttered. '*You?* Really! Is this some sort of tasteless joke?'

He seemed about to say more, but his visitor had begun to look around the room, as if noting its contents.

'*Mais non*, Sir Henry. You wrote. I came. It is as you see. No joke.'

My host had grown extremely red in the face by now, both with outrage and embarrassment. But he tried again.

'My letter, madam, was addressed to *Mister Laurence* Martin. A man. There is no mistake about it. It must have been misdelivered. Or perhaps,' he suggested hopefully, as though glimpsing an escape from the confusion, 'perhaps he has sent you as his representative? You are his wife, perhaps?'

'No, monsieur. I am unmarried. I am Laurence.'

Said in a French accent, the name was transformed from a prosaic English one into something foreign and exotic.

'But I understand your puzzlement, monsieur. In France,' she went on, '*Laurence* is a name for a woman. It is different here, *non*? And in France, *Martin* is a common family name, more common than in England, I think.'

'But how can you be…?' Sir Henry, it seemed, was still struggling to grasp the situation, but suddenly a clear thought struck him. 'Why, madam, then you are a fraud!' he declared. 'You have been hiding behind a man's name to attract the business of customers who would not dream of entrusting their affairs to a woman!'

Mademoiselle Martin, who all this time had been holding in her hand a tiny little reticule of French silk, now transferred it to her other hand, and the gesture seemed to signal a change of mood.

'Monsieur, I am who I have said I am. I do not ever play games and pretend to be someone I am not. But if you do not feel you can trust a woman in this matter, I shall of course bid you farewell.'

She began to move away, but before she could depart, another voice, much louder and more commanding than my host's, caused everyone to turn and look.

'Henry!' Lady Catanache had risen from her seat, and was looking across at her husband with a thunderous expression. 'Henry! You are not to let that woman leave this room!'

She let out a long, unsteady breath, then continued.

'Our son's life is at stake, Henry. Unless something is done, he will be hanged for the most horrible of crimes. If this young woman is really the Mr Martin who has achieved such astonishing feats, then I beg you to let her help us!'

She turned then to the young woman near the door.

'Please, Miss Martin. We had assumed, as the whole of London had assumed, that Mr Martin was a man. But now we know differently. Tell us, you know a little of the case already, do you really think you can save our son?'

I watched Mademoiselle Martin's face soften and she gave, at the same time, a little smile and a little shrug.

'Madame,' she said simply, 'I give you my solemn word that I can.'

—

I think all of us, with the exception of Mademoiselle Martin, took a little while to recover our equilibrium that afternoon.

Before that day, I would have hotly denied sharing any of Sir Henry's prejudices against the female sex. Yet, undoubtedly, I had been every bit as taken aback as he had been by the revelation of Mr Martin's true gender. As Lady Catanache guided her visitor further into the drawing room, my mind was still trying to adjust. A woman could be a detective – of course she could. I simply hadn't expected it.

However, I was a model of composure compared to Sir Henry, who remained flushed and incoherent as though doubly embarrassed – firstly, for having to prostrate himself, in his hour of greatest need, not at the feet of some solid fellow from the same school or the same club, but at the rather petite slippers of an undeniably attractive young woman; and secondly, for having previously attempted to throw that same young woman out of his house.

Lady Catanache, however, rose to the occasion. I remembered that she and her son had both enjoyed following the career of Laurence Martin in the newspapers, and now, with her son in such great peril, she seemed perfectly willing to forgive Mlle Martin her gender.

'But, tell me,' she asked gently, when Mlle Martin was seated and tea had been sent for, 'how can it be that a young lady such as yourself comes to embark on such an, er, *masculine* career?'

'But it is very simple,' Mlle Martin assured her with a smile. 'I come from a wealthy family in the Languedoc, a quiet and rural corner of France. My father is a prosperous man and I am his only child. My mother died when I was very young, and he and I have lived a quiet life, in what in France is called a chateau, but which in England would only be a very old country farmhouse. But even in our quiet corner of France, we have heard of Baker Street, and of the great English detective who lives there. My father developed a huge passion for reading accounts of his cases. He sent for them all, and between us, in our little French wilderness, we studied his methods, at first for fun, but in time, as we thought about the future, with more seriousness. We thought, why could we not do the same, move together to Paris or London, and apply the methods of Mr Sherlock Holmes, but perhaps with some additions of our own, a little bit of French intuition, perhaps?'

She looked across the room at me, and smiled, then paused pointedly.

'My apologies, Miss Martin,' Lady Catanache intervened. 'In the excitement of your arrival I failed to introduce you to Miss, er... to an associate of the detective you've been referring to, Mr Sherlock Holmes. This is Miss...'

She looked across at me appealingly, having clearly forgotten my name.

'But of course no introduction is needed.' Mlle Martin waved her hand in my direction as though it were she, not Lady Catanache, who alréady knew me. 'This is Mademoiselle Flotsam, of Baker Street. You see,' she said, smiling directly at me, 'when first in London, I had time to do some investigating of my own. I walk the streets, I ask questions; I make, as you say, the connections that a good detective needs. And of course, as on a pilgrimage, I go to Baker Street and talk to the gendarmes and the street boys, and I hear the rumours that tell me Mlle Flotsam has distinguished herself on many occasions. But of course,' she went on, turning to Lady Catanache, 'you know this also, my lady, which is why you have invited her here today, and I applaud you for your common sense. I shall look forward to working with you, Mademoiselle Flotsam.'

Lady Catanache looked both surprised and embarrassed at this unexpected twist.

'Well, I believe Miss Flotsam was here simply to… Well, to pass things over to you, Miss Martin…'

But Lady Catanache was spared the necessity of further explanation when her husband interrupted her.

'You mentioned your father, Miss Martin. Did I understand you to say that you and he came over here together?' There seemed to be a little glint of hope in his eye. 'Of course, had you mentioned that you and your parent had been working *in tandem* over the last few months, I would have seen things very differently!'

But Mlle Martin simply raised her eyebrows.

'*Mais non*, Sir Henry. My father's health began to decline last year, and he is now an invalid being cared for in the chateau by a loyal and ancient servant. But it was his dearest wish that I should make our dream come true by travelling to London and advertising my services as a detective.'

She gave a little sigh.

'This I did, but in this country all depends on who you know. Without friends in high places you are nothing, and so my advertisements, they achieve nothing. Nobody writes. Nobody knocks on my door. I almost despair, but then I think of poor papa, and I think, 'Laurence, if nobody will bring cases to you, you must go out and find them.' So I turn to your newspapers, and find in them many opportunities to demonstrate my talents. I read, I draw conclusions, I write letters, and *voila*! I am suddenly famous.'

She looked across at me with a slightly impish smile.

'It was clever of me to start with the dog, *non*? In England, everybody is your friend if you are kind to the dogs.'

Sir Henry gave a little cough.

'This is all very well, madam, but you are not playing games in a French chateau anymore. My son's life hangs in the balance. Now, my wife here believes that you may be able to discover some evidence that exonerates him of this murder, and God knows, we have nothing to lose! That man in Baker Street…' and here he cast a dark look in my direction, '…has practically put the noose around Oscar's neck already. You can hardly make things any worse. So what course of action would you suggest?'

But Mlle Martin simply looked at him with her eyebrows raised – an amused look of mock-astonishment.

'This murder, you say, Sir Henry? This *murder*? Poof! There has been no murder. Two lovers argue. The woman

202

is scorned. She plots her revenge. She takes her revenge. She goes. It is a story as old as time. In France, we all know this story. It is only in England, where you button up your feelings into the starched shirts, that you cannot see this. But I feel it in my bones. And when the world knows it too, then your son is set free.'

She examined her beautifully gloved fingertips for a moment.

'I have written to you explaining my terms, Sir Henry, and as you wish me to collaborate with Mlle Flotsam here, I assume you will agree similar terms with her. A woman should not work for free, however much a man may wish it. There is no fee, of course, should your son be executed. I am not a monster. But that will not happen. If you assist me in every way I ask, if you allow me to come and go in this house as I please, speaking to whoever I like, without hindrance of any sort, then I give you my word that your son will be exonerated of all crimes before the month is out.'

'Madam,' Sir Henry declared, and he said it with an earnestness and fervour that impressed me, 'if you can indeed achieve what you promise, then you can ask anything at all of me, any recompense you like, and I will be only too delighted to grant it. Now, when can you start?'

'But now, of course.' Mlle Martin rose to her feet, and the rest of us rose with her. 'First, I wish to talk to Mlle Flotsam, so you may leave us for a few minutes. Then, Sir Henry, I will ring that little bell, and you will please spare me, say, fifty minutes of your time? Also I will need to speak to your son very soon, either in his dungeon, or should he be released, here in his home. Please arrange it. I will also speak to all your servants. Your maids, your housekeeper, the man who looks after your son, everyone who ever comes upstairs. The cook and the bootboy? *Mais non, monsieur*, there is no point. What can they know of your son's affair, of the great passion between man and maid, living always, as they do, only in the heat and smoke of the regions below?'

She managed to make the kitchen at Cuthbert Square sound rather like the underworld itself, while in reality, as kitchens in townhouses go, it was really quite a pleasant one.

'And after that...' Mlle Martin shrugged. 'Well, who knows? We will see in which direction the wind carries the seeds. But it will not take very long.'

–

Left alone with Mlle Martin, I suddenly felt rather small. Quite regardless of her skills as a detective, and quite regardless of her striking and easy elegance, it was her confidence which struck me most forcibly – the effortless way in which she had handled Sir Henry, her assumption of equality, if not superiority, when talking to that gentleman, and her apparent certainty that she could obtain Oscar Catanache's acquittal. These things were admirable and impressive, and made me want to applaud – but they also put me a little in awe of her.

However, relieved of the presence of Sir Henry and his wife, Mlle Martin changed quite markedly. As soon as the door was shut behind them, she turned to me and smiled then threw herself backwards into Sir Henry's armchair like a child testing its springs.

'Ah! That is good, *non*? You English have so many boring hours of formality! Do you never wish to take off your shoes and bounce up and down on all this oh-so-heavy English furniture?'

I grinned back at her – I couldn't help myself – as she got up again, dragged a little footstool over to the armchair, flopped back a second time and lay, semi-sprawled, with her feet up and her ankles showing.

'So, Flotsam,' she began. 'It is acceptable to you that I may call you that? The policeman in Baker Street who told me very much about you and everyone else in your household, he told me that Flotsam is your first name *and* your surname, *non*? Which I like. It is very not-English.'

It was true. I had arrived in Mrs Hudson's care with only one name and had never acquired another, so that one did for both. Just like Mlle Martin, I had come to like it too.

'And you must call me Laurence,' she went on. 'But in the French way, please, not in the way of the crusty English gentleman. And now, please, I want you to tell me everything you know.'

So I did, from my strange encounter by the area steps and my finding of Miss Trubshaw's handkerchief, to everything I had learned from Mrs Fenton and Miss Evans about the vanished housemaid. When I had finished, she swung her feet back to the ground, rose from the chair, and began to smooth down her clothes.

'But this is all truly excellent, *ma chère*,' she told me happily. 'With so much information, this Oscar will be free in no time. But tell me one thing. When this Trubshaw woman came to you in Baker Street with her story of being so afraid, could it perhaps have been, not truth, but performance? Was she perhaps just a little bit like on the stage, making drama for an audience?'

I considered this carefully. Of course, when viewed from a distance, the whole incident did rather smack of melodrama, but if you live with Sherlock Holmes dramatic things *do* happen, and quite often, so you just get used to it. Now, suddenly, I couldn't be certain.

'And the handkerchief, Flotsam, so conveniently shown to you, then left behind – could that not have been a way of making certain she could be identified? Perhaps, Flotsam, you have never been spurned in love, but for me it seems very simple. My lover casts me aside. I seek revenge. I visit the house of a great detective and tell a servant that my lover plans to kill me, knowing that my words will be remembered. I leave my handkerchief so I can be identified, then leave another, just like it, to be found at the scene of the so-called crime.'

She looked at me, and gave that little smiling shrug of hers.

'To me, Flotsam, it seems as certain as swallows in spring that we shall find this Trubshaw, and we shall find her alive. Our problem when we find her will be to prove that she truly is the vanished housemaid, for she will deny it through her teeth. We have no picture of her, no photograph. The young man here can identify her, but will not be believed. As for his parents, they are not the sort who notice housemaids. This Trubshaw could no doubt promenade before them this very day without them recognising her. There is only the housekeeper and her friend who can be certain, and without them at our sides, no way for you and I to prove she is Miss Trubshaw.'

But I could already think of a way. I reminded Mlle Martin of the burn I had seen on the young woman's wrist, the burn mentioned also by Miss Evans. Such a scar could be hidden, but it could not be removed.

This problem of identification had clearly been troubling Mlle Martin, for her face brightened and she beamed at me.

'You see, Flotsam! I knew that between us we would have all the answers!' Pushing away the footstool with her feet, she levered herself a little more upright in the armchair and began to smooth down the lace of her gloves. 'Now, *ma chère*, before I talk to Sir Henry, is there anything you wish to ask me?'

It was the sort of question for which I had too many answers, because there were a great many things I would have liked to ask Mlle Martin, from her childhood in France to her theories about where to look for Thomasina Trubshaw. So in the end I simply grabbed at the first question that presented itself.

'Please, Miss. Please, Laurence. I've wondered for ever so long, just how did you know so much about Mr Jones' dog?'

She laughed aloud at that.

'Ah, Flotsam! You see! You are English to your very centre! It is not the diamonds that interest you, or the young man facing the noose! It is the dog! But of course, it was all most simple.'

She perched herself very informally on the arm of Sir Henry's chair, and wriggled a little to make herself comfortable.

'The advertisement in *The Clarion*, you see, it told me all I needed to know. This dog, this Scrap, was an unusual breed, you remember? One you do not see often on the streets. And even for dogs of his kind, he was unusual, with a red coat, *non*? But he was old and infirm in his legs, so what reason would anyone have for stealing such a dog?

'It was *certainement* not to sell the animal for money,' she went on. 'Even the most stupid criminal could see no profit was to be made from such a creature. So kidnap, perhaps? I think there is much money to be made by taking the beloved dogs of the English. But on this occasion no demand for ransom had been made.

'So what other reasons could remain? It is obvious, *non*? But only perhaps if you step away from the facts and think for a moment like the thief! It is clear that the only reason to steal Scrap is if you have an oh-so-strong desire to own such a dog for yourself. But why? Such a motive is surely unusual when the dog is old and decrepit, and probably a little bit smelly. What strange passion was at work to make this Scrap such an object of desire?'

I watched Mlle Martin turn her face to the ceiling and assume an expression of deep thought.

'So I shut my eyes and imagined, Flotsam! And I imagined a person mourning the loss of their own beloved Trawler Spaniel, who comes, by chance and without warning, upon one that resembled theirs so closely that it seems uncanny. The same rare breed, the same unusual markings. Their emotion would be very great. But would such a person boldly untie the animal and lead it away? I thought not. Many people lose beloved pets, but, even in England, very few then steal others to replace them.'

Mlle Martin shook her head sadly, then theatrically stabbed the air with her finger.

'But, Flotsam! What if their grief was for more than just a dog? What if, I asked myself, someone had lost a beloved spouse, a spouse who doted upon their pet dog, a red-coated Trawler Spaniel? And what if then that pet itself were to pine away and die? Imagine then the explosion of feeling in a young husband, say, now unexpectedly a widower, pining for his wife, who turns a corner near Regent's Park and sees, as though waiting for him, a dog that is the spitting image of his beloved wife's favourite!

'To kneel, to pet him, to call him by that other dog's name – these things would seem natural to one deranged by grief, almost as natural would be to un-tie the creature from the railings, perhaps to allow him to be more easily petted. From there, how natural to desire once again to walk a few paces with this so familiar companion. And then a few more, and a few more, until going back unnoticed is impossible, and in panic and grief, a theft has been committed!

'Of course, it was all most simple to test. My thief would be a man – a woman, she would take the dog back. My intuition told me so with great certainty. He would be of young or middle years because in later years, when the prospect of loss is more familiar, the nature of grief is not the same. And as a recent widower, he would still be wearing mourning. Where would one look for such a man? Well, at his wife's grave, of course, but there are a great many places in London where one may bury a wife, and very few where a beloved pet may be interred.

'And so I came, in my mind's eye, to the place in Hyde Park, the place where the little animals are laid to rest. I imagined my widower's pilgrimage, every weekend, to the graves of those he loved. I saw him make the journey, first to the grave of a wife, then to the grave of her favourite. I saw him with his new dog, perhaps already knowing this stolen animal could not take the place of those he had lost. So I wrote to Mr Jones of *The Clarion*, telling him where to watch for his pet, and begging him to be merciful to the man who had purloined it. If I were wrong, poof! It makes no difference. I am unknown. But if I were right…! And I *was* right, Flotsam. And now even men such as Sir Henry will pay for my services, although I am a woman and Sir Henry thinks women are for bearing children only. Perhaps also for pleasure,' she added doubtfully, 'but with Sir Henry I think perhaps he gets more pleasure making speeches.'

With that slightly uncomfortable thought still hanging before me, she rose from the arm of Sir Henry's chair, brushed at her rear with both hands in the way a lady shouldn't, and looked at the clock.

'Now, my little friend, I must speak to the man himself. It is not to learn anything, you understand, it is simply to win his confidence. We cannot succeed if Sir Henry wishes us gone, but if I am allowed fifty minutes in his company, I am determined he will begin to find my presence acceptable to him.'

And having spent nearly as long alone with her, I had little doubt that she was right. Mlle Martin was a very winning person.

I left the house in Cuthbert Square that day wondering how I would explain to Mrs Hudson that I had somehow been engaged by *Mademoiselle* Martin to assist her in her investigations. As I made my way down the front steps, through the open window of the drawing room I could hear Sir Henry guffawing with laughter.

Chapter Fifteen

I didn't go straight home that day. Instead, I headed south, to Piccadilly, just to check that Scraggs was not still waiting for me, although I knew he couldn't be, not after so long. I found many pedestrians and sightseers scattered around the Statue of Eros but none of them were Scraggs, so instead I headed up Regent Street and along towards Wigmore Street, where on such an afternoon Scraggs was often to be found with his barrow. But there was no sign of him there, nor in half a dozen other places I tried, so eventually I sighed to myself and turned for home.

I think I must have been very eager to pour things out to Mrs Hudson, because when I found she wasn't in, I was surprised by the little wave of disappointment that swept over me. Instead of my familiar companion, I found Mrs Macfarlane, the housekeeper from three doors down, seated at the kitchen table eating a slice of bread and butter and reading one of the pamphlets about poisonous food colourings that Mrs Welland had left for us.

'Amen to all this,' she declared, waving it at me as I appeared in the kitchen doorway. 'I've been saying for years that more should be done, Flottie, child. It's terrible the things you read about, just terrible! There was that case in Surrey last year – the whole family was poisoned, and all three children nearly died, just because the cook had bought green food colour that turned out to be something horrid! And remember the Bath Bun case in Bristol? Or that fancy dinner in Bradford with the poisonous trifle? What I always say is, if something's green that's not meant to be green, or blue that's not meant to be blue, or red that's not meant to be red, don't eat it, Flottie, don't eat it!'

Mrs Macfarlane was the sort of woman who was anxious when Mrs Hudson was calm, and bony where Mrs Hudson was rounded, and I rarely saw her eat anything but bread, butter and dry biscuits; so avoiding sweets and puddings of any colour was probably not, for her, a very great hardship. But she was a good-hearted woman for all that, and one who Mrs Hudson trusted with polishing the brass, which said a great deal in her favour.

There had been various callers, Mrs Macfarlane told me, all for Mr Holmes, and none of them very pleased to be turned away. Inspector Merivale, Lady Hastings and Sir James Croxton were the names she listed, as well as a chimney-sweep with a message for Mr Holmes that was something to do with fish. The latter had been sent on his way, and scolded for leaving dirty footmarks on the front step. Intriguingly there had also been a visit from a fair-haired young man with spectacles who hadn't left a name but had promised to call again in the evening.

The only other person to cause her any trouble, according to Mrs Macfarlane, had been a young scamp who'd knocked on the kitchen door asking for me, but hadn't left a message.

'Though something did arrive for you, Flottie. Over there on the side.'

It was a thick creamy envelope address to 'Miss Flotsam' in handwriting I recognised, and inside was a card with a simple message. '*I am so sorry for making you miss your appointment today. The fault was all mine. Not deserving of, but hoping for, your forgiveness. GD.*'

Oddly, perhaps because I'd been hoping Mrs Hudson would be at home to put an arm around me, the note affected me in a peculiar way. It made me smile, a quiet, inside sort of smile which Mrs Macfarlane couldn't possibly have noticed. But also, just for a moment, it made me want to burst into tears. I don't know why. I don't think Mrs Macfarlane could have noticed that either.

By the time Mrs Hudson *did* come home, around an hour later, I was fully recovered. I'd polished and dusted in Mr Holmes' study, swept the stairs, done all the doorknobs, even the ones that didn't really need it, had swept and mopped the kitchen floor, and had generally made myself feel better through vigorous action. Before she had even taken off her coat, I had the kettle boiling.

At first, I didn't think to ask where she'd been, so eager was I to tell her about all that had befallen me at the Catanache house in Cuthbert Square. But when I came to my great revelation, it fell rather flat.

'If you are going to tell me that Laurence Martin is a young lady, Flotsam, then it is only fair to confess I already know.' She pulled her cuffs back from her wrists and settled down next to me. 'On my errands today, you see, I happened to be in Kensington, and it struck me that it might be interesting to call at the address in Cornwall Mews listed in Mr Martin's advertisements. Of course, Flotsam, it was just idle curiosity. I knew that the detective was with you in Cuthbert Square. But I was interested to see the manner in which he lived, and I even went so far as to ring the bell.'

I had known Mrs Hudson long enough to know that it could not have been pure coincidence which had taken her in that direction that day, and nor was it simply idle curiosity that had caused her to ring the bell. Something about Mademoiselle Martin's cases had intrigued her, I knew that. I think Mrs Hudson had sensed something unusual. But now, of course, all was made clear.

'I suppose you spoke to her maid, ma'am. She must be growing used to it by now – I mean, to callers being astonished when they discover her employer is not a man.'

'On the contrary, Flotsam, she is not used to it at all. Her name is Margaret and she seems a sensible girl. She previously worked for the Harringtons, which reflects well on her. But she had never before been confronted with a caller asking after *Mr* Martin, for the simple reason that no callers ever come to the house.'

'Ah, I can explain that, ma'am,' I told her. 'That is exactly what Mlle Martin said. Even when she advertised, no one came.'

I had warmed the pot and made the tea, and now I poured for both of us.

'But that was before her recent triumphs, Flotsam. Her advertisements invite clients to write to her, and there is nothing unusual in that. But it is surely strange, now that she is so well known, that she has never invited any client to call?'

But I couldn't agree. As a woman living without a companion, it would be difficult for Mlle Martin to invite male clients to her house, and possible that very few female clients had yet presented themselves.

'Perhaps she simply meets them elsewhere, ma'am? She gave me the impression that she is often out and about.'

'Indeed she is, Flottie. Margaret tells me that for the first couple of weeks of her employment, Mlle Martin didn't come home at all except on Sundays, and never for the night. She would send Margaret instructions about the piles of new clothes that were being delivered to the house, but Margaret had no way of replying. That was because of the nature of her work, Mlle Martin said.'

I wasn't sure what Mrs Hudson was implying, or even if she was implying anything at all, but I felt obliged to speak up in Mlle Martin's defence.

'She told me, ma'am, that at first it was very hard for her over here, and that she spent her time making investigations of her own. I think she meant that she was getting to know the city and getting to know some of the people in it. She found out all about us, for instance.'

'She did, did she?' Mrs Hudson examined me thoughtfully for a moment over the top of her teacup. 'Well, anyway, Flottie, that all changed a couple of months ago. Margaret says that from then on Mlle Martin, although often away, was at Cornwall Mews a great deal more.'

I tried to sort out the chronology in my head.

'That does make sense though, doesn't it, ma'am? These last couple of months are the ones when she has been following the cases in the papers and scoring all her triumphs!'

'Yes, I suppose so, Flotsam.' Her teacup was empty, so I added a dab of milk and refilled it from the pot. 'Margaret says that Mlle Martin is an unusually good mistress to work for. One of the best she has *ever* worked for, in fact. Exacting, but knowledgeable, and understanding of the difficulties. I would say that Margaret rather likes her.'

But this didn't seem surprising to me at all. It was easy to imagine that Mlle Martin was a likeable mistress. I thought of saying as much, but instead decided to broach a subject that was worrying me.

'Mrs Hudson, ma'am,' I began. 'Mlle Martin is certain that Miss Trubshaw is alive and well. She says that everything I saw at Salisbury Street was part of her revenge on Mr Catanache, that it's all a plot to get him into trouble. Could that be true, do you think?'

Mrs Hudson drained her second cup of tea, then rose. I had expected a prompt reply, but instead she began to gather up the tea things.

'I must confess, Flottie, that the thought has certainly occurred to me. But it doesn't seem to explain quite everything, does it? The burnt cuff, for instance. Or the fact that witnesses are certain it was Mr Catanache they saw, carrying something very like a body from the building.'

And of course it was true. Neither of those things fitted Mlle Martin's theory, and when I considered them, the young man began to seem very guilty again. I wondered what Mr Catanache would have to say in his own defence.

That evening, an hour after Sherlock Holmes arrived home, and barely twenty minutes after Dr Watson's return from Aldershot, I was to find out.

–

I didn't actually hear the knock at the door that heralded Oscar Catanache's arrival in Baker Street. I had clambered through the little trapdoor in the kitchen floor into the tiny cellar below, trying to find a spare bottle of Marsden's oil which was going to be needed for the picture frames, and from the cellar you can't hear very much. It was only when I emerged that I heard voices on the stairs and realised that Mrs Hudson must be showing someone up.

216

I confess to a pang of jealousy, because I was sure from Mrs Macfarlane's description of the earlier, fair-haired caller, that this must be the young man himself, returning as promised – and I was ablaze with curiosity to see him again.

But I need not have feared, because Mrs Hudson returned with a twinkle in her eye and the news that I was wanted upstairs.

'Not by our two gentlemen, Flottie, though I'm sure they'll be delighted to have you. No, it was the caller – young Mr Catanache himself – who requested that you should be present. No doubt he will explain himself. But first, off with the apron, and you'd better give your face a quick wipe first, because that looks suspiciously like a cobweb across your nose.'

I found Mr Oscar Catanache standing with his back to the fireplace in Mr Holmes' study, polishing his spectacles with a small red cloth. He was, as I remembered, a nice-looking young man with a pleasant face, and, like his mother, clearly had no recollection of my presence on the night of his arrest. When I entered, Mr Holmes and Dr Watson rose from their armchairs, and Mr Holmes made the introductions.

'Mr Catanache is aware, Flotsam, that you became acquainted with Miss Martin earlier today. It was her suggestion that you should be present when he told us his story.'

'Then you have met, Mlle Martin, sir?' I asked our visitor brightly, pleased to hear that her investigations were continuing according to her plan.

'Indeed I have, Miss Flotsam.'

Oscar Catanache had a light, tenor-ish sort of voice and tended to speak rather softly. That, combined with his pleasant smile and spectacles, did not give the impression of a man given to violent murder, although Mr Holmes would no doubt have been able to point me to the case of the Watford Whisperer or the Merton Mumbler, or some such thing, to convince me that a soft voice did not always preclude an appetite for slaughter.

'I was released at three o'clock this afternoon,' he went on, 'by a rather glum Inspector Merivale, who told me not to undertake any journeys outside the capital. When I arrived home, Mlle Martin was waiting for me in the drawing room. I fear it took a few minutes for me to really understand who she was, because it seemed incredible that such a person could be *the* Laurence Martin, but she told me her story and explained that my father had rather fallen out with Mr Holmes and, unaware of her sex, had summoned her instead. That was when I determined to call here in person, to apologise for my father's behaviour.'

'Very good of you, sir!' Dr Watson declared. 'Bit of a shock for my friend here to be told that his services weren't required.'

The doctor was back in his usual armchair as though he had never been away, although I noticed he was still slightly grimy from his journey. Quietly, without being asked, I moved over to the drinks tray and began to mix him a brandy and shrub. It was good to see him.

'Sir Henry is perfectly within his rights to consult whoever he wishes, Watson,' Mr Holmes replied, although it struck me that he was very pleased that Mr Catanache had called. 'Tell me, sir, what did you make of this new rival of mine?'

For a moment, I thought Mr Catanache looked a little embarrassed, because he undoubtedly paused before answering. But when he did speak, it was with the conviction and certainty of a man who has decided to be honest.

'To tell the truth, sir,' he admitted, still fiddling with his glasses, 'I found Mlle Martin rather remarkable.'

I think he was preparing to elucidate further, but Mr Holmes was suddenly impatient to get to the matter in hand.

'Yes, quite so. I have been rather too busy to read about her triumphs in any detail, but she would appear to have demonstrated a very respectable grasp of deductive principles. Now, sir, you told us that you wished to give us your version of events. You will no doubt be aware that the evidence against you mounts alarmingly, so I would urge you to give us as full an account as possible, omitting no detail of your acquaintanceship with Miss Trubshaw and of the events which followed.'

So, while I silently handed Dr Watson a brimming glass, then took up position on the little footstool by the window, Mr Catanache placed his spectacles on his nose, shuffled a little awkwardly on the hearth rug and began.

It struck me at once how clearly and coherently he spoke, in a way that would have struck many as an indication of his openness or honesty, and many others as proof that his story had been often and carefully practised. As for me, I found it hard to decide, swinging from one position to the other as his tale unfolded.

The first part of his account concerned the arrival of Thomasina Trubshaw in the Catanache household, or rather his growing awareness of the new housemaid – a chance encounter when he was looking for a book in the library, a conversation about the Suffrage when she had taken a leaflet from a caller, a meeting of the eyes in the drawing room when guests were present, followed by another, and then another, until hers were the first eyes he looked for on entering a room.

'We were foolish, Mr Holmes. After four months of clandestine meetings, we declared our love for each other, declared that neither of us could ever love another. For a time I entertained the idea of placing things openly before my father, telling him of our love and begging for his permission to marry. But I know my father too well, sir, and brought Thomasina to understand that any such approach was doomed. Instead I promised her that we would find another way.'

He removed his spectacles again and polished them vigorously, although it was impossible that they could already be in need of such attention.

'But of course, no such way existed,' he concluded sadly. 'My father and I, sir, are very different characters. Our politics, our pastimes, our beliefs – in all these things we are complete opposites. We argue endlessly, over everything. Yet somewhere, underneath, there is a bond. He has never been less than generous to me – so generous, in fact, that even without an allowance from him I would be an extremely wealthy man, able to support a lavish establishment and to live as I please. But perhaps because of this generosity, as I explained to Thomasina, I feel it is my duty as a son to marry in a way that meets with his approval.'

'Love versus duty, eh?' Dr Watson mused. 'Can't say I've ever had that problem myself, but I've met one or two who have – nice fellows, too – and no easy way out. You have my sympathy, sir!'

I think, however, I was less sympathetic, and at my age Dr Watson would probably have been less sympathetic too. What price a dry old stick like Sir Henry, set against the burning flame of a perfect love? Also, it seemed rather unfair on Thomasina. Oscar Catanache could go back to being an unattached gentleman of means; Thomasina Trubshaw would go back to scrubbing floors. My heart hardened against him a little.

'So I take it then,' Mr Holmes asked, 'that your engagement was broken off, and that the young lady took it badly.'

'I fear so, Mr Holmes.' The young man hung his head. 'In a month's time, you see, I shall be leaving England for a number of years. My family has business interests in Singapore, and it has long been arranged that I shall move out there and take up the supervision of them. They are, I fear, barely profitable, and I believe that by running them in a more enlightened way, by sharing with the workers a certain proportion of the profits, I can prove to my father that the business will become more prosperous, not less. Thomasina knew of this, and had entertained some hopes that she could travel with me as my wife. But the day came when I had to concede it was impossible, and explain to her that, when I quit these shores, it would be goodbye forever.'

'Pretty bitter pill for the young lady,' Dr Watson observed sadly. 'Very upset, I imagine.'

Mr Catanache nodded.

'She was indeed, sir. And it was in the weeks that followed that I realised I had been mistaken about her. The carefree, understanding woman I had come to love was replaced by one consumed with anger and with jealousy. You must understand, sir, that I did not plan to utterly cast her aside. I had the means to establish her in comfort, anywhere she wished it. I even spoke of purchasing for her a villa on the Cape, for she had often talked about quitting England for a new life in South Africa.'

On my little footstool by the window, I heard this and began to reconsider. Perhaps I had been hasty in condemning the young gentleman? Perhaps Mr Catanache had been reasonable throughout, after all. I thought back to the letters that had been found in Salisbury Street, the letters from Oscar Catanache to Thomasina Trubshaw, which gave considerable support to his account. His had been patient, pleading letters, begging for calm, trying to soothe a young lady who seemed barely in control of her emotions. The Thomasina Trubshaw who received those letters had been the one Mlle Martin imagined – vengeful and vindictive and furious.

But then I remembered Mrs Fenton telling me that Thomasina had been tearful for a little when she and Mr Catanache agreed to part, but was resigned to the fact that the two must go their separate ways, and even felt optimistic for the future. The more I heard, the less sense it all made.

'In the end, Mr Holmes, I had no choice but to insist that we severed the connection altogether. The threats she was making against me and my family were too alarming. Not legal threats, for there had never been any formal understanding between us. But darker threats, of ruin and disgrace and lives cut short.'

'You have those letters?' Mr Holmes asked sharply.

'I burned them, sir,' Mr Catanache replied. 'At my club. Or else tore them up and discarded them. They were too horrible to keep. I feared for myself and my family, but also for Thomasina herself. A complete break seemed better for all concerned. And I went to Salisbury Street that night to tell her so.'

Mr Holmes began to speak again, but Mr Catanache held up his hand.

'Oh, I know, sir, that when asked by Inspector Merivale, in front of my family, I denied that I had been there. It was very wrong of me. I panicked, you see. My instinct was to conceal from my parents the sordid situation in which I had become embroiled. But now I'm not afraid to speak the truth, sir, and the truth is that I was at Salisbury Street that night.'

'We don't need your confession to convince us of that, sir,' Mr Holmes told him coldly. 'Flotsam here had already proved it, to the inspector's satisfaction and to mine.' He leaned forward a little in his chair. 'Now, you were observed entering the building at around eleven o'clock that night, wearing a distinctive waistcoat and carrying a stick with a round, silver knob. Is that correct?'

'It is, sir.'

I sensed that the atmosphere in the room had changed. We were no longer listening to Mr Catanache's story, but to his interrogation.

'The same witnesses state that you stopped to arrange your scarf over your face a few yards before the entrance of the house. Now, why, sir, on such a warm evening, would you think of doing such a thing?'

Mr Catanache looked a little embarrassed.

'Well, if you must know, Mr Holmes, I had seen a couple of fellows I knew, walking down The Strand. A bit of a gathering had been arranged to celebrate George Dashing's return to London, and I'd forgotten that they were all meeting at The Savoy. I even thought for a moment that Dashing himself had spotted me – he and

I are friends, you know, for all that my father despises him – and I confess I was embarrassed that someone like him might see me frequenting a place like the house in Salisbury Street. So that is why I stopped to cover my face.'

'And you found Miss Trubshaw at home?'

'Of course. She had suggested the meeting, and even the hour. She said my presence in the building would excite less remark were I to arrive later.'

'And what passed between you during your visit?'

'Well, Mr Holmes, you will perhaps find this part hard to believe, but in fact our encounter was not angry or acri-monious.' He shook his head as though a little bewildered. 'In fact, it was a little like things had been before, when we first grew close.'

'Indeed?' The great detective considered this for a moment. 'And how do you account for that?'

Another shake of the head.

'It's very hard to say, sir. But as soon as I arrived, I sensed that Thomasina was in a different mood – a forgiving, even a rather tender one. She told me that she fully understood why my father's approval meant so much to me, and that she had been wrong to torment me so. She cried and asked for my forgiveness, and some comforting words were said on both sides. It was, I felt, a touching and rather lovely ways of saying our farewells.'

'I see.' Mr Holmes looked away, apparently focusing his attention on a small scorch mark on the wall, a little to the right of Oscar Catanache's head. 'But I have been informed, sir, that one Elsie Tanner, a neighbour, was disturbed at around midnight by Miss Trubshaw shouting the words '*No, Oscar, no! Please! Please don't! Please! No!*'

That doesn't sound particularly touching, does it, Mr Catanache?'

I watched the young man frown, then suddenly his brow cleared.

'Yes, Mr Holmes! She did say something of the sort! We had been reconciled by then, and our words were fond. So fond, indeed, that I even went so far as to reconsider things. I said something to her about how perhaps I was wrong, how perhaps, after all, I should put the whole thing before my father and let him decide. But by then our positions had switched, and she tried with all her heart to dissuade me. I remember at one point she grew quite animated, saying that my father would never forgive me. 'No, Oscar, no! Please don't! Please don't!' Yes, I believe she *did* cry out something a bit like that.'

Mr Holmes blinked and turned back to him.

'So you maintain that you took your leave on amicable terms?'

'We did, sir. I stayed until a little after midnight, and then I left.'

'According to the witnesses who saw you arrive,' Mr Holmes pointed out, 'you left considerably later than that, carrying something heavy over your shoulder.'

'They are mistaken, sir.' Mr Catanache spoke very firmly. 'I left a little after midnight, and I carried nothing.'

'Did anyone see you leave?'

'Not that I am aware.'

'Even though three witnesses claim they were observing the front door for the entire duration of your stay and did not see anyone depart till one o'clock?'

'It definitely wasn't that late. I'd say quarter past midnight at the latest.' Mr Catanache's eyes suddenly opened a little wider. 'But, of course! There was some sort of disturbance taking place when I left – a fist-fight or something, on the other side of the road. Perhaps that distracted them?'

'And where did you go, at a little after midnight?' Mr Holmes' eyes were firmly fixed on him now. 'Straight home, I assume?'

'No, sir. When I said goodbye to Thomasina that night, I felt rather confused. In some ways I felt supremely relieved that it was all over, but also incredibly sad, because I *had* loved her, Mr Holmes, or I had certainly imagined myself in love with her. I was certainly in no mood for sleep, or for joining in any celebrations. So I walked down to the river, and must have wandered this way and that for well over an hour. I returned home at around two in the morning.'

'Tricky, that, ain't it, Holmes?' Dr Watson observed. 'Not many people around at that time, so it can be a dashed hard thing to prove. I don't suppose you happened to bump into anyone, did you?'

'Alas, no, sir. I couldn't even tell you exactly where I walked.'

'But you had your stick with you, I take it?' Mr Holmes asked. 'Or did you leave it at Salisbury Street?'

'I took it with me, I think.' Mr Catanache appeared to be searching his memory. 'Yes, I'm sure I had it when I left.'

'And yet now it cannot be found, either at your home or, at your valet's suggestion, at your club.'

Again, the young man appeared to be struggling to recollect the events of that evening.

'I can only think… Yes, that's right! There was one point in my excursion when I paused on one of the bridges – Blackfriars, I think it was – and looked down at the water. I remember propping my stick against the rails. I can only assume that I must have left it there.'

'And, tell me, sir...' There was something quite menacing now about Mr Holmes' questioning. '...During your amicable evening with Miss Trubshaw, did she make any comment about the state of your jacket?'

I knew exactly what this question meant, and watched Mr Catanache carefully to see how it affected him. But he didn't look at all put out by it, or at all guarded, he simply smiled broadly.

'I should say she did! It was in a terrible state. You see, I'd come straight from watching a lightweight bout in Stepney, and something had splashed over me that frankly defied description. A mixture of water, sweat, blood and who knows what else, judging by the odour. Miss Trubshaw said I smelled as though I'd come direct from an abattoir. It was so bad that when I got home I had my man give it away for rags.'

'And your cuffs, too, presumably?' Mr Holmes' gaze had returned to the scorch mark on the wall. 'I imagine they did not escape this inundation?'

'My cuffs?' Mr Catanache looked surprised. 'No, I don't remember any of it getting on my cuffs.'

'Yet you discarded your cuffs too?'

The young man looked slightly bemused.

'No, I don't think so. Just left them on the floor with my other things, I suppose.' He paused. 'Look here, Mr Holmes, I came here to apologise, because it struck me that my father had probably lost his temper with you and behaved rather badly when you were only trying to help. And of course I'm happy to go through all these questions again, because the more people who know the truth the better. But it does rather feel that, whatever I say, you have me down as a murderer. At least Mlle Martin seems to believe I'm telling the truth.'

Mr Holmes returned his gaze, unflinching.

'Mlle Martin no doubt has her own methods. I have mine.' But then his mouth softened slightly and he rose from his armchair. 'Come, sir. I apologise for so many questions, but they have to be asked, and if I don't ask them, someone else certainly will. Contrary to what your father believes, I simply want to arrive at the truth. And if I find myself any closer to it, you will, of course, be the first to know.'

And with that, the interview was over, and Oscar Catanache left Baker Street with the air of someone who had emerged from a bruising bout, not victorious, but at least still standing. I watched him go, then instinctively returned to the study, never thinking to wonder whether or not I was invited.

However, neither Mr Holmes nor Dr Watson appeared to wonder either. I found them both in thought, Dr Watson still seated, Mr Holmes in his favourite position, leaning against the mantelpiece.

'Well, I don't know about you two, but it's a fishy story if you ask me,' Dr Watson opined after a moment or two. 'Oh, I daresay it all hangs together, but, well, I'm just not sure I like the smell of it. The lost stick… That shout in the night…'

'Indeed, Watson,' Mr Holmes concurred. 'It is all *possible* but quite a lot of it seems unlikely. We are being asked to believe that Oscar Catanache left unseen at just after midnight and was replaced by an individual of similar build, who entered unnoticed by the inquisitive neighbours, caused incredible carnage, wrapped his victim in a blanket and left, leaving no clue as to identity or motive. But even that doesn't work, does it, Flotsam?'

'No, sir,' I told him firmly, because at that very moment, just as he was speaking, I suddenly understood his exchange with Mrs Hudson. 'It doesn't work because of the blanket.'

Mr Holmes nodded approvingly but Dr Watson looked bewildered.

'Eh? The blanket, Flotsam? What do we know about the blanket?'

'We know it should have been on the bed, sir, because Thomasina Trubshaw always slept with a blanket over her, because she didn't like the cold. So someone must have taken it *off* the bed, before wrapping up the body and carrying it out.'

'Well, Flotsam, that sounds perfectly reasonable.' Dr Watson rose with his empty glass in his hand and headed towards the drinks tray.

'But there was all that blood, sir. Huge great pools of it. All over the sheets. If the blanket had been on the bed when the blood was spilled, then it would have been soaked too. Whoever carried out the body, sir, would have been carrying it in a blanket that was dripping with blood. I mean, really, actually dripping, sir. But we didn't see any drips of blood leading to the door of the room, or on the landing outside, or on the stairs, or anywhere. Also, sir, a person carrying something heavy on their shoulder, wrapped in that blanket, would have got blood all over themselves, on their arm and hand and face as well as on their clothes, and even late at night somebody must have noticed that.'

'Ah, yes, Flotsam, I see your point.' Dr Watson began to help himself to a small glass of port, then changed his mind and helped himself to a large one. 'Our man must have thought of that. He must have removed the blanket first so it didn't get stained.'

'Oh, really, Watson!' Mr Holmes sounded a little impatient. 'How likely is that? Are we to believe that Mr Catanache or some other stranger arrived in Miss Trubshaw's room, carefully removed the blanket from the bed in the lady's presence, and only then bludgeoned her to death? If he was able to show that amount of forethought, Watson, he might more sensibly have brought his own blanket. Besides, there *was* no bludgeoning, was there, Watson?'

'Ah! Now, that's a very good point, Holmes!' Dr Watson looked pleased to have been asked. 'I was thinking about that on the train. There did seem to be an awful lot of blood, didn't there? But judging by the stains it had flooded out over the bed and floor in pools. In other words, it had *flowed*. There seems to be a lot of talk about that cane with the silver handle, but if someone had been beaten with a stick of that sort, I don't think the room would have looked like that.'

'But, sir,' I pointed out, 'there *were* some small splashes of blood on the letter Miss Trubshaw was writing.' I thought about this for a moment and then realised the true significance of my statement. 'But the letter was on the desk, and the desk was on the wall opposite, as far from the bed as it could have been. And I didn't see any other drops of blood on the desk, only the ones on the paper...'

'Precisely, my friends!' Mr Holmes clapped his hands together in a single, resonant clap. 'Someone has done some deep thinking, and has gone to a great deal of trouble, but they have mismanaged the blood! And, never fear, where there has been one mistake, there are likely to be others.'

It was a heartening rallying cry to send us to our beds. But as I tidied up the study that night, my brain awhirl with thoughts of Oscar Catanache and Thomasina Trubshaw, of bloodstains and bludgeons, and of dark, horrible doings in that dark, horrible room, I could only hope that Mr Holmes was right. Because a knife can be small and easy to conceal, and will make blood *flow*, and the heavy stick might simply be sending us in the wrong direction. It was not impossible that the young housemaid had died that night in Salisbury Street after all, and, as the house fell quiet, I found it harder and harder to put the thought out of my head.

So, instead, I tried to remember the warm sunshine on my face that morning, and the waters of the Serpentine quivering in the sunlight. If I stopped and shut my eyes, Mr Dashing was smiling at me, and I was laughing, and the world felt safe again.

Chapter Sixteen

The next day was one of those days when, at first, nothing seems to happen.

I don't mean that I wasn't busy, or anything like that. In fact, I was more than usually busy, because there arrived on the milk train from Petworth a half-barrel of autumn raspberries, an annual offering to Mrs Hudson from Lord Wyndham's head gardener, in recognition of her help in unmasking the person behind the Duncton tree-murders that caused such a stir a few years back.

These late raspberries were not considered suitable for the table, because they were small and fell apart very easily, but they made the most perfect jam, and every year their arrival signalled the start of a frantic rush to get the fruit preserved and bottled and stored within the day – an undertaking shared by half the houses in our street, because there was simply too much fruit for any one house to manage. It was hard work, but enjoyable too, with every household doing its share, and I found myself running from kitchen to kitchen, moving supplies of sugar loaf to anywhere they were running short, and ensuring that enough jars were hot and ready for filling at the very moment they were needed.

But this year, I was unable to give myself over to the frivolities of jam-making with quite as much enthusiasm as usual. After the previous day's excitements, it seemed impossible that Mrs Hudson and I should simply ignore the problems of the Catanache family, and the challenges facing Mlle Martin, and the threats to Mr Dashing, simply because it was necessary to make jam.

To make matters worse, Mr Holmes seemed quite happy to ignore those things too. Word reached him at breakfast that a fifth hieroglyph had appeared in Romford, and before he had even been able to put down his toast and reach for his hat, a carriage had arrived, sent by the Keeper of the Royal Antiquities, to whisk him and Dr Watson away on the journey eastwards. It seemed to me, just at the time when new inquiries into the Blue Daisy Affair were most needed, we were all stopping to do something else.

'Don't you worry so, young lady,' Mrs Hudson reassured me, on discovering me looking slightly glum in the cavernous kitchen of No 17. I was stirring an enormous jam pan for Mrs Cripwell, the housekeeper there, who had disappeared upstairs looking for labels. 'Mr Catanache is safe from arrest for a few days at least. Inspector Merivale is putting up posters with Miss Trubshaw's name on all over London, and his men are still searching the river, but there'll be no arrest because the inspector can't risk a repeat of that time Lord Plumpton was found in his own greenhouse, potting up herbs, ten days after his nephew was arrested for his murder.'

She dipped a wooden spoon into the bubbling jam pan, lifted it out, then studied very closely the red mixture on the tip of the spoon.

'I hope Mrs Cripwell has her jars ready,' she mused, 'because I'd say we're three minutes off the setting point. As for George Dashing, Flotsam,' she continued, 'Mr Holmes feels he is safe enough for a little while too.

The Paternoster Lecture isn't until the first Friday in November, and it's Mr Holmes opinion that any Russian assassin – if there *are* any Russian assassins – won't strike till the very eve of the lecture at the earliest. He's arguing that those assassinations we heard about weren't really about punishing individuals, they were about sending a warning to the world, so they will definitely want to wait until the whole world is watching.'

I confess I did find these words slightly reassuring, because that morning's *Times* contained a message that had rather disturbed me.

> Maya to Aldan – The end is nigh. By the side
> of the water in the heart of the park. That is
> our place. I shall give the word.

Reading that, I couldn't help recalling Mr Dashing's jocular remark of the previous day about assassins lining the shores of the Serpentine. It had been a joke, of course it had, but now it began to worry me a great deal, and I found myself hoping fervently – for Mr Dashing's safety, of course, and not for any other reason – that he had no more appointments to row young ladies on the lake.

Once Mrs Cripwell's batch of jam had been safely bottled, I moved to No 31 to help with boiling the jars, then to No 20, where everything was a little behind because of an argument over pectin, then finally home again, where Mrs Hudson and I had yet to start work on our second batch. I was greeted by the housekeeper with a smile, but also a raised eyebrow that made me wonder straightaway what task I had neglected.

'Scraggs has just been in,' she told me. 'He seemed sorry to have missed you yesterday.'

My heart sank a little.

'It was my fault, ma'am,' I confessed. 'I didn't want to be late for Sir Henry, and after seeing Miss Peters and Mr Dashing I was running short of time.'

'Ah, well,' she responded briskly, 'not to worry. Scraggs says he has some important business to do today, but he'll pop back tomorrow. He's very anxious to see you though, Flottie, because he wants to ask you something, or show you something, I'm not sure which. He was in his suit again, and looking very serious. Now, let's get this last bucket of fruit in the pan, and when we're finally done and have washed all the juice off, we can sit down with a slice of Dundee cake. And then, Flotsam, you must run over to Bloomsbury Square. Mr Spencer's uncle is very partial to the Petworth jam and likes to say he's always the first to taste it, so don't worry if it's still warm and hasn't set yet. He enjoys it more that way.'

What with bottling and labelling, and clearing up, and scrubbing pans then scrubbing myself, and celebrating the end of Raspberry Day in the kitchen of No 17 with a very small glass of sherry and a very large piece of cake, it wasn't until half past six that I arrived in Bloomsbury Square, only to find that the Earl of Brabham was at Newmarket for the week, having left instructions for the Petworth jam, should it arrive in his absence, to be sent on by special messenger.

'Miss Peters *is* in, however,' Reynolds informed me, 'and would no doubt like to see you. You will find her in bed.'

'In *bed*?' It was generally quite hard to persuade Miss Peters to go to bed even at bedtime, and, once, when laid low by a fever and ordered to stay in bed for a week, she had attempted to climb out of her sickroom window on the very first night, because she couldn't bear the idea of missing the Montmorency Ball.

'Yes, Miss.' Reynolds looked grave. 'After your visit yesterday, her condition worsened considerably. News that Prince Andrei had been wounded at Borodino affected her very badly. But things grew really serious later in the evening, during the evacuation of Moscow, when she stopped talking and refused all food, then disappeared to her bedroom. I'm told the crisis came at about four in the morning, and by dawn she was able to sleep a little. But now she appears to be through the worst of it and is comfortable enough, although exhausted, and very far from her usual self.'

'Goodness, Reynolds! Who would have thought it? I can't help thinking that we really must read this book for ourselves.'

But, at this suggestion, the butler simply shut his eyes and looked pained.

'There is no need, Miss. I have *lived* it.'

I found Hetty Peters in her bedroom and still in bed, propped up against an enormous bank of pillows. She looked pale and had little dark smudges beneath her eyes but she managed a smile when she saw me.

'It's all over, Flottie,' she told me wanly. 'Natasha has married Pierre and all is well, although all doesn't *feel* well, it feels as though someone has taken out all my insides and replaced them with an enormous damp flannel that has been wrung out and abandoned. I really don't know what I am to do now. Tonight there is a gathering at the Gascony Rooms and I had chosen a very lovely rose-pink dress to wear, with the most beautiful spider-web lace, but what's the point of spider-web lace when Andrei is dead, especially when he could have lived much longer and perfectly happily if he had only *tried* a bit harder?'

That was a question I really couldn't answer, and I was spared answering it by a polite knock at the door and the entrance of Mr Rupert Spencer. He was carrying a large bunch of grapes in a glass bowl and a copy of *The Times*, and he looked amused.

'How is the war veteran feeling now?' he asked with a smile, only to be met with a long groan from Miss Peters.

'No, really, Rupert! Please go away. There is nothing at all to smile about. While you have been studying beetles or whatever, I have been enduring things you cannot even imagine. And you cannot possibly sympathise because you have never truly *suffered*. Has he, Flotsam?'

Mr Spencer ignored this and waved his copy of *The Times* at me.

'Have you seen the latest from Maya to Aldan, Flotsam?' he asked. 'This one rather grabbed my attention, because I happened to spend an hour or two with George Dashing last night, and he mentioned that he'd spent a very happy morning boating on the Serpentine.'

My heart gave a little leap at this, but only for a moment, because almost immediately I felt myself grow wary, wondering what had been said, wondering if I was to be teased, or warned, or questioned. But Mr Spencer simply carried on talking without even particularly looking at me, and I realised that he had no idea at all about the identity of Mr Dashing's boating companion.

'That's why the Maya message worried me,' he went on. '*By the side of the water, in the heart of the park.* It seems to me that someone may have been spying on George.'

He tossed the newspaper down onto the bed, and Miss Peters picked it up idly.

237

'I *had* seen that message, sir,' I told him, 'but Mr Holmes thinks Mr Dashing is quite safe until much nearer his lecture in November.'

Next to me, Miss Peters had shuffled upright and was studying the agony column with a good deal more interest and enthusiasm than she had shown for either Mr Spencer or the grapes, but it was the expression of surprise on Mr Spencer's face that really captured my attention.

'Why, Flotsam! It sounds as though old Sherlock really has been busy with other things, hasn't he? Have none of you heard the news? George Dashing is to fight the Winchester by-election in November, so there was a special meeting of the Paternoster committee and the date of the lecture has been brought forward. It is now to take place this Friday. That is to say, in three days' time.'

I think it is fair to say that I rushed from Miss Peters' room that day with unseemly haste. The shock of discovering that Mr Dashing's much-awaited public appearance was so imminent unsettled me greatly, and I felt a strong and urgent need to return to Baker Street to tell Mrs Hudson the news. Because if the date of Mr Dashing's lecture had been brought forward, then the plans of his enemies would be brought forward too, and my mind raced with horrible imaginings of dreadful plots already being put into motion.

I was in so much of a hurry that I barely had time to mumble proper goodbyes, and no time at all to wonder why, as I left the room, Miss Peters had thrown aside her copy of *War and Peace* and was demanding that she should be brought all back-copies of *The Times* for the last two months.

I rushed home to Baker Street that evening hoping for sound counsel and good judgement, but found only darkened rooms, a very large quantity of jam, and a note from Mrs Hudson on the kitchen table informing me that our two gentlemen were remaining overnight in Romford, that she and Mr Rumbelow were spending the evening in the West End, and that she would probably be back quite late.

This was undoubtedly peculiar. Neither she nor Mr Rumbelow were, to my knowledge, regular frequenters of the theatres, and even if they had been, it was very hard to imagine them attending together. They were, of course, very old acquaintances, and it was easy for me to picture them sitting up very late at our kitchen table chatting about old times, but very difficult for me to picture them squeezing into the stalls together, side by side.

Her absence left me at a loss. There was nothing in particular that she could do, early on a Tuesday evening, that would significantly contribute to Mr Dashing's safety but it would have been reassuring to pour out my concerns. And now there was nothing I could do, either. But the thought of lingering alone in the quiet house, doing nothing, seemed intolerable. I thought about returning to Bloomsbury Square. I thought about calling at No 17 to see if the jam celebrations were continuing. Then I thought of George Dashing, at home perhaps, perhaps preparing his lecture, unaware of the new message in *The Times*.

Well, at least that was something I could do. Miss Peters' lovely outfit from the day before still hung beside my bed because I'd forgotten to return it. It would be the work of a moment to slip it on, and to slip outside and to stroll over to Weston Square on the off-chance that

Mr Dashing might be in. If he were out, no harm was done, and I should have had a good walk. It was already almost dark, but the evening was warm. There was no need for any hurry.

But I did hurry. The thought that perhaps someone sinister had been watching Mr Dashing – watching both of us – from the edge of the Serpentine made me feel prickly and uncomfortable, and the sooner he were warned of it the better. And then, of course, the longer I went without warning him, the greater the danger seemed to become, until I was weaving my way along the crowded pavements in almost panicky haste.

Then, when I was crossing Old Bond Street, I heard someone call my name. Scraggs. Running towards me with a smile.

'Hello, Flot! I thought it was you. Didn't recognise you at first, all dressed up like that.'

He was still in his best suit, but this time it looked a little dusty and crumpled.

'Oh, Scraggs! I'm so sorry about yesterday. I ran out of time and...'

But he just smiled and waved away my apology with a little sweep of his hand.

'It's all right, Flot. I thought it must be something. But it's good to see you. Look, there's something I've been really wanting to show you. I haven't shown anyone yet, not even Mrs H. It's just a couple of minutes away.'

'Oh, but Scraggs...' I was aware of the time ticking, and getting to Weston Square still seemed the most pressing thing imaginable. 'I've really got to rush. There's a gentleman I'm calling on...'

I saw his face fall slightly, and immediately regretted the stupid way I'd put things.

'It's just that, well, it's a Mr Holmes thing, and I really should… Couldn't you just tell me about it instead?

He gave a little shrug. 'Better to show you, but you need to go, Flot. We can find another time.'

'No. No need. It's fine. I'll come now.' Sometimes, when we make a terrible mess of something, we then make it worse by rushing to make it better. 'Is it far?'

It wasn't the happiest of walks. He led me into Burlington Gardens, the two of us awkward and barely talking, nothing quite right, then along Vigo Street and across Regent Street, to Bridle Lane, where we stopped outside a small dark shop with empty windows, apparently almost derelict.

'What do you reckon, Flot?' he asked.

'The shop, you mean?' I replied, taking in the cobwebs in the windows, and the peeling paint. More than one of the panes was cracked. 'It looks a horrible, musty old place.'

He was standing in shadow so I couldn't really see his face, but he bent down and felt around inside the bottom of a rusty down-pipe before straightening and showing me a key.

'It's mine,' he said quietly. 'Let's go in.'

The door grated against the floor as it swung open. By the light of the streetlamps, I could make out the shapes of old shop fittings, some draped with dirty dust-sheets, some just draped with cobwebs. A high counter of the old-fashioned kind was thick with dust, and behind it I could make out rows of indistinct display cabinets and pigeonhole shelves.

'It's all my savings, Flot. Everything. All in this.'

But he didn't say it regretfully or anxiously. He just said it.

'Oh, Scraggs,' I whispered, appalled and anxious, but desperate not to sound it. 'Why…?'

'Can't push a barrow forever, Flottie,' he replied. 'And this place has beautiful bones. Honestly, you may not see them now, but they're there. I've got a crate of cleaning things coming tomorrow, and next week I'll make a start. It will brush up fine, I'm sure.'

'A shop, Scraggs?' I just hadn't expected this. 'What are you going to sell?'

'Well, that's just it, Flot. Behind the back wall, this place goes back miles. There's plenty of space if I need it. So I'm going to sell everything.'

Suddenly his voice was confident. It was as though, in his own head, everything was clear and simple and made sense.

'Think of it, Flot! Instead of going to Throok's and Ostermann's and Bromley's, you could find everything here, in one place. And people will come because the things will be good, which is why they look out for my barrow – because they trust me to find the good stuff to sell. And when they're here, they'll buy the cleaning paste they've come for because it's better than Bromley's, and then they'll see we've got feather dusters that are as good as Throok's and candles that are smarter than Ostermann's, and they can buy them all here and save themselves half a mile of walking. Do you see, Flot?'

I did see, sort of. But I also saw a rundown old shop that no one would want to visit.

'But, Scraggs,' I replied, desperately trying to work out how much I should and shouldn't say, 'Ostermann's and Bromley's are awfully good at selling things to people. That's why they do so well.'

But to my surprise, he was nodding enthusiastically.

'Exactly, Flot. They're good shopkeepers. They're good at selling. But it's something I've been thinking about a lot, and you know what? It isn't the selling that makes the biggest difference, Flot. Not in the end. It's the buying. Getting out there and finding the right stuff, the stuff people want, before other people find it. Better stuff. Cheaper stuff. Different stuff. And that's what I'm good at.'

I watched him looking around, the dream bright in his eyes, then the shadow forming when he turned to me.

'So what do you think, Flot?'

'You *are* good at it, Scraggs,' I told him, truthfully. But I felt terrible. Terrible because I'd been so reluctant to come; terrible because I hadn't realised how much it all meant, so had said the wrong things, in the wrong way; terrible because I thought Scraggs had made a dreadful mistake. And also terrible because a little part of me, however much I tried to push it out of sight, was still desperate to get to Weston Square.

Of course, when I got there, Mr Dashing was out, and all my haste in saying goodbye to Scraggs had been pointless and foolish and embarrassing, and it would have been so much better if I had just stayed at home. So I left a message saying that Miss Flotsam had called, and that I would call again the following afternoon. Then I went home, and I do believe I felt a little teary, because everything just felt wretched.

But the following morning, things seemed brighter and my spirits revived. To start with, there was nothing at all from either Maya or Aldan in *The Times*, which made me feel a little better. Then there was a short note from Mr Dashing, thanking me for calling, and telling me he would be delighted if I were to call again that afternoon.

But in the end I had to send him an apologetic reply asking if I could call at a different time, because I had been summoned to Cuthbert Square by Mlle Martin. Her message, brought by a small boy and not written down, was a little garbled. Something about cuffs and a waistcoat.

Chapter Seventeen

The first thing I noticed about Mlle Martin when I arrived at Cuthbert Square was how radiant she looked. She was wearing another elegant dress, but this time a pale one, and a different pair of very beautiful gloves, and she seemed to glow with an energy and a vitality that put the rest of us in the shade. She had promised to spend her time investigating, and investigating clearly suited her.

She welcomed me into the drawing room where we had talked before, where she was sitting at one end of a richly upholstered sofa, with Oscar Catanache at the other, a tray of tea on a small table between them. The gentleman rose when I entered, and I thought that he too looked greatly improved since our last meeting, for his face and shoulders seemed more relaxed than they had been in Baker Street, and his smile a little warmer. But it was Mlle Martin who commanded the scene as she rose to greet me, and folded me in a very Gallic embrace. That afternoon her face was carefree and full of laughter, and it changed her. Previously I had found her pretty; today I thought she was rather beautiful.

'Ah, Mlle Flotsam! How delighted I am to see you. Thanks to you, and all the invaluable information you gave me when we met, I have been... How do you say? Busier than a bee. I have asked a great many questions and found a great many answers, and, as I have just been telling the gentleman, they were answers that were very much to my liking!'

She spun away from me and favoured him with a bright and happy smile.

'I promise you a happy ending, sir. But you will have to wait just a little bit longer, because first I must go and find Sir Henry and his lady. I gave him my word that they would miss nothing. Also, we must wait for the inspector to call. There are many things that he must certainly hear. One moment only, I promise...'

And with that, she swept out, leaving the room feeling calmer and quieter and a great deal emptier.

I had never before been alone with Oscar Catanache, and I confess I felt a little bit awkward. When you have once allowed yourself to imagine someone as a murderer, it can be a hard thing to put out of your mind. But the gentleman seemed completely unembarrassed, and he watched Mlle Martin depart with a look of undisguised admiration.

'Quite a woman, is she not, Miss Flotsam?' he asked, and I agreed that she was certainly in remarkably good spirits.

'I believe she is working miracles,' he told me, and he said it without a smile, as something he truly believed. 'Take my father, for instance. He has, as you know, extreme views about the limitations of the female sex. He would no more consider a woman the equal of a man than he would a chimpanzee or an orang-utan, and no one who held an opposite view has ever really be allowed across the threshold. Yet now he not only tolerates the presence of Mlle Martin, he seems to rather enjoy it. He tells me she's a charmin' gal and a lively young thing, and that someday soon she'll make someone a damned fine wife, which in his book is the ultimate compliment.'

'Although, sir, none of those are qualities you look for in a successful detective,' I pointed out.

'And when I made that exact same point to my father, Miss Flotsam, he simply snorted with laughter and said I shouldn't be too sure, because most people would be a damned sight happier answering questions posed by her than by a morose old bloodhound like Sherlock Holmes.'

Before I could jump to Mr Holmes' defence, we were interrupted by the return of Mlle Martin with Sir Henry and Lady Catanache, who both acknowledged my presence with surprisingly friendly nods of the head, and were closely followed by Inspector Merivale, who looked as crumpled as ever, with his sandy hair a little out of place and his collar not quite straight. He greeted me with a formal 'Good day, Miss', but seemed pleased to see me, and took the seat next to mine.

'No Dr Watson today, Miss?' he asked quietly. 'No Mr Holmes?'

I explained to him that both gentlemen had been detained in Romford and that, anyway, Sir Henry had chosen Mlle Martin as his consultant in the Salisbury Street case.

'I was told that, Miss, although it's quite hard to believe, especially given what we know of Sir Henry's views. But there's nothing like a murder to muddy people's waters, is there, Miss?'

It was at that point that Mlle Martin cleared her throat in a rather pointed fashion and the rest of us fell silent. She had returned to her original seat, on the same sofa as Mr Catanache, and, after a little glance across at him, she began to speak.

'Mesdames and Messieurs, were I an English detective, I would no doubt embark on a little speech to explain my methods, but you know I am not, so I shall not bother. Let us instead go straight to the facts. I am here to show you that this young English gentleman beside me is innocent of any crime.'

She allowed herself the luxury of a little pause, so her statement could have its full effect.

'I know, of course, you will all say, 'But how can this foreigner, this *woman*, succeed in this when all English detectives have failed, when all male detectives have failed?' And the answer is simple. *I believe.*'

She chose this moment to rise to her feet, only to find that all three gentlemen present began to do the same, causing her to roll her eyes in exasperation.

'Please, messieurs, be seated. And remain seated. I shall sit, I shall rise, that is my choice. But today you have no choice, you must all of you sit and listen. Now, as I say, *I believe*! By this I mean that I do *not* begin with an open mind, seeing where the facts may lead me, like Mr Sherlock Holmes, like the inspector here. No. Sir Henry tells me that his son is innocent. I believe Sir Henry. For if I did not believe him, how could I, in good conscience, agree to act on his behalf?'

I watched Sir Henry, who was listening to this with a rapt expression, nodding vigorously.

'So,' Mlle Martin went on, 'I do not listen to Mr Oscar Catanache and ask, 'Is this man telling the truth?' No, I listen to him telling me the truth, and then I ask, 'Why do the facts seem to hide this truth from view?''

When she heard these words, Lady Catanache gave a little, almost blissful, sigh, and I thought Sir Henry might actually start to applaud. Even Inspector Merivale shrugged his eyebrows.

'So, *mes amis*, let us look at these so-called facts, at the evidence that the good inspector here finds so convincing. Many of these are not in dispute. Mr Catanache wished to be rid of his former paramour, who was tiresome and making unreasonable demands. True, he admits this. But to do this he does not require murder. He can send her to South Africa, where she has often told him she wishes to go. Such a woman will always go to South Africa in the end. She may be difficult, she may threaten, she may seek her vengeance, but, if all else fails, she will go.'

Mlle Martin looked around at us and held up both her forefingers, as if in warning.

'I know what you are all now thinking,' she told us. 'You are thinking, "But Mr Catanache visited this Trubshaw woman in her rooms on that fatal night." True. He was seen arriving, his waistcoat was noticed, he left behind a button. He now denies none of this. At midnight, this Trubshaw was heard to cry out as if begging something of him. True, and Mr Catanache has explained why. And so it goes on. To save much time, let us talk only of the facts that are in dispute.'

She held up her gloved forefinger.

'Firstly, Mr Catanache was seen to leave her oh-so-ugly house in Salisbury Street in the earliest of hours, carrying something heavy, something wrapped in a blanket. This is not true. I know it, because Mr Catanache tells me so. He tells me that he leaves at midnight, carrying nothing, and I believe him. So why does this good inspector not believe him? Because the busybodies in Salisbury Street tell him otherwise. I ask myself, how can these witnesses be so mistaken?'

Mlle Martin gave an exaggerated shrug.

'I do not know, so yesterday I take myself to Salisbury Street and I talk to them. But first of all, I talk to a different neighbour in Salisbury Street, one who does not spend his evenings spying on his fellows. This neighbour is called Corbett and he makes his living putting the stuffing into dead animals. I ask him if, that night, there was any disturbance in the street, and he says yes, because at midnight he was woken by two boys fighting. This makes me happy, because Mr Catanache has already said the same.'

There was no doubt that she had her audience's attention. All eyes were upon her, and on Oscar Catanache's face there was a look of unabashed admiration.

'So I go to the Mrs Grace and the Mr Wickes, and to the Mr Boldacre who lives across the road, and I ask them if they saw the two boys fighting, and all three say, yes, they saw the two boys. I ask them if it was a fierce fight. All three say it was not. I ask them to describe it. All three say it was more slapping and pushing than punching. I say, "While you watched the fight, you did not watch the door. So it is, after all, possible that Mr Catanache left while the boys were fighting." All three look cross and say they are certain he did not. But it is possible, I ask? Yes, they say. They say it very reluctantly, like it is poison I am squeezing from a wound. But they say it. It is possible.

'But then they brighten, because they remember something. It is possible, they say, but it did not happen. We can be sure, they tell me, because we saw him leave later, at one o'clock. Ah! I say, but the man who left at one o'clock wore a scarf so you could not see his face, and he did not carry Mr Catanache's big stick. What, then, tells you it was Mr Catanache? His waistcoat, they begin to say, but then they stop. Already I have noticed that when they gave to the policemen their accounts, they did not mention the waistcoat. On the way in, yes. On the way out, no. And when I make them remember, all three confess they did not see the famous waistcoat on the man who left at one o'clock. Perhaps it was too dark, they say. Perhaps his jacket was buttoned. But he was the same size and the same shape as Mr Catanache, they say. In fact, as I soon understand, they have only one reason to think they saw Mr Catanache going *out*, and that is because they all saw Mr Catanache going *in*. So, poof! This evidence against him collapses.'

'Let me get this straight…' It was Inspector Merivale who broke the spell. 'Are you asking us to believe, Miss, that Mr Catanache left Miss Trubshaw alive and well just after midnight, and after that someone else slipped in, murdered her and carried out the body?'

But the look of derision on Mlle Martin's face told him immediately that was not the case.

'Murder? Poof! I say it again, there was no murder!' And she wagged her finger at the inspector in reproach. 'This Trubshaw was a woman deranged. First, she thinks she loves, but then she hates. She hates with passion. She is offered a house, travel, a life of comfort such as so many dream of. But no, she chooses hate. She will make her Oscar pay. She will destroy him.'

'And so she sets her scene. She travels to Baker Street and tells a tale of fear, making sure she will be known by her handkerchief. Then she lures her lover to her room, knowing he will be seen. While he is with her, she finds a reason to shout words her neighbour will hear, words that will incriminate him. When they embrace, she tears away a little button, which later she hides where it will be

251

found. When he is gone, she writes a letter to show again her fear. She knocks over her little table. And then, for drama, she reaches for the pigs' blood sold to her by the butcher. There are many butchers in London, too many to speak to them all. And they sell much blood for the making of your horrible English black puddings. Even in Spain, the blood pudding is not so horrible as here. This Trubshaw has that very morning bought blood, and now she pours it on the bed, the floor, and because she is one that likes the drama, a tiny bit is splashed upon her letter too.'

Sir Henry Catanache was still nodding, his smile growing stronger with every word Mlle Martin spoke, while his wife held her hands together over her heart and his son continued to look up at the young French woman with a blend of gratitude and awe. But Inspector Merivale still looked troubled.

'That's all very well, Miss,' he said, 'but Thomasina Trubshaw didn't wrap herself up in a blanket and carry herself down the stairs, did she, now?'

'Oh, Inspector! But that is the easy part. There are so many men in this city looking for work, especially for easy work of only a few minutes, for which they will be paid as much as for a day. Such a one could be found on the docks as quick as a click of the fingers! Perhaps one day, if you search very hard, your men will find the one this Trubshaw found. She tells him he must come to her house. He must wait till she is alone. Perhaps she tells him he must climb in through her window at the back of the house, to be sure he is not seen. She tells him to touch nothing, because she does not want Mr Holmes with his microscope finding the little marks made by his fingers. Then she bids him roll her in the blanket, which she has set aside already, of course, because she does not wish to be hidden in a blanket full of the blood of a pig. Then he carries her from the building to some nearby alley where nobody sees. There he sets her down, he takes his money, he goes, poof, forever.'

At this, Lady Catanache clapped her hands together in triumph, her eyes fixed on Mlle Martin in a look of unashamed adoration.

Inspector Merivale, however, remained more cautious.

'Very well, Miss. You have cast some doubt about the reliability of the witnesses. You have given us another explanation for things, albeit a rather fanciful one. But what about Mr Catanache's behaviour that night? The missing cane, the missing jacket, the cuffs burned in the grate?'

'Ah, Inspector!' Again Mlle Martin wagged her finger at him. 'Still you do not believe! The jacket was most horribly soiled, so it was given away. The cane was mislaid on a walk. These things I believe and you must believe them too, and even if you do not, you cannot show them to be false. But then there are the cuffs! You say the cuffs are a sign of guilt. You cannot find cuffs, but you find ash, therefore Mr Catanache burned the cuffs, therefore he was hiding the bloodstains, therefore he is guilty. Always Mr Catanache is asked about the cuffs! What did you do with the cuffs? Was there blood on the cuffs? Where are the cuffs now? Always he doesn't know. He simply took off his cuffs as he took off his collar, he discarded them to the floor as he does his shirt and his undergarments. But no one says to him, what of this ash? No one asks him to think back, to remember, because no one *believes*! So I ask him, what of this ash, sir? How can it be? And then, with the questioning more gentle and more feminine, he recalls. Please, monsieur, tell them.'

All eyes turned to Mr Catanache then, and he met them with an apologetic smile.

'It's true. I came back that night pretty done in, I can tell you, what with all the emotion and the walking and everything. It all seems a bit dream-like now, and I don't really remember going to bed. And all the questions anyone asked me about my cuffs made no sense to me. It was only when Mlle Martin here asked me if I attempted to light a fire that night, that I recalled a little detail that, in all the horror and shock, had previously escaped me.'

The two exchanged a little look.

'You see, that night, in the pocket of that dirty jacket of mine, I found a little keepsake Thomasina had given me in happier times – a little strip of linen she'd once worn in her hair like a ribbon, in the park one day, on her afternoon off. At the time I had treasured it, but finding it that night, when all was over, I felt like a cad to still have it in my possession. So I simply dropped it in the grate and put a match to it, and to be honest I never really thought of it again.'

He smiled again, as though this simple account would complete the proof of his innocence. But, judging by his frown, even Sir Henry could see that it was a little lacking, and Inspector Merivale was quick to question it.

'Well, you may say that now, sir,' the inspector began with a frown, 'and I daresay people do sometimes remember things that they've previously forgotten. But we only have your word for it about the ribbon, sir, and while those cuffs are still missing...'

'Oh, Inspector!' Mlle Martin interrupted him. 'You and your cuffs. For you, now, it is all about the cuffs. If I find the cuffs, all your evidence has disappeared, *non*?'

She looked around the room, smiling at each of us in turn, still lit up by that air of happiness and confidence.

'When I came to London,' she told us, 'my father said that I would have to be very brilliant to solve the mysteries here. Like Sherlock Holmes, he said, only even more brilliant, because I am a girl. And in the case of the dog, and the Knibling diamonds, and the Hatton Garden plot, yes, perhaps I am a little brilliant. I have to think very hard, to deduce, to connect things. But this Blue Daisy Affair, as people are calling it, I do not have to be brilliant at all. I only have to believe. Then everything is so simple. Almost, Sir Henry, I feel I do not deserve all the money you will pay me. Now, let me tell you a little story...'

She returned to her place on the sofa then, sitting neatly and demurely, and the mood in the room grew confidential.

'Once, when I was small,' she began, 'I had a little silver thimble. It had belonged to my mother, and it was very dear to me. I used to keep it in her old knitting bag, along with all the bits of wool and pieces of tiny blankets that my mother had left unfinished.

'One day, I need this thimble for something urgent. I cannot remember what. But I do remember rushing to the bag and feeling for it amongst the wool, and disaster! I cannot find it. So I think to myself of all the other places I have played with the thimble those last few days, and I search each one in turn, but it is not there. So then I search all the other places, places a thimble may be, places a thimble may have fallen, places a servant may have placed a thimble. I ask the servants to help.

Between us we search the chateau from top to bottom, but we find no thimble. Finally, in tears, I go to my father. Maman's silver thimble is lost, I tell him through my tears.

'But Papa is not upset. He is very calm. He takes my hand in his and he asks me where is the first place I looked for the thimble, and I tell him in the knitting bag. So we go to the knitting bag, and very carefully he empties out all the wool, and there, in amongst the wool, we find the thimble.'

She rose gracefully from the sofa and moved over to the bell-pull, still talking as she tugged it.

'You see, *mes amis*, in my hurry to find my oh-so-precious object, I had thought it missing, and, still in a hurry, I had rushed into my search. From that day forward, though, I had learned my lesson – that when something is lost, the best place to search is the place you looked for it first.'

The footman had appeared in the doorway, and she smiled across at him.

'Please, you may ask Mr Grimsby to join us now.'

Mr Catanache's valet had clearly been waiting for the call, for he appeared in the drawing room almost immediately, and at once I was struck by the way that he too appeared to have been touched by Mlle Martin's magic. When I'd seen him last, in the presence of Mr Holmes, he had seemed an old man, teetering on the brink of despair. Now he entered the room with his head held high, and his chest out, on his face a look of great satisfaction, and, in his hand, an object that immediately caught and held the attention of every person in that room.

Not a very striking object in itself, but at that moment, in that place, as wonderful and as mystifying as if he had been carrying a phoenix in his hands.

It was a simple cardboard cuff-box.

—

I seem to remember a stir of noise as Mr Grimsby advanced into the room that afternoon – a sighing and a shuffling, even, perhaps, from Lady Catanache, a gasp. But we were quickly silenced by Mlle Martin, who once again held up her hand.

'Please, my friends, one moment!' she commanded, then addressed herself to the ageing valet. 'Mr Grimsby, I am most certain that everyone in this room has already guessed what it is that you hold in your hands, but please tell us anyway.'

'Yes, Miss.' Grimsby paused for a moment while he opened the box, revealing to the assembled company a pair of perfectly starched and laundered gentleman's cuffs. 'These belong to Mr Catanache, sir,' he continued, addressing his remarks to Sir Henry. 'They are the pair he wore on that terrible night.'

Beside me, Inspector Merivale rose to his feet with an exclamation of anger.

'No, this is too much, Miss!' His sandy moustache quivered. 'You ask me to believe that these have suddenly been found, just now, just at the moment when you need them?'

'But, of course, Inspector.' Mlle Martin spoke soothingly. 'I ask you to believe.' Then she turned back to the waiting valet. 'When Mr Holmes asked you about the cuffs, Mr Grimsby, I imagine you were upset and very worried? You had begun to think that the innocence of your master depended upon them?'

'Why, yes, Miss. From the questions about the jacket and things, I could tell how important they were. I think I must have been in a bit of a state, because I hurried to the dressing room and checked the drawer where the cuffs were kept, and, when I couldn't find them, I began to panic. I searched all the other drawers, and then the laundry baskets, but there was no sign of them, and I knew I couldn't keep Mr Holmes waiting, so I had to go back and confess to him they were missing.'

Mlle Martin smiled and looked around at her audience for a moment.

'Of course. And after that?'

'I went straight round to the laundry in Delph Street, Miss, and demanded to know where they were. But they showed me their books, which showed the cuffs had been sent back, and then, because I insisted, they allowed me to search their premises for myself. But Mr Catanache's cuffs were not there. They had simply disappeared.'

'Like my little thimble, non?' Mlle Martin whispered softly to the room at large. 'So yesterday I sit with Mr Grimsby, just the two of us, no scary policemen or gentleman detectives, and I suggest to him that we go back to the drawer together, the first place he looked, and look again. He gives me a look that tells me he is offended, that I do not trust him, that I think him an infirm and helpless old man. But I am gentle, and so we go, and carefully we remove all the cuff boxes, and there, hidden a little by the soft paper that lines the drawer, is the missing box, and in it are the missing cuffs. This is all so, is it not, Mr Grimsby?'

The valet confirmed that it was, then let out a deep sigh of relief.

'I don't know how I missed them first time, sir,' he explained to the inspector. 'I would have sworn on my old mother's grave that I'd searched properly. But it's certainly true that I was in a hurry and very flustered, and I can't tell you what a relief it was to find they had been there all along. I can only apologise and say that I was in a terrible rush, and when they weren't in exactly the place I was expecting, well, I suppose I just feared the worst.'

'And so, *voila*!' Mlle Martin concluded, with a gesture towards the old man. 'Inspector, your cuffs.'

And then she rose, as calm and unflustered as though we had been exchanging polite commonplaces about the weather.

'But my work is not finished, of course. Until we find this Trubshaw woman, the world will think the worst, because it always does. So now I will find her. And when I do, we will know her by her by the little burn on her arm, the scar she cannot hide. This morning, at the cracking of the dawn, I took a train to the countryside and met with the women Evans and Fenton who once worked in this house, so they too could describe her to me. They are kind, and the woman Evans gives me a very good description of this Trubshaw, including her scar, so already I think I know her. And already I send a great many telegrams to a great many places, to the people who make lists and take names in the great ports. In time – I think a very little time – I will find her.'

'We've done that already, Miss,' the inspector told her wearily. 'All the companies that sail to South Africa, for instance. And we've had no luck yet.'

'Ah, yes, Inspector.' Mlle Martin looked utterly unconcerned. 'But maybe I will succeed because I ask a different person. Or maybe, of course, because I ask a different question.'

I looked around the room then, taking in the expressions on the different faces around me: Mr Catanache beaming at his saviour as though she were an angel and a saint, all rolled into one; Lady Catanache, almost the same, as though she wished to step across and embrace the young lady; Inspector Merivale, thoughtful and nodding, and chewing his moustache, but not yet perhaps entirely convinced; and Sir Henry – well, it's hard to put into words. It was as though a tide of relief so great had sprung up inside him that it had washed away all the *hauteur*, had dissolved all the arrogance, leaving him a simple old man, drained and exhausted, no longer angry with anyone, but breathing freely for the first time in days.

It couldn't last, of course. As the company broke up, and Mlle Martin led me down the front steps for a little walk in the shade of the garden square, we heard Sir Henry's voice raised again, addressing his son with at least some fraction of his old vigour.

'Of course, I would still give the lecture!' he was announcing fiercely. 'If the chance arose, why wouldn't I? Can't let a little misunderstanding like this one blow me off course! If that libertine George Dashing loses his nerve, I'll be up there like a shot! As for you, Oscar,' he went on, 'you are a fool. A stupid, naive fool, and you've thrown away a brilliant opportunity. She won't have you now, of course, after your shoddy little dalliance, but if you'd never fallen into the embrace of that dreadful little servant, you could have tried your luck with our French friend. A woman with a head on her shoulders, and good-looking too! I don't care that she's foreign, she'd have made you a damned fine wife!'

–

And so, it seemed, the Blue Daisy Affair was explained and Mr Oscar Catanache exonerated. Mlle Martin had been right when she said that the solution hadn't really involved any brilliance. In fact, it had all been so simple, and the case against Mr Catanache so easily demolished, that I almost felt a little disappointed. Such dramatic events, I felt, should have required a more dramatic explanation, some great triumph of detective genius. Were this case ever to be written about by Dr Watson, I thought, it would leave his readers extremely disappointed.

But that was only until I returned to Baker Street, and found Mrs Hudson busy folding laundry. Dr Watson, she informed me, had returned from Romford and was spending the evening at his club. Mr Holmes had also returned, only to depart almost immediately for the Beauchamp estate.

'I think it very likely that he will stay at Beauchamp Maltravers overnight,' Mrs Hudson told me, 'then return directly to the British Museum. Now, how were things in Cuthbert Square?'

So I told her the full story, all the details of Mlle Martin's investigations and interviews, her discovery of the lost cuffs and her determination to find Miss Trubshaw, even to the point of travelling to Market Steepleford to confirm the details of the young woman's appearance.

Mrs Hudson listened quietly throughout, although it seemed to me that more than once her eyebrow twitched, and, when I came to that last part, she put down the towel she was folding and looked at me sternly.

'She did what, Flotsam?'

'Went to Market Steepleford, ma'am, by the early train.'

'Did she?' For a moment she remained still, one eyebrow raised, before returning to the discarded towel. 'That is very interesting indeed, Flottie. And you know what, young lady? If we ever have time to pay her another visit, I'm sure Mrs Fenton would appreciate some of this jam.'

I allowed her to line up the corners of the next towel before saying anything else, and when I did, I think I spoke a little nervously.

'You don't sound very pleased, ma'am,' I told her reproachfully. 'About Mlle Martin's explanation of the Blue Daisy Affair.'

'I'm neither pleased nor displeased, Flotsam,' she told me firmly, completing the folding of the last towel, then picking up the whole pile in her arms. 'I'm just intrigued, that's all. And the reason I'm so intrigued, Flottie,' she added, pausing by the door on her way to the airing cupboard, 'is that I don't believe a word of it.'

Chapter Eighteen

The next morning, I awoke to find two messages waiting for me on the kitchen table.

The first was from Mrs Hudson, telling me that she had left very early but hoped to be back late in the morning or early in the afternoon, and asking me to look after Dr Watson in her absence. I confess to feeling a little disappointed, because I'd spent a little part of the night lying awake, pondering what she had said about Mlle Martin's ideas, and was keen to resume the conversation. Lots of what I'd heard the day before *was* hard to believe – Mr Grimsby finding the cuffs so suddenly and so conveniently, for instance – but I had been there and had watched the old valet tell his story, and I was convinced he'd been telling the truth. If Mrs Hudson had been there herself, I was certain that she would have believed him too.

The second message was from Mr Dashing, thanking me for my note of the day before and saying he would be delighted to receive me at half past eleven that morning if I still wished to call. He ended with a rather less formal post-script:

> PS. Busy working on my speech for tomorrow, so not going out today. Safe from the assassins for another twenty-four hours at least!

It wasn't really a joking matter, and I should really have felt cross about it, but it did make me smile. It also reminded me that I needed to check *The Times* for new messages in the personal columns, since Mr Holmes seemed to have lost all patience with them. So after making sure that Dr Watson was still sleeping, I popped out into the sunshine and bought myself a copy of *The Times*, then returned to examine it over a cup of tea.

But I never did drink my tea that morning, for the message I found nestling in the heart of the agony column was much longer than any that had gone before it, and was one that demanded my full attention.

> Maya to Aldan – Our story reaches its climax. We must meet today; tomorrow this story ends. He will no longer hinder our happiness. Find me at ten in the place by the water, in the heart of the park, where Lancaster is left for the Temple. A red carnation tells me our plans bear fruit and you shall be mine forever.

Dr Watson was roused from his sleep that morning by the sound of me clambering on chairs in Mr Holmes' study, attempting to find the London atlas that was not where it should have been, in the low bookcase by the door. I eventually located it folded into the pages of a book about explosives, and by the time Dr Watson had washed and dressed and had come to look for me in the kitchen, it lay open on the kitchen table while I hastily and carelessly slapped the components of a basic breakfast onto a tray.

'Goodness, Flotsam,' he declared. 'You seem in a right kerfuffle. Whatever is the matter? And where's Mrs H?'

'Mrs Hudson's out, sir,' I told him breathlessly, accidently slopping tea from the pot onto the tray. 'I've laid you some breakfast – just some bread and tea and, er, a pineapple – but I really must be getting out. You see, sir, those Russians – the two secret agents Sir James Croxton warned us about, the ones planning to attack Mr Dashing – they are going to meet today, at ten o'clock, and I think I know where, and it's nearly nine already, but if I can find them, and perhaps call a policeman, then the danger is over.'

Dr Watson had picked up my copy of *The Times* and was examining the personal column.

'Maya and Aldan, eh?' he mumbled. 'But surely, Flotsam, this could be any park, anywhere in the country? In fact, it might not even be a park at all. Those might be code words. They might be meeting in a forest by a river.'

'Yes, sir,' I agreed, 'but I'm sure it *is* a park, and I'm sure I know which one. Look here…' And I beckoned him over to the book, open on a map that included Hyde Park and Kensington Gardens. 'Here, sir, in Bayswater, running down from Lancaster Gate, that path is called Lancaster Walk. And here, just here…' I tapped a particular point on the map with my fingernail, 'that's where a path splits off Lancaster Walk and runs down to Queen Caroline's Temple and the Serpentine.'

'*Where Lancaster is left for the Temple…* My word, Flotsam! I think you may be on to something! It's certainly worth us taking a look. Wait one moment while I fetch my hat.'

'You're coming with me, sir?'

I hadn't even thought to ask, because no one but me seemed to be paying much attention to Maya and Aldan, or to the perils faced by Mr Dashing, but the thought of having Dr Watson at my side as I dashed to Bayswater was enormously comforting.

'Of course, Flotsam! Didn't think I'd let you go alone, did you? Besides,' he added, looking at his breakfast tray, 'I'm not really that hungry. But, tell me, don't you think we should perhaps be stopping on the way to arrange some sort of assistance? If these fellows really are the people Sir James Croxton says, they are murderous brutes of the very worst kind.'

'Well, sir, Sir James says that his people are keeping an eye on the Maya and Aldan messages, and if someone like me has worked out where their meeting place is, surely they will have too, and then there'll be plenty of big, strong officers to grab them if they appear. But just in case they haven't guessed the right park...'

Dr Watson pulled a face.

'Hmm, Flotsam, I'm not sure I like the sound of that. But Sir James or no Sir James, we can't just turn a blind eye, so of course we must go. We'll just have to be careful, that's all. No rushes of blood, Flotsam! No letting valour triumph over wisdom!'

I promised him I'd stay very calm. Then we left a note for Mrs Hudson, telling her where we'd gone and why, grabbed Dr Watson's hat, and set out.

–

Despite the heat of another golden September day, we walked briskly, and by twenty-five to ten we'd reached the park gate in Bayswater. There we paused and spent a moment or two deciding on our next steps, agreeing in the end that our best policy would be to stroll arm in arm along Lancaster Walk like any pair of park-goers enjoying the sun, all the while keeping a lookout for anything – or anyone – strange or suspicious.

'That way we can see without being seen, Flotsam,' Dr Watson concluded, apparently satisfied, 'which is by far the most prudent course.'

I think we had both expected our vigil to be a test of patience as well as a test of nerve. The foreign agents described by Sir James Croxton, the ones who used the agony columns to hide their secret communications under the very noses of the public, would surely be on their guard, and would not be easily trapped. We had expected disguise, wariness, even perhaps, if they had cleverly merged into the crowds, a state of semi-invisibility.

We had not expected to see a man of forty-five in a far-from-new suit, with a very large red carnation in his buttonhole, pacing up and down in front of a park bench at precisely the spot indicated by the message in *The Times*, muttering to himself as he did so.

I felt Dr Watson place his hand on mine and grip it very tightly.

'My word!' he whispered excitedly, trying to conceal the direction of his gaze. 'That must be the fellow!' Then, a little less excitedly, 'He's not really what I was expecting.'

'I don't suppose a good assassin looks like one,' I countered. 'Can we try to go closer, sir, to hear what he is saying? He might be giving out some sort of message.'

So, still arm in arm, we walked in a gentle circle, until we came within only a few yards of the man in question, close enough to be able to make out the phrase he was repeating under his breath, each time with slight variations.

'Maya,' he said, 'my dear darling, Maya! We can be happy at last! Maya, my *darling* Maya, at last we can be happy! Maya, my darling Maya, he has fled! We can be happy at last!'

As we moved further away, his words became inaudible, but he continued to pace.

'Some sort of code, do you think?' Dr Watson asked quietly, when we were sure we were out earshot, but I could only shrug in reply. I really had no idea what to make of it.

We repeated our small circle twice more, and each time the man was repeating a phrase to himself that was the same or almost the same, like an actor deciding upon his best way to deliver a line. But as we were beginning to circle him for a fourth time, we saw him stop and look at his watch, then begin to scan the milling crowds around us.

I felt myself tense a little. If the man before us was Aldan, then the mysterious Maya was about to make her appearance.

'Don't like this, Flottie,' Dr Watson whispered. 'Hard for us to do anything against two of them. But it's not too late. Is he armed do you think?'

I had no idea, and said so.

'Then follow me!' And before I could protest in any way at all, Dr Watson had released his arm from mine and was striding towards the man with rapid steps, his stick raised to the height of his shoulder.

At first, the man with the carnation didn't see him coming, because he was facing the other direction, looking up Lancaster Walk and away from the lake. But when Dr Watson was only ten or twelve paces away, the man turned, blinked with astonishment, then began to back away, his hands raised in the air.

But Dr Watson closed inexorably. I saw the look of surprise on the man's face change to one of fear, and he took another step backwards, failing to realise that the

268

bench lay directly behind him. As Dr Watson reached him, the man fell back heavily, his bottom landing firmly on the seat of the bench, his hands still in the air.

'Please, don't hurt me!' I heard him gasp.

I confess that none of this was what I had expected from a murderous Russian assassin, and the same thought had clearly occurred to Dr Watson because he lowered his stick and cast me a worried glance.

'We believe, sir, that you are known as Aldan,' he said firmly, turning back to his victim. 'Is that true?'

'Yes.' The man nodded, stilling looking astonished, while he slowly lowered his arms. 'How did you know?'

'We have been following your messages,' Dr Watson explained, his voice still firm, and very different from how it generally sounded in Baker Street. 'We know your game!'

'Good lord!' the man replied, looking even more aghast. 'You haven't been sent by May's Uncle Bertram have you?'

That was the point at which Dr Watson lowered his stick completely, and I knew without him telling me that he and I had arrived at the same conclusion. Whoever he was, and whatever he was, the man in front us was surely *not* a highly trained foreign assassin, plotting how to murder George Dashing in a gruesome and spectacular way.

--

The full story was made clear to us over a pot of tea and some scones in a little teashop just off the Bayswater Road, where Mr Alastair Snell and his wife May agreed – very graciously – to join us for some refreshment.

'You see, May and I married in our middle years,' he explained to us. 'It had been a long engagement because we first met when we were barely twenty, but May's father was an invalid, and it was always understood that she would care for him, so we waited, didn't we, May?'

'He was ever so patient!' Mrs Snell told us proudly. She was a narrow shouldered, narrow faced woman, who had appeared in the park carrying a red carnation and wearing, for dramatic effect, an enormously think veil. 'But we lived just over the road from each other in Ealing, so we saw each other every day, and Alistair had his work – he's a salesman at a very good furniture company – and I had Father to look after, so the time just passed really. But we both knew that when Father died we'd marry, and we did, two years ago last June, although my Uncle Bertram didn't like it, because I got all Father's money, and if I'd died a spinster it would all have gone to him.'

Mr Snell took his wife's hand and gave it a squeeze.

'And very happy we've been, haven't we, May?'

Mrs Snell nodded and smiled, and turned to Dr Watson.

'It's true, sir. We have a happy life. And one thing we often do, in the evenings, is look at the agony columns together, and we always marvel at the exciting lives some people have, with all their problems and dangers, and one day we fell to wondering what it would have been like for us if Uncle Bertram had been a despot with a castle, and we'd had to conduct our romance through secret messages, instead of just chatting over the hedge. We decided I would have called myself Maya, short for May Amelia, that being my middle name, and he would have been Aldan, for Alastair Daniel, and then we had a good chuckle at the whole idea.'

As if to prove it, the pair both chuckled. A part of me was still disappointed that they weren't ruthless killers, but I had to confess that they made a rather endearing pair. It was Mr Snell who continued the tale.

'You can imagine my amazement, Doctor, when one day, a little while later, I sat down with the paper one evening after work, and there it was – Maya to Aldan – in bold print on the front of *The Times*! A little message hinting at all sorts of mysteries, it was. Well, I laughed aloud, I'll tell you that much. But I didn't let on I'd seen it, did I, May?'

'I thought he hadn't noticed it,' she confessed. 'But I didn't say anything because I thought I'd try again in a few weeks. And then, there it was, the very next day – Aldan to Maya. Well, I don't think I stopped smiling all day!'

'But we never talked about it, did we, May? Not a word, not till today, even though we both knew that that the other knew! We'd sit down together, and I'd say, 'Anything interesting in the agonies, May?' and she'd shake her head and say, 'Just the usual,' but when I looked there'd be a message from Maya to Aldan, hinting that Uncle Bertram had discovered us, and that I would have to fight a duel with him if we were to be happy!'

'In the end, I just couldn't go on pretending any longer,' his wife explained, 'I was so longing to sit down and have a good laugh about it. So I decided to arrange a meeting. And that's what happened today.'

Dr Watson shuffled a little uncomfortably.

'Very touching tale. Heart-warming. Nothing to do with Russian rivers at all. Thoroughly ashamed of ourselves for intruding so rudely, aren't we, Flotsam?'

'Oh, no, Doctor!' Mrs Snell looked horrified. 'You mustn't think that! It's thoroughly made our day, having

271

you surprise us like that. When I came to the bench and saw Al being thrown to the ground by a brute with a stick, why, it was like the whole story we'd made up was true!'

'Gave me a nasty turn,' Mr Snell admitted, 'but as soon as I knew I wasn't being robbed in broad daylight, I could see the funny side. And May is right. If we'd planned to end our little bit of nonsense in the most memorable way possible, we'd never have come up with something half so dramatic! We'll be talking about it for the rest of the year!'

'Longer than that, Al,' his wife corrected him. 'Every time we read about Sherlock Holmes in the newspapers we'll say to each other, 'Do you remember that time Dr Watson mistook us for Russian spies!''

Dr Watson paid the bill, and we left Mr and Mrs Snell chuckling together over the last scone. That was the last I ever saw of them, although I do sometimes wonder if Maya and Aldan were ever reborn, and are perhaps still at work, under different names, weaving ever more complicated stories in the pages of *The Times*.

At Lancaster Gate, Dr Watson and I went different ways. Perhaps remembering the pineapple that awaited him in Baker Street, he seemed very keen to go and breakfast at his club. And even though it was still much earlier than the time he had suggested, I was more than a little inclined to head straight to Weston Square, to inform Mr Dashing that the danger he'd been warned about was actually no danger at all. But if I arrived early, I reflected, he might well be out, or engaged, and I would once again feel foolish for calling. Instead, I resolved to linger in the park a little, until the appointed hour was nearer.

So I found a bench halfway between Queen Caroline's Temple and the Bayswater Road, and sat down in the sunshine, alone with my thoughts. In front of me a little girl of perhaps five or six, very smart in a crisp white dress, was skipping in little circles with a book in her hand, while an elderly woman, perhaps her grandmother, paused to chat to an acquaintance. Further away, two young gentlemen in boaters swaggered towards the lake. A blackbird was singing in the bushes and all was calm, and the absurd melodrama of my earlier adventure became gradually less vivid, my embarrassment at the thought of it, gradually less acute.

I was shaken from my reverie by the sound of my name being spoken, and there, approaching the bench, was Mrs Hudson, still in her travelling clothes and smiling fondly.

'It's a beautiful morning, Flotsam,' she began, 'and you've found a beautiful spot. Would you mind if I sit down and enjoy it with you?'

I shuffled over a little, and she sat down beside me then patted my hand.

'I found your note,' she explained, 'and when I saw that message in *The Times*, I put two and two together. So I thought I'd stroll over in this direction to see how things turned out. No, don't worry, there's no need to tell me. I bumped into Dr Watson on the Bayswater Road and was given a full account. It sounds as though the two of you have given Maya and Aldan some excellent memories to take back to Ealing.'

In the end, I had to smile. After all, it wasn't really my mistake; it had been Sir James Croxton and his team at the Ministry who'd first decided that the Maya-to-Aldan messages were a threat to the nation, and judging by the absence of special policemen in Kensington Gardens that morning, they hadn't even been able to work out where the pair were meeting. So, consoled by the thought, I allowed myself a little grin, and when Mrs Hudson nudged me, I nudged her back.

'But what about you, ma'am? Where have you been this morning?' I asked.

'Well, Flotsam,' she began, settling more comfortably onto the bench, 'as I said last night, I was greatly intrigued by the fact that Mlle Martin had made a special journey to Market Steepleford yesterday, and, as I was awake long before dawn, it struck me that I too could catch the first train down and have a word with Mrs Fenton and Miss Evans. They were surprised to see me, and I must say, Flottie, I found a great change in them.'

The little girl with the book had finished skipping in circles, and, finding that her grandmother was still chatting, she settled herself down on the grass just in front of us and started to read. Two more young men, both in boaters, sauntered past us, whistling.

'You see,' Mrs Hudson continued, 'when we called upon them, it seemed to me that both Mrs Fenton and Miss Evans were very worried indeed. And who could blame them? They were both clearly extremely fond of Thomasina Trubshaw and considered themselves, in some ways, *in loco parentis*. Hearing of that terrible scene in Salisbury Street, it is hardly surprising that they feared the worst.

'But this morning, when I called, I was struck that both seemed in much better spirits. They confirmed that Mlle Martin had called, and said that she had completely reassured them that Miss Trubshaw was safe. It is a little strange, Flottie, is it not?'

'You mean strange that she reassured them, ma'am?'

'I mean, strange that they were both so completely reassured.'

I considered this for a moment.

'Mlle Martin does have a very reassuring manner, ma'am. It's her confidence, I think. Even Sir Henry has been won over by it. If you'd ever met her, you'd know what I mean.'

'You may be right, Flotsam.' Mrs Hudson pulled out her watch and checked the time. 'I really should be going, I think. But first, Flottie, tell me again why it was so important for Mlle Martin to visit Mrs Fenton and Miss Evans yesterday?'

'Well, ma'am, she's very determined to find Miss Trub-shaw, to prove that she's alive and well. But she's afraid Miss Trubshaw will deny that she *is* Miss Trubshaw, and Mr Catanache doesn't seem very good at describing her – he can't seem to get beyond dark and fairly pretty – and I only saw her once, so Mlle Martin wanted a description from one of the servants who worked with her. She says Miss Evans gave her an excellent, detailed description.'

'But, Flottie, surely you can anticipate the question I'm going to ask next?'

The little girl with the book looked up and appeared to study Mrs Hudson for a moment. The blackbird, which had fallen silent, began its song again with new energy. I frowned.

'Look, Flottie,' Mrs Hudson went on, 'Mlle Martin has been extremely busy. Her feet must barely have touched the ground since you first spoke to her. And she was fully aware of the staffing arrangements in Cuth-bert Square, you've told me that yourself. But when she wanted someone other than Oscar Catanache to give her a description of Miss Trubshaw, this hugely busy woman hopped onto an early train and travelled all the way to Market Steepleford. But *why*, Flottie? Why go to

275

all that trouble when there was a person to hand who could perfectly easily provide the description she needed? Someone who had worked alongside Miss Trubshaw for quite as long as Miss Evans and Mrs Fenton had? A person just downstairs, who could have been summoned in a moment. So that's the question we must ask, young lady. Why didn't Mlle Martin simply ask the cook? Why on earth did she ask Miss Evans?'

A little silence followed. On the grass in front of me, the girl in the white dress closed her book and stood up, and I realised her grandmother was calling her, in an amused, kindly voice.

'Now, Aggie! We can't have you spending your visit to London sitting on the grass! Come, let's find a nice warm bench to sit on.'

And the two of them walked off together, leaving me to ponder Mrs Hudson's question without distractions.

–

I was still pondering it when, half an hour later, I arrived in Weston Square to call on Mr Dashing, only to find that he was, indeed, dashing. When I was shown into his drawing room by the rather silent Smithers, he already had his hat in his hand.

'Ah, Miss Flotsam, thank goodness you're here! I promised to be in when you called, and look! I'm as good as my word. But I can't deny that I'm in something of a hurry to go out. You see, I've still got quite a lot of my speech to write before tomorrow, but word has reached me that Lady Hastings is threatening to call. She is throwing a special dinner for me tomorrow, before my speech, you know. It's been planned for ages, and I understand there is very elaborate catering, so I can't very well refuse to see her.'

He sighed, but it was the sort of sigh that was also half-smile, as though he was sharing with me a tiny, guilty secret.

'But Lady Hastings is a great one for talking, and if I *do* see her, she will beg me to alter my speech. She wants me to talk about Votes For Women, you see, and she will spend a very long time trying to persuade me. By the time she's finished, there will be barely enough hours left in the day to finish the speech I've already started, never mind to begin a new one. My only hope is to leave here before she arrives, and to finish the speech at my club.'

He had waved me towards a rather lovely chaise longue of sky-blue velvet, but I only perched on the edge of it because it seemed my visit wasn't to be a very long one.

'But wouldn't Votes For Women be a good thing to talk about?' I asked. 'Ever so many people get to read the Paternoster Lecture.'

'That's certainly true, Miss Flotsam, but lots of people are already giving speeches about the suffrage, and the only people I'd really annoy would be Henry Catanache and his cronies. But by having a poke at the Tsar, I can stir up a veritable hornets' nest, and I rather enjoy that sort of thing. Besides, I have a by-election to think about, and the good people of Winchester are probably divided over the suffrage, but they'll all enjoy a Dashing young man denouncing evil foreigners.'

I wasn't sure this was the best of reasons, but he smiled so winningly that I was quite willing to forgive him, and when he suggested that we could continue our conversation in his carriage on the way to his club, I was more than happy to agree.

'I want to hear how Mr Holmes is getting on with preventing my assassination, Miss Flotsam, and there'll be plenty of time for you to tell me because my usual man has been called to Scotland by a family bereavement and his replacement seems to drive everywhere very slowly indeed.'

The Dashing carriage was a very sleek, modern vehicle, and tremendously luxurious inside, with seats so soft you seemed to sink into them. I was handed up by a rather dour coachman who did indeed seem to navigate the streets with a good deal of caution, so I was able to tell Mr Dashing the full story of how Maya and Aldan were actually Mr and Mrs Snell from Ealing – a tale he enjoyed immensely.

'Well, that's one in the eye for old James Croxton!' he declared when I'd finished. 'I had him around at my place only yesterday telling me I was an irresponsible young gadfly, single-handedly threatening the balance of power in Europe, and that it was him who'd have to clear up all the mess if I did go and get myself assassinated. I think he meant that figuratively, Miss Flotsam, because I'm pretty sure he has people working for him who would do the actual clearing up.'

I was able to laugh with him this time, knowing that Sir James' fears really had been very ludicrously misplaced. By the time we reached Baker Street, where Mr Dashing insisted on dropping me, we had moved on to other things, and I was telling him all about the exploits of Mlle Martin in the Blue Daisy Affair. Mr Dashing insisted on handing me down from the carriage himself, and there was a little moment as he did so when his eye met mine and mine met his, and I felt his hand tighten very slightly over my hand. Only it was such a tiny, fleeting tightening, that afterwards I couldn't decide whether or not I'd imagined it.

And twenty minutes later, when Mlle Martin and Inspector Merivale arrived at our door in a hansom cab, I had plenty of other things to think about.

Chapter Nineteen

The brief interlude between my return to Baker Street and the arrival of our visitors was a busy one. Mr Holmes had returned from his travels not half an hour before, still deep in thought about the latest developments in Romford, and he was now in the process of changing his shirt and briefing Dr Watson while Mrs Hudson sliced bread and pressed me into service to help with the sandwiches. As I laid down the tray in the study, I could hear Mr Holmes in full narrative flow.

'…And so it could not have been Lady Galbraith. But equally, it could not have been the fishmonger. And yet, Watson, they remain the only possible culprits…'

I'm afraid Mr Holmes was not greatly pleased when I interrupted his explanations to announce the arrival of Inspector Merivale. However, when I added that the inspector was accompanied by none other than the famous Laurence Martin, it was conceded that perhaps the pair should be shown up.

By the time I had accompanied the new arrivals to the study, Mr Holmes and Dr Watson were already there to greet them. No one seemed to notice when I followed them in and closed the door behind me. The first meeting of the two detectives was a moment I didn't want to miss.

But it was, perhaps, a little bit of an anti-climax. Inspector Merivale made the introductions, Mr Holmes bowed, Mlle Martin gave a little curtsy, then the two shook hands. I believe both mumbled some sort of commonplace greeting, but I couldn't hear what. Then Mlle Martin took the seat Dr Watson offered her, Mr Holmes took up his position by the mantelpiece, and Inspector Merivale started to speak. It is hard to imagine it of two such confident people, but I suspect each was a little wary of the other.

'Thank you for seeing us, gentlemen,' the inspector began. 'This call is more of a courtesy really, seeing as Dr Watson here was present at the start of it all. And Miss Flotsam, too,' he added, with a little nod to me, still hesitating in the shadows by the door. 'We just thought we should tell you, sir, that thanks to the efforts of Mlle Martin here, Scotland Yard has now finished its invest- igations of the Salisbury Street business. No charges are to be laid, as it would appear no crime was committed. I suppose we could caution Miss Trubshaw over wasting police time, but seeing as she's in Canada now, I really don't think anyone will bother.'

'In *Canada*?' Dr Watson exclaimed. 'My word! Hear that, Holmes? She's been found! Alive and well, I take it, Inspector?'

'Yes, sir. Made the crossing from Liverpool on one those fast two-screwers. Docked this morning. Thanks to Miss Martin here, we'd already cabled the port authorities and they let us know straight away.'

He half turned towards Mlle Martin, who wafted her beautifully gloved hand at him with a dismissive wave.

'Ah, monsieur, it was, you see, a very obvious thing. Everyone was very interested in South Africa – the South African steamers, the South African shipping companies. But why? Because in the days when Mr Oscar Catanache and the Trubshaw woman were more amicable, this Trubshaw spoke often of South Africa. And so it was, of course, most obvious to me that, of all the countries in the world, she would not go to that one. She is angry, she seeks vengeance, she wishes the whole world to think her dead. She must disappear somewhere no one will look. Immediately, I think of the New World. So I twist at the arms of the inspector and we send our description to all the obvious ports.'

The inspector winced slightly.

'Not a cheap business to wire out that long description to so many places. But in the end, we didn't need it. Seems she was travelling under her own name. They picked her up in Halifax this morning. And it's her, no question.'

'How can you be so sure?' Mr Holmes asked sharply.

'Well, sir, quite a lot of telegrams have gone backwards and forwards today on that subject. The thing is, the woman isn't trying to deny it. She's spilled the whole story to the Canadian officials, how she was angry, so she bought a lot of blood from the butchers, then spread it around and disappeared, all to get Mr Catanache into trouble.'

'Eh? Confessed to that, did she?' Dr Watson looked a bit shocked. 'Shameless type, clearly.'

'She even told them all about her visit here,' Inspector Merivale told him. 'Says she talked to a housemaid with some parcels from Throok's in her hand and a red ribbon in her hair.' He turned to me again. 'Was that you, Miss?'

I nodded, embarrassed, because I *had* worn a ribbon in my hair to go and meet Scraggs that day, even though it was hardly part of the uniform.

'And, of course, there was the burn mark on her wrist. She showed that to the Canadian officials and said that proved who she was, and they could ask the people back home. Told them she was looking forward to making a new start.'

Dr Watson raised his eyebrows and gave a slight shake of his head.

'Well, that's that! Turns out it was all as Miss Martin here said. A woman scorned, and so on. Can't say I approve, but at least she's come clean now, and we can all put the whole thing behind us.'

I heard Mr Holmes clear his throat.

'Indeed. It is a great relief, as it leaves me free to concentrate on weightier problems. Flotsam? I think now would be a good time for you to join Mrs Hudson downstairs. I believe, from something she said, that she has some ideas about…' He trailed off, aware that Inspector Merivale and Mlle Martin were watching him. '…Some ideas about tonight's dinner.'

So I bobbed politely, and went downstairs, and told Mrs Hudson everything that had just passed, and hoped that she did indeed have some ideas about it all, because it seemed to me that Dr Watson was right, and everything really had worked out exactly as Mlle Martin had predicted, and again I was aware of a terrible sense of anti-climax. Although I liked Mlle Martin very much, I was afraid that all the newspapers would make it look as though Mr Holmes had failed and his rival had succeeded. And I suppose, if I'm honest, I thought all the newspapers would be right.

But Mrs Hudson simply nodded as I talked, and carried on folding pillow cases. When I finished, she nodded again.

'That's very much as I expected, Flotsam.'

'But is that all, ma'am? I thought you had your doubts about Mlle Martin.'

She picked up a fresh pillow case and gave it a little shake.

'I never had any doubts that she would find Miss Trubshaw,' she told me solemnly. 'Nor that she would prove Mr Catanache innocent. Incidentally, Flotsam, I never told you about my night at the theatre the other day. Mr Rumbelow and I had a very interesting evening, and we met some very interesting people. Remind me to tell you all about it when our visitors are gone. In the meantime, we should finish this pile of laundry, then find out if the gentlemen have any plans for dinner.'

And that's what we did. It felt like a very tame end to such an exciting day, especially knowing that the following evening Mr Dashing would make his speech without fear of assassination, and then would disappear to Winchester to fight his by-election, leaving London a quieter, drabber place.

It occurred to me that I might never see him again.

–

But the very next morning, a thick, creamy envelope was delivered to Baker Street with my name on it, containing tickets for two people to attend the Paternoster Lecture at the Prendergast Hall in Kensington. With it came a little note – '*So you can watch me tweak the Tsar's nose*' – which I thrust hurriedly into my apron pocket.

It had never occurred to me that I might actually attend the famous lecture itself, and even though a little part of me wished that Mr Dashing had agreed to speak in favour of Women's Suffrage, the thought of watching him give such an important speech was more than a little intriguing. So many people would be there, and so many people would read his words in the newspapers the next day, but very few of them would ever share a rowing boat with the speaker. The thought of being there in person, at his invitation, made me feel special and a little bit excited.

And Mrs Hudson seemed to think that it was quite all right that I should go. The two gentlemen were to be out all evening, and although Mr Holmes had mentioned to Mrs Hudson that he might drop in at the Prendergast Hall at some point, when he heard that I was to attend the lecture he seemed happy to change his mind. But when I asked Mrs Hudson if she would accompany me, she declined with a shake of the head.

'I'm not in the mood for speeches tonight, Flotsam,' she told me. 'And besides, Mr Rumbelow and I are going to the theatre again. But perhaps Miss Peters would like to keep you company? I know Mr Spencer has been invited to the lecture, and when I bumped into him yesterday he was telling me that Miss Peters was cross that she hadn't been invited to go with him. This mystified him somewhat, as she is not generally one for a lengthy lecture, but apparently she has developed a sudden and passionate interest in Russian politics.'

So I explained about *War and Peace*, and asked if I might be allowed to slip out to ask her. But, when I got to Bloomsbury Square, Miss Peters was not at home, so I left a message about the tickets, saying that I would call for her at six o'clock if she wanted to come with me. The lecture didn't begin till eight o'clock, and that seemed plenty of time to get Miss Peters out of the house and into a carriage for Kensington, even allowing for her astonishing capacity for delay.

My visit having been much shorter than I'd expected, and Mrs Hudson having allowed me a generous amount of time, I was in no particular hurry to rush back, so I'm afraid I rather lingered on Oxford Street, looking into the windows of the great shops and wondering whether my Sunday-best clothes would be suitable for an event like the Paternoster Lecture. The morning was sunny, but there was already a sense in the air that these were the last few days of heat – that it would only take one thunderstorm to break the spell, and bring the Indian summer to an end. Already the window-dressers had moved on, and the sumptuous window displays were full of autumn fabrics and autumn colours. They seemed but a short step away from the first frost.

It was while I was gazing into the huge plate-glass windows of Plumley's that I heard my name being called, and looking up I saw behind me, reflected in the window between passing carriages, the neat figure of Mlle Martin, smiling and waving from the other side of the street. As I turned to wave back, a gap opened in the traffic, and she crossed to join me. After the turmoil and the worries of the previous few days, I was struck by how serene and contented she looked.

'Ah, my Flotsam!' she began. 'I noticed you doing the window-shopping and felt certain I should say "hello". Although I cannot linger, as I must go and prepare myself for tonight. I have been invited by Sir Henry to join his party for this big and most-boring sounding lecture tonight. For me, such an invitation seems like a great punishment, but I know it is meant as an honour, and so I say yes, because Sir Henry is now being kind to me like a favourite uncle.'

Mlle Martin laughed prettily at this, and seemed greatly surprised when I told her that I too would be attending, as a guest of Mr Dashing.

'But that is excellent news, my little Flotsam!' Mlle Martin declared. 'Then I shall see you again this evening.' She paused for a moment. 'And perhaps then, it is just possible, I think, that I will have some news to tell you. But, no, do not ask questions! It is nothing bad, and that is all I shall say!'

And on that cryptic note, she said her farewells and left me outside Plumley's. More than one gentleman's head turned to follow her as she went.

When I returned to Bloomsbury Square at five minutes to six that evening, Reynolds showed me straight up to Miss Peters' private upstairs sitting room, where I found her in a state of high excitement and wearing the most extraordinary costume – a huge, hooped gown of the sort that was at least twenty years out of fashion, if not much more.

'What do you think, Flottie?' she asked excitedly. 'It is my tribute to Natasha – you know, who married Pierre – because I feel it is just the sort of dress she would have worn. Don't you think it's rather marvellous?'

She gave a little spin around, watching herself in the mirror as she went.

'Of course,' she went on, 'I know Patricia Hartley-Palmer and Georgina Trapperton and, well, everybody, really, will say it is an eyesore and so old-fashioned, but I simply shan't care, because from now on I am going to live more *deeply*, and their silly ideas about fashions and things are hair-brained and frivolous and even, to be honest, a little bit sad. Although it *is* quite a difficult thing to wear, Flottie, as it's simply enormous, so going through doors and things is quite a challenge, and it's incredibly heavy too, which makes it a bit exhausting, and, also, my uncle says that I am not allowed to be seen anywhere near his carriage in a garment like this one, so we shall have to walk, or something.'

A thought seemed to strike her, and she frowned a little.

'Although perhaps the evening is just a *little* bit too hot to walk all the way to Kensington in a dress as heavy as a suit of armour, so perhaps I might have to change it after all, and find some different way to honour Natasha. What do you think, Flotsam?'

I pointed out that I wasn't as familiar with the young lady as she was, and tried to suggest that perhaps not very many people in her circle of friends would be either, and that Miss Peters' tribute, whatever it turned out to be, might very well be misunderstood.

'Oh, but I think you are wrong there, Flottie, I really do!' she told me brightly. 'Now that I've got my eyes open to them, I see all sorts of references to Natasha and Andrei and Pierre, I really do. Take that thing I saw in *The Times*, for instance. For a little bit, that might have been the real Natasha and Pierre exchanging messages, although after a bit it all got rather odd and a bit disturbing, so perhaps those two hadn't really read the book after all. And, yesterday, Rupert mentioned someone who'd given a talk about the Battle of Austerlitz, and how impressive he was, and how deeply he'd studied, and all that, but, between you and me, Flottie, I'd be prepared to have a hefty wager that he'd just read the same book that I've read, and thought he could get away with it.'

Politely, in order to change the subject, I asked if Mr Spencer was in, and if he would be travelling to the lecture with us.

'He certainly won't, Flottie, and I wouldn't let him even if he wanted to! Rupert is a beast. He simply wouldn't believe that I wanted to go tonight, and even when I'd persuaded him that I did, he said it was too late to get any tickets. So now he's gone off to Mayfair, to Lady Hastings' special dinner for Mr Dashing at the Granby Rooms in Brunton Street, which I wasn't invited to, just because I like to look nice and dance with handsome young men, and because one of the handsome young men I danced quite a lot with last year was Lady Hastings' nephew. But I don't think looking nice and flirting with young men at the Balliol Regatta, and sometimes having rather too much champagne, means that you don't want to vote, does it, Flottie?'

I agreed that it didn't.

'And, anyway, I think it's very bad of Rupert not to come back here specially, just to escort us, because we are actually risking our lives by going, and if the assassins who are after Mr Dashing get carried away and slaughter lots of us, and if one of the ones they slaughter is me, then Rupert will jolly well wish that he'd spent these last few, precious hours at my side, and he'll regret forever that he hasn't married me yet, because he won't be able to say 'my darling wife' at the funeral, which is always such a moving thing to hear, isn't it?'

So I broke it to her very gently that there weren't going to be any assassins, because Maya and Aldan had turned out to be Mr and Mrs Snell from Ealing, and that if there *had* been any assassins plotting to attack Mr Dashing, they'd have been pretty peeved to discover that there were already two Russian rivers sending each other messages in *The Times*.

'Well, really, Flottie, I don't think proper assassins would be put off by something like that, would they?' Miss Peters told me scornfully. 'They'd just think of different names.'

Then, suddenly, her expression changed, and she stood looking at me, blinking. So abrupt was this transformation that I even wondered if it were caused by some sort of seizure, especially when she spoke.

'Natasha and Pierre,' she said in a whisper. 'Natasha to Pierre. Pierre to Natasha. Andrei.'

But then, just as suddenly, she blinked again and her former animation returned, greatly amplified.

'Quickly, Flottie! The bell! Call Reynolds!' But even as I did just that, she ran to the door, opened it, and yelled, at the very top of her voice, 'Reynolds! Reynolds! I need those copies of *The Times*! It's incredibly urgent!'

'But what's urgent, Hetty?' I asked her as she started to pace up and down.

'Those messages in *The Times*, of course, Flottie! The ones I've just been telling you about! They caught my eye at once, obviously, because, well, they just *would*, wouldn't they? Natasha to Pierre... I thought they must be star-crossed lovers, desperate to meet against the dictates of the universe! And so, of course, once I'd seen those names, I read all their messages, every line, right from the beginning. But it soon became clear that they weren't really lovers, because they were plotting to get rid of Andrei, so I thought they must be those pitiful sort of people who read a book, and get so caught up in it they go a bit mad.

You know the sort, Flottie, they start skipping meals and weeping and being a terrible nuisance to all their friends and family. But, of course, talking to you, it seems so obvious that the people leaving those messages don't really think they're Natasha and Pierre, they've just chosen those names, and the person they're plotting to kill isn't really Andrei, it's Mr Dashing!'

Just then, in astonishingly quick time, Reynolds appeared with a large bundle of newspapers under his arm, and stood panting while Miss Peters threw herself upon them.

'Let's see, let's see, let's see…' she muttered, throwing them to the floor, then kneeling and beginning to spread them around her. 'This one, and this one, and this one. Yes, and this one, too. And those two. Those are probably the most important ones. Oh, Reynolds, do *please* move your feet, because they're getting in the way!'

I confess I was still gaping at her when she began to get up, still in a hurry, an armful of newspapers gathered to her chest.

'Come on, Flottie! We'll look at these on the way! Reynolds, would you mind very much running down-stairs as quickly as you can without killing yourself and telling Carrington to get the carriage out straight away. Flotsam and are going to Lady Hasting's dinner in Brunton Street!'

Chapter Twenty

The sun was low by the time Carrington had brought round the Earl of Brabham's carriage, but there was still enough light for us to make out the print in *The Times*, and as the heavy coach lumbered westwards, into the worst of the Oxford Street traffic, Miss Peters and I studied avidly the perplexing texts she'd brought with her.

The first of these seemed relatively benign.

> **Natasha to Pierre – Awake! The great spirit calls to us. It is time to strike a blow for our love. Prepare!**

'Not at all the sort of thing the real Natasha would say,' Miss Peters sniffed. 'But at least, at that point, she doesn't seem to be planning to kill anyone.'

As I read on, the messages, although still cryptic, grew darker.

> **Pierre to Natasha – My love burns bright. I am ready. Command me.**

> **Natasha to Pierre – Andrei has returned. Seek him out and learn. Wstnsq. His departure must shake the world.**

> Pierre to Natasha – I have seen Andrei. He is
> not cautious. It will be the end of him.

'It all seemed quite all right up to there,' Miss Peters told me. 'But from then on it all became a bit too *Russian*, as Reynolds would say.'

> Natasha to Pierre – He must not speak! But
> intends to speak sooner than we thought. Are
> we prepared?

> Pierre to Natasha – I am. Trust my devices.
> He dines before he speaks, then his carriage
> alights and Home, James!

> Natasha to Pierre – But we must certainly
> spare the horses, my love, lest friends and
> enemies alike turn against us. Remember
> where we stand!

> Pierre to Natasha – All is arranged. Brntn.
> Grnby. Tomorrow!

> Natasha to Pierre – All the mysteries of the
> rainbow await him. He trifles with us no more!

'So you see!' Miss Peters exclaimed triumphantly as the sequence concluded, the last message published that very morning. 'I felt all along it had become a bit horrid. But it wasn't until just now that it dawned on me that it was all about Mr Dashing!'

'But is it, Hetty?' I wondered. 'Couldn't it be about anyone? Perhaps it just fits Mr Dashing's case because we're thinking a lot about Mr Dashing?'

Miss Peters lifted her nose slightly.

'You must speak for yourself, Flotsam. Personally, I rarely think of him at all. I used to, perhaps, long ago, but when you have been in love with Prince Andrei, a man such as George Dashing fades to nothing.'

She sniffed again, but then the carriage jolted over a pothole and she was forced to grab my arm to keep her balance.

'To be honest, Flottie, I was only coming to his lecture so that I could shout at him when he started being rude about Russia,' she added in something much more like her usual tone. 'But, of course, now there probably won't be a lecture, will there? Because if the assassins don't actually kill him, he will probably be wounded or bleeding, and far too shaken to get up and speak. And they probably *will* kill him, because they know he lives in Weston Square – they actually *say* so, although the penny didn't drop until just now – so they could have set upon him with cudgels or something whenever they liked, but they didn't, because they were so sure they could do it tonight. Which, I confess, seems rather extreme and not very sporting, even though he probably deserves it. So I think we probably should save him if we can, and you're very clever at that sort of thing, Flottie, so you probably will.'

I think she was a little surprised when, by way of reply, I threw my arms around her neck and told how clever I thought *she* was, and for a moment I think both of us were a bit emotional, until we remembered that we had no idea what we were going to do when we got to the Granby Rooms in Brunton Street.

'Go in and tell Mr Dashing everything, I suppose, Hetty,' I decided, 'because even if he tries to make a joke of it, we'll have the newspapers to show him.'

But entering the Granby Rooms to warn Mr Dashing of his danger proved a good deal more difficult than we had anticipated. I'd thought that the impressive sight of the Brabham carriage pulling up outside would have been enough to guarantee us entry, but when Hetty and I knocked we were confronted by a burly footman of very broad dimensions who told us that we would not be admitted under any circumstances.

'Strictest orders, Miss,' he explained. 'Lady Hastings, who's throwing this here party, is very worried about her guest of honour. Seems this Mr Dashing fellow has a few enemies, and her ladyship has been most insistent that absolutely no one should be allowed to set foot indoors unless they're on the list. And as everyone on the list is here already, you ain't coming in, no matter how prettily you ask.'

Miss Peters, who was capable of asking very prettily indeed, seemed to find this hard to believe, and she continued to plead our case while I looked about to see if there was any alternative way of entering the building. As I looked, an unmarked delivery van drawn by an unimpressive grey cob pulled up beside us, and the driver called out something indecipherable to the burly door-keeper.

'Round the back,' he replied roughly, signalling with his thumb, and the driver replied with a wave of his hand, then directed an equally indecipherable command to the cob, which acknowledged it by walking on.

'But *he's* being allowed in!' Miss Peters complained, outraged.

'That's because he's delivering an absolutely enormous jelly, Miss.'

Miss Peters and I looked at each other, and without a word, set off after the van, which led us around the corner of Brunton Street to the mews at the back, where a rear door to the side of the stables gave access to the back of the building, including, presumably, to the kitchen. There we watched two rather surly-looking men emerge from the van and, under the direction of the driver, begin to unload what was truly an extremely large dessert – about three feet high under an enormous glass bell-jar, resting on a silver platter, which in turn was standing on a wooden panel with poles attached to it. It was shaped like the dome of St Paul's Cathedral, but made of different layers of jelly in different colours, and it wobbled rather alarmingly as the delivery men manoeuvred it out of the van.

The arrival of such a remarkable object was clearly something of an event, and a little crowd of domestic staff had begun to gather at the rear door to witness it. Sensing an opportunity, Miss Peters was quick to join them, beckoning me to follow.

'Please, everybody,' she called in her brightest, happiest voice, 'please make way for the dessert. It's very fragile, so the gentlemen here are going to need lots of space to get it safely indoors. Now, if one of you would be good enough to point us towards the kitchen, my assistant and I will make sure there is a safe surface to receive it...'

And with that, she sailed through the parting crowd and through the open door, dispensing very charming smiles as she went, while I scuttled rapidly behind.

'Thank you, so good of you! Straight on and down the stairs, you say? Thank you!'

I followed her into a narrow and rather dingy corridor which led to a flight of stairs leading downwards with a closed door on either side of it. Miss Peters chose one of the two doors, apparently at random, and led me through it, down a further corridor, towards another door.

'This way, Flottie!' she hissed excitedly. 'It's bound to lead somewhere. I think the dining rooms are upstairs, so we need to find some steps going upwards.'

And with that she threw open the next door and ran straight into the arms of the burly footman who had thwarted our entry through the front of the building.

'Oh, no, you don't, Miss!' he told her calmly, retaining hold of her wrist while very deftly grabbing mine too.

Looking around, I realised we had blundered through a servants' door into the opulent front hallway. To our left, a broad and beautiful staircase of dark but highly-polished wood led upwards to the formal dining rooms where, no doubt, the company was already toasting Mr Dashing, unaware of the dangers that threatened him. But the footman's hold was very firm, and our chances of reaching them seemed very slim indeed.

Miss Peters seemed to think so too, because she sighed a rather sad sigh and shook her head.

'I'm afraid this gentleman has been too clever for us, Flotsam,' she told me, mournfully. 'We will never get to see the famous Mr Dashing after all.'

She sighed again, the sigh of someone so gently but utterly forlorn that even I felt quite moved.

'You see, sir,' she went on, turning to the footman, 'everyone in London has been talking about Mr Dashing ever since he got back from abroad, going on about how handsome he is, and how charming, and, well, how *dashing*. And I live such a quiet life, looking after father, who is quite an invalid, and very crotchety, and relies on me so utterly for every little act of care, so I very seldom go out, not even to the shops, and sometimes, in winter, I barely see the sunlight at all except through the window, and so I thought, when I heard all about Mr Dashing,

297

that perhaps the life I lead, looking after father, listening to his scolding and putting up with his cruelties, well, perhaps it wouldn't all feel so unbearable if only, just for a few moments, I could get a glimpse of Mr Dashing, and perhaps even exchange a few words with him, just to tell him how much joy it brings me, in my little room, to read of his exploits...'

I watched the footman's face, looking for the inevitable signs of softening, then held my breath as he opened his mouth to reply.

'Hop it!' he told us brusquely. 'Both of you, hop it! And if I see you hanging around the front door again – or the back door for that matter – I'll call a constable.'

At this, Miss Peters' expression changed again, to one of indescribably hauteur.

'Very well! In that case, I'm afraid you leave me no choice.'

Then, with surprising vigour, and even a little bit of venom, she kicked him very hard in the shin.

I think it probably hurt both of them equally, for the footman let go of both of us and began to hop backwards on one leg, endeavouring to grasp the other with both hands, while Miss Peters uttered a most unladylike word under her breath and began to hop in the other direction towards the front door.

'Quickly, Flottie,' she cried, waving at the stairs. 'Go and save the day!'

But unfortunately, the stairs she was waving at no longer offered an easy route upwards. The footman, in hopping backwards, had stumbled onto them, and was now sitting on the third step, still holding his shin, clearly extremely angry as well as in pain. For a fraction of a moment I considered attempting to rush past him, but his large frame was a formidable obstacle and if he caught me again there would be no escape. So instead I turned back, the way we'd come, in search of the servants' stairs. The other door, the one Miss Peters hadn't chosen, would surely lead me to them.

I found that second door open and could see the steps leading upwards, but before I could set foot on them, I heard voices and the sound of heavy boots hurrying down.

'Big jelly, that, Jim,' one voice said.

'Bloody enormous,' the other confirmed. 'Now let's get out of here.'

Afraid to be seen, and a little worried that they might cannon into me on the narrow stairs, I stepped back behind the door, and waited until I was sure they'd left the building. Then, the moment I felt it was safe, I slipped from my hiding place and ran up the back stairs three steps at a time, to a little landing with a window that overlooked the mews.

I don't know what made me look out of the window. By rights, so great was my haste, that I should have rushed straight on, through the green baize door which now lay ahead of me. I think perhaps it was the sudden movement in the mews that caught my eye and made me pause, or perhaps it was simply luck. But when I did look out, it was to see the unmarked van that had brought the jelly accelerating out of the mews at alarming speed, its driver urging on the cob with shouts and a wave of the whip.

I distinctly remember that my first thought was just a fleeting sense of disapproval. It was rare to see a delivery van being driven so recklessly, because bad driving reflected badly on the company. 'Perhaps that's why they use an unmarked van,' I thought idly, even as I began to move on, 'so nobody can complain about their driving.'

And then, from nowhere, the image appeared before me of Mrs Macfarlane sitting in our kitchen reading a leaflet, her voice raised in warning:

'*If something's green that's not meant to be green, or blue that's not meant to be blue, or red that's not meant to be red, don't eat it, Flottie, don't eat it!*'

And then – the two voices almost overlapping in my brain as I slammed through the green baize door without even pausing – Miss Peters in the carriage, reading out the agony columns:

'*All the mysteries of the rainbow await him. He trifles with us no more!*'

As the door banged back behind me, I was aware of a great silence ahead, and I stopped abruptly to look up and take in my surroundings.

It was a memorable moment, one that seems every bit as clear in my mind now as it did at the time. The great dining salon lay in front of me, its long table laden with huge platters of fruit, every seat filled, and the occupant of every seat, astonishment written all over their faces, turned towards me, gaping.

The only person not seated was Mr Dashing, who was standing at a trestle table only nine or ten feet away from me, with the great multi-coloured St Paul's in front of him and an over-sized spoon in his hand. I noticed at once an alarming crater below the dome, at about the level of the Whispering Gallery, and an equally alarming blob of treacherous red jelly on the spoon.

It was the work of a moment to stride over to him, knock the spoon from his hand, and then to shove the whole amazing cathedral off its platter and onto the polished floor.

–

It is fair to say that the commotion which followed was considerable.

Several ladies screamed, I believe, and at least as many people, both ladies and gentlemen, rose to their feet in consternation. Lady Hasting rose, sat down again, rose, sat down again, and then remained seated with one hand over her eyes, while a very stern looking woman wearing a rosette marked 'Votes for Women' seized a large fruit salad spoon and advanced upon me threateningly. Behind her, I noticed Mr Spencer endeavouring to assist the lady next to him who, in the confusion, had placed her elbow into her cold cherry soup.

Mr Dashing simple raised an eyebrow, smiled, and said, 'Good evening, Miss Flotsam. I hadn't expected to see you until later.'

I don't know if I replied, but he probably wouldn't have heard me, for by then the uproar had risen to tumultuous levels and I was aware of different opinions being shouted across the room, the debate being whether or not I was a political protestor or simply a lunatic.

By then various footmen had joined the woman with the fruit salad spoon, and I think I would have been seized on the spot had the main doors of the room not been opened by a hugely dignified butler, a man with the presence of mind to bang a gong to restore some calm. With the attention of the room thus diverted, the noise subsided enough for him to announce to Lady Hastings that the van from McClintock's, having been delayed when their horse was found to be lame, had now arrived with a second jelly, and that the driver, who was known to him personally, vehemently denied any knowledge of the first.

A real silence fell then, and every eye in the room turned to the rainbow ruins of St Paul's, still quivering slightly where they had fallen.

Mr Dashing, who still stood beside them, was the first to speak.

'So, if the second jelly is the one that was actually ordered, then this one must be…'

'Poisoned!' Lady Hastings was the first to say the word, and she said it with such conviction that I don't think anyone in the room remained unconvinced. 'By all the Saints!' she went on. 'The attempt we feared has been made! And came within an inch of succeeding!'

The mood of the room changed very quickly after that, her ladyship's voice quickly drowned by a rising babble of speculation and surmise, and I found myself surrounded for a second time, this time by a crowd profuse with its congratulations. Questions were fired at me from all sides – far too many for me to answer – and Lady Hastings shook my hand with the enthusiasm of a thirsty man pumping water. I believe one or two individuals even slapped me on the back. Mr Dashing, who had at first appeared rather bemused by my intervention, was now regarding me with a raised eyebrow and a smile. For all his calm exterior, I did wonder if perhaps he was a little shocked to discover that the dangers predicted by Sir James Croxton had proved a reality. But his manners remained most charming, and he thanked me for saving his life in a way that was simple and sincere, but made me blush terribly.

'I really don't think the jelly would have killed you, sir,' I told him in reply, anxious that my achievement shouldn't be exaggerated. 'Not unless you'd eaten all of it. But it would probably have made you ill, I think.'

The questions continued to come all at once, until Miss Peters appeared with the bruised footman at her side, the two having apparently buried their differences when the uproar from upstairs filtered down to them. With her to assist me, explanations became a great deal easier, although also a great deal longer. Miss Peters commanded the floor with great confidence, and her tales of assassins and secret messages, liberally salted with references to the Battle of Borodino, entertained and baffled quite as much as they enlightened.

However, before she had even begun to get into her stride, I was aware of Mr Dashing checking his watch.

'Thanks to you the danger is past, and now I have a speech to give,' he reminded me in a whisper. 'My carriage should be here by now, and I want to make sure I'm in good time. Would you care to accompany me, Miss Flotsam?'

I looked at Miss Peters holding forth to an enthralled audience, and saw that she had Mr Spencer in attendance, and remembered that she still had her uncle's carriage waiting for her outside. I didn't think she'd miss me very much, at least not for a little while. So I said 'yes', and allowed Mr Dashing to lead me to his carriage.

After all the excitement indoors, it was something of a relief to emerge onto Brunton Street. It is never the busiest of streets, and at that hour of the early evening the pavements were almost empty but for one or two pedestrians, and few vehicles were passing. Mr Dashing's luxurious carriage was waiting directly outside the front door of the Granby Rooms, and as we descended the steps I began to explain to Mr Dashing the full story of the exchanges between Natasha and Pierre. The taciturn coachman I remembered from the day before was still on duty, and, before we had even set out, he informed us that there'd be a short delay while he changed the horses.

'One's cast a shoe,' he explained, 'but the people here can lend us a fresh pair, so I won't be a moment.'

But I was so full of the story I was telling that I barely heard him. Mr Dashing handed me into the carriage, then settled himself next to me, and listened in flattering silence as I listed for him the various messages that Miss Peters had brought to my attention. It was pure coincidence that I came to the end of my explanation just as the coachman began to lead his pair away. Otherwise, it might never have occurred to me.

I've read a number of novels over the years in which the heroine rescues the hero in dramatic circumstances. But I've read very few where she does it twice, the second time within minutes of the first. After all, such a tale would simply be too silly, and unnecessary, and would over-stretch the belief of even the most dedicated reader.

But that evening in Brunton Street, I honestly did just that.

You see, as I watched the coachman go – the rather dour, temporary coachman – I was, by pure chance, repeating to Mr Dashing the penultimate message from Natasha to Pierre.

'*But we must certainly spare the horses, my love, lest friends and enemies alike turn against us.*'

And there he was, sparing the horses.

It must have taken a moment for all the pieces to fit together in my mind, and then, when they had, there certainly wasn't time to explain them. To this day I can't remember how I opened the door, or whether or not I shouted a warning. I rather think I pulled Mr Dashing out of the carriage by the lapels of his jacket. Certainly, we both landed awkwardly on the pavement, clutching each other, off balance and stumbling. But that helped, because it carried us a little further away, and before Mr Dashing could object, or even say anything at all, I was able to drag him further still, into the doorway of the Granby Rooms, just before a passer-by in scruffy workman's clothes casually rolled something beneath the coach.

The effect was immediate – less an explosion than a sudden conflagration, the carriage simply erupting into flames like tinder tossed onto hot coals.

As I watched it start to burn, I found myself repeating in a whisper the penultimate message from Pierre to Natasha. '*He dines before he speaks, then his carriage alights and Home, James!*'

Chapter Twenty-One

The uproar that followed was considerably greater, and of a very different nature, than anything that had gone before. Within a few moments the street was crowded, and briefly chaos reigned, with police whistles sounding, people shouting, and coachmen rushing to their vehicles to calm their horses and lead them away from danger. I don't know what sort of incendiary mixture had been used, nor how it was ignited (although Mr Spencer did in fact spend quite a long time explaining the chemistry to me a few days later) but Mr Dashing's carriage burned almost silently and very quickly, with a fearsome heat. It was a peculiar sight, because the fire seemed very contained, never threatening the buildings or the passers-by that gathered to watch, until gradually we were standing around a neat circle of flaming wood, burning brightly in the gathering gloom, no different or more dangerous than a Guy Fawkes bonfire, but in a strange place, and a few weeks early. The person who'd started it – the non-descript passer-by in workman's clothes – had simply vanished into the evening, and so had Mr Dashing's temporary coachman.

It was Lady Hastings who took charge. She had clearly recovered from the initial shock of my assault on the jelly, and was now at her best – giving orders, insisting on calm, explaining to the arriving constables what had happened, to whom and why. It was also Lady Hastings who took Mr Dashing to one side, reminding him of the time, and insisting that he should set out for the Prendergast Hall.

'For if you don't leave now, you will be late, and Sir Henry Catanache will get to make his dreadful, damaging speech, and the people who did this will have triumphed. It is up to you, young man, to show that murderous thugs of this sort do not emerge victorious in *this* country, no matter what atrocities they may commit elsewhere. When people read of this tomorrow, they will swell with pride when they hear that you took to the podium regardless.'

It was a rousing little speech, witnessed by a number of the onlookers standing closest to us, who greeted it with a low rumble of approval.

'Good for you, sir!' one of them called, and another cried, 'You show them, Mr Dashing!'

Perhaps not surprisingly, the gentleman himself looked considerably more shaken this time than he had after the jelly affair, but, aware of the urgings of the crowd, he nodded in acknowledgement.

'You are right, my friends,' he told them. 'The show must go on! We need a cab. Miss Flotsam, given what has just happened, I hardly dare ask you to accompany me, but I should be delighted if you would, all the same.'

I nodded breathlessly. I still felt a little battered after falling out of the carriage, and my clothes were certainly a little dusty, but it never occurred to me for a moment to abandon him.

'Please, sir – Mr Dashing, I don't think a hansom's the right thing.' I kept my voice low deliberately, so that only Mr Dashing and Lady Hastings could hear me. 'It's getting dark, and the traffic will be bad, and if… if anyone with ill intentions were still in the vicinity, then they would surely expect you to continue your journey in a carriage.'

'Then what are you suggesting, girl?' Lady Hastings asked sharply, as though she suspected me of trying to dissuade him from continuing. 'Why, good Lord!' she went on, her tone very altered. 'I can place you now! You're Sherlock Holmes' maid! How very enlightened of him to entrust this business to you!'

I gave a little bob of acknowledgement, then rushed on.

'You see, I was thinking, my lady, that it's almost dusk but the park gates are still open. If Mr Dashing and I were to take the Grosvenor Gate and cut across the park to Kensington, we could easily make it in time, and no one would expect him to arrive that way, on foot, in the dark.'

Mr Dashing appeared to hesitate, but Lady Hastings decided for him.

'An excellent plan,' she declared. 'You must go at once. I shall sort things out here, and then come on when I can. I'm not quite sure of the procedure for dealing with the remains of burning coaches on public highways, but no doubt I am about to find out.'

So we slipped quietly away from the crowd, into the gathering dusk. I left a message with Lady Hastings for Miss Peters, telling her to meet me at the Prendergast Hall, although she now appeared to be giving an impromptu lecture of her own from the window of the Granby dining room, about the devious machinations of Natasha and Pierre, and about how they had been thwarted. The throng below seemed strangely fascinated. No one really noticed us go.

In Park Lane, the lamps were lit all along the side of the park, touching the thickening darkness with pin-points of magic. Omnibuses trundled past, pedestrians were coming out for the evening, and Mr Dashing offered me his arm. Suddenly, after the astonishing dramas of Brunton Street, the world seemed normal again, and the evening serene. I suppose, inside, I was still shaking from our narrow escape and I found myself letting out a very long breath.

Perhaps Mr Dashing felt the same, because he smiled.

'Close shave, wasn't it?' he said softly.

'Far too close. If I hadn't seen those horses... If Hetty hadn't shown me those messages...'

'If I'd never met you,' Mr Dashing added simply.

Neither of us spoke for a little after that. As we passed through the park gates, I leaned a little closer to his arm.

Hyde Park was almost empty, and the pedestrians who remained were in the process of leaving, drifting in ones and twos towards the various gates and exits. After the bright lights of Park Lane, the park felt much darker, its intermittent lamps exacerbating the gloom more than they dispelled it.

'I never really took Sir James Croxton seriously,' Mr Dashing said at last. 'I thought it was great fun to throw sticks at the Tsar, because I knew it annoyed a lot of annoying people, and made other people think rather well of me. But I never thought for a moment it would come to this. I owe you my life.'

I didn't really know what to say, so I didn't say anything. A strange numbness had settled over me – the fear and the anxiety and the dreadful racing against the clock had all come to an end, and I felt certain now that Mr Dashing was safe, and here I was, alone with him in the park in the first reaches of the night, with what looked suspiciously like a new moon peeping down at us. I wondered if the numbness was really relief, or exhaustion, or something else. And then I wondered if perhaps it was just happiness.

We had reached the edge of the Serpentine, by the little dell, when Mr Dashing stopped to look over the water. I stood by his side, listening to the noise of London in the distance, thinking it was like a bit like your own heartbeat – always there, in the background, but something you rarely really listened to.

'Flotsam,' Mr Dashing said suddenly, turning to me, his face very close to mine. 'It is foolish of us to pretend. There is something that passes between us – a feeling – and I recognise it for what it is, even if you do not. And it's as strong as I have ever felt it. You are wasted in your current life, Flotsam! You cannot be a housemaid for the rest of your days, not when, with me, you could have so much more!' His tone was low and soft, but urgent. 'I own a little apartment, just north of the park, and if you say the word, it could be yours. I could visit you freely there, whenever we wished, and we could stop all this pretence of propriety and politeness. Think of it! Days and nights together whenever we want, with no stern employers peering over our shoulders!' And he reached out with his other arm to draw me closer to him.

But I pushed him away. Suddenly the night had lost its magic and the Serpentine was just a faceless sheet of water.

'No, sir! Mr Dashing. I would not… I'm honoured, of course… But, no! That isn't…'

'But surely you feel it, Flotsam! Yesterday, in my carriage. Today, when you pulled me into that doorway, and we were pressed so close together, our bodies…'

I took a step back, still blinking in surprise.

'Really, sir! Yesterday… Today… No! I mean, of course I like you. Liked you. You've always been so kind to me. And sometimes perhaps I *do* let myself imagine things. But never that! Never a flat in Bayswater, waiting for a man to come. And never that sort of man. I don't care if I *am* a housemaid for the rest of my life.' I took a deep breath to calm myself. 'I may be a housemaid now, but I have a life full of things so very, very much better than I could ever have dreamed of, and I would never give them up for a life such as that. Not with *anyone*.'

I thought my words might hurt him, that he would withdraw with wounded pride. But to my surprise, he was nodding and his eyes were still bright.

'Yes, of course. You're right. I see that now. The mistake is mine.' He edged a little closer. 'You're right to think you're better than that, Flotsam. You're destined for so much more. Please, let me withdraw my clumsy and tawdry offer and apologise. But for God's sake, let us not miss our moment!'

He made a sweeping gesture with his arms that seemed to take in him, and me, and the whole of the park.

'Look! We are alive, Flotsam! Both of us! Against the odds. We were an inch from death, but we're still alive, still breathing! Still *feeling*. And none of the others out there are going to understand that feeling, Flotsam. No one else. Not tonight. So tonight, there is no one else on earth I can imagine being with. No one else on earth I *want* to be with. Come with me! Now! For one night, at least, let us leave the rest of them to their prattling, and hold each other!'

'Tonight? Now?' I struggled to take it in. 'But you have a speech to make, and if not, Sir Henry…'

'Oh, damn the speech! And damn Sir Henry! He can talk till Doomsday for all I care! I don't give a fig about the Tsar or about Russia, or about any of the so-called liberal causes. It's all just a game, Flotsam, a game to see who is cleverer. So I bait Sir Henry and Sir James Croxton and all the rest of them, and the angrier they get, the more people love me – people I've never heard of, who don't even know me.'

He shook his head as if in disbelief at their stupidity.

'But I could just as easily have chosen to argue for the opposite side, Flotsam. It suited me to be a radical because the other side was older and uglier, and the radicals get all the best lines, and because the young ladies I meet who like radical young men tend to be prettier and better company, and are often pleasingly liberal in other ways too.'

I must have been looking terribly shocked, but he simply confirmed it all with a nod.

'Yes, that's right. That's all part of the game as well, I don't deny it. That's why I sent you marigolds after our first meeting, because marigolds always work with pretty young housemaids, and you seemed just the right sort. Perhaps even when I invited you boating, because I was amused by the idea of seducing Sherlock Holmes' maid, just as it amused me once to seduce Sir James Croxton's niece. I don't deny any of it, Flotsam, because I've been playing that same game my whole life. And the trouble is, it's a game I forget I'm playing. And then suddenly, tonight, with that coach in flames, it was as if I woke up and looked around, and all I could see was you!'

I think he thought his honesty was making things better, but really he was making them much, much worse.

'So all those other speeches you've made, all those things you've said in public…?'

'Forget those other speeches, Flotsam. They're all just words! I'll make any speech you like, just come with me tonight!'

And he reached out to take my hand. But this time I pushed him away properly, a good old-fashioned shove, and the force of it caught him off balance. I watched him step back, stumble, and reach behind to try to steady himself. But there was nothing behind him, nothing to catch hold of, and, with a surprisingly loud splash, he fell, full-length, into the dark, murky water.

It covered him completely, but only for a few seconds, and I quickly realised the water wasn't very deep, because when he righted himself and stood up, he was no more than hip-deep in the lake. As I looked at him standing there, blowing and coughing, and coated with mud up one side of his body, right up to his cheek, I felt, first of all, a little stab of horror, because now it really was impossible for him to make his speech, so Sir Henry Catanache would talk instead, and it would be my fault that the cause of Women's Suffrage was going to be set back thirty years.

But as he stood there, angry and dismayed and totally speechless, wiping things out of his hair that may have been mud but may have been newts, I realised I was glad. However wrong Sir Henry was, however prejudiced or misguided or misinformed, however downright *stupid* he was, at least he believed it all. And afterwards he could be argued against, and his points refuted, and his arguments rebutted, and the more stupid his arguments, the easier they would be to rebut, and there were plenty of people ready and eager to do the rebutting. So perhaps it wasn't all as bad as Lady Hastings thought. And anyway, it had been worth it.

Still in the lake, Mr Dashing spat out another mouthful, then looked up and scowled at me.

'Damn you, Flotsam!' he spluttered. 'And damn the bloody lecture!'

It was the first time I'd seen him scowl, and it made him look mean and a bit ugly, and it seemed a good note to part on. As I turned and left him there, I was aware of a terrible stench behind me – of pond mud, and dead leaves, and foul, slimy things. A part of me still felt upset inside – and hurt, and angry, and perhaps also a bit tearful and a bit confused – but that smell made me smile.

Chapter Twenty-Two

I arrived at the Prendergast Hall in Kensington at five minutes before eight o'clock, to find the foyer packed and the whole building abuzz. A little, self-appointed Committee of Welcome had formed on the steps outside, looking this way and that with increasing anxiety. Among them I recognised Folkestone, Lady Hastings' coachman, and the scary looking woman with the rosette who only an hour or so earlier – although it seemed like a lifetime – had come at me armed with a fruit salad spoon.

This time she gave me a much warmer reception. With a little cry of 'there she is!' she bounded down the steps towards me, while the others followed amid a babble of questions. I was introduced hastily to a frowning and upset looking gentleman, who turned out to be Jeremiah Hildegard, the secretary of the Paternoster Society.

'But where is Mr Dashing?' he asked me, his pocket-watch clutched in his hand, still looking around wildly. 'Lady Hastings sent word of the terrible events earlier, but we were assured Mr Dashing was on his way. However, he really should be here by now! I can only delay another five minutes at most. At eight o'clock, Sir Henry will claim the podium, as he has every right to do.'

'Mr Dashing will not be giving the lecture,' I told him, sounding much firmer and calmer than I felt. 'He has had a change of heart.'

Immediately the babbling rose in volume, but I had nothing more to say and nothing I was going to add, and eventually I saw Mr Hildegard shrug.

'Very well! As Mr Dashing is not here, and as this young lady informs us that he has no intention of giving the lecture, I shall inform Sir Henry that the podium is his. In these exceptional circumstances, I am happy to give him some extra minutes to prepare, as I have no intention of claiming the podium myself. But you should all be taking your seats, nonetheless. We shall begin in, say, ten minutes' time.'

So I made my way up the steps to the Prendergast Hall, listening to the rosette woman muttering the words 'Judas' and 'Dashing' under her breath, and, at the entrance to the foyer, I found Lady Catanache and her son and Mlle Martin peering out into the gloom. When they saw me, their faces brightened.

'Miss Flotsam!' Mr Catanache exclaimed. 'Is it all true? We've just heard that George Dashing isn't coming. Father has rushed off to prepare. And is it really the case that there was an attempt on his life?'

I told him that all those things were true, and Mr Catanache let out a low whistle.

'A failed assassination attempt, by Jove! Well, that's the by-election in the bag, then!' he declared. 'The British public will love that.'

He may have been right, but we never found out, because the newspapers next day, when reporting on the evening's events, announced that Mr Dashing had withdrawn his candidacy for the Winchester by-election and intended instead to winter in the south of France. From the reports I heard of that winter, and of his subsequent years spent travelling on the Continent, Mr Dashing found no shortage of young ladies in those parts who enjoyed playing the game quite as much as he did.

But I had no time to ponder those things just then, because Mr Catanache had taken me by the hand and drawn me closer into his little circle, and was telling me that he was the happiest man alive.

'You see, Miss Flotsam, Mlle Martin here – Laurence, I should say – has confounded me utterly by agreeing to be my wife! I know it's quick, but I just can't believe my luck, and Laurence tells me that she knew from the first moment she saw me in Cuthbert Square!'

He beamed as he spoke, and it was impossible not to beam back.

'And Mother's ever so, pleased, aren't you, Mother? And, of course, Father was always going to be the challenge, but when we told him he just laughed and patted me on the back and said that for the first time in my life I was doing something sensible. And it's all arranged! My passage to Singapore has been brought forward because of a little bit of trouble over there, so Laurence will travel with me down to Plymouth, and we're going to get married there by special licence before we sail, with the ship's cat as witness, or something like that, because Mother and Father say they don't care less if they're not at the ceremony, so long as I get on with it!'

So I offered them both my sincerest congratulations, and Mlle Martin embraced me and called me 'her dearest Flotsam', and looked so happy that even Lady Catanache became a little teary. It did seem a remarkably short romance, but seeing them together that night, so easy and happy with each other, I couldn't deny that they appeared a well-suited couple.

But then a little bell rang to remind us of why we were there, and the crowds in the foyer began to trickle away, into the Great Hall. Mr Catanache, still smiling, produced tickets from his pocket and insisted that I should join their party.

'You shall have Father's seat, Miss Flotsam,' he told me. 'I've been telling everyone I'm the happiest man on earth and couldn't be happier, but of course I'd be a lot happier if I didn't have to sit down and listen to the old man spout his views for the next hour! But you know what? Given the circumstances, I'm prepared to forgive him even that!'

As there was no sign of Miss Peters or Mr Spencer, I agreed to join them, and we took our seats, and very good seats they were, in the front two rows, close to the podium. Mlle Martin and Mr Catanache sat in front, with Lady Catanache and I just behind them. And there was no time for any further conversation, because almost straightaway the lights dipped a little and Sir Henry Catanache took the stage to deliver his famous Paternoster lecture.

–

So much has been written about Sir Henry's speech at the Prendergast Hall that there is little need for me to describe it here. So surprising were his words, so eloquent his description of his conversion, that the newspapers next day, and for many days to come, devoted column after column to it, and reports of the attack on Mr Dashing were pushed towards the bottom of their crowded pages.

I don't actually remember very much of what he said, only my growing astonishment as I listened and understood what I was hearing. But I do remember how he began, because as he spoke Lady Catanache grasped my hand and held it very tightly. But her eyes never left her husband's face, so I'm not even sure she realised she was doing it.

'Mr Secretary,' he began, 'Members of the Society, ladies and gentlemen. It has been said that it takes a wise man to know when he is wrong, and a brave man to admit it. For a very great part of my life, I suspect, I have been neither of those things. But recent events have caused me to re-examine many of the beliefs I have always held, and as a result I stand before you – I hope – a little wiser and a little braver than ever before...'

I remember looking around at the audience during the middle part of his speech. Two rows behind me a lady with her handkerchief grasped tightly in her hand was breathing very fast and nodding along with every word he said. In the gallery, Lady Hastings wept openly. Behind her, the salad-spoon woman waved her rosette in the air and cheered every time Sir Henry paused for breath.

But it was something else I remember most clearly about that night at the Prendergast Hall. Something that was nothing to do with Sir Henry's speech. In fact, it happened just as that speech was drawing to its close. I'd been looking up at the podium, but a movement in front of me caught my eye, and looking down I saw that Mlle Martin was holding her right glove in her left hand while her other, un-gloved, hand was reaching for her fiancé's. While Sir Henry continued to talk, the pair sat very neatly and demurely, holding hands.

I don't suppose anyone else noticed. And I don't suppose they'd have minded if they had.

But I minded. Because it wasn't their hands I was looking at. It was Mlle Martin's wrist, and the narrow scar I saw there. The sort of scar that might be made by accidentally brushing against a very hot grate.

–

'I first suspected something of the sort a few days ago,' Mrs Hudson told me, as she laid a little cloth over one corner of the kitchen table, 'when I called at her house in Cornwall Mews.'

There was a fire burning in the kitchen at Baker Street because the night had turned cold, and I was glad of it. I was cold too, and, by the time I'd arrived home, I was feeling rather wobbly. I couldn't remember when I'd last eaten, and it felt as though the day had lasted about a thousand years. So, before Mrs Hudson would let me tell her anything at all, she had insisted on feeding me, and on wrapping me in her alpaca shawl, the one sent to her from Peru by the Marquis of Dundee. Only when she was certain that I was properly fed did she let me begin, while she occupied herself clearing away the supper things and laying out glasses for the Warburton port, which, she told me, in small quantities would cure a great many ills.

'You see,' she mused when I had told her everything, 'there was something a little odd about the career of the great Laurence Martin. The dog, the diamonds, even the Hatton Garden plot. In none of them did Mr Martin ever appear in person, Flottie, but it wasn't that which bothered me. After all, you and I have seen Mr Holmes solve all sorts of puzzles from his armchair. No, it was the lack of any *culprits* that struck me.'

I considered that for a moment, while Mrs Hudson carried on.

'The dog thief was said to be a poor widower who must be pitied and released rather than held accountable for any crime. The diamonds had been dropped by accident into the bushes while their rather silly owner drank champagne. The Hatton Garden plot involved anonymous messages, a mark on the cellar wall, and some old tools, but no actual gang. The only person known to be involved with it was the person who rented the cellar, who had convenient disappeared without trace.'

I nodded, watching Mrs Hudson decant the port. It was certainly true that Laurence Martin hadn't risen to fame by bringing criminals to justice.

'At first, Flotsam, I just suspected that Mr Martin was cleverly manufacturing these things for himself, his motive being fame, and success in his chosen profession. It would have been easy enough for him to follow the editor of *The Clarion* and to have someone steal his dog, and easy enough to pay some ne'er-do-well to dress in mourning and deliver it to Hyde Park. Easy enough, too, to post those messages in *The Times* and to rent the cellar in Hatton Garden and to fill it with tools.'

'But what about the Knibling diamonds, ma'am?' I asked.

'Yes, they were a good deal more interesting, Flottie. Patricia Knibling had clearly mislaid her diamonds at that party, and it would have been easy for someone to find them and then conceal them again, with a plan to reveal their whereabouts later on. But, of course, that would mean the person who did the hiding was one of the Knibling's guests, as the Knibling servants appeared to a particularly long-serving and trustworthy troupe. So, when I called on the house in Cornwall Mews and discovered that Laurence Martin was someone who could not possibly have been at the Knibling's ball, I knew she must be working with an accomplice, and a well-connected one at that.'

The port decanted, she carried the decanter over to the table and placed it in front of me, then took the seat next to mine.

'But there was something else I learned in Cornwall Mews that set me thinking, Flottie. Margaret, the maid there, was a sensible young woman and an experienced housemaid, and she told me that Mlle Martin was the best employer she'd ever worked for. Now, that's high praise indeed. I've worked for many different ladies in my time, Flotsam, but very few of them have really properly understood the difficulty of a housemaid's work in the way that Margaret described. Those that had were generally hugely experienced in the management of a big house, and none of them was even remotely as young as Mlle Martin. That set me to wondering, Flottie, how Mlle Martin had come to acquire her unusual insight into maids' work, and at such an early age.'

I thought of all the stories I'd ever heard from other housemaids, about mistresses who had no idea how long it took to black a grate or scrub a roasting tray. Mlle Martin would certainly have known both those things.

'And then there were her strange hours, Flotsam. Margaret told me that at first she'd only ever appeared at Cornwall Mews for a few hours each week and every Sunday, ostensibly because of her detective work. But those hours didn't sound like detective work to me, they sounded very much like the days-off of someone holding down a regular post. And then, two months ago, the regular hours disappeared, and Mlle Martin was around much more often – although still very regularly away. It was unusual, to say the least.'

I remembered that day in the drawing room in Cuthbert Square when Mlle Martin had bounced around on the furniture – furniture she had once been required to clean. I remembered how readily I had put her merriment down to high spirits. I had been fooled completely.

'But, Mrs Hudson, ma'am, she seemed so very *French*,' I pointed out.

'And, of course, Flottie, that is something Thomasina Trubshaw would have been able to achieve quite easily, having spent most of her life moving between France and Italy. Mrs Fenton gave us something of a clue when she talked about how comfortable Miss Trubshaw had been playing the role of a parlour maid. Mrs Fenton perceived she was a natural actress and, as we know, she was a very good one. In many ways, I think, it was Oscar Catanache who gave the game away.'

'In which ways, ma'am?'

'Oh, through no particular fault of his own, Flottie. But there were one or two flaws in their plan. Very early on, for instance, you told me that he had been seen wrapping a scarf around his face before entering the house in Salisbury Street. Inspector Merivale maintained he'd done that to hide his identity because he was about to commit a murder. Mr Catanache argued it was because he didn't want to be recognised by George Dashing and his friends, who were hanging around on The Strand. But neither of those reasons make sense, do they, Flotsam?'

I thought about it.

'No, ma'am, they don't. Because of the waistcoat.'

She smiled and poured a thimbleful of port into the glass in front of me. It smelled of strawberries and nutmeg and old brick walls in summer.

'Exactly! Only an idiot goes to the trouble of hiding his face while continuing to display, in full view, what seems to be the most recognisable waistcoat in London. And nothing I've ever heard suggests Mr Catanache is that sort of idiot. I could only conclude that Mr Catanache *wanted* to be recognised, and, more perplexing still, that he wanted to be seen to be hiding his face. But why? It struck me there were odd things about the behaviour of both Mr Catanache and Mlle Martin, and their paths seemed strangely connected. Miss Peters confirmed Mr Catanache had most definitely been present at the Kniblings' ball in Sussex, and Mr Catanache, before his arrest, had made sure that his mother was fully aware of the meteoric rise of Laurence Martin. That would, very nicely, have paved the way to employing her – for instance, if he were suddenly and dramatically arrested.'

I thought about everything Mrs Fenton had told us about the arrival of Thomasina Trubshaw in London, and about her affair with Oscar Catanache.

'I suppose the plan might have formed by accident, ma'am. They must have told each other that if only Miss Trubshaw hadn't been a housemaid, there might have been a chance that Sir Henry might come round.'

'I think that's right, Flottie. Once they'd realised that Mr Catanache would never be allowed to marry Thomasina Trubshaw the parlour maid, their only hope of happiness was for Thomasina to disappear, and then to reappear as someone else – and ideally as someone who could win Sir Henry's admiration and respect. So they decided to kill Thomasina off.'

I imagined the pair of them sitting together, in love and desperate to be together, hatching the plan, embellishing it, working out the details. Even though they had lied to all of us, it was hard to not to feel a little bit of sympathy.

'But, of course, they couldn't really kill her off completely, could they, ma'am?' I pointed out. 'Because they needed her to be found alive, so that Mr Catanache could no longer be accused of the crime. I suppose it was a sort of genius to come up with the idea of a crime for which Mr Catanache was the only suspect, but one which Mlle Martin could prove he didn't commit.'

Mrs Hudson nodded and filled her own glass.

'Thereby winning the eternal gratitude of Mr Catanache's obstinate but loving father, and paving the way to their marriage. Your good health, Flotsam.'

Our glasses touched with a satisfying, musical clink, and I took a sip.

Mrs Hudson sipped too, and gave a contented sigh.

'It was certainly an audacious, perhaps even a brilliant plan, Flottie,' she continued. 'But it only really became possible when the scullery maid left to get married and the footman ran off to join the army. Taken along with the retirement of Mrs Fenton and Miss Evans, it meant that, by September, hardly any of the staff at Cuthbert Square had ever set eyes on Thomasina Trubshaw.'

I couldn't help but recall that moment when Mlle Martin had entered the drawing room in Cuthbert Square for the first time, to stand in front of Sir Henry and Lady Catanache. For Thomasina Trubshaw, all decked out in her Parisian fashions, it must have been the most agonising and nerve-wracking moment, but she had never seemed anything but perfectly composed and at ease. And neither Sir Henry nor his wife had shown one flicker of recognition. Thomasina the parlour maid really had been invisible to them.

'I would have to say,' Mrs Hudson went on, a little note of admiration in her voice, 'that the pair of them seized their opportunity with great panache. The scene at Salisbury Street was planned very beautifully, so that Mr Catanache's arrival and departure couldn't fail to be noticed and would appear as suspicious as possible. They arranged the pig's blood in advance, of course, and the made-up letters, and all the other details, even down to Miss Trubshaw crying out when they were certain the neighbour would hear. It was vital to them that every detail pointed to Mr Catanache's guilt, yet allowed Mlle Martin to argue his innocence. I imagine they paid a couple of lads to fight outside at midnight so that Oscar Catanache could say he'd been able to slip away unnoticed. But he didn't really slip away, of course, Flottie, because he had to carry out Miss Trubshaw in the blanket – the *un-bloodied* blanket – at one o'clock in the morning.'

I looked back on how the story had unfolded.

'Those letters, ma'am... The ones from Mr Catanache that were found in Miss Trubshaw's room. The ones that made it sound as though the two had come to hate each other...'

'Yes, Flotsam?' Mrs Hudson rolled her port glass very gently between her fingers.

'Well, there was a moment when Mr Catanache was here, ma'am, being questioned by Mr Holmes, when he was asked what had happened to the letters written to him *by* Miss Trubshaw, and he said something about burning them at his club. It struck me as strange at the time. But I see now that there never *were* any letters from Miss Trubshaw. He was just thinking on his feet. And then there were those cuffs, ma'am...'

'Ah, yes, Flottie, those cuffs!' Mrs Hudson nodded approvingly. 'They were a lovely touch. It was easy enough to get rid of a jacket and a cane in ways would attract a certain amount of suspicion. I imagine the cane ended up in the river somewhere. But burning a pair of cuffs so that just a little remained to be found, well, that was inspired.'

Sitting in that calm kitchen with Mrs Hudson, it all seemed very simple.

'And Mlle Martin was free to move around the house, wasn't she, ma'am? So it would have been easy for her to replace the real cuffs, all nicely laundered, somewhere where Grimsby could be made to find them.'

Mrs Hudson raised her glass, as if to toast the cleverness of the plotters.

'It was nicely done, wasn't it, Flotsam?' Our glasses touched and we drank again, another tiny sip each. 'I think it was our trip to Market Steepleford that really began to stir my suspicions. The letters found in Salisbury Street, the ones from Oscar Catanache, suggested that Miss Trubshaw had turned into a terrible harridan after they had parted, but Mrs Fenton refused to believe that. And because I trust Mrs Fenton's judgement, Flottie, I had to assume that Miss Trubshaw was not in fact a vengeful harpy, and that those letters were misleading us – and misleading us in a way that would deliberately throw suspicion upon Mr Catanache.'

She raised her eyebrows for a moment, then refilled our glasses with another thimbleful.

'So, Flotsam, I had to wonder why a young man would go to such great efforts to incriminate himself. After all, there was no other suspect he might be trying to protect in some way. I confess I was puzzled. Until I thought about the cook.'

'The cook Mlle Martin didn't wish to interview, ma'am?'

'Exactly, Flotsam. The cook she took such great care to avoid. The cook who had worked with Thomasina Trubshaw for a year, and who would surely have recognised her again, despite her French finery.'

I found myself thinking of that day in Baker Street, by the area steps, when I'd found the lost handkerchief.

'So the young woman I met, ma'am, wasn't Thomasina Trubshaw at all. She just looked a bit like her. But who was she really?'

Mrs Hudson gave a little shrug.

'We may never know, Flottie, but I think we can be sure she's now living in Canada in some comfort, under the Trubshaw name.'

'So you think they just found someone to play the part, ma'am?'

'I do, Flotsam, and it was vitally important that they did. If young Mr Catanache wasn't going to live the rest of his life under a terrible cloud of suspicion, they had to be able to produce Thomasina Trubshaw alive and well. So they looked for someone who was not unlike Miss Trubshaw in appearance, and who was willing to take up a new life in the New World.'

It seemed a long and lonely journey, and I found myself frowning.

'But would that really be possible, ma'am? Would anyone be willing to do that?'

But Mrs Hudson only grinned and ruffled my hair.

'I suspect that was the easiest part, young lady. Mr Catanache is an extremely wealthy man, and he was prepared to spend lavishly to pull off his scheme. And it wouldn't be hard to find a struggling actress willing to take on the part if the reward were a smart home in Ontario and an allowance that would allow her to live in comfort for the rest of her life. Of course, there was one painful procedure to be undergone. Before catching the boat, the successful candidate would have to burn her own wrist, just like Miss Trubshaw did. But I think you'll find there are a great many young women who would think that a small price to pay for the reward on offer.'

The thought made me wince, and I found myself rubbing my own wrist.

'Is that really true, ma'am?'

'Well, Flotsam, Mr Rumbelow and I have made two excursions to the West End in the last few days, and have been able to meet a number of members of the acting profession, and persuade them to ask some questions on our behalf. So we've heard tell of a certain Myfanwy Price, an unemployed member of the chorus, who some months back went to see a man about a part, and came back over the moon, with money to spend, saying that she'd landed a role that would set her up for life. We've no way of knowing if Miss Price was the woman you met, but about a fortnight ago she showed her friends a first-class ticket to Halifax on one of the fast steamers, then wished them all fond and final farewells.'

'So their plan worked perfectly.' I considered this for a moment, rolling the thought round and around in my head. 'At least until Mlle Martin took off her glove.'

Mrs Hudson nodded, and we sat in silence for a few moments.

'So, tell me, Flotsam,' my companion asked eventually, 'what do you want to do?'

'Do, ma'am? You mean about Mr Catanache and Miss Martin?'

I hoped she might prompt me in some way, but she simply waited.

'Well, they've told a lot of lies, ma'am, and caused an awful lot of trouble. But I like Mlle Martin. She can't be *all* bad.'

'I don't think she is, Flotsam.' Mrs Hudson drained her glass. 'Her trip down to Market Steepleford... That wasn't really about getting descriptions, was it? In fact, I thought it rather a feeble excuse. But she knew Mrs Fenton and Miss Evans were terribly worried about her mysterious disappearance. So she found the time to go and reassure them, to share her plan and to explain. It was a kind thing to do.'

'But making up that story... Making fools of Sir Henry and his wife... That can't be right, can it?'

'And yet, Flotsam,' Mrs Hudson said softly, 'there must have been opportunities tonight when you could have told Sir Henry what you had discovered.'

It was true. After his speech, while I was still waiting in the foyer with the Catanache party, wondering what to do and what to say, Sir Henry had made a point of seeking me out and shaking my hand, and thanking me for all the help I'd given him.

'He even asked me if there was anything he could do to repay me,' I told her. 'I couldn't think of anything to say, so I told him about Mrs Welland and the food colourings, and asked if he would spare her half an hour of his time, and he laughed loudly and promised me that he would, and that he needed a new cause to champion.' I took another little sip of port. 'He seemed so happy, ma'am, that it didn't seem right to say anything, not just then.'

'It strikes me that they're all happy now, Flotsam,' Mrs Hudson observed. 'Somehow they've found their way. We may not approve of the methods, but perhaps we should find some joy in the outcome.'

And I think she was right.

But there was no time to discuss it further, because just then our peaceful little moment was disturbed by noises in the street.

'Blimey, ma'am!' I exclaimed. 'Is that Mr Holmes?'

She smiled. 'A young lady does not say 'blimey', Flotsam. But I think you're right. And it's sounds as though Dr Watson is actually singing. I'd suggest that the two gentlemen have had a very successful day.'

And so it proved. Mr Holmes and Dr Watson stumbled into the hallway that evening in an unusually celebratory mood, both looking a little dishevelled.

'You must forgive the late hour, Mrs H,' Mr Holmes declared. 'We have been delayed by an excellent pint of ale at the Museum Tavern.'

'More than one, Holmes!' Dr Watson corrected him. 'Celebrating, you see, Mrs Hudson. The business with the Romford hieroglyphs. Holmes here got his man!'

Mr Holmes smiled, and looked pleased.

'Got his man, Watson, yes. Or rather his woman. And what an admirable adversary she has proved! Had it not been for her error with the herring receipts…'

He passed his hat to Mrs Hudson, and, as the two of us began to offer our congratulations, he reached into his pocket.

'The real congratulations don't belong to us, though, do they, Watson? This telegram managed to find us at the British Museum, Flotsam. It's from Sir James Croxton, thanking me profusely for thwarting this evening's assassination attempt on George Dashing. Lady Hastings has informed him that it was one of my agents who saved the man's life.'

He held the slip of paper out to me.

'Here, Flotsam. You should keep this. I have already replied to Sir James, telling him who he really needs to thank. Now, an evening like this calls for further celebration. Watson, where's my violin?'

As quickly as the excitement started, it passed, and Mrs Hudson and I were once again alone in the kitchen.

'They'll both be heading for bed very soon,' she predicted. 'And we should do the same. Hot milk before you go, Flotsam?'

But I shook my head.

'Actually, ma'am, would you mind at all if I went out again?' I asked her. 'There's something I need to do. And I might not be back till very late indeed.'

Mrs Hudson looked at me for a moment, and I wondered if she were going to ask for explanations. But she simply smiled very gently.

'If it's something you need to do, Flotsam…' And she nodded towards the door.

—

Bridle Lane was almost deserted by the time I reached it, and the dark, dusty shop looked no darker than those around it. The key was in the drainpipe, where I'd seen Scraggs place it, and the door seemed to make a terrible noise as it opened.

I'd brought a storm lantern with me, and it cast a pale, pessimistic glow. Perhaps that's why, looking around at the dust and the dustsheets and the ancient fittings, I felt a little shard of the hopelessness I'd felt before. But this time, alone and without distractions, perhaps I understood a little better what Scraggs had seen there. Beautiful bones, he'd said. And if they were there, I was going to find them.

First, I lit the great oil lamps that still hung by chains from the ceiling. Only one of the three refused to light. Then I lit the various smaller lamps I found in corners and in cupboards, until the place was bright with a yellow, flickering glow. The crate of cleaning things Scraggs had mentioned stood unopened by the door so I prised it open and unpacked. Then I got to work.

I suppose I was tired. I certainly should have been tired. But I was in no hurry, working slowly, methodically, finding my own rhythm, almost in a trance, and thinking of nothing but the movement of my own hands. Bit by bit, with every scrub or brush or dash of polish, a tiny portion of order was reclaimed. One brass knob on a drawer behind the counter; then the front of the drawer, dusted and polished to a deep mahogany glow; then the next drawer, then the next. Gradually something old and honest and rather noble began to emerge.

I took no notice of the time. When I knelt and began to work on the floors it must have been around five o'clock because, outside, the dark figures of early workers were sliding through the gloom. I barely noticed the dawn, until suddenly it was bright outside and I rose to put out the lamps.

In daylight, it all looked different. But Scraggs had been right. It did have beautiful bones. He had seen it all along.

The clocks were striking seven when I locked the door and returned the key to the drainpipe, then hurried home to bed.